Mirror's Ecko

A Mirror Walker Novel by

A. C. Mooney

Hodge Publishing LLC
Conroe, Texas
info@hodgepublishing.com

ISBN: 979-8-9907439-0-8

Mirror's Ecko

And what is a reflection but a mirror's echo?
A silent image that echoes back from the looking glass
Meant to be seen with the eyes,
Not heard with the ears.

Re•flec•tion

the throwing back by a body or surface of light, heat,
or sound without absorbing it

Ech•o

a sound or series of sounds caused by the reflection
of sound waves from a surface back to the listener

Table of Contents

Prologue

The woman sits on the edge of the stained and lumpy mattress, listlessly staring at the dirty, discolored walls of her borrowed room. She is beautiful, breathtakingly so, but her face is pinched with fatigue, pale and drawn. Fear, exhaustion, and despair have taken its inevitable toll on her. She can barely scrape up enough energy to properly care for her newborn infants. Giving birth to not one, but two babies all alone in that terrible Black Forest had been almost more than she could bear. Worse, the hardships hadn't stopped when the labor pains had ceased either.

After the birth, she'd walked for two days before finally making it to this small, dilapidated town. Most of the inhabitants proved to be a rough and untrustworthy lot, harsh and hardened as only the truly desperate tend to be. She'd fearfully kept to the shadows, hiding herself and the babes from evil eyes even as she desperately sought a friendly face. She needed help; they would not survive without it.

Eventually her gaze had settled upon an elderly couple, and she'd watched them closely as they bickered back and forth. Before they could wander off again, she'd crept out of hiding and cautiously approached them. Of course, they would be happy to take her in, they'd said. For a price. She'd given them one of the priceless rings from her fingers as payment for allowing her to stay in their extra bedroom.

A single jewel from that ring was worth more than their entire home, but it was a price that she'd been more than willing to pay. Shelter, secrecy, and three meager meals a day, that was all she'd needed, and time. Time to heal, time to love, and time to say goodbye.

She's been hiding in here now for three weeks, recuperating and showering her newborn babies with as much love as she possibly can. She spends hours whispering into their ears, telling them how much she loves them. She rocks them in her arms and tells them all about herself and about Irredarr, her beloved home world.

When she sleeps, she curls herself around them, cuddling them as close to her as possible. She holds them all day, all night. Every single moment is precious, for she knows that every second is borrowed time. She wishes with all of her heart that she could stay here in this dumpy little house forever, just a normal mother raising her children. But she knows that it's too dangerous to remain here, and that she'll soon have to send her babies away from her. The Lokskell, the Shadow Lord will stop at nothing to have them all recaptured and brought back to him. She knows that the only way to evade him is to split up and hide the children. Even now his spies have entered the town and are combing the streets, diligently searching for them. She is all out of time.

The woman begins to cry as she feels the darkness of the Lokskell closing in on her. She must hurry! The spell she's working on must be completed! "Avalduma... Reveal" she whispers and suddenly the energy force surrounding herself becomes visible. Her aura is luminous, swirling with kaleidoscopic, iridescent rainbows shimmering in the light. She reaches into it and painfully extracts two glittering strands and plaits them into two thin locks of her hair.

She then snips off the braids, severing not only hair, but also those glimmering threads of her aura and further weakening herself. She quickly ties them around an ankle of each child. All that remains now is to initiate the binding spell. She recites the enchantment and the bracelets dissolve and melt into her babies' skin. They giggle and coo at the tickling sensation as the spell anchors itself to their very DNA. The bracelets morph and transform into golden tattoos, one with a shimmering blue strand of her mother's aura and the other a purple one. Although it had cost her dearly, a permanent spell of protection now winds around their ankles. The new mother knows that it will not be enough, but it's all that she can do to help her beloved daughters. She sheds a thousand more tears as she holds them both close one last time.

The dour-faced old man and his frumpy wife walk into the room. They're both extremely worried and fretting about being discovered by the Shadow Lord and they're anxious for the deal to be completed. "You must leave now! The longer you remain, the more danger you place us all in. Give us the child...and the jewelry. Don't forget the jewelry! And then be gone with you!" the man insists.

She does not hesitate. She gives him all that she owns, everything except the few items that she has set aside for her girls. She hands the old woman a small, cloth-wrapped bundle and tells her, "These are for the child. I am entrusting you not only with my precious daughter, but also with the task of ensuring that she receives these things. This is very important. There will come a time when she will need to know the truth of who she is and where she comes from. The truth is all that I have to give her. When she's old enough to understand, give her these and tell her about me. You will know when she's ready."

The mother sobs uncontrollably as she reluctantly hands one of the babies to the old woman. She bends down and gives her daughter one last kiss, her tears dripping onto the infant's face. She glances back up at the elderly couple through blurry, tear-filled eyes and gives them a final command, her voice loud and resonating with power. "Her name is Samara Mikelle Zyanya. You are not to change it in any way. Tell her that it means Beloved Miracle and that I give her this name as a reminder that no matter what happens, there was someone out there that loved her, completely and unconditionally."

With tears streaming down her face, the broken-hearted mother turns away saying, "Now if you'll just give me the mirror, I can be on my way. I have lingered here for far too long. The sooner I am gone, the safer you and Samara will be." The old lady removes a small hand-held mirror from her apron pocket and hands it over to her. Feeling a sudden deep compassion for the grief-stricken mother, the elderly woman clumsily pats her shoulder and assures her that she will take good care of her daughter. She promises to love the girl as if she were her own child.

Unable to bear it any longer, the inconsolable mother desperately clutches her other daughter to her breast and hurries away. She runs as fast as she can, out of the house, down the broken cobblestone streets, right out of the town. She does not stop running until she reaches the shores of the Dead Sea, and she can go no further. She falls to her knees in the wet sand, protectively cradling her babe close.

She kneels there beside the sea, struggling desperately to calm herself. Her breath scrapes harshly in and out of her lungs and her tears refuse to cease. Her heart beats frantically with apprehension and an all-consuming dread when she hears the sounds of pursuit coming from the direction of the town. She must have been seen fleeing! There's still time to do what must be done before they catch up to her, but it would be close. She must hurry! She affixes the destination that she's chosen firmly in her mind and begins to murmur the spell.

She lifts the mirror up into the air and... freezes in shock. The mirror is broken! A long, jagged crack runs from top to bottom, right down the center. That old couple had never once mentioned that the mirror was damaged. This would make things very difficult. Difficult, but not impossible, and it will take everything she has to accomplish it. She may not even survive. But what else can she do? She cannot go back and demand restitution, and she can't go in search of another, more suitable looking glass. She has no time left. The shouts from the search party that's hunting her steadily grow louder. They're closing in and will soon be upon her. She has to make this work, now, with the mirror that she has available to her. Whatever happens to her doesn't even matter. The important thing, the ONLY thing, is saving her daughter. She would gladly forfeit her life to keep her baby safe.

Even with her enemies advancing and the tremendously daunting task ahead, the woman still takes a moment more to love her remaining daughter, just one last time. She strokes the girl's soft, downy cheeks, memorizes every detail of her tiny face. She instinctively knows that this is the last time she will ever get to hold her in her arms. She feels her heart cracking inside her chest, just like the broken mirror in her hand.

She kisses her beautiful baby for the last time and whispers, "My whole life I dreamed of being a mother. You are all I ever wanted for myself, a daughter to love and call my own. Now I have you and you are perfect, everything I ever dreamed of." Her breath hitches in her chest as she continues, "I wish with all my heart that I could keep you with me forever, but I must send you far away. You are the next Wandelaar, the new Mirror Walker heiress. My beloved Irredarr will rise or fall with you. The fates of entire worlds will one day depend upon you. So much magic and power reside within you, and there are those that will stop at nothing to take it from you. You must remain hidden and safe until you grow into your abilities and can protect yourself. I am so sorry that I won't be there to help you." The baby stares intently up at her mother, listening to every word.

The ferocious baying from some hellish version of a dog rings out over the water. The Lokskell's hunters that are tracking her have made it onto the beach. A huge group of nightmare creatures howl and fight to be the first to reach her, to be the lucky one that gets to claim the reward for capturing her. The distraught mother lifts the mirror back up, staring into it and frantically searching for the man... the one that she's chosen to entrust her child with.

There! He's there, sitting on a park bench right where her magic had directed him to, quietly staring out into the night... waiting. She urgently speaks the words that will allow her to open the portal and send her daughter through to that other world. She focuses all her powers on the image of that remote land far away from this, and all other worlds.

It is a strange place, overpopulated with a primitive race of people. Accessing this particular world is extremely difficult because of its lack of magic; that is the reason why it has never been explored by her own people. Because this world is closed off from so many others, it will be the safest place to send her daughter. But now she has to access it with a broken gateway, turning a difficult task into an almost impossible one.

It takes every bit of power inside of her to open up the passage. Sweat beads on her brow and her hands shake from the mental exertion. The mirror finally starts to glow, but the crack begins to spread outwards, making the way unstable. She has to do it NOW! This is the only way to protect her child, but it's simultaneously tearing her apart inside. She glances back down at her daughter and sees that her baby is silently crying too. Glittering silver-tinted tears stream down her baby's face.

This sight almost undoes the grieving mother. Barely able to choke the words out, she whispers, "I give you the name Adrina Ecko Zyanya. On Irredarr it means Love Repeats Forever. And I do love you, more than I ever thought was possible. Goodbye my daughter, my sweet little girl. I pray that one day we will meet again. For now, you must stay safely hidden. All of Irredarr's hopes and dreams go with you, precious one." Quickly, before she loses her resolve, the woman gently pushes her baby through the glowing mirror to the world on the other side, and she lets her go.

A crippling sorrow fills her the instant that she loses contact with her baby. Her heart can't bear it; her mind cannot accept it. A desperate wail of despair and absolute anguish bursts out from the very depths of her soul. She feels her mind cracking as the agony overwhelms and begins to consume her. She grabs onto her head, the mirror still clutched tightly in her hand, as she desperately tries to keep a grip on her sanity.

But wave after wave of sorrow crash over her, one after another, threatening to drown her. She can't breathe. She can't escape the torment. She cannot fight the darkness threatening to pull her down, down, down. Her mind fractures further and the tiny bit of magic that she still possesses explodes out of her and into the mirror. She screams so loud and so long that the mirror in her hand is shattered and blown to dust. The echoes of her magic-infused, wounded cry reverberate throughout all the mirrors in the land and shatters every single one.

The broken mother rocks back and forth and stares out to sea. She is lost, gone mad from grief, her mind trapped in a hellish purgatory. Fittingly, the last thing she sees before the Shadow Lord's monsters overtake her is the Isle of Despair where the most fractured souls go to wait out eternity. A tiny, heartbroken creature curled up on the shores of that island watches as the monsters converge on the apathetic woman and carry her away. It lays its head back down in the sand and continues its vigil as its own ceaseless tears fall and get washed out to sea.

Two weeks later, the woman is unmercifully dumped onto the cold stone floor, completely unaware that she has been returned to the Lokskell's castle. She has withdrawn so far into her own mind that she doesn't even acknowledge that HE is shouting at her. He stands over her, every inch of him drenched in sweat and blood.

He'd spent the days waiting for her return down in the dungeons, taking his fury out on his prisoners. All of his servants had scattered and hidden, terrified that his wrath would extend to them next.

The half-witted Grunter, (half man, half swine creature) triumphantly jabs his finger at the dispirited woman and crows gleefully, "I got her M'lord! It was me, Groik, what done it! I caught her and brought her back to you!" Dumb as the creature is, it nevertheless realizes that all is not right when the Shadow Lord just stands there, silently glaring down at the woman. "Why is M'lord not pleased?" it squeals with its nasally, grating voice. "This IS the female you requested, is she not?"

The Shadow Lord's face is terrifying to behold as his rage grows. Groik backs away as far as he can get and cowers against the wall. The very air grows thick and heavy, the Lokskell's madness becoming a terrible, palpable thing. When he finally speaks, his voice is so loud, so powerful and full of malicious intent, that Groik's eardrums instantly rupture. The swine-man lets out an agonized squeal as blood spills from its ears.

"Where. Are. The. Infants?" the Lokskell thunders.

The sniveling Grunter's eyes go wide with shock as a debilitating fear grips him tight. "There weren't no infants, M'lord! I swear there weren't none. No one said nothing about no infants!" he whines, as he presses his hands against his ears. The Lokskell throws back his head and roars his rage to the rafters. Unable to restrain himself, he reaches out and slams his hand onto the cretin's chest.

Suddenly, the flesh of Groik's face begins to melt, as if it's made of wax. The flesh around its eyes starts to droop and its nose slides down into its mouth, which has opened wide in a silent scream. Its eyeballs plop loose and hang down on its melted cheeks, dangling by the optic nerves. The Lokskell holds his hand in place until the creature has been liquified to such an extent that it can no longer support itself or stand upright. It slides to the floor with a sickening squishing/plop sound. The Shadow Lord then brutally snatches the woman up and steps over the puddle that had just moments ago been a living creature. Groik is somehow still screaming from the depths of the goo as the woman is dragged back to her cell.

For the next several days, the Shadow Lord tries everything he can to make the woman tell him what she'd done with his son and her daughter. Hypnosis, mind control, hallucinations, even torture; nothing works. She's buried the truth too deep in her crazed, tormented mind. Or, she has erased the memory completely. He cannot tell which. Interrogating her is nothing more than a waste of time, and it gets him nowhere, although he has enjoyed it immensely.

The rage inside of him is now absolute. It knows no bounds and threatens constantly to consume him. It grows inside him with every passing moment that he is forced to go without those infants, and it has nowhere else to go. He's running out of prisoners to torture. He calls out for his spies to come to him. He knows that there are always several of them hiding close by.

A small roach-like beetle crawls out of a crack and waits for his command. "Those brats are mine and I will have what belongs to me. I want them found immediately. Go. Tell your Collective to spread the word to every corner of this land. I will inform my Shades to gather all my forces on every single world that I hold dominion over. Everyone will search until those infants are found and returned to me. Someone, somewhere knows where they are. And when I find the one responsible for hiding them from me, I will turn him inside out until he is reduced to a ball of living meat."

The Lokskell's face changes from that of a man's and becomes that of the Shadow. He reaches up and plucks an inky wisp of his Shadows from around his head and sends it slithering off. He does not have to command it; it already knows exactly what must be done. He can at any moment separate pieces of his Shadow form from himself, and each fragment will remain sentient. They're extensions of himself, as are all of his Shades. The black, vaporous tendrils are nothing more than tiny parts of his collective consciousness, almost like a visible thought.

The roach-beetle begins to scurry away to carry out his Master's orders but skitters to a stop when the woman starts laughing. It turns back to see how she would be punished. It has to watch; it just can't resist the allure. The Collective spies for the Master, because it must. Gossiping and causing misery and dissent are truly what it lives for. This was a juicy tidbit of gossip that the bug creature just can't ignore. It crawls a bit closer and watches in complete incredulity. It cannot fathom how the woman is still alive after all it had seen the Master do to her, much less where she found the courage to laugh in his face.

But laugh she does, hysterically so. The Lokskell stands over her, his anger skyrocketing. The woman stops her mad, howling laughter long enough to say, "Go ahead and search. Have your Night Shades and your spies and all of your men tear every single world apart searching. You will never find my daughter." Convulsing with laughter and gasping for breath, she adds, "And I promise you that you will never find your son."

The Lokskell becomes so enraged that he loses control of his forms. One second, he's a man, the next he's shifted into the Shadow. He flashes back and forth between the two for several seconds. With half formed, skeletal hands that are engulfed in shadows, he grabs the giggling woman and lifts her high up into the air. With a sudden roar that reverberates throughout the entire castle, he throws her with all his tremendous might against the far wall.

She never once cries out as she slams back down to the ground and lays still, her body now as broken as her heart and mind. The Lokskell reforms as a solid man and calmly smooths his hair back into place. He kneels down in front of her and strokes the hair back from her lovely, bloodied face. "Then I guess I really don't need you anymore, since you are of no more use to me," he calmly replies. The woman smiles a tired, peaceful little smile before everything goes dark and all the pain fades away.

Can You Spell NORMAL?

Before The Bad Thing

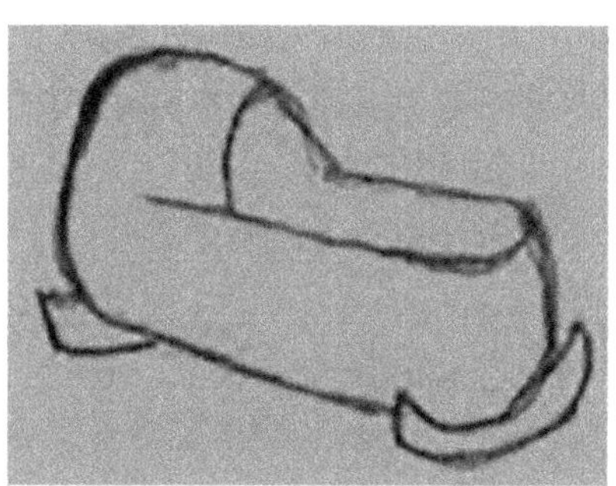

Daniel Roberts, Dan the Man, as his friends call him, is your typical every day, ordinary man. He's exactly six feet tall, with brown hair and brown eyes. He is unremarkable in every way and that is exactly how he likes it. He had enough unwanted attention as a child to last a lifetime. Two lifetimes, if he's being honest. Now that he's a grown man, he wants nothing more than to blend in and go unnoticed. The only time he cares to stand out is in the courtroom.

Dan is one of the most prominent corporate lawyers at Proctor and White's Law Services, one of Houston, Texas's largest law firms. At the office he's quiet and reserved, and mostly keeps to himself. But when he takes that first step into the courtroom, he transforms into someone else entirely, someone that people take notice of. He's bold, confident, and memorable. His co-workers say that it's like watching him pull off a magical mask, or put one on. The change is so drastic that it's almost as if he has two totally opposite personalities living inside him. He just loves his job, and he's very good at it, that's all. And he never loses. Ever. He earns an insane amount of money and drives a brand new, albeit very ordinary and inconspicuous car.

Early on in life Dan had set goals and constructed a strict plan for himself, and he has diligently stuck to it. He's worked hard to overcome his troubled past and become the successful man that he is. He's built a solid, stable world to live in, and he is very proud of his ability to provide his family with a good life. He avoids any and all things that are the slightest bit *strange*, as if they somehow carry the bubonic plague with them. He wants nothing more than to follow The Plan and live out a simple, mundane life with a nice, normal family.

He'd met his wife seven years ago at a colleague's Christmas party. Rachael was a good looking, but also very ordinary elementary school teacher. Dan had taken one look at her and immediately knew that she was the one for him. She was perfect. He'd plucked up the nerve to ask her if she would like to go out to dinner with him sometime. And when she said yes, they made plans for the following evening. That was all it took. After that first date they were inseparable. Even so, they were very practical with their relationship growth. They'd sat down together and came up with *The* Plan. They mapped out their whole lives, planned every major detail. They spent a year dating and another year engaged before they were married. During that first year of marriage, they both worked hard and saved every extra penny so they would be able to buy a nice home to raise a family.

Dan, in the meantime, made quite a name for himself in the corporate law field by winning every case he took on. Hence, the nickname Dan the Man. He was given the incredible opportunity of hiring on at Proctor and White's law firm and became one of the company's highest paid lawyers within his first year there.

During their second year of wedded bliss, Dan and Rachael had decided that it was time to move out of the city and start their family. They bought a large, two-story house in a crowded, upscale suburb on the outskirts of Houston. It was very big and very pricy, and it looked exactly the same as all the other houses on their street. It was packed in too close to their neighbors and the front yard was tiny, almost nonexistent. But the backyard more than made up for all that. There was a large deck, a pool, and plenty of room for future family activities. However, it was the view beyond the backyard that ultimately made them decide that this was where they wanted to grow old together.

Beyond the fenced in backyard lay a thick patch of woods where all manner of wildlife could be seen going about their daily lives. They loved to sit out on the deck with their coffees each evening and watch the animals scamper about, especially when they received the news that they were expecting their first child.

Rachael continued to work until the baby was born. She took one look at that tiny, squalling baby girl and decided then and there that she would stay home to be a full-time mother. Dan was more than happy with her decision and had supported her in every way that he possibly could. The happy new parents named their daughter Karen after his mother. Dan could not have been happier with his life. He adored his wife and baby girl beyond reason and lavished affection on both of his ladies, showering them with gifts and attention.

Dan and Rachael had quickly adjusted and settled into life with their new family addition. The time virtually flew by, and they watched as Karen grew like a weed. Their angel is now a healthy, happy, and *typical* three-year-old little girl. She has big dreams of being a princess and living in a castle, and she absolutely adores the color pink. She loves tea parties and dress up and play dates. And tiaras… she *adores* tiaras. As their first and only child, she is very much loved and doted upon. Life in the Roberts household was perfect. Their dreams were coming true, and they were enjoying every minute of it. All they had ever wanted was to raise a nice, normal family in a safe, conventional home. And that is exactly how it was. Everything was going according to The Plan. Nothing strange or unexpected ever happened to them and that was just how they liked it. But that was all about to come to a sudden, shattering end.

When Dan woke up on that dismal, overcast morning, he felt completely out of sorts, grumpy and unrested. He had not slept well at all. Although he couldn't remember any of the details, his dreams had been strange and disturbing. He tried to shake the unpleasant feelings plaguing him as he made his way to the coffee pot. He needed a jump start to get him going. He cheered up considerably as he remembered that it was Thursday. He always treated himself to breakfast at Momma May's Cafe every Tuesday and Thursday, without fail. It was also a treat for his wife, as she didn't have to get up early to make his breakfast. She got to sleep in on those two days, at least until Princess Karen woke up demanding 'mashmano' cereal (marshmallow, in grown up speak). So, Dan kissed his sleeping wife and daughter goodbye, grabbed his umbrella, and quietly went on his way.

Maggie Reynolds was the morning waitress at Momma May's Cafe. She'd gotten the job a little over a year ago when the previous waitress ran off to Vegas with her boyfriend. Maggie was a very sweet and reliable worker. She was there greeting the customers with a tired and somewhat sad smile every single morning. After several months of Tuesdays and Thursdays, the same order of scrambled eggs, toast with no butter, and cup of black coffee, Dan and Maggie had become quite good friends. Conversation between them always came easily.

He talked to her about his wife and daughter, and she told him all about Ally, her thirteen-year-old girl. Dan had even brought Rachael and Karen in a time or two. He was proud of his family, and he took every opportunity to show them off.

As Dan headed to Momma May's through the drizzling rain, he couldn't help but think back on that morning six months ago. Maggie hadn't been there to greet him when he walked through the door. It was an extremely flustered Momma May that snapped, "Morning, Dan. Go on and tell Bobby you're here, so he can get started on your order."

Momma May had bustled around the room refilling coffee cups and wiping tables. She was trying her best to run the whole show as the greeter, the waitress, and the cashier. When Momma May had stopped for a moment to catch her breath, Dan asked if everything was ok with Maggie. That was the day that Dan learned the truth.

Maggie's daughter, Ally had been fighting cancer for the past two years. It was actually the only reason Maggie even worked at the cafe. She'd needed the extra income from a second job to help pay for the outrageously expensive medical bills. She worked mornings at Momma May's, because it was the only time she could spare. She already worked a full-time job, downtown at a thread factory. Maggie had been unable to make her shift that morning because Ally had been rushed to the hospital during the night. Dan's heart had ached for his friend and her daughter, but he never let on that he knew her secret. She would talk to him about it, if and when she was ready. He did, however, start leaving better tips though. And he was not above sneaking extra money onto other customers' tables when she wasn't looking. Momma May caught him a time or two, smiled and shook her head at him, but she never said a word about it either.

When he walked into the cafe that morning at precisely 7:00, Maggie smiled and said, "Good morning, Dan. I'll have your usual out in just a few minutes."

He sat down in the same booth he always sat in, looked up and said, "You know what Maggie? I'm feeling a bit...different today. I think I want the pancakes. Yes. Let me get the short stack. And orange juice along with my coffee please."

Maggie turned back towards him and frowned. "Is everything ok?" Dan smiled and assured her that he was fine. But he wasn't fine. He felt strange and restless, sort of itchy under his skin. As he watched Maggie walk away, he had a startling realization. It felt like someone had their eyes on him, watching every move he made. He had the unsettling feeling that someone had, in fact, been watching him all morning. But that was crazy. It made absolutely no sense at all. Who would even want to watch him? Why? And how? There was *no way* anyone had been in his house this morning, spying on him. After nervously searching his surroundings, he shrugged it off and chatted with Maggie while he ate his unconventional breakfast. He left his usual $50 tip, then anxiously drove himself to work.

As foolish as he felt, Dan still just couldn't shake the thought that he was being watched. He quickly became jumpy and irritable, and he was exceedingly grateful that he didn't have to appear in the courtroom that day. He stayed shut up in his office until he just couldn't stand it any longer. He decided to call it a day and head home early. He wasn't making any real progress on the case he was currently working on anyway. In fact, he'd only been staring blankly at the computer screen and shuffling papers around for hours.

He drove home slowly, constantly checking his mirrors and glancing around, trying to spot anyone that looked suspicious. He felt extremely vulnerable and uncomfortable and when he got home, he locked the doors behind him. It was an eerie feeling, one that he could not understand or explain, but which he still felt compelled to take heed of.

Later that evening, as Dan was sitting at the table eating dinner with his family, something odd happened. He suddenly had the strangest compulsion to get up and leave. He felt an overwhelming urge to just *Go!* He wanted nothing more than to leave the dinner table, get in his car, and drive away. He ignored it as long as he could until he finally HAD to obey. He had no other choice. He calmly set his fork down and wiped his mouth with his napkin. Without a single word of explanation, he stood up and walked out of the house. He didn't even shut the door behind him. Hours later he returned home, soaking wet, red faced and ashamed…with a very big, very strange life altering secret. *And a six-week-old baby that he claimed was his.*

The wonderfully simple life that the Roberts had thus far been enjoying suddenly and drastically morphed into some sort of unreal nightmare reality. Rachael went into total mental shut down. The shock of Dan's betrayal was such an unexpected blow, she just couldn't wrap her mind around the whole situation. Dan had been unfaithful? He'd made a baby with some other woman? WHAT HAD HAPPENED TO THE PLAN? She never would have thought him capable of such treachery. She was happy and quite satisfied with her life and had thought that he was equally happy as well. She'd trusted him completely. How could he do it? How could he have an affair? And to have a child result from that affair... and then expect her to take that child in and raise it as their own? The nerve, the *unmitigated* gall of it.

It all seemed so surreal to her. And then, not one word of explanation. Not. One. Word. The only thing he would say was that the baby was his, and he could not/would not put her and Karen in danger by discussing it. Whatever *that* was supposed to mean. Time after time he insisted that he loved her, loved her more than life itself, and that he had *never been unfaithful*. That was it. That was all the explanation that she got, and it was a strange explanation at that. How could he say that he'd never been unfaithful, but still claim that baby as his? It made absolutely no sense at all.

But Dan had cried and begged her not to leave him. He told her that he would understand if she never wanted to see him again, but just please, *please* forgive him. Rachael had only seen him cry twice before in the seven years that she'd known him. He broke down when they had buried his mother, and he cried his eyes out when their daughter Karen was born. Rachael couldn't stand the sight of his tears. She did not like seeing him broken.

For a while she existed in a strange mental fog as she struggled with indecision about what to do. Should she leave? Should she stay and see if they could work through this? Could she ever forgive him? Sure, Dan had done a terrible thing. He'd broken her heart and then he wouldn't even give in to her demands for answers. But even though he stubbornly closed his mouth and kept it closed, she could tell that he was going through his own private hell too. She wasn't sure if they could make it work. She wasn't sure of anything really, but in the end the deciding factor was that strange baby girl. She could not reject a tiny, helpless baby. It just wasn't in her. And no matter what, she loved Dan, and that baby was a part of him.

Adrina Ecko Roberts was NOT your typical six-week-old baby. Everything about her was just a little...odd. She was a tiny thing, much smaller than she should have been. Her facial features were a bit ethereal, giving her an almost pixie-like appearance. With emerald-green eyes flecked with silver and a headful of flame-colored curls, she was as pretty as a doll. As silent as one too. She never cried. She just quietly watched everything that went on around her. It seemed as if she was always looking for something. Her eyes wandered everywhere, searching. Always searching.

It also became quite evident that the color red intensely disturbed her. Any time she saw an object that was predominantly colored red, her eyes would tear up and her little bottom lip would start to tremble. She never made a sound, but tears would course down her silky-soft cheeks until the red object was removed from her sight. It was so *strange.*

Another perplexing characteristic was that she didn't emit that baby smell that all infants seem to have. Instead, she perpetually smelled like some sort of exotic flower, something subtle and slightly sweet but with an underlying hint of spice. Even her name was exceedingly abnormal. Peculiar, but somehow charming too.

Dan and Rachael realized right away that Ecko, as they called her, was not going to fit right into The Plan. She looked different than them and she behaved strangely too. Even the way she'd joined their family was bizarre. But there was something about her that undeniably drew them in. There was an air of expectation about her, as if the world was holding its breath, waiting for… something. She was like a mysterious puzzle that they just couldn't quite figure out. And although their lives had been drastically altered, there was no denying the allure of this strange little girl. Those peculiar eyes of hers drew them in and captivated them.

As drawn as they were to her, it seemed like nothing ever really affected *her*, other than the color red. She expressed no other emotions whatsoever. She didn't cry. She didn't laugh. Although they tried their hardest, they couldn't even make her smile.

Late one night, when Dan thought that his wife was fast asleep, he got out of bed and tiptoed down the hall to her nursery to check on her. Ecko was wide awake, staring up at him. Dan picked her up and hugged her close to his heart. He kissed her soft baby cheek and whispered, "Hello, sweet girl. I'm your dad now. I promise I will always do my best to protect you. No matter what, I will always be here for you. You ARE wanted. I love you Adrina Ecko Roberts, my sweet baby girl."

One tiny tear rolled down Ecko's face and then her eyes lit up and she smiled the most beautiful, soul-shattering smile. She giggled and cooed up at her father, then settled down in his arms and instantly fell back to sleep. The tears on Dan's face glittered in the moonlight from the window as he lay his daughter back in her crib.

Rachael, who was quietly watching from the doorway, felt her heart practically melt into a puddle inside her chest. She smiled to herself, wiped away her own tears, and silently crept back to bed. She'd made up her mind. She was going to fight. This was her family, and she was not going to lose it. No, Ecko didn't fit in with The Plan, but they were just going to have to make a new one.

In those first few weeks after their new arrival, Dan and Rachael spent a great deal of time in silent observation. They watched Ecko gazing curiously around at everything. They watched Karen. Their daughter did not like all the attention the new baby was garnering, and vocally protested her displeasure with not being the center of everyone's attention. And they watched each other.

Rachael's eyes often reflected the hurt, betrayal, and confusion that she felt. Dan's held fear, regret, and a deep, endless sorrow. They wondered if their little family would survive this sudden traumatic upheaval in their perfectly constructed lives. Those weeks were the hardest times they had ever faced. They were constantly on edge, their marriage tested to the breaking point.

Their friends made things even more difficult for them too. They were determined to find out all the juicy details about Dan's infidelity, his 'mystery' woman, and their love child. They whispered and gossiped incessantly behind Dan and Rachael's backs. When Dan refused to speak about any of it, he was treated like a leper and shunned by all but a few loyal friends.

They made Rachael feel stupid for letting Dan stay and for taking his baby in. Eventually she stopped seeing all of her friends too. It broke Dan's heart to see the hurt that just kept slamming into his wife like waves during a high tide. Although he knew that he could never heal the pain that he had caused, he did everything he could to make it up to her. His love for her grew even more and he knew that if he could somehow do penance for a thousand years, he would *still* not deserve her.

Time passed, and as the saying goes, life went on. Eventually they fell into a functioning routine and some semblance of their former life. They all did their best to put aside the hurt and the emotional disorder that Ecko had unwittingly caused in their lives. The Roberts family banded together and did their very best to continue with The (slightly altered) Plan. And although Rachael's eyes never regained all of their former sparkle and Dan's exuberance for life had been subdued a bit, they mostly succeeded. Before they knew it, months had gone by and everyone had, if only reluctantly, accepted Ecko's presence in their lives.

Rachael and Dan had noticed right away that Ecko loved looking in mirrors. She was completely and utterly transfixed with her reflection. It was the only time she showed any kind of emotion whatsoever. She would reach her tiny hands out and babble her baby talk to herself, kicking her legs excitedly all the while. It was her favorite thing to do. It was strange, but they figured it was harmless and she would eventually move on to other things.

But Ecko never did outgrow her interest in mirrors and her reflection. In fact, it became more like an obsession than a fascination. And then disturbing incidents began to occur...The first time it happened was a complete, panic inducing shock. Dan had been at the office putting the finishing touches on a case that he'd been working on when his secretary, Barbara burst into his office without even knocking. She wrung her hands in distress as she informed him that Rachael had just called. Dan immediately wondered why she had called the office instead of his personal phone.

"She was crying hysterically and babbling gibberish. I couldn't understand what she was trying to say! All I could make out were the words baby, mirror, and crying. Then she yelled 'I don't know what to do. I need Daniel!' And then the call disconnected. I tried to get her back on the line, but there was no answer." Barbara threw her hands up and wailed, "What should I do? Should I call the police?"

Fear clutched Dan's heart tightly in its grasp. His face turned ashen, and his legs went weak. He suddenly couldn't get enough air into his lungs, and he dropped down onto his chair. A hundred horrific thoughts ran through his mind about what could be happening to his family at home, because he knew things that no one else knew. There were secrets, *dangerous* secrets that no one else could discover. In a panic, he gathered up the paperwork and files on his desk, stuffed them all into his briefcase and rushed out. "I'll take care of it," was all he said to Barbara as he sped past her.

By the time Dan got home he was in total panic mode. He burst through the door yelling for Rachael as he ran from room to room, searching for his family. He finally found them sitting on the floor in Karen's bedroom, but he was running so fast that he couldn't stop. He passed the room up, sort of skidded across the floor, and bounced off a wall before he managed to halt his mad dash.

He scrambled back to the doorway, his eyes darting wildly around the room trying to locate the threat. After all the awful scenarios that had run through his head, he fully expected the worst. But there were no intruders, there were no monsters, and there was not a single drop of blood to be seen anywhere. "What Rachael?" Dan shouted. "What is it?!"

His wife stood up and ran to him. She was crying, her breath hitching in and out. "Oh Dan. I can't make her stop. I don't know what to do. She's breaking my heart!" She put her head on his shoulder and just bawled. Dan smoothed his wife's hair back, kissed her forehead and gently moved her aside.

As he walked into the room, his gaze landed on Karen. She was sitting in a pile of princess dresses and there were shoes strewn all around her. Her pretty face was smeared with her latest attempt at beautifying herself with her makeup kits. She looked up at him with irritation clearly stamped on her little face. She pointed an accusing finger at Ecko as she demanded, "Daddy, make her stop. She's ruining my fashion show!"

Dan smiled and promised to do his very best. Then he turned his attention to his youngest daughter. Ecko, who was now ten months old, had a small mirror clutched in her hands and she was staring intently into it. Whatever she saw in there distressed her immensely. She had tears streaming, just pouring down her face. The whole front of her purple princess dress was soaked from her tears. She didn't make a sound, just silently cried as if her heart was breaking and her world was ending.

Dan worriedly glanced back at his wife. "What's going on? Why didn't you just take the mirror away from her?"

Rachael, who was now hiccupping from crying so hard replied, "I did! I took it from her, and she freaked out! She screamed and cried and threw herself backwards. I was so shocked that I didn't move fast enough to catch her. I think she banged the back of her head on the floor. But she didn't even care! She sat up and crawled to me and tried to take it from my hands. She screamed so loudly that I didn't know what else to do but let her have it back. What do we do Dan? This is *not* normal!"

Dan didn't say so, but he silently agreed that this was extremely bizarre behavior. He tried talking to his daughter, but it was as if she was in a trance and couldn't hear him. He was at a total loss as to what he should do but standing there just watching her was tearing him up inside. His heart ached at the sight of his baby in pain. Not knowing what else to do, he sat down on the floor, picked his daughter up, and held her close. He hummed softly as he slowly rocked her back and forth. It was all he could think to do. He just wanted to reassure her that she was not alone and that she was safe and loved.

He had no concept of how long he sat there humming and whispering to her that everything was going to be ok. He must have done something right though, because eventually Ecko dropped the mirror to the floor. She turned and flung her arms around him and then snuggled her face into his neck. Dan felt her breath on his face and was overcome with a fierce surge of protectiveness. He had never been a violent man, but in that moment, he knew he would do great bodily harm to anyone that tried to hurt her. But how was he to protect her from what only she could see?

After that disturbing episode, Rachael and Dan noticed that Ecko started to act a bit more like a normal child. She would smile and laugh sometimes. She even cried once when she didn't get her way. One evening, a month or so later, Rachael had been giving her a bath when she caught sight of the mirror above the sink.

Little Ecko tried as hard as she could to get out of the tub and get to it. Rachael had been forced to scoop her up and finish bathing her in the kitchen sink. Not wanting a replay of the previous experience, Dan decided that it was best to try and keep her away from mirrors. It had been absolutely terrifying and also a bit traumatizing. But more importantly, he didn't want Ecko to hurt like that ever again.

Rachael moved all the small mirrors out of reach and Dan took down the big one in the hall. They removed every mirror that she had easy access to and limited her exposure to the remaining ones. But children are surprisingly resourceful creatures, and in that one aspect, Ecko was no different.

She found ways around all of their blocking attempts. One time, she found a compact makeup mirror in Karen's toy box. When Rachael came in to get the girls for lunch, she found Ecko holding it up and giggling at it. Rachael's heart missed a beat, then sped up to double time. She tried to act normal, but she could hear the tremble in her own voice as she cheerily called out, "Lunch time girls. Let's put our toys away and go eat! I think a picnic is a good idea. Doesn't that sound like fun?" Ecko immediately put the mirror back into the toy box and came running, just like that. If there was one thing she adored more than looking into mirrors, it was being outside.

Another time, Dan caught her standing on the sink in the guest bathroom, laughing and babbling at her reflection. Lifting her up into her arms and tickling her belly, he'd told her, "Sinks are not for climbing on. You could hurt yourself. Let's go get your sister and see if she wants to help us build a fort instead!"

After several of these slightly less stressful mirror incidents, Dan and Rachael began to relax a bit. They still found it disturbing and perplexing, and it *always* made them a little uncomfortable, but they were learning to deal with it. They prayed that they'd never have a repeat of that first terrifying event. But always in the back of their minds were whispered thoughts of something worse to come.

Samara

(5 years old)

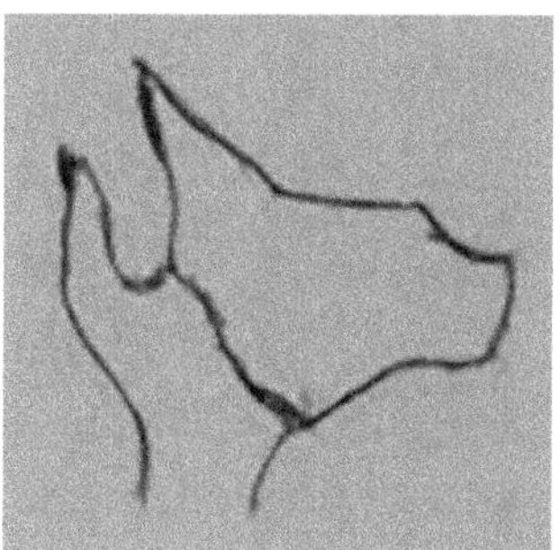

I watch the empty room inside the looking glass, waiting for her to come. I'm sitting on the cold, hard floor of my own bedroom with my back pressed against the door, blocking the way, in case one of the old ones try to come in. This little piece of broken mirror in my hands is the only thing I have of my very own. I keep it hidden away, because I stoled-ed it from Lekjaz the Leech. He owns the Popalickary (Apothecary) shop in town. It's my favorite place to snoop around in, because he always has the bestest stuff, *magic* stuff.

But I can't go back in there anymore. Last time he chased me away because I exploded all his stupid Ribbitters. I had accidentally (on purpose) knocked their cage onto the floor because they started screeching at me when came in. They always do that when they see me; I don't know why. I don't like it. Something about their screaming bothers me in my head.

I asked Lekjaz once why they always scream like that. He'd scrunched up his face all ugly like and scoffed, "The only sounds they make is 'ribbit' and they certainly do *not* scream." I don't know why the stupid man lied to me. This time they started their shrieking as soon as I walked in the shop. They hadn't even seen me yet! And they just got louder and louder.

So, when I walked by them, I made sure Lekjaz wasn't looking at me and then reached out and shoved their cage off the table. But then it busted open, and they all started jumping on me and licking me with their long, sticky tongues. It was grosser than gross, but the worst part of it was that I felt like I was getting weak and sleepy. They were somehow stealing the invisible parts of me, the parts on the *inside* of me, slurping all the energy right out of me, lick after yucky lick. I wanted to lay down on the floor and take a nap.

But then I got mad…really, super mad! And suddenly, I knew exactly what to do. I saw it first in my head and I just knew that I could make it work the same way *outside* my head. I lifted up my hand and made it into a fist. I pretended my fist was giant and that all the Ribbitters were inside it. And then I just gave it a big, hard squeeze.

Guts and Ribbitter brains squirted everywhere. It even got in my hair. And It. Was. Awesome! Then the stupid old leech-man yelled and tried to grab me. But he couldn't catch me. I run super-fast, and he is so old and slow. I zigzagged around crates and cages filled with strange creatures and shelves of bottled herbs, powders, poisons, and who knows what other mysterious gunk. I slid and crawled underneath the tables of all Lekjaz's operation tools, the pinchers and clampers, the needles and knives and saws, as well as his prized bottles of blood sucking leeches. I dodged it all with the old coot slipping and sliding in the Ribbitter ooze behind me.

The door was right there in front of me. I was almost free! But suddenly a bright, shining light coming from one of the shelves flashed into my eyes. I was running so fast, trying to escape, that I almost ran right past it. I had never seen a real mirror, but somehow, I knew that was exactly what it was. The old lady that takes care of me had told me all about my mother and the magic she could do with mirrors.

My feet stopped instantly, like they suddenly got stuck in sink sand, but the rest of me didn't understand what was happening. The top half of my body kept going forward and I fell face down onto the floor. I oomphed really loud as all my air left me, but I jumped up and snatched that mirror off the shelf anyway, even though I couldn't breathe. And then I ran out the door so fast that old Leech man never had a chance of catching me. I looked back and laughed as I sped away. Old Lekjaz was standing in the middle of the street, shaking his fist in the air at me. He screamed that if I came back, he would change me into a snail and eat me. He can do it too, so I'll stay away until I am big enough to explode *him* too, just like I did to his Ribbitters.

That was a month ago and I have learned that while I don't have my mother's ability to go through my stolen mirror, I do have enough of her magic to see through it into other worlds. That's how I found *her*, the girl that looks exactly like me. Now that I can't go to the Popalickary shop no more, all I can do is watch her, that *other* me through the mirror.

I have to wait forever this time, but finally she appears. She sits on the floor over there in that fancy room, while I'm stuck here in my stupid boring bedroom. She's staring into her own mirror, same as I am. I know that she can see the Otherlands too, same as me. I can see her, but she can't see me. Why? I have tried so hard to get her to see me. I wish voices could go through mirrors. I would scream at her. *That* would get her attention.

I watch as a man comes in and sits on the floor beside her. Her father, I guess. He looks into the mirror too, points right at me and says something. My heart leaps, jumping just like all those Ribbitters had, right before they got splattered everywhere. Can he see me? The other me just keeps looking off to the side, still watching the Otherlands. Disappointment fills me. He doesn't see me at all. All he can see is HER. Always HER! I wish it was me over there in that nice house, with the nice family. Why does she get to have everything, while I'm stuck here with these stupid old people, in this ugly house, on this nasty world?

Anger burns inside me as I watch the man smile down at *her* and scoop her up in his arms. He hugs her tight and kisses her forehead. Then he stands up and carries her from the room. I can tell that he really, really loves her. ***I hate her***.

Through Dangers Untold and Hardships Unnumbered

Things settled down and the Roberts family somehow managed to move forward with their lives. Ecko continued with her bizarre inclinations of seeking out (and finding) every mirror in her vicinity. It was uncanny how she could always locate them, even if they were tucked away and hidden from view. It seemed almost as if the mirrors called to her. Aside from all her strange little quirks, Ecko was an absolutely delightful child. She was sweet, polite, and respectful at all times. Karen was her complete opposite, a sassy, bossy little thing.

Dan and Rachael did their very best to make sure that they all lived happy, normal lives. Even though Rachael was never quite the same as before 'the incident', she eventually forgave her husband… Even the worst pain dulls, given enough time. Dan became an even more attentive husband, a more involved father.

They tentatively made a few new friends, and for the most part, this newly modified Plan worked out great. So what if their youngest daughter was slightly odd and saw things no one else could see? What did it hurt that she stared into mirrors every chance she got? Was that really so bad? Teenagers spend an extraordinary amount of time in front of mirrors too. See? Not so strange when you look at it that way.

Years passed quickly by, as they tend to do. One day Ecko was a tiny baby, and then they blinked, and she was turning five years old. Dan and Rachael had discovered early on that Ecko had a huge love for storybooks, fairy tales, and old fantasy movies. The bookshelves in her room were filled with all sorts of adventures. The Never-Ending Story, The Brothers Grimm, The Dark Crystal, The Wizard of Oz, Willow, Mary Poppins, Coraline; she loved them all.

She was extremely advanced for her age and could already read several of her books on her own. When she wasn't mirror gazing, she was usually immersed in a book or watching one of her favorite movies. She never really played with toys much, although she had a ton of them. She had a whole room full of things that most little girls would love to own. Karen certainly loved them anyway. Ecko, not so much. Dress up and tea parties just weren't her thing. The two girls were nothing alike at all. Karen was the princess, Ecko was the adventuress.

At first, Dan (who admittedly enjoyed building forts and fighting off trolls a great deal more than finding and kissing princes) had tried to find some sort of middle ground activities for them all to enjoy together. He wanted his girls to get along and to be close. So, he made up games that included the best of both worlds to encourage the girls to play together, romance AND escapades, heroes AND happily ever afters. It was a good plan. It just didn't work out very well.

The girls were just too different. Karen refused to do anything that was not princess-y, but then she got too bored watching the heroes fight their way through enemy forces to come rescue her. Ecko, exhausted after all that damsel in distress saving, napped during the celebration for the return of the princess. No, that strategy to bring the girls closer didn't work as well as Dan had thought it would. That plan got discarded entirely and filed under 'Disastrous Failed Attempts' the day that Ecko accidentally slung mud all over Princess Karen's favorite ball gown.

Dan had no idea that his eldest daughter could scream so loud. He was actually kind of terrified. After that last unsuccessful attempt, Dan gave up and just played with his daughters individually. He figured that was the safest course of action anyway. With Karen, he played dress up, make overs, and fashion shows. He escorted her to numerous balls and tea parties. He was even known to wear lipstick and a tiara a time or two.

With Ecko, he went on daring and dangerous escapades. He built her a treehouse in the backyard, and together they slayed countless hordes of nasty, bloodthirsty creatures.

Dan spoiled his daughters, and he was constantly on the lookout for things that he knew they would love. For Karen, he always tried to find beautiful and unique porcelain dolls to add to her collection. The glass dolls were the only things Karen had consistently asked for throughout the years...other than clothes, make up, and jewelry. Also, tiaras. There were so many tiaras…

He was always happier to buy the dolls and avoid the tiaras. At last count, there were thirty-three porcelain dolls in her collection, most of them vintage and worth quite a bit of money. Whenever he brought a new one home, he was always careful to present it to Karen when they were alone, without her sister present. Not that Ecko would have been jealous; she wasn't the petty or jealous kind. No, the reason he gave the gifts in secret was because Ecko was terrified of the dolls. They never knew why, but she had a deeply ingrained aversion to them. She wanted nothing to do with *any* dolls, but porcelain ones were the worst. She couldn't stand to even look at them.

Karen had been thoroughly tickled when she first discovered Ecko's irrational fear of her dolls. She had tormented her for days, carrying them around and leaving them in random places for Ecko to find. Every yelp, every scream, every whimper encouraged Karen to think of new ways to frighten her sister. For a short time, it was the highlight of her life. That is, until her fun came to a bitter end. Karen had snuck into Ecko's bedroom and placed her favorite doll into the bed, under the blankets. It was a vintage Ashton Drake bride doll made in the early 1900s, and Ecko was especially afraid of it. She ran every time she saw it.

That night when Ecko had crawled into bed and saw it lying there, she barely managed to swallow back the scream that tried to escape. For a moment, as her heart thudded painfully in her chest and she gasped for breath, she honestly believed that she was dying of fright. When she calmed down enough to realize that she would live to see another day, she decided then and there to put a stop to Karen's mean games. She just wouldn't give it back, that's all. She would hide it and pretend that she had never even seen it.

Ecko picked the doll up by its dress, so that she wouldn't have to touch any more of it than she had to and hid it in a dresser drawer. Then she went to sleep. The next morning, she got up before anyone else was awake. Karen would surely find it if she hid it anywhere in her room, so she took the doll out and tiptoed downstairs to find a better hiding spot. But she stubbed her toe on a chair and when she stumbled, the doll flew from her hands and fell to the floor.

Dan heard the noise and when he came downstairs to investigate, he found Ecko sitting on the floor, crying next to the shattered doll. "I didn't mean to!" she cried. "I was just going to hide it, so she would stop putting them in my bed. I didn't mean to drop it, Daddy!" Ecko covered her face with her hands and sobbed.

Dan sat down on the floor beside her. "I know you didn't mean to break the doll. But I'm glad that you're finally trying to stand up for yourself. I wondered if you were going to let her continue to bully you forever. I know that you're a lover, not a fighter… except when you're fighting off hordes of drooling trolls, that is. *Then* you're ferocious and fearless and unbeatable.

But you're different with people, especially with your sister. You don't want to hurt her, because you love her. Eventually though, enough is enough. Sometimes, fighting back is necessary. I don't want you to ever start a fight, but you can't back down and allow a bully to abuse you either. Not even if it's someone that you love. Now here's what we're going to do. *You* are going to act like you don't know anything about this doll. You never saw it in your bed, and you certainly didn't break it. Understand?"

He gathered all the pieces up and tiptoed into Karen's room and dumped the remains at the foot of her bed. The next morning, Karen predictably started hollering that Ecko had broken her doll. Dan calmly looked at her and said, "That doll was on the floor in the hallway this morning. I didn't see it and I accidentally stepped on it. Hurt my foot too. Why are you trying to get your sister in trouble when you just forgot to pick up after yourself, like usual? I don't understand why you're blaming Ecko. We all know that she hates your dolls. She would *never* go into your room and take any one of them. Now, young lady. You know that those dolls are expensive. Maybe we should find someone else that wants them more than you do, someone that will take care of them properly."

Dan winked at Ecko as Karen stomped back up the stairs. The plan had worked marvelously. Karen decided she'd better find other ways to torture her little sister. She didn't want to risk losing any more of her beloved dolls.

As much as Dan enjoyed searching for new dolls to buy for Karen, he loved shopping for Ecko even more. There was such a broad array of things that she found interesting. But mostly he searched for fantasy books and movies, intricate puzzles, and *anything* pertaining to fairies. She absolutely adored the Fae and all its surrounding folklore.

Dan had discovered her fairy infatuation when they'd come across an old and scuffed, leather bound book of the Fae at a neighborhood group yard sale. Ecko had been drawn straight to it, almost like something had led her there. Dan and Rachael watched intently as she dug through a box, shuffling books aside until she reached it. It seemed as if she'd been searching for *that* particular book.

Dan went on high alert, his protective instincts kicked in by her very un-Ecko like behavior. She was always very observant of everything around her, but she tended to keep her hands to herself. She *never* picked things up without permission. But she hadn't even hesitated on this particular instance. With an angelic smile on her face, she'd lovingly ran her tiny hands over the worn leather, over and over again. It wasn't a typical, mass-produced book. The pages were thick, old, and yellowed, the pictures and writing all beautifully done by hand. It didn't even have a title, seeming more like a personal journal of some sort.

When Ecko opened the cover, her eyes had instantly filled with awe. She'd sat down right there in the grass and immediately became immersed in the world of Faeries. When half an hour passed and Dan announced that it was time to leave, Ecko, who had never asked for anything before, had quietly and shyly asked if she could have it. "Well, let's see," Dan murmured with a twinkle in his eyes. "How much is it?"

They searched for a price tag but were unable to find one. He had every intention of buying that book for her; he didn't care how much the sellers were asking for it. With those big green eyes pleading up at him, there would have been no way he could have denied her anything. So, the Roberts family each carried their findings to the cash out table.

Karen's arms were so full that Dan had to walk behind her and pick up the things that she dropped. He pulled out his wallet as the prices were being totaled. "My daughter would like to purchase this book, but it doesn't seem to have a price tag. Can you tell me how much it is?" he asked the ladies handling the cash boxes.

Ecko reluctantly let go of the book long enough for them to look it over. "I don't even know who's selling this," one of the women said. "There's no tag at all. Hey Dana, do you know who this belongs to?" she carried it over to a tall blond-haired lady that was busy refolding shirts on a table.

"No. It's not mine. I've never seen it," she replied. Ecko watched anxiously as each person involved in the group sale was questioned about the book. There was quite a bit of confusion; nobody seemed to know where it had come from, or how it had gotten there.

Fearing that she wouldn't be allowed to have the book, Ecko began to cry. "Aw, don't do that. Don't cry, Kiddo. We'll get it sorted out." Dan assured her. The lady holding the book finally made her way back to them.

"Well, no one knows where this thing came from." She looked down at Ecko, handed her the book, and smiled. "We all took a vote and decided that, not knowing who the actual owner is, we really can't sell it. But we still want you to have it. It's our gift to you."

Ecko smiled shyly. "Oh, thank you!" she told them in her tiny, quiet voice. She did not take her eyes off of that book the whole way home. When they got there, Dan and Ecko sat on the porch swing and went through the book together. It was extraordinarily beautiful, and very, very old. The hand-painted art was truly remarkable. There was no story line whatsoever. It simply listed different types of Fae. Each page depicted a hand drawn image, the name of the Fae, a description of their looks and traits, and all of their known magics.

When they reached the end of the book, Ecko turned back to the first page and started over again. Dan laughed and asked her why she was so fascinated with the fairies. Her precious little face had scrunched up with a look of intense concentration while she thought it over. "I don't know" she'd finally whispered to him. "They just feel like family." Dan felt his blood run cold and he shivered. He was suddenly reminded of secrets and promises from the past.

A couple of weeks before her fifth birthday, Ecko had solemnly asked her parents for her very own mirror for her bedroom. Her little voice was so quiet and serious when she said, "I won't ask for anything else ever again. I promise I will do my chores and be good forever. I won't look *all* the time, just a little bit of times. And I won't cry, so you won't get mad at me."

Dan picked her up and settled her onto his lap. He told her, "We have never been mad at you. We've been worried about you and scared, but never mad. We love you and your sister more than anything. We just want to protect you and do what is best for you. Now, let's get you to bed. Your mother and I will discuss this birthday request of yours."

The concerned parents did discuss it and in the end Dan and Rachael reluctantly decided to give her what she wanted. After all, she had access to mirrors every day and nothing terrible had happened thus far. So, the very next day they bought a mirror and hung it above the girl's dresser. She watched her reflection as she jumped up and down on her bed and giggled uncontrollably. "Just look at how happy she is," Rachael whispered. "Such a strange thing to bring a 5-year-old so much pleasure."

Dan put his arm around his wife and smiled, trying his best to hide his nervousness. Despite his unease, nothing odd happened that night, or the next night, or the one after that. So, mom and dad eventually began to relax their guard.

Dan was overly excited for Ecko's birthday to arrive. He'd found the perfect movie and he just *knew* that she would love it, and he was right. The moment she got it unwrapped, she begged to watch it.

Dan smiled to himself as the excited birthday girl settled onto his lap to watch Labyrinth. She sat still as a statue, totally absorbed and mesmerized for the entire two hours and five-minute duration. She even had to listen to the song while the credits rolled. When it was over, Dan poked her in the ribs to get her attention and make her giggle. "Well kiddo, what did you think? Did you like it?"

She turned, threw her arms around his neck, and gave him a sloppy cake-smeared kiss. "That was the best movie ever! I love the Hobglin King! And the Fire Gang! Oh, and Sir Didymus! Oh, thank you Daddy. You are the best Daddy in the whole wide world! Can we watch it again? *Please* Daddy?" Dan may or may not have had tears in his eyes as he picked up the remote and restarted the movie.

When it was time for Ecko to be enrolled in kindergarten, Dan and Rachael had a difficult time deciding what to do. Should they put her in a public school or a small private school? They went around and round about it; they just didn't know what would be best. Rachael was worried and said, "Maybe we should just homeschool her. I do have a teaching degree, after all. Instead of going back to work as we planned, maybe I should just teach her here at home… where it won't matter if she goes weird."

But Dan didn't want her to stay isolated, kept away from other people just because she was a little bit different. "No Rachael. I don't think that's the way to go. She needs to be around other people, other children her own age. If she interacts with others and watches how *they* act, maybe she can learn how to fit in too." Dan sighed and shook his head. "I just don't want her to get bullied. Because she IS different, and people don't like different. Kids are mean. You know they are."

In the end, it was finally decided that Ecko would go to the same public school that Karen attended. They could always change the plan later if it didn't work out. As Dan walked her to her classroom that first day, he couldn't help but notice that she was scared, even though she was clearly trying so hard to be brave. "What's wrong Baby Girl? You're going to have lots of fun here. Why are you scared? Talk to me."

Ecko nervously glanced around at all the kids in the classroom. Some were running around like wild animals. Some were crying for their parents. Three of them were crawling around and plowing into anything that got in their way. One boy was even picking his nose and eating what came out. In a timid little mouse voice she whispered, "I can't stay here. I'm not like them. They're going to hate me."

Dan got down on his knees and took her in his arms. "No, you're not like them. You *are* different. But that's not a bad thing. You don't have to be like everyone else. Why would you even want to be? All you can do is try to make friends. They very well may not like you, but only because they won't understand you. Look at me now. You are perfect. Your mother and I love you just the way you are. Don't you ever forget that. Now put on your brave face. You have fought scarier monsters and survived way more dangerous situations than this!" Obviously unconvinced but resigned to her fate, Ecko nodded and bravely walked into the classroom. Then she turned and gave him a sad little wave goodbye. Dan cried all the way home.

School turned out to be everything Ecko thought it would be. She *didn't* fit in. The girls all wanted to play girl games. She tried to play along, to pretend that she liked them too. She really did. But somehow, she always ended up trying to bring fire breathing dragons and trolls to their princess parties. She would have played with the boys, but they'd all laughed and said that she had cooties.

So, she spent play time alone, either reading or staring out the window, but *always* wishing that she were somewhere else. She quickly became bored and lonely, but the real trouble began for her just a few months into her first year of school. She'd been washing her hands in the restroom with several other girls when she suddenly climbed up on top of the sink to stare intently into the mirror.

She lost all awareness of her surroundings, never even responded to the girls yelling out their "oohh's" and "aahh's" and their "You're gonna get in so much trouble's!" The girls were scared, because she seemed to not even hear them. She just stood there staring until the teacher had to come find her and drag her away.

The kids all teased her mercilessly about it. It went on for weeks and weeks. They were relentless. Until one day on the playground, she finally got mad. She'd never been mad before. All the kids went running to the teacher, crying. They told her that Ecko's eyes had flashed silver, like mirrors, and then everyone had been pushed to the ground. They insisted that *Ecko* had knocked them all down with her mind. After that, the kids called her a witch, and made it a point to stay as far away from her as possible. At that, the die was cast, and the roles were all set. She'd been labeled Freak, the outcast that no one wanted to know. School proved to be a very lonely and trying time for her and would remain so for the duration of her years in the public education system.

One night, not long after she'd become the kindergarten pariah, Dan woke to find Ecko standing next to his bed, crying, and trembling all over. Not wanting Rachael to awaken and worry, he quietly got out of bed, scooped his daughter up in his arms and tiptoed out of the room. He held her and rocked her until she'd calmed. "Did something scare you?" She nodded her head yes, her face pressed into his neck. "Did you have a bad dream?"

She shrugged her little shoulders and whispered, "I don't know." "You don't know? You don't know if it was a dream?" he asked. He patted her back and continued, "I understand. You were dreaming, but it seemed like it was real. Something scared you?" Up and down went her shoulders again as a tiny whimper escaped her. "Well, can you tell me about it? What was it that scared you? I may not be able to fix it, but I can at least listen. I love you and I am always here for you. I want you to trust me. Perhaps just telling me about it will help."

Ecko sat back and looked him in the eyes. She balled his shirt up in her tiny hands and her face scrunched up. "It was a dream, but it was real too. It was me, Daddy! A different me, in a bad world. The real me was here, in my bed, looking at myself in the mirror. But my reflection wasn't looking back. The me in there was asleep. She was asleep and dreaming, and it was HER dream that scared me. The other me was screaming at a scared old lady and she looked really mean! Her eyes turned gray, like they were filled with smoke, and then a big black shadow got off the wall and came up behind them. Then the REAL me got out of my bed and walked to my mirror, *without my permission!"*

"I tried to stop them, but they didn't listen! My hands just lifted right up and pressed against the glass! The shadow stood over that other me, but it looked at real me through the mirror as it turned into a big, scary man. He just looked and looked at me. He didn't say anything at all, but I heard his voice in my head anyway. He said, "I found you." And then he laughed and laughed, and it was *so scary!* It made my heart hurt. I couldn't move but I wanted to. I wanted to run and find you, but I was froz-dened!"

"And then, his face started getting all strange, like it was disappearing. But his smile got bigger, and bigger, and bigger! It was all I could see! And...and he bent down and gobbled the other me up! Then he turned back into his shadow self and flew out the window!"

Her voice rose higher and higher with every word. By the time she'd finished her tale, she was hysterical and nearly inconsolable, and Dan was more frightened than he'd even been in his entire life. It sounded like a horrible nightmare, but he didn't try to tell her that it was just a dream or merely her imagination. He never once doubted that it happened, just like she described it, because he'd immediately recognized the shadow man.

It was the same evil being that had haunted his dreams since the day he'd bought Ecko home. Dan felt incredibly helpless. He didn't know how to protect his little girl. "What can I do to help, Baby Girl? Do you want me to take your mirror away? I can get rid of every mirror in this house if you want. Will that even stop it?"

His daughter's eyes filled with panic. She frantically shook her head back and forth. "Oh, please no, Daddy! Please no!" She started to cry again.

"Hey! I won't take it down if that's not what you want. I'm *asking* you what you want! It was just an idea. I can't stand seeing you scared and upset." He hugged her tight and murmured, "I just want to help."

They were silent for a long time while Dan simply rocked her back and forth in the rocking chair. Finally, he said, "This is the first time that you've been scared of what you see in the mirrors, isn't it? What have you seen inside there before tonight? Can you tell me?"

His little girl lay there on his chest and whispered, "Everything. I see everything, everywhere. Different worlds with all kinds of people. Strange animals and creatures and even trees. So many places, and they are all so different from here! Some worlds are beautiful, some are scary, and some are sad. I call them the Otherlands."

She told him that she remembered the very first time it had happened, the first time that she'd seen one of those Otherlands. "That time when I was just a little baby, and I was crying so much that it scared you and momma. There was a lady. A sad lady that sat in her chair crying and looking out the window every day. That's all she did, because her heart was brokdened in half. She was all alone.

There were people there with her that loved her, but in her heart she was alone. Understand?"

"Then that Otherland place disappeared and there was a different one instead, an island. Everyone there had brokden hearts. They were crying on the inside, in their hearts, and on the outside too. It was a place just for the saddest, lostest people to go to when they died. There was a little old black and brown dog laying in the sand on the beach. And she was crying and crying and crying. She was laying there waiting for that woman in the chair to come for her, and she was just crying! They loved each other and missed each other so much, it brokeded my heart too."

Ecko had choked up and started sobbing then. Dan had tears streaming down his face too. He could not imagine such sorrow, and his young daughter had lived with these images inside her mind all this time, bore it all alone. He held her close and stroked her hair. He told her to go ahead; cry and let it all out. He would cry with her. And that's just what they did.

They stayed up late into the night talking about all the wonders that she had seen through the looking glass, all from right here inside her home. He knew without a doubt that she was telling the truth and that she really could see the things she spoke of. "I wish I could see the things that you see," Dan told her. He'd been amazed by what he'd learned, but he was also terrified.

If she could see out to the Otherlands, could someone look back at her, find her somehow? Who was this 'other' girl in the mirror and what of this shadow man? *He* was obviously a very evil being. The verdict was still out on whether or not the 'other' girl was bad, but something deep inside warned him that she was just as evil as the shadow man. Dan had no answers, but he knew one thing for sure. He would die protecting his little girl if they somehow found their way here.

Exhausted from her ordeal, Ecko had finally fallen asleep cuddled up against him. He could tell that her dreams were uneasy. Her eyes rolled back and forth under the closed lids and her legs twitched frantically, as if she was running from dream monsters.

Dan lifted her into his arms, and she started sleep-mumbling. The words were said so quietly that he had to lean in and strain to hear them. "The Red Room. The Red Room." That was all she'd said, over and over again. He held her just a little bit tighter and soothingly stroked her back. After a few minutes, she seemed to calm and go into a deeper sleep. He could only hope that the dreams couldn't reach her there.

Dan awoke sometime around midnight, stiff and sore from falling asleep sitting up in the rocking chair. He carefully stood up and shifted her limp form into a better position before making his way to the hallway closet to retrieve the surprise that he'd hidden there. Then he carried his daughter back to her room and laid her down in her bed. She woke up and gave him the sweetest smile. "You were right, Daddy. I do feel better now. Thank you for loving me."

He got all choked up and had to clear his throat a couple times before he could speak. "Don't go back to sleep just yet, Kiddo. I have a surprise for you. I bought it to give to you for Christmas, but I think you need him now."

She held out tiny, eager hands. "Gimme," she said, and her excited grin nearly melted his heart. He pulled the scruffy stuffed animal with the eye patch out from behind his back where he'd been hiding it and placed it into her hands. "Sir Didymus!" she squealed and launched herself from the bed, right back into his arms. She hugged her new toy close while she covered her dad's face with sweet little girl kisses.

His face flushed with pleasure, he laughed and tucked her back under the blankets. "I want you to listen to me now. This is very important. If you ever feel like something bad is going to happen, or if you ever see that shadow man again, you run. In a dream or awake, it doesn't matter. You just run. Come and get me as fast as you can. If I'm not here, you take Sir Didymus and you hide. I will do my very best to keep you safe, always. I don't know why you see things that no one else can see. I don't have the answers. I wish I did. But never doubt this for a second. You Are. Special. And there is a reason for *all* of this. One day, you will know exactly who you are and why you were chosen for this." He'd reached out and tweaked her nose before continuing. "Until then, Sir Didymus will help me protect you. Hold him close when you get scared, or when you're sad. He'll help you feel better. He's a knight, you know, and has taken a sacred oath. He is sworn to do his duty. Sir Didymus will protect you, Through Dangers Untold and Hardships Unnumbered. And so will I."

Dan waited until his daughter fell back asleep, then he laid down on the floor next to her bed. There was no way he was leaving her in there all alone tonight. But what was he to do about tomorrow night?

Samara

(7 years old)

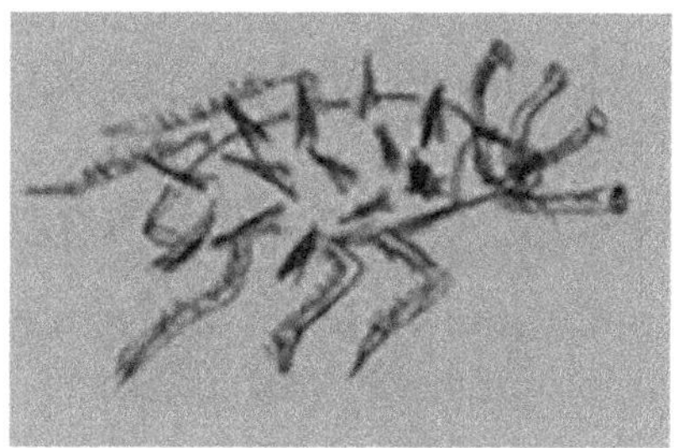

They've come for me, the Shadow Lord's henchmen. The house is full of his nasty, smelly minions. They tell me that he's my father. They say that he's had all his people searching for me, ever since I was born. They couldn't find me because all that time, they'd been looking for a boy. He was supposed to have had a son, not a daughter. Oops. They said that a Vika Vakooja, a roach-beetle, had seen me practicing my squishing power on some fish in the market and reported it back to the Shadow man. So, he'd sent his Night Shades out to 'feel' me. They surrounded me, a dark, swirling cloud of shadows, swarming around my head. I fell to the ground and tried to scream, but I breathed them in instead. They went in my nose and my mouth, making me choke. I could feel them slithering around inside my head. It felt terrible and it took forever. Then they poured back out, like I was puking out smoke. I heard a man's voice inside my head. He laughed and said, 'I found you." I should have run away, but somehow, I knew that it would have done no good to run. There was nowhere I could go to hide from him. Not if he could just send his voice into my brain.

Now my father's goons are keeping me trapped here in my room while they question the old couple that took me in when I was a baby. They're wasting their time on those two old fools. They know nothing. When that doesn't get them answers, they search the house and find my mirror.

They ask all kinds of questions, scream them in my face. What kind of powers do I have? How did I squish the fish? Could I squish anything I wanted? Why did I have this mirror? Where had it come from and why was I hiding it? What do I see in it? Can I travel to other places through it?

I tell them, "I can only squish little stuff. I have tried and tried but I can't squish anything big, or even little things on big stuff. Like, this one time, I tried to squish the old man's head, but as you can see, he still gots his head so *that* didn't work."

They also wanted to know if I could go through the mirror. "I wish!" I screamed back. "There's no way I'd still be here, forced to look at your ugly faces if I could do that!" And now they're mad. "Well, I'm sorry!" I yelled back, just as loud as they were shouting. "I thought you *knew* you were ugly." I couldn't help but laugh out loud at the anger in their eyes. I think they wanted to hurt me, but they knew they couldn't, because my father, their Shadow Lord would kill them if they tried.

They'd finally gotten tired of questioning me and stormed back out to start on the old couple again. I *really* wish I could see what was happening, but they have me locked in and refuse to let me out. The Shadow's men must be torturing them, though because they've been screaming out there for hours. I wonder if they took the old people's guts out. I wonder if they've cut them open. I wonder if their guts are old and wrinkled like they are.

The Goons have told me that my father is extremely happy that he's finally found me and that he's *glad* that I'm a girl. He wants to be with me, but he can't. He's cursed, trapped in a castle so he can't come get me. I could go to him, but then I would be trapped in the castle too. He's been trying to find a way out so that he and I can be together. They tell me that he wants me to learn to use my magic, grow strong and powerful so that I can rule the worlds at his side. I want to believe them. I want my father to love me, more than anything I have ever wanted before.

But then they ruin everything. They say that my father wants to know if I've met any *other* little girls. Did I have a friend, or maybe a sister, somewhere? Have I ever seen another girl that looked like me through the mirror?

I've told them over and over, "No! I haven't seen any dumb girls!" But somehow, they know that I'm lying. I think one of my father's roach- beetle spies caught me watching the *other* me, saw me trying to get *her* to notice *me*. The nasty little thing must have snitched on me! Well, so what? They can't make me tell them anything!

So now my father's men are trying to force me to use the mirror. I don't want to. It's none of their business! But I know that I'll do it soon; I'll have to. I'm so hungry. They won't let me eat! They say they'll give me food only when I show them what I'm hiding. I don't want them to find out about that 'Other' me. I don't know who she is, but I know that I don't want the Lokskell, Lord of Shadows to know about her. If he really is my father, then I want him to see *me*. Not her. She already has a family to love her. All I have is some old people that are scared of me. And they smell funny.

I finally did it. I couldn't help it. I just had to eat. I used the mirror but none of the men guarding me (holding me prisoner) saw her. They made me watch as she lay there on her bed reading a book. And then they made me watch and watch some more, just stare at her like she was doing the most interesting and exciting things. Gah. Boring.

How long did I have to watch her do nothing? Besides, I was *starving.* I made the mirror go blank and set it down. "I want food," I tell them. But they don't care. They start yelling questions at me again, asking about *her.* So. Many. Questions.

"I don't know! I don't know anything!" I scream back as I start to cry. I *never* cry. I absolutely hate crying. It's such a disgusting weakness. I just want to eat something. If I don't get food soon, I'm going to take a bite out of one of *them.* We'll see how they feel about starving me then.

Father is a big fat liar. He doesn't love me, and he doesn't really want me to rule by his side. All he cares about is HER! I am to remain a prisoner here and learn everything I can about the *other* me. A few of his creatures stay outside my house at all times to keep me here. His Night Shades and roach-beetles are always in here with me. They never leave. They spy on me as I spy on HER.

I can't hurt his Night Shades, but I have squished 327 roach-beetles with my magic. They just keep sending more. That's ok. I need the practice. Father doesn't care at all about the things that I can do. I've realized that is a *good* thing, because he doesn't know that I'm learning how to become shadow too.

When his Night Shades got in my head to 'feel' me, well, I felt them too. I learned stuff about Father and how his shadow form works. If I think about it and try really hard, I can become shadowy too. Just my hands, but I know I can learn to do better. I practice every chance I get. I have alone time for bathroom stuff and that's when I get to work on it. But I get tired real fast. Being tired makes it hard to spy on *her* and that makes Father angry.

They make me watch her room all the time, even while she sleeps. Sometimes they wake me up in the middle of the Pitch, when the world is dark and everyone else is sleeping to check in and see what she's doing. "Stop waking me up! She's just sleeping, you big stupids. I want to sleep too!" I tell them again and again.

I even have to watch when she's away from her room. Sometimes she's gone for hours and hours, but they make me watch anyway. At first, I hated staring at an empty room. It was so boring! But one time, I got really mad because I had to wait so long for her to come back. I was tired of staring at her dumb toys.

Then it came to me, just like the time I realized I could squish the Ribbitters. I could *make* her notice me. I knew how! I could rearrange her room, from my side of the mirror. Well, the reflection of her room, anyway. That way when she looks in the mirror, the reflection would show that her stuff had been moved all around! She keeps her room neat, everything always in its place. She would definitely notice if I moved her things.

So, I tried to do it. I tried to do it just like how I saw it in my head, but it was a lot harder to do than squishing stuff. I had to try and try for weeks, months. I almost gave up. It took so long, and it was really hard for me to concentrate that much, especially in secret. I think that Father's goons were starting to get suspicious too. But I finally did it! All I managed to do was knock that dumb, dead dog thing off her bed. But it *is* her favorite toy, so I know that when she comes in and sees her bed reflected in her mirror, she'll definitely notice it missing. Then, she'll know things are not what they seem through the looking glass.

I'll keep practicing and I will keep it all a secret. I'll work on my powers and grow bigger and stronger. And when I'm finally powerful enough, they'll all be sorry for how they've treated me. Father the liar, who doesn't really want me at all. Who thinks spying is all I'm good for, like I am just another of his roach-beetles. That my only use is to watch and then report information about *her*. The special one. They will learn, in time. I am so much more than they realize. He'll be sorry...soon. And so will *she*. I hate them both.

I Spy Something Scary

Ecko loathed school, mainly because she learned things far too easily and completed her assignments too quickly. Then, she was forced to wait for everyone else to catch up. To top it off, she also didn't have any friends; all the other kids thought she was a freak. She was bored all day and she never had anyone to talk to. So, even if she hadn't been so very different, so *strange*, she was far more advanced than the average second grader. While all her classmates were busy peeling glue off their hands and learning sight words, she was immersed in books that she'd brought from home. She absolutely despised the babyish books for her grade level.

There was talk of moving her up a few grades, but it was eventually decided that they would wait a bit longer to see what would happen. She was already alienated from classmates of her *own* age. It would be even worse if she were three or four years younger than the rest of her class.

So, she gritted her teeth and did the work that her teachers doled out, tedious as it was to her. She stayed quiet and kept to herself, always watching the other kids, learning what to do, what to hide. She'd quickly figured out that she had to take as few bathroom breaks as possible during school hours. Bathrooms were the only places on campus that had mirrors, so she avoided them as much as possible. When she had no other choice but to go, she kept her eyes lowered down at her feet and got in and out as fast as she could. She didn't care what wonders might be waiting for her in those mirrors; she couldn't afford to have another incident like the previous one.

In fact, she'd learned to ignore public mirrors almost completely. The only mirror gazing, (as she called it) that she allowed herself was while she was alone in her bedroom. Rachael was extremely pleased with how things had turned out. She thought that putting Ecko in public school had really helped her and that she was outgrowing the whole mirror phase.

Dan knew better. His daughter had certainly learned to control when and where she did her mirror gazing, but she hadn't outgrown it. She'd merely adapted. It had helped her to... not fit in exactly, but it had helped her blend in a bit. He encouraged her to always tell him about the Otherlands and about any dreams she had. He was constantly worried about the Shadow man returning, whether by dream or by mirror. If she ever saw him again, she kept it to herself.

Still, she *did* confide in him about many of her dreams. Especially Red Room. Or more precisely, Red *Door*. She'd confided that in almost every single dream she had, a red door would make an appearance, not random ones either. It was always the same mysterious door. In some dreams it would suddenly appear in her path, blocking her way. She could never get it open. She could knock, pound on it, kick it. Nothing worked. She'd get so frustrated that she'd even tried to scream it open.

Sometimes, she dreamed that she was in a huge room and the only way out was to go through that door, but it was locked. It was *always* locked. But there were thousands, *hundreds* of thousands of keys locked inside with her. They took up every inch of wall space. They hung from strings on the ceiling. They covered the entire floor in a layer at least an inch thick, like a blanket of metal snowflakes on the ground. She would die long before she could ever possibly check that many keys. In other dreams, she only saw it in passing, as if it were simply an innocent door, minding its own business and had nothing to do with her. But it was always there, *somewhere*, in every dream... like a bloodstain in her mind.

Dan hated that Red Door, absolutely despised it. He knew that it really disturbed her, and he wanted to fix it. He wanted answers, damn it. He wanted to know what it all meant. But he WAS glad that she was comfortable talking to him about these things now. At least she had someone to confide in. But he noticed that the older she got, the less she talked about the Red Door.

"I try not to think about it anymore," she'd told him the last time he asked about it. "It makes me so mad! And sad. And scared. I can never figure out how to get through it, or why I even *need* to get through it. And I can't make the dreams stop. So, I just try not to think about it anymore."

She also stopped talking about the Otherlands as often too. If he asked about them, she would shrug nonchalantly and say that she hadn't seen any new places, just the same ones that she had already told him about. Dan knew that something had changed, but he didn't want to keep at her and possibly push her away. Ecko was grateful that he didn't pry. Avoidance often felt dishonest to her, almost like a lie. She wasn't lying, exactly. She just wasn't telling him the whole truth and nothing but the truth, so help her God.

She didn't even really know what was going on, but something *had* changed. Ever since she'd turned eight years old, her mirror had begun to show her different things. Oh, she still saw the Otherlands, but now there was something else too. Something strange was going on with her own world inside of the glass. She had started to see the things in her room get rearranged, but only in the mirror's reflection! It was little things at first. Every day she came in, looked into the mirror, and found that something had gotten up and moved out of its place.

Yesterday it had been little Janey-Bug, the old glow worm that her father had found on eBay for her last year. She'd come home from school, hung her backpack up, then sat down on her bed. She looked everywhere except at the mirror as she mentally prepared herself. Her eyes assessed everything in the room, everything that she possessed, assuring herself that things were exactly how she had left them that morning and that everything was still in its own place.

Everything was right where it was supposed to be, like always. She took a deep breath and reluctantly raised her eyes to the mirror, slowly and meticulously searching for any discrepancies between the mirror world and her own world. She had spotted it immediately. Her green, glowing caterpillar plush was not where it was supposed to be. Janey-Bug lived on the shelf beside her bed where she kept all of her favorite things. *But she was missing from the mirror's reflection.* She slowly turned her head to look behind her, back into the real world, and there she was, sitting on the shelf just where she was supposed to be.

She turned back to recheck the mirror. Yep, still gone from the reflection. Always before when this happened, the thing that had gotten moved had done just that. It only moved out of its place. It was never gone altogether. Usually, it was knocked down onto the floor. Sometimes it was lying on a different shelf or even on the bed. But this time she couldn't see the toy anywhere. Janey-Bug was just gone, and Ecko was very, very scared.

She ran from the room and spent the rest of the evening outside on the swing. She swung as high as she could and pretended that she was flying, flying, flying, just like a bird. The next time she checked her mirror, Janey-Bug was back where she belonged! Ecko was glad that she was back, but she certainly didn't feel any better. She went to bed that night feeling troubled and uneasy, and her tummy hurt. She absolutely refused to look into the mirror. She didn't think she could handle seeing something else amiss that night. For the very first time, she was afraid of the mirror. But the tension from restraining herself was almost unbearable. It took forever for her to fall asleep, and then her dreams were troubled, full of shadows and crawling things and cartoon inchworms with sharp, snapping teeth...

When she woke up the next morning, like always, her eyes automatically went straight to the mirror. Janey-Bug was gone again! She searched the whole reflection twice, before her eyes were drawn to the shelf in the real world. She just stared, mouth open in disbelief. Janey-Bug was really gone. Really, really gone! She couldn't believe it. The toy was missing, from the mirror world as well as the real world.

How could she just disappear? In total panic mode, she jumped out of bed and ran around the room, searching everywhere.

She pulled out all the drawers on her dresser, checking them in the real world and in their reflection. Not there. She tore open the doors on her closet. No Janey-Bug. She had just gotten down on the floor and lifted up the duvet to search under her bed when her sister burst in with the toy in her hand.

"Why is your dumb toy in my room? You *know* you're not allowed in there. And why have you pulled its head off? Were you planning to tell Dad that I did this to get me into trouble? Well, it won't work! I am *not* taking the blame for this. And stay out of my room!" she yelled. Then she threw the toy to the floor and stomped out, slamming the door behind her.

Shocked speechless, Ecko picked up the two pieces of the severed glow worm and sat there on the floor staring down at it. Someone had cruelly and maliciously decapitated Janey-Bug! This was all too confusing and frightening. She didn't understand what was happening at all, and it was really starting to scare her. She didn't know what she should do.

Eventually, she got up off the floor and went in search of her dad. "I don't know what happened, Daddy. I think it just fell off!" It wasn't a lie, not really. She truly *didn't* know what had happened. "Can you fix her?" she pleaded.

Dan had taken one look at those tear-filled eyes and that wobbly bottom lip and set his work aside to perform emergency worm surgery. He carefully stitched the head back to the fuzzy green body while Ecko watched anxiously from beside him. When he'd put in the last stitch and cut the string, he said, "Here you go, Sweetheart. She's good as new."

Ecko threw her arms around her hero's neck, causing Dan to beam with pleasure. "Oh, thank you Daddy! I knew you could do it! You are the best Daddy in the whole wide world!" She hugged Janey-Bug to her chest and scampered back up the stairs to her room, but she kept the toy close to her for the rest of the day.

At bedtime, she reluctantly placed her back on the shelf. "Don't you move from this spot, Janey-Bug. Don't you dare," she whispered to the worm. She turned away and just happened to glance up at the mirror as she took her bedtime clothes out of the dresser. She didn't even mean to look; it was an automatic thing. She never even realized how many times a day she looked into the mirrors. She saw herself standing there with her pajamas in her hands, and for a split second it appeared as if her reflection was smiling. But when she looked closer, everything was exactly how it should be. It was just her normal self. She hurriedly got dressed and jumped into bed to await good night kisses from her parents.

Unfortunately, she had to listen to a lecture from her mother on respecting other people's privacy. She didn't even try to defend herself by saying she hadn't gone into Karen's room, (even though she would never willingly step foot in there with those dolls). No, there was no use trying to explain. The truth was too strange, even for her.

After that incident, Karen must have made it her life's mission to torment her little sister every chance she could get. Christmas morning soon came and Ecko was shocked to find a gift from Karen under the tree. When she saw her sister's nasty little smile, she knew that whatever was inside that package wasn't going to be anything she would be happy to receive.

Dread filled her as she slowly unwrapped the gift. She held it as far from her body as her arms would allow as she carefully opened up the box. She was right. It was one of the most horrifying things that Karen could have possibly given her… other than a porcelain doll, that is. It was a fluffy, brown teddy bear. Karen knew that she didn't like teddy bears and that they'd always creeped her out. All that false cuteness, hiding behind those dreadful glass eyes... *dead* eyes. She hated it. But even before the gift was fully unwrapped, she had decided on a course of action.

First, no matter what it had turned out to be, she would try to hide any fear or revulsion. It could (and would) be used as further ammunition against her later. Second, she would pretend to be thankful. Her parents would be angry if she acted ungrateful.

So, she forced herself to reach in and take the hideous little thing from its box. The feel of it in her hands made her skin crawl, but she smiled and hugged her sister as if it were the greatest gift she had ever received. The angry frown on Karen's face almost made up for her cruelty. Almost.

Later, her dad helped her carry her new things up to her room. He made sure the teddy bear was in the stack that he carried. Apparently, he wasn't fooled by either of the girls' actions/reactions. He said, "Karen knows that you don't like teddy bears. I know she only bought it to mess with you. I'm going to have a talk with her, but I wanted you to know that I am very proud of how you handled it. It was very mature, not to mention smart of you to hide how much it bothered you. You did good. Now, where do you want me to put it? How about here on the nightstand by your goldfish? Oh! Squishy the Fishy has gotten so big!"

Ecko frantically shook her head as he bent down to study her pet. "No! If I put it there, I'll have to see it every time I feed Squishy. Besides, that wouldn't be fair. Squishy doesn't want to have to look at that freaky thing all day either."

Her eyes darted all around the room, searching for a good spot. "What I really want to do is throw it away. Or burn it in the fireplace. But I know I can't. Karen would know I was faking and tease me if I hide it in the closet, but I don't want to put it where I have to see it all the time either."

They finally decided on letting it take over Jareth the Hobglin King's chair. They moved Jareth to the shelf next to Janey-Bug, set the teddy bear into his vacated seat, and moved the whole setup to a spot that was out of sight from the bed. Ecko spent a lot of time sitting on her bed and she didn't want those 'creepy dead eyes' staring at her. Dan laughed as he hugged her and said, "I sure do love you. Merry Christmas, Kiddo."

Throughout the next several months, Ecko kept a close eye on the mirror world. Things steadily got more and more strange with every passing day. Her belongings continued to play musical chairs and hide and seek, sometimes two or three different items a day. She became even more obsessed with her mirror, but she was no longer watching the Otherworlds. She had started watching *herself.*

She couldn't determine exactly what had changed, or even when it had changed. But there was definitely something different about her reflection now. It was still her, but sometimes her image seemed a bit...off somehow. So late one night, when she couldn't sleep because she was so worried that she was going crazy, she came up with a plan. She determined that if nothing came of it, if she couldn't figure out what was wrong tomorrow, then she was going to stop searching for answers all together. She would just let it all go. She couldn't continue this way. She really was making herself crazy.

With a course of action planned out, she was finally able to relax enough to fall asleep.

The next afternoon, when she got home from school, the reflection showed one of her books lying on the floor with all the pages ripped out and scattered all over the room. But only in the reflection. There was absolutely nothing on her floor in the real world. No book, torn apart or otherwise. Perfect! She went over to the bookshelf and saw that that particular book was indeed missing. Show time.

She started looking around the room, acting like she was searching everywhere for it. She pretended to get mad and then proceeded to throw a royal fit. She stamped her feet and put her hands on her hips. Scrunching up her face, she threw her head back and acted like she was screaming at the top of her lungs. She stomped around the room, knocking things to the floor and kicking them to scatter them around. She grabbed Sir Didymus off the bed, lifted him up over her head, preparing to toss him across the room, then she spun around as fast as she could, her eyes zeroing in on her reflection…and just about died of shock.

There it was. The proof that she'd needed to convince herself that she wasn't imagining things. Her reflection self-stood there in the same position as her real self, with Didymus held up above her head. But her face was completely wrong. Her eyes had the look of a crazy person, and she was laughing, smiling from ear to ear. Mirror girl froze in shock when she realized that she'd been discovered. Her face instantly flashed with a terrible anger, but then she was gone as if she'd never been there. Her reflection had reverted to normal, showing nothing more than what was supposed to be there.

Ecko now knew for certain that there was a girl living on the other side of her mirror. One who looked exactly like her, or pretended to anyway. After that, she watched that mirror girl like a hawk, always trying to catch her. She *had* to find out who she was. She just had to know. She stared into the mirror constantly, and most times her reflection behaved just like it should. She did all the things that *she* did, exactly as she was supposed to, at exactly the right times. But sometimes, every once in a while, there would be a discrepancy.

The next real incident occurred just a few days later. Ecko had been sitting in front of her mirror, turning this way, then that way, looking at herself from different angles. She pushed her face right up close to the glass. "Who are you," she whispered. She was startled when she heard a snorting noise coming from beside her. She jumped back and spun around with a little squeak of fright.

Karen stood there in the doorway staring at her with a look of pure annoyance. "I'm telling Mom that you're in here talking to yourself. I *told* her that you weren't getting better," she taunted as she started to turn and walk away.

Ecko panicked. She didn't want to cause her parents any more worry and she did *not* want her mom to keep thinking that she was strange. Most of all, she didn't want her parents to take her mirror away. "Wait!" she cried out. "Please don't tell. You don't understand! There's a girl in there, a girl that looks just like me. But it's not me, I swear it's not!"

Karen snorted again, such an un-princess like sound. "That's just your reflection, dummy. Man, you sure are stupid," Karen sneered.

Ecko did her best to explain about the mirror girl, and how she knew that it wasn't just her reflection. She insisted that it wasn't just her imagination either. But her sister just stood there, silently glaring at her for the longest time, trying to process everything she'd just been told.

While Ecko waited for her to say something, she had the craziest thought. She imagined that she had somehow switched places with the mirror girl and that when she spoke, her words came out as mirror-speak. After all, images in a mirror are seen reflected backwards. If words *could* come out of a mirror, wouldn't they be reversed too? Like some sort of backwards speech.

That thought process screeched to a halt and derailed as Karen's face twisted up with disgust. "*Why* do you have to be such a weird little freak? You need to stop this. You're not a baby anymore. Stop playing these dumb little games. Stop giving everyone reasons to hate you. You don't have any friends, because everyone thinks you're crazy. You know, I can't even have sleepovers because you would scare everyone away. Pretty soon *I* won't have any friends left either. I wish Dad had never brought you here! I'm telling Mom you're acting crazy!" Then Karen turned and ran down the stairs yelling "Moooomm!" at the top of her lungs.

Ecko slowly sank back down onto her chair. She couldn't understand why her sister was always so mean to her. Sisters were supposed to look out for one another. Now, thanks to Karen, her mom would soon be up here with that sad, slightly terrified look on her face that she sometimes got when it was just the two of them.

She sighed and glanced back up at her reflection… and there she was, sitting there staring back with a creepy little smile on her face. After all that time spent trying to see the mirror girl again, of course *now* was the time she chose to reveal herself. It HAD to be the mirror girl because Ecko definitely wasn't smiling on this side of the glass. With her mom coming to have one of their *talks*, there was no reason to smile at all.

She reached up and touched her face, just to be sure. Mirror girl's hand went up and traced her lips, just like her own did. But mirror girl's little fingers moved over lips that are curved upwards in a smile, while Ecko's fingers touch a mouth that's slightly opened in a round O of surprise. "Who are you?" she asked again, just as she heard her mother's footsteps starting up the stairs.

Not wanting her mom to see her standing there in front of the mirror, she took several steps backwards until her legs bumped into her bed, never taking her eyes off the other girl. Her reflection mimicked her movements exactly, but just as her mom reached the top of the stairs and started down the hall, mirror girl's mouth shaped a single word. A voice whispered through her mind like a wind whispering through the leaves. Ecko dropped down onto the bed, her heart beating frantically and gasping for breath just as her mother entered her room. The hardest thing she had ever done in her entire life was pull her eyes away from the mirror at that crucial moment. Mirror girl had a name, and it was Samara.

Ecko started talking to Samara all the time. She asked hundreds of questions, always trying to find out who she was and where she lived. Was anyone else able to see her? How did they even see each other? *Why* did they see one another? She asked about everything. She talked whether she knew Samara was there or not. Sometimes Samara would reveal herself clearly. She'd frown when Ecko smiled, or laugh when Ecko was upset. Sometimes, she would even lift her hand up to wave. Occasionally, she'd turn her head to look at something behind her, while Ecko remained perfectly still on her own side of the glass.

It seemed as if Samara enjoyed playing a game of cat and mouse, catch me if you can. For some reason, she liked to hide her presence. Ecko wondered how many times Samara hid from her and she never knew about it. How long had it been going on with her being completely unaware of it? Sometimes though, every once in a while, Ecko caught her at it.

There were times when she'd move or talk and Samara's movements were sluggish, slightly out of rhythm, almost as if time had slowed down on her side by a few seconds. It reminded her of those old Japanese films she liked to watch with her dad, the ones where the actor's mouths didn't match up with the audio. Ecko did everything she could think of to communicate with Samara. She even wrote questions on her little chalkboard, just in case she couldn't read lips, but Samara ignored every single one of them.

Aside from the time when she'd revealed her name, mirror girl didn't try to communicate again.

Things continued in this fashion for years, with Ecko constantly speaking to Samara, questioning her, and searching for answers. She tried her best to get to know the girl in the mirror, while Samara played her games of cat and mouse and hide and seek. Ecko eventually learned that Samara enjoyed seeing her frustrated and upset. It always seemed to make her smile when she showed any signs of displeasure. The day would come when Ecko would wish she'd never seen the girl in the mirror named Samara. If she'd only known how things would turn out, she would have never tried to get to know her at all. If only she had known….

I'm So Bored

(Samara 10 Years Old)

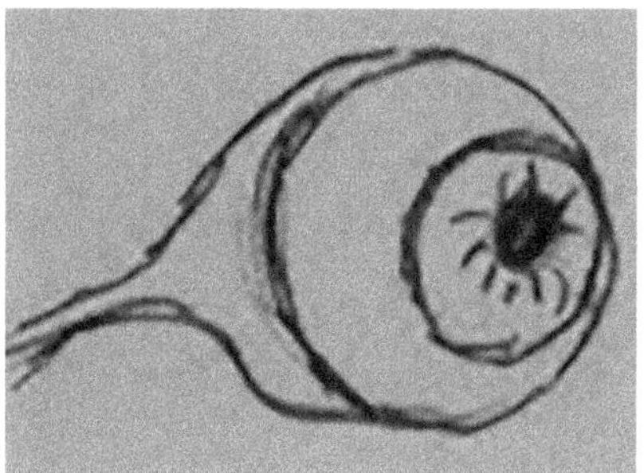

I've decided to take matters into my own hands. Literally, into my own hands. I want answers and I won't be ignored any longer. I *refuse* to be that kind of girl. I'm ready. I've worked so hard.

Hours upon hours I have practiced my magics, pushed myself to do more, to *be* more. I've endured so many failures and suffered through my father's relentless anger, his fits of rage and the resulting punishments. I'm tired of his never-ending displeasure of me. I'm done with being his whipping girl. And I am beyond bored with redecorating *my sister's* room and playing hide and seek with her.

Yes, my sister. I learned *that* little secret during one of my father's many, many fits of madness. All this time, he's only cared about *her*. I'm nothing more than a puppet, a tool for him to use to get closer to *her*.

I'd already come to that conclusion long ago, but knowing that she's my twin makes it worse, somehow. I'm a thousand times better than her! She has no magic that I've ever seen, other than the fact that she can see the Otherlands, same as me. She can't Squish. She has no Shadow form. She's not special. She can't do anything at all! It infuriates me that *she's* Father's chosen one when I'm the one who's been here all this time, doing everything he demands of me. Well, no more! I'm tired of his secrets, of his commands and his abuses. I'm tired of his lies. I want answers. I *demand* them.

Why? That's what I really want to know. Why *her*. Why not me? I'm determined to find *that* out, if nothing else. Striking out at my father is pointless as I can't even get close to him. Besides, he would just refuse to answer my questions and all I would get for my efforts is another beating. But I know a couple people that won't refuse. Well, I won't *let* them refuse, I should say. The two old fools that took me in all those years ago *have* to know something more than what they've revealed to me. They'd told me all about my mother and her abilities ages ago, but they never once mentioned that I had a sister. I don't know why they kept my twin a secret, but I do believe that it's time to find out, at long last.

I feign sleep as my current guard settles himself into the chair that blocks my door. I crack one eye open, just a sliver, to watch while he shifts around in search of a comfortable position. He grunts and then lets out a loud fart that startles a cry from my lips. I freeze as fear of discovery washes over me but all he does is snort and scratch at his privates.

A small eternity passes before his loud, steady snores assure me that he's fallen into a deep sleep. Opening my eyes, I sit up and look him over, contemplating how big he suddenly seems. He'll be too heavy to move and besides, he'll wake up if I try it. I have no weapon to use against him. The only things I have in my room are my mattress and a rickety old dresser to hold my pitifully small wardrobe. And I have my chunk of mirror, of course. I could stab him with it, I suppose, but I'm not willing to risk damaging it further. I can't squish something as big as him. I've tried and tried but I just can't manage it. *Yet.*

I'll have to use my Shadow form, somehow. I've gotten better at it. I can change my whole body now. But it's not nearly as helpful as I'd thought it would be. I'd had great aspirations of being able to pass through doors and walls, just like a spook can. I'd tried so hard to escape that way, but if that ability comes with the Shadow form, I'm a long way from figuring out how to go about it.

I *have* learned that my hands are my strongest assets while in Shadow form. They're the only part of me that I've managed to pass through another object, and that had only happened once. I'd been feigning sleep, practicing turning myself to Shadow under the cover of my thin, raggedy blanket. I'd somehow managed to pass my hands into the wall beside me, but I panicked and pulled them right back out. What if my hands re-solidified and got stuck inside the wall? What would I do then? I'd decided that it was a risk I would have to take if I wanted to get better at it. But so far, I hadn't been able to get it to work again.

There's also the issue of how long I can hold onto the magic. I can only stay in Shadow form for a few short moments before I'm completely drained of energy and revert back to myself. I don't know if it'll last long enough to overpower the guard. And then there's the problem of me being too weak afterwards to extract my answers from the old ones. Oh, what to do?

I glare my hatred at the drooling guard with mounting frustration. But then I have it! The instructions, the brilliant master plan is suddenly there, already worked out in my mind. And it's so *very* simple, I don't know why I didn't think of it before now.

I quietly stand up and tiptoe to the guard. With every bit of my concentration, I *will* myself to change into Shadow form, but just my hands. That's all I'll need. I raise my Shadow hands up to his face and slowly plunge my vaporous thumbs deep into his eyeballs. He feels nothing at all… until I suddenly return my hands back to their natural state. *Now,* he is instantly awake and screaming his fool head off.

I jerk my re-solidified thumbs back out, and his eyeballs come with them. They pop right out of his face with a wet, squelching sound. Giving myself two thumbs up for a job well done, I hold them up and inspect the bloody globs impaled on them in morbid fascination. I'm momentarily distracted as I slip them off my thumbs and squeeze them gently. I've always been curious as to how squishy eyeballs would be. How much pressure can they withstand before they burst, just like a vine globberberry does when I toss it into my mouth and bite it. Hmmm, I wonder what they would taste like….

I come back to awareness when I feel a painful kick to my side. The unfortunate guard has fallen to the floor and is thrashing about, his hands over his empty eye sockets. But he can't hold back the sheer amount of blood pouring out of his face. It leaks out between his fingers and runs down his arms to pool on the floor. I turn the eyeballs so that they're facing outwards and pointed down at him, so that he can look at himself.

"Look!" I tell him. "Just look at what you've done! Look at the mess you've made of my room." I giggle as I turn to go. "Oh well," I say as I toss them back over my shoulder. "I'm not cleaning it." Ha, ha, I crack myself up. Now, on to find the old ones and get some answers.

Hours later, I am finally satisfied that they'd told me everything they possibly could, which isn't much more than I already knew. I am my father's heir and as such, have inherited his dark abilities.

My twin is supposedly our mother's heir. My father had desperately wanted my mother's magic, but he knew that he couldn't steal it from her any more than he could force her to use it to help him.

So, he'd captured her and forced her to bear us with the intent of stealing the magic from her defenseless daughter. I was just a side effect of his true purpose. And to top it all off, I am not *at all* what he'd expected to get out of the deal. Surprise! I'm a girl, not the boy that he was supposed to have spawned. The old geezers told of how my mother somehow escaped and brought her babies here, before he could get his hands on them. They had agreed (accepted a huge bribe) to take me in and raise me. Then Mother dearest had run away with her other baby and that was the last time they had ever seen her. I only learned one other thing. My sister's name is Adrina Ecko. I laughed so hard when they told me that. I'm so glad I didn't get stuck with such a dumb name. At least I have one thing to thank my mother for.

I released the old ones as soon as I got all I could get from them. I didn't hurt them. *Much.* I certainly didn't do any permanent damage. I may still need them. In fact, they're in my room scrubbing it clean right now. The guard has been removed and has finally quieted his squalling. Occasionally, he lets out a whimper, but whether it's from the pain or from fear is anyone's guess, because I know without a single doubt in my mind that he's terrified.

My father surely has replacement guards on the way. His gossipy roach-beetles will have notified him of my actions immediately. I'm surprised they aren't here already. When they finally do arrive, they'll dole out my father's punishment to their guard mate for falling asleep and failing to keep me under control. I know it, the old farts know it, and the blinded guard knows it too. Poor fellow. I honestly don't think he will survive the retribution he's about to receive for his negligence. I hope they let me watch this time. I *could* use this opportunity to run, but I won't even bother.

I know that it wouldn't do me any good. I'm not strong enough to escape my father. Yet. Oh, but I'm working on it.

Slime and Snails, Puppy Dog Tails

Ecko soon realized that the girl in the mirror was not her friend, nor did she ever want to be her friend. Samara was *not* a nice girl. She didn't play well with others, and she was downright scary sometimes. Mirror gazing was no longer something that she looked forward to. It had started to leave her feeling lost and confused, even more so than usual. Samara's games, the mean, little pranks had all started to feel threatening and ominous.

But the scariest thing was that when she looked into the mirror now, she never knew who was looking back at her. She didn't recognize herself anymore, couldn't see through the lies to find the truth. After studying Samara's behavior for so long, she'd started to suspect that maybe she should put some distance, literally and figuratively, between them. Her encounters with the girl in the mirror had gotten uncomfortable and she'd steadily grown more and more uneasy with their interactions. Something sinister lurked behind Samara's eyes, and her smile had become a chilling thing to witness. It always seemed to be slightly unbalanced, just a little bit south of sane.

Sometimes she could have sworn that Samara's grin held too many teeth, sharp and pointed and deadly. Seeing them gave her a dreadful feeling in the pit of her stomach, like a premonition of terrible things heading her way. For those reasons, she had made up her mind to get some alone time, and as it was her favorite time of year, that had been easy for her to do.

She'd always had a great love of Autumn and all it had to offer, so she found herself spending less and less time sitting at her mirror with Samara. She stayed outside roaming the woods behind her house as much as possible, fully embracing all the changes that the Autumnal Equinox brought with it. The Fall season always sparked such strong emotions inside her. Something about the trees wearing such vibrant colors spoke to her. The sound of the wind in the leaves tugged at her heartstrings. Hiraeth, a longing for a home that she had never known, whispered through her, like a memory just out of reach.

It had been the most wonderful day, the best day she'd had in a long time. Her mom and her sister had gone out on an all-day shopping spree and her father had spent the whole day with her, just the two of them. First, they had raked the blanket of leaves in the yard into massive piles, taking turns jumping into them and rolling about, laughing hysterically up at the sky. Then they'd gathered them all up again and moved them to the burn pile for later.

She told her dad about a secret place that she had recently discovered, a beautiful, babbling stream, hidden deep in the woods. She said it was her new favorite place and that she wanted to show it to him, but only if he could keep it a secret.

Dan had solemnly promised, crossed his heart, and hoped to die, and suggested that they pack a lunch so they could have a picnic when they got there. So, together they wrapped up sandwiches, apples, cookies, and juice boxes. Then they set out with Ecko pointing out all her favorite landmarks along the way.

They walked for a long time and Dan started to worry about her going out so far by herself. She just laughed and told him not to be so silly. She could always find her way home, sort of like his GPS. When they came upon the hidden stream, Dan saw a look of pure joy wash over her face. He'd never seen her look so at peace. All she could say was that it felt like home there.

They had their secret picnic, Dan solemnly swearing to never disclose the location of her special place. It would forever remain their little secret.

Then they headed back home, hand in hand. They'd both enjoyed their day together and neither one was quite ready for it to end. They decided that as soon as it got dark, they would burn the leaves they had gathered and have a weenie roast. "With s'mores?" Ecko begged.

"Of course! How can we have a weenie roast without s'mores?" They had just stepped out of the woods when Rachael and Karen pulled up in the driveway. Dan glanced down at Ecko and smiled. "Our secret," he assured her. Then he sighed and added, "Now let's go help those ladies carry in their latest haul. I sure hope they didn't wear out the credit cards again!"

They ended up having to make four trips to carry everything into the house. They both giggled the entire time, leaving Rachael and Karen confused and clueless, which just made the whole thing even funnier. Ecko told them that they were going to roast weenies and make s'mores, and sweetly asked them if they wanted to come outside and have some too.

Rachael smiled at her eagerness. "What a fantastic idea! It's the perfect weather for a bonfire. And I'm starving after all that shopping! It's still a bit early though. Let's sit down so I can rest for a bit first. I'm exhausted! Shopping is hard work, you know. We can watch a movie while we wait for it to get dark out there. Ok?"

Rachael made popcorn while everyone voted on what movie to watch. After a short, but fierce battle of wills, (which Dan and Ecko won) they all settled in to watch Mulan. Dan just loved that movie. Mushu cracked him up every time. Before the end credits even started rolling, Ecko had jumped up off the sofa and ran to gather the things needed for the s'mores.

Dan laughed and followed his overly eager daughter to the kitchen, where she was attempting to reach the top shelf in the pantry. He picked her up and lifted her so that she could snag the marshmallows. (Even at 12 years old, she was still a tiny little thing.) Rachael came in and said, "It's getting a bit chilly out there now. Why don't you run on up to your room and put on a sweater while Dad and I gather everything up. We'll meet you outside." With a happy burst of excitement, Ecko threw her arms around her mom and squeezed tight for a moment. Then she ran up the stairs to her room.

She burst through the door and never even paused to glance at the mirror. Usually that was the first thing that she did, but she was so excited that Samara never even entered her mind. And as she soon discovered, that was a very bad thing to do. She'd just reached into her closet and grabbed the first sweater she saw and had one arm in when she felt something hit her right in the middle of her back! It felt just like someone had put their hands out and shoved her. She flew forward and with her hands trapped halfway in the sweater, there was no way to catch herself. She fell flat on her face, banging her nose on the ground and biting through her lip.

Crying out in pain, she untangled her hands enough to stand back up. Fear like nothing she had ever felt before washed through her. It was Samara that had pushed her; she knew it without a single doubt in her mind. She could *feel* the mirror girl standing right behind her, malice radiating off of her. Waves of dread coursed through her as she spun around to look behind her.

There was no one there. She was all alone in her room. Her eyes immediately darted straight to the mirror. Samara was there, still on her own side of the glass, laughing as the blood dripped down both of their chins. Ecko knew that somehow, Samara's anger had reached across worlds to physically hurt her. She had never been so terrified of anything in all her life as she was in that moment. She heard the sounds of Samara's crazed laughter echoing inside her head as she ran from the room, crying for her dad.

She ran into the kitchen and Dan turned to smile and assure her that they were almost ready to go outside for their campfire. The words died before they ever left his mouth when he saw all the blood that covered her. He'd snatched her up in his arms, checking her all over for injuries. He was relieved to see that there were no life-threatening wounds. It all seemed to be coming from her nose and lip. "What in the world happened, Kiddo?" he asked as he cleaned her up.

Ecko had never outright lied to her father, but for some reason she didn't want to tell him about Samara. In her young mind she thought that she was protecting him. In the end, she just said that she was running and that she'd tripped and fell. She had to go back to her room to change her clothes, but thankfully her dad had gone upstairs with her to clean up the mess she'd made. She hadn't wanted to go alone and find that Samara was still there waiting for her.

She grabbed her clothes and changed in the bathroom as her dad cleaned the blood off the floor. Later, while everyone was laughing around the fire, Ecko just couldn't get the incident out of her mind. What should have been a great ending to such a wonderful day (aside from the part where she got shoved) was instead spent in pain and fear. A trickster Samara that enjoyed playing mean spirited but harmless games was one thing. She didn't know what to do about a vindictive Samara that could reach through the mirror and physically hurt her. She had learned a valuable lesson that day, though. She'd learned that allowing Samara to feel ignored and neglected was not a smart move on her part.

Things steadily got worse after that. Samara continued to move her belongings around her room and sometimes even went so far as destroying them. Whatever magic she held had grown considerably, and she stopped bothering with just making it *look* as if things were moved around in the mirror. Everything actually *was* moved around the room. She had learned how to physically affect things in Ecko's world, and she was no longer interested in pretending otherwise.

It seemed to be her new favorite game; destroy stuff and then sit back and laugh as Ecko got upset and was forced to clean it all up. She also seemed to have outgrown the desire to play hide and seek. She no longer mimicked Ecko's movements or tried to hide in any way. It seemed that she now enjoyed blatantly putting herself on display every chance she got. One day, Ecko walked into her room and found an outrageously huge mess. It looked as if a burglar had snuck in and ransacked her room, searching for hidden valuables. Everything she owned had been thrown onto the floor.

She had stopped in the doorway, frozen in disbelief and unable to make herself move forward. She'd almost jumped out of her skin when Karen came up behind her and said, "Oh man, you are in so much trouble now. Mom is gonna be so mad!"

Ecko just let out a tired sigh as she muttered, "Let me guess…you're on your way right now to tell her. Am I right?"

Karen laughed. "Of course," she called over her shoulder as she descended the stairs. It had taken Ecko hours to clean that one up, and she'd gotten grounded for a whole month on top of it!

By the time she turned 12 years old, Samara had thankfully outgrown rearranging and destroying things, probably because Ecko had stopped reacting to it. She'd quickly grown bored once Ecko showed her that it didn't bother her anymore. Every day she would come in, quietly clean up the mess, and then went on about her business as if it had never happened. She never actually ignored her, she just refused to let Samara know that her actions bothered her.

It was a tricky balance because she didn't want Samara to feel like she was disregarding her. Bad things happened when she did that.

But she also knew that, like a small child, Samara was acting out for attention. Ecko was determined to not play into that game in any way. So, she made sure to spend at least a little time each day with her. She would sit down at the mirror and talk to her, telling her all about her day. Even though she never received any answering replies, she always asked Samara how her day had gone and if she was doing ok over there on her side of the glass.

She always encouraged her to speak, but Samara never seemed to have anything to say. She even whispered, "Goodnight, Samara" each night as she turned off her lamp to go to sleep. Although she knew better than to ever trust Samara again, it seemed like they'd come to some sort of unspoken truce. She made sure she included Samara in her life just enough so that she wouldn't feel neglected, and in return Samara stopped playing all of her cruel little games.

Things had calmed down considerably, and life went along rather smoothly for several months. Ecko's bedroom returned to the peaceful and uneventful haven that it used to be. She knew that she should have been happy with the newfound tranquility, but instead it just felt like the calm before the storm. She never let it show, but she was scared. Instead of feeling relief, a sense of urgency had taken root in the pit of her stomach, and it grew stronger with each passing day of their 'truce'. A storm was on its way. Ecko knew it, and she could only hope that she wouldn't get swept away in its wake.

The school year had finally, mercifully come to an end and it was the very first day of summer vacation. She had been looking forward to this day since the first day school had begun! She hadn't enjoyed elementary school a bit, but this first year of intermediate school had been excruciatingly miserable. She'd hated every minute of it. Little kids were mean, but teenagers were brutal. They were especially unkind to anyone that didn't fit in with their little cliques. Summer break hadn't come soon enough, if you asked her.

Ecko had already decided that the very first day of her freedom would be spent lounging about in her pjs and reading her new book. Her dad always gave her and her sister an end of the year gift. This year he had presented her with Miss Peregrine's Home for Peculiar Children, and she'd so been looking forward to reading it. She'd gone to bed that last night with high hopes for a perfect day filled with lounging, reading, and snacking.

But her night had been restless and full of terrors. She dreamed that she was standing in front of the mirror, looking at Samara through the glass. She whimpered as Samara stepped right through it and walked towards her with a cruel smile twisting her lips. Ecko had been frozen in place, unable to move at all. All she could do was scream as Samara drew closer and closer.

Then Samara crawled right into her opened, screaming mouth and disappeared inside of her! Samara had then been able to use her to walk around and torment everything in her path. She'd forced Ecko to do terrible things... unspeakable things. She'd kicked tiny little kittens and squashed snails in between her fingers and then played in the resulting slime that they made, and so much worse. Samara had laughed and laughed using Ecko's mouth, and all while Ecko was trapped inside her own body, unable to do anything but scream.

When she finally jerked awake, she was trembling all over and gasping for breath. She'd been unable to do anything but lay there in her bed and try to calm her racing heart. "It was just a dream," she told herself over and over. "Just a dream. It could never happen for real."

After a few long minutes spent trying to convince herself, she eventually believed it enough to get up and get started on what was STILL going to be an amazing day. Nightmares would *not* ruin it for her! She stretched and rolled about on her bed, just enjoying the fact that she didn't have to rush around and get ready for school. When her tummy growled loudly in complaint of being empty, she sat up and slipped her feet into her green dinosaur feet slippers.

"Good morn…" she'd started to say, but the words died on her lips.

What she saw in the mirror had shocked her to the core. Samara was standing there (thankfully on her own side of the mirror) with her arm held up, her hand closed into a tight fist. Something gross oozed out from between the cracks of her fingers. As terrible as her dreams had been, Ecko knew that she didn't want to see what was inside that fist. Samara smiled cruelly as she slowly opened her hand, and what was left of Ecko's pet goldfish, Squish plopped back into the fishbowl. It was the most horrible, gruesome thing that she had ever seen. She'd never felt such pain as she did in that moment.

Her dad had won the fish at a carnival when Ecko had been only four years old. The whole family had laughed when Dan had handed it to her, and she'd immediately christened it Squish the Fish. Dan offered to win one for Karen too, but she'd merely wrinkled her nose in disgust. "No, thanks. I don't want a stinky, disgusting fish. You can buy me a tiara instead!"

Squish had been Ecko's only friend for a long time. She'd read all her favorite books to him. They'd gone on countless adventures together, even if Squish hadn't realized it. She just couldn't believe that her little friend was gone forever, she *wouldn't* believe it. She knew that Samara could be a bit callous and mischievous at times, but was she actually capable of something so wretched and vile? More importantly, was what she'd just witnessed in the mirror true or was it just another one of Samara's reflection games? "Please, *please* let it be a reflection game," Ecko quietly begged.

As soon as her feet became unglued from the floor, she ran over to the fishbowl and peered into it. She hoped with all her heart that Samara was just being mean and playing a new, cruel game and that Squish would be fine on this side of the mirror. But there was

Squish, floating belly up at the top of the bowl. There was no evidence that he'd been maliciously murdered. Squish was clearly dead, but he was whole and fully intact, not squashed with his insides on the outside. Loud screams filled her consciousness, one long continuous shriek after another reverberated throughout her mind. She didn't even realize it was *her* that was screaming out loud until her dad grabbed her by the arms and shook her to snap her out of it.

He was kneeling on his knees, searching her for injuries. She just pointed towards the fishbowl with big fat tears welling up in her eyes before she tucked her head down and buried her face in his shirt. "Ah Kiddo, I'm so sorry" he murmured when he realized what was wrong.

"What? What is it?" her mom yelled from the doorway.

"Poor Squish the fish has gone up to fish heaven," Dan murmured. Then he snuggled Ecko in close and stroked her hair, trying his best to comfort his grieving child.

Karen could always be counted on to try and make things worse for Ecko. "*That's* what all the screaming's about? Why does she always have to be so crazy? It was just a dumb fish!" Ecko whimpered miserably as her dad sucked in an outraged breath.

"Karen! Apologize to your sister this instant!" her mother insisted. "Can't you see she's really upset?" Dan stood back up, arms held protectively around his sobbing girl.

"No, Rachael. That was cruel and completely uncalled for," he said as he turned to Karen. His face had turned bright red with anger and his voice was unsteady when he ordered, "Karen, you will go to your room immediately. You just got yourself grounded on the very first day of summer break. I'm sick and tired of you always digging at your sister. Don't think I don't notice it. She doesn't even fight back! She does nothing to you! Go. Just go to your room. Now! Before I lose my temper for real!"

Karen's eyes flew open wide, before she turned tail and ran. He hugged Ecko again and promised, "It's gonna be ok, Baby Girl. We're gonna get through this. You'll see."

After she'd calmed a bit, Dan found a small box to use as a coffin and they gave Squish the fish a nice burial under the old oak tree in the backyard. Ecko never said a word about what had really happened that day, and no one ever suspected that a sadistic killer had open access to their home.

Ecko was so traumatized and broken hearted over the loss of her little friend that she could barely function. She moped around for days, feeling lost and disillusioned. Dan and Rachael did everything they could think of to help their daughter heal, but nothing seemed to work. In a final, hopeful attempt to cheer her up, they'd decided to buy her a puppy.

She had always wanted a dog of her own but had, until now, been denied one. Her parents hadn't wanted to take on the extra responsibility of owning a dog, but they were now desperate for anything that would snap her out of her depression. They chose the fluffiest, most playful puppy at the shelter and brought it up to her room. She'd been lying on her bed hugging Sir Didymus, listlessly watching a movie on the tv, but she glanced up when she heard her parents call her name from the doorway.

A little squeal of surprise escaped her lips as her eyes darted straight to the wriggling ball of fluff in her dad's arms. Dan set the puppy on the floor and stepped back, anxiously waiting for her reaction. She sat up and could only stare with stars in her eyes. Her hands twitched with the urge to run her fingers through all that soft fur. She could practically feel that rough little tongue licking her face. She wanted that pup in the worst way.

She'd started to jump up and run to pick it up, but then she remembered. Her eyes shot over to the mirror. Samara was there, grinning with such a malevolent look on her face that she immediately knew there was no way she could possibly keep that sweet baby; it would, without a doubt, die a horrible death. As long as Samara was around, there was no way she could ever have another pet.

It was hard, *so hard*, and it absolutely broke her heart to do it, but Ecko laid back down on her bed and refused to even look at her parents. "Thank you, but please take it back. I don't want a dog anymore," she listlessly informed them. But Dan had seen the look of joy that had filled her face, however brief it had been. He knew that there was more to this than her suddenly no longer wanting a dog.

Hoping that she'd change her mind, he told her to at least hold the pup, just for a minute. "I don't want it Dad!" she screamed. She had never, ever raised her voice to him before. Shocked and hurt, he picked the puppy up and left without another word. Dan and Rachael had no choice but to take the sweet boy back to the shelter. What else could they do?

Ecko knew that she'd hurt her dad's feelings. Her parents had only wanted to help, but all it had done was add another crack in her already damaged heart. She hugged Sir Didymus against her chest, buried her face in her pillow, and cried herself to sleep. She had never wanted anything like she'd wanted that beautiful, perfect puppy.

Savages, Savages Barely Even Human

(Samara 12 years old)

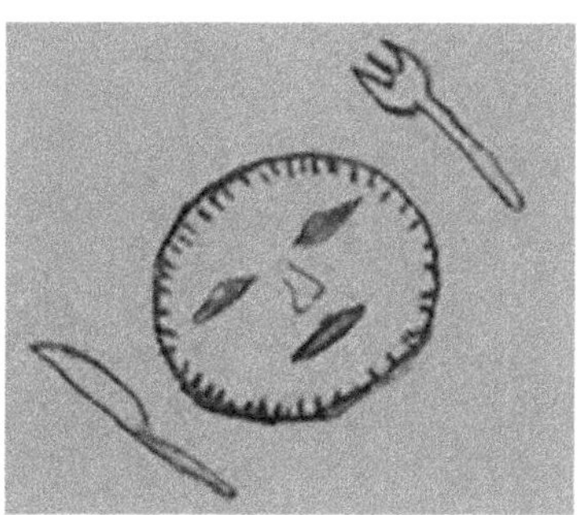

I met someone my own age, a boy someone. My guards caught him peeping into my window, spying on me. They'd dragged him inside and questioned us both. 'Who was he? Where had he come from and how long had we known each other. Why was he snooping? What did he hope to learn?' At first, they'd refused to believe that we've never seen each other before. They thought that we'd been secretly plotting my escape. New Boy explained that he'd felt the magic radiating from inside this house and he'd seen all the guards constantly coming and going. He'd been curious, that's all.

He just wanted to find out what was happening in here. Once the guards were finally satisfied that he was telling the truth, they deemed him an insignificant inconvenience, nothing more than a pest that needed to be terminated and disposed of.

But I wanted to keep him. He was kind of cute, in an almost deadish, but not quite way. He was tall, nearly as tall as the Sluggeellian guard that had him shoved up against the wall during the interrogation. Other than the light blue-grey skin and the overly large, clawed hands and feet, he looked (mostly) humanoid. And the two tiny horns just barely poking up out of his hair were simply adorable. But best of all was what I sensed *inside* of him. A malevolent wickedness that called to my own darkness, coaxing it to come out and play. I saw the depravity lurking behind his innocent smile, the devilry shining in his eyes. Looking at him, I felt a tiny thrill deep in the pit of my belly, a dark, delicious excitement in my breast. Yes, I wanted him. I wanted what he had to offer. I refused to let them kill him. I wanted to play with him first.

I nodded at him, a tiny, barely perceptible dip of the head to prepare him for what was coming. That subtle hint was all it took. He understood. I focused all my will on the troll-like guard that had done all the questioning. I lifted my hand and made a fist, imagining with all my might that the troll-man was the size of a Ribbitter and that I had him caught tight within my grip. Then I just squeezed.

I watched the panic enter his eyes as the pressure built inside of him and his bones crushed. I had never felt such exhilaration, such joy, in all my life as I did when I squished all of his insides to the outside of him. When he thumped down to the floor, I turned my fist to the Slug-man, but he was no longer a threat.

In fact, he no longer even had a throat. In the sixty seconds or so, that it had taken me to squash the troll-man, New Boy had used those deadly claws to remove it for him. Slug-man dropped to the floor too, just as dead as his guard mate. It was then that our eyes met, the two of us standing there over the bodies.

His smile was the most beautiful thing I'd ever seen. I grabbed his hand, and we made a mad dash out of the house and into the dark, laughing like deranged lunatics. As we passed by the town's only diner/bar, both of our stomachs simultaneously let out a loud grumble of protest. Without even discussing it, we both turned right and busted through the doors, startling an old drunken Wartal so bad that he fell off his stool.

The Chopping Block Eatery serves the best meat pies. The owner, Storver, peels the unfortunate meat donor's skin off and uses it for the pie crusts. If you're lucky, and have the coin to pay, you can purchase the pie that has the face for the top crust. It's always the one made with the juiciest, tastiest body bits, or so I've been told. I have never had one with a face. The old geezers are poor, and stingy with the little coin they have. They only buy the old, stale leftovers from Storver.

We ran back to the kitchen and New Boy grabbed everything he could get his hands on in the little time we had. I went straight for the cooling rack full of pies. Three guesses on which one I snatched, but you're dumb if you need more than one.

Storver came barreling around the corner wearing his bloody apron, screaming and swinging his cleaver at us. Just before he reached me, I grabbed a pot of boiling...something, and tossed it right into his face. We turned and ran with our spoils, Storver howling in agony behind us.

New boy led me to where he lived, in one of the many abandoned houses on the edge of town. Away from prying eyes, we sat and ate our pilfered dinner (I knew the face pie would be delicious. I just *knew* it!) and introduced ourselves. He said his name was Krispin, and he had no idea who, or what he was. In all his life, he had never met anyone else like him. He'd been told that someone had abandoned him on the steps of the orphanage, years ago when the town still *had* an orphanage, that is. When it closed down, all the kids had been turned out into the streets. They'd been given no choice but to live like wild animals. It was either fight and steal or die. Most died.

I told him who I was, and who my father was. For some reason, I kept Ecko a secret. I wouldn't take the chance of him wanting *her* more than me, just like everyone else always did. He was mine. I refused to share him with *her*. But his next words made me suspect that he already knew about her.

"I lied to that ugly Sluggeellian," he whispered, a gleam in his eyes. "This isn't the first time I've seen you. I've been watching you for years. I used to follow you around when you were still free to come and go. When I realized that you were being held captive in your house, I started watching you through the window. I do it all the time. I only got caught today, because I *let* them catch me. The old ones were gone and there were only the two guards. I figured it would be easy to free you, and I was right," he bragged. Then he asked, "What did you do to that troll- man? *How* did you do it?"

I just shrugged. None of his business *how* I do what I do. Although he did show me how his claws pop out and how he can pull them back in whenever he wants. We stuffed ourselves as full as we could possibly get while we got to know each other. Then we set out to see what other mischief we could get into together. How much trouble could two adolescent hooligans cause? The answer is plenty.

The two of us shook that town up and left its citizens traumatized. They *will* remember us, and they'll run the other way and lock their doors from now on whenever they see us coming. It was the best time of my life. We did whatever we felt like doing and took whatever we wanted and there was no one that could stop us. We were wild things, free and savage and beautiful. Until my father sent his Night Shades out to get me. But until then, I'd been free, and it had tasted as delicious as Storver's face pie.

When the Night Shades had caught up with us, they ignored Krispin and immediately surrounded me. They slithered around me with their revolting *ick*, filling me with the dread that they bring with them. They wrapped themselves around me, up my legs, around my waist and chest, binding my arms to my side. I'm sure I resembled a mummy, wrapped head to toe with an inky black, shadowy fog instead of white cloth.

Father commanded his Night Shades to invade me, to go in and seize control of my mind and body so that he could control me. They poured themselves into my mouth, my ears, and up my nostrils. I felt them slithering inside me, searching me, reading me. What they found shocked my father. I could feel it in their 'thoughts', because just as they could read me, I too, could read them. They soon found that they couldn't get past my defenses to gain control of me.

"Why so shocked, Father?" I mentally spat through the Night Shade's collective awareness. "I *am* your daughter. Surely you knew I would inherit some of your magic. I may not have Night Shades of my own. *Yet*. But I have my own Shadow magic that I've been practicing and strengthening. I will *not* be a puppet on a string, not even to someone as powerful as you."

I felt my father's anger rip through the Night Shade's awareness, and terror filled me, despite my earlier bravado. I turned my eyes to Krispin then and whispered, "Run, New Boy." Despite the fear that was coursing through me, I watched in admiration and a bit of envy, as Krispin backed away and somehow changed, altering himself to blend into the walls of the nearby building, like a chameleon.

Within seconds he was gone from sight completely. I couldn't tell if he was still there, masterfully disguised or if he had fled. But I hoped he was gone. I hope he didn't stick around to witness me being dragged back to my room by twelve of my father's lackeys. I hope he didn't follow behind and watch as they brought dozens of

Ribbitters in and turned them loose to crawl all over me. To run their slimy, energy stealing tongues all over me.

My father had his men leave me to the nasty creatures for hours and they took so much from me that I was left pathetically weak and lethargic. Then, when I was too drained to fight back, my father had his men punish me for daring to defy him, thoroughly and painfully so. Now I'm stuck back in this dreadful room with more guards than ever, back to staring into this mirror at a sister that I despise almost as much as I loathe our father. I'm so ashamed that I wasn't strong enough to fight dear old dad. I'm weak. I'm pathetic. And I hate myself for it.

But oh, I am pissed too. "One day you will pay for it all, Father. I promise you that," I'd whispered to his Night Shades as they were unwinding themselves from my body, once I'd been properly punished. Again, I was blasted with my father's enormous rage. But I was surprised when I felt something else mixed in with the anger. Admiration. He couldn't hide the fact that he felt the tiniest bit of pride at my will and determination. Not that I care about that at all.

The only thing I *do* care about is that Krispin had gotten away. Oh, he'll come back for me. I know it. Until then, I will try to do exactly as I'm told, play the meek, dutiful daughter. I'll watch my dear, sweet sister and I'll practice using my magic to torment her. Her misery is like a balm on my dark little soul.

The more I hurt her, the better I feel about being weak and so easily controlled by our father. Every passing hour I grow stronger... and every passing hour I grow angrier. I want my freedom. I want my father defeated, at my feet and begging me for his life. I want Krispin back. There are things I want to do with him, things I want to do *to* him. Most of all, I want to go to Ecko's world and leave *this* place behind forever. But until that time comes, I'll amuse myself with what little pleasures I can sneak in.

I want to watch my sister's face as I torture the light and the *good* right out of her. Squishing her little pet fish had been satisfying and so very exhilarating. Seeing her scream her fool head off over a dumb creature made my little heart sing with joy. Watching her cry and mourn for weeks has been the absolute highlight of my life. How very stupid of her to love something, *anything*, that much. Love is weakness. I will never, *ever* allow anyone to have that much power over me. Especially not something as fragile as a stupid pet fish. Besides, fish are food, not friends anyway.

Doll Parts and Growing Pains

Ecko's broken heart slowly stitched itself back together, but it never healed up quite right and now bore a gruesome scar. Her family didn't know what to do. They just couldn't figure out how to help her. Trying to get her to talk to them no longer did any good. She looked straight through them like they weren't even there. She'd always been a quiet girl, but losing Squish made her go silent. It seemed as if her voice had shriveled up and died right alongside her pet.

Even Karen had started to worry about her, not that she'd ever admit it, though. Ecko avoided being around any of them as much as possible. She kept to herself, taking long walks and spending hours at a time at the public library. She'd also become afraid to go to sleep at night and did everything she could to keep herself awake. She could keep the nightmares at bay, only when she fell into such an exhausted sleep that dreaming was impossible.

When she began to lose weight, (tiny as was she couldn't afford to lose a single pound) Dan put his foot down and told her that he was going to send her to a therapist. He'd had enough. He wanted his daughter back and he didn't care what he had to do to achieve it. His heart ached when she cried and begged him not to make her go. He acknowledged that help from a stranger might not be the best idea, given all the weirdness that surrounded their family. But he knew that he had to do *something.*

He decided to start with a less extreme tactic than getting professional help. He passed all of his ongoing cases to his coworkers, took some time off from work, and then spent every waking hour with his daughter. He watched movies late into the night with her. He started accompanying her on her daily walks through the woods. He didn't speak at all, just walked quietly by her side. He didn't try to pry into her thoughts. He made no demands, put no pressure on her. He just let her know that he was there for her, whether she wanted him there or not. And somehow that seemed to slowly get through to her.

She began to interact again, bit by little bit. One day she pointed out a flower peeking out from a pile of leaves. Dan kept quiet but smiled and felt his heart light with hope. The next day it was the tiniest, lonely blue mushroom that caught her attention. In a gentle, hushed voice he simply remarked that it was beautiful.

Dan watched as her face started to light up with wonder over the smallest traces of beauty again, and an idea came to him. That evening, after they'd returned home, he went out and bought her a digital camera. On their walk the next day, Ecko stopped and pointed at a small patch of bushes. A little brown rabbit was peeking out at them, almost completely hidden amongst the foliage.

Dan squatted down and snapped some photos before it scampered away. He showed her the images he'd captured, and when she smiled for the first time in months, he began to believe that his girl was finally on her way back to him. Things would be okay now. *She* would be okay. He gave her the camera and showed her how to operate it. Then they spent the rest of the day searching for hidden treasures to photograph.

When they returned home that evening, they showed the pictures to Rachael. Dan was surprised to see that there was an image of him sitting on a large rock with his pants legs rolled up, his bare feet dangling in their secret stream. His heart swelled with love when

Ecko quietly said that it was her favorite photo. Every day she took her camera out and every day she came back to herself more and more. Although she still didn't have much to say, she had rediscovered her love for the beauty of the world around her. She also cherished her father just a little bit more for not making any demands on her, for just being there when she needed him the most.

Ecko's life went on and she adjusted to the loss of her beloved friend. She knew that every living thing eventually had to die; that was just part of life. She'd just never felt the loss of a loved one before and needed to learn to cope with it. With time and her father's help, that's just what she did. But what she couldn't come to grips with was *how* Squish had died.

She just couldn't believe that Samara could do something so dreadful, but apparently at some point the girl in the mirror had turned nasty and had become completely hostile. Ecko didn't know what to think. She questioned everything. Had Samara always been this way? This cruel? Or had she herself done something to make Samara want to hurt her? That ability she had to affect things on Ecko's side of the glass had obviously grown stronger over the years. Had Ecko somehow had a hand in that? And most importantly, how was she going to get her to go away?

She thought about breaking her mirror but was terrified of taking things that far. She got a horrible feeling in her belly every time she considered it. She was convinced that if she shattered that glass, Samara would be set free and would then be able to step into her world for real. She could ask her dad to get rid of the mirror and he would do it, no questions asked. But she just didn't have the heart to worry him any more than she already had.

Also, she knew that Samara was not restricted to just her bedroom mirror. She could find her through any mirror, at any time. It could be disastrous if Samara got angry and showed up in a mirror with other people around her. No, Ecko decided, the safest bet was to leave the mirror in her bedroom where she could keep an eye on things. She would leave it until she could figure out what to do, but she wanted nothing more to do with the girl on the other side of the looking glass.

The months passed with Ecko completely ignoring the mirror. She missed the Otherlands but wouldn't take a chance on looking for them. She knew that Samara was there, watching her. She could *feel* her watching. Ecko no longer spoke to her. She didn't ask about her day. She didn't wish her good morning or tell her good night.

In fact, she avoided looking into the mirror as much as possible. Ecko had come to realize a few things. 1. Samara was mentally unbalanced and *very* disturbed. 2. Samara hated her beyond all reasoning and took great pleasure in tormenting her. 3) Things had to change. She couldn't ignore the girl forever and she couldn't live the rest of her life like this, passively waiting for bad things to happen. Samara was quiet for now, but she wouldn't be silenced forever. Ecko had no way of knowing when she would strike again, but she had no doubt that the hit was coming.

For the next whole year, the only contact Ecko had with the other girl was through her dreams. Samara seemed to be focusing all her energy on entering her mind while she was asleep and taking control of her dreams. There was no limit to the things Samara could do in Dreamland, and each night she sent all sorts of depravity to visit her. Terrible, disgusting things that haunted her for weeks afterwards.

Aside from those nightly terrors, there was nothing else from Samara. There were no games, no rearranging her belongings or trying to get her attention. But she was still there. Ecko felt the weight of her eyes staring out at her any time she had to be in her room. Samara's hate and madness radiated out, right through the glass and permeated her bedroom like an unseen disease floating on the air.

Subconsciously, Dan and Rachael had begun to feel it too. To them it presented itself as a bad feeling, an unpleasant, cloying scent perhaps. Without even realizing it, they stopped entering the room altogether. But Ecko noticed, not that she blamed them one bit for their avoidance. She was sure that Samara noticed it too.

One night, just a few weeks after her fourteenth birthday, Ecko suddenly woke in a cold sweat, frozen in place and unable to move. With her body completely paralyzed, her mind raced to discern what the danger was and where it was coming from. It definitely wasn't time to be up yet. It was still dark out; the only light was from the full moon shining through her window. She hadn't been dreaming. Her sleep had blessedly been Samara free.

But *something* had woken her. She shivered as unexplainable chill bumps broke out over her entire body. Something was very *wrong*. Her heartbeat doubled, then tripled its normal rhythm. She heard something moving around, a small rustling whisper coming from somewhere beside her. Fear swept through her, keeping her limbs locked down. She closed her eyes tight and tried to feign sleep.

"Be still. Be so still and so quiet," she whispered to herself. She felt the blankets move ever so slightly and her eyes shot back open like they were spring loaded. She stared up at the ceiling, not moving, not even daring to breathe. She felt another barely-there tug on the sheets beside her, then the feel of some tiny *something* lying down on the pillow, right next to her face. She had to look. She had to, but she just *couldn't* look. Her eyes, indeed, her entire body refused to do anything that her brain commanded. She was just too frightened.

The sound of a high pitched, maniacal giggle in her ear convinced her eyes to cooperate faster than any scenario her mind was conjuring. She tried to swallow past the lump in her throat and slowly turned her head. There, lying on the pillow right beside her face was Sigmund, the teddy bear that Karen had bought for her. It giggled over and over again, a sound of pure, unadulterated evil, while she remained completely immobilized by terror. All she could do was lay there, unable to move, mouth opened in a silent scream.

As God above was her witness, that thing that was supposed to be an inanimate child's toy somehow sat up and turned its terrifying fuzzy little face towards her. She watched in absolute horror as its glassy, dead eyes turned blood red and *oh please dear God help her*, it opened its mouth full of sharp, deadly teeth and growled, literally growled at her. Ecko managed one sharp scream for her father before the bear leaned over her and tried to bite through her throat.

Feeling those sharp little teeth chewing into her neck was excruciating. The pain they inflicted was all consuming and overwhelming, and for a moment, all she could do was lie there in shock with him latched onto her neck. When at last she came to her senses, she grabbed the demented teddy with both hands and rolled out of bed. She instinctively yanked the little monster away, but unfortunately it had clamped its teeth down tight. When she jerked it away from her neck, a wide strip of flesh came with it, exposing the underlying muscles and tendons. Blood poured from the open wound.

Ecko stared in horror at the stuffed bear in her hands and knew that if she survived this, she would have nightmares for the rest of her life. Sigmund was glaring at her with red demon eyes, the fur of its face soaked with her blood. The swath of skin it had bitten off was hanging out of its mouth. "Nnurung Nnurung Nnurranggg," it growled at her as its teeth gnashed and chewed furiously.

She was horrified to see that the little monster was consuming what it had taken from her. Sigmund was *eating* her. Thoroughly disgusted and horrified, she dropped the nasty little thing to the floor and kicked it away from her. She heard the sound of crazed laughter, and her eyes automatically flew to the mirror.

Samara was there with her hands pressed to the glass. There was some sort of dark smoke flowing out of her hands, coalescing on her side of the glass. She was laughing hysterically, her eyes lit with unholy, maniacal glee. Ecko was dying, literally bleeding to death while Samara laughed. The girl in the mirror had tried to murder her and might still succeed if she didn't get out of there and get help fast.

She took one unsteady, wavering step towards the door, then another before she faltered. Her dad burst in, just in time, as the room began to spin. Her eyes rolled back as he rushed in and caught her, thankfully before she hit the ground. Dan didn't waste time trying to find out what was happening. He didn't think about anything at all. His mind in panic mode and body on autopilot, he yanked a drawer out of the dresser, grabbed a handful of t-shirts, and pressed them against the wound.

He yanked a sheet from the bed and wrapped it around her neck to hold it all in place. Then he scooped her into his arms and just ran for it, racing through the hall and thundering down the stairs. They needed medical help, and fast. His daughter was fading in and out of consciousness in his arms, her eyes fluttering and her breath hitching.

She tried to assure him that she was okay, but her lips had somehow forgotten how to form words. She was cold, and her limbs felt heavy. As if from a distance, she heard her father yell at her mom and sister to get into the safe room, ordering them to not come out until he came back for them.

Dan waited just long enough to ensure that Rachael and Karen were locked in, safe and secure. He didn't know what or where the danger was, and he couldn't just leave the rest of his family unprotected. He laid Ecko in the back seat of his car and drove as fast as he dared, telling her over and over that help was on the way and that she had to stay awake.

Ecko tried to listen to her father, but it felt like the air around her was no longer breathable, almost as if it had turned to water instead. She struggled desperately to keep her head above the surface, but something was pulling her down, down, down into the darkness. Consciousness came to her in waves, and she was vaguely aware of being picked up and carried. She heard banging and her dad yelling.

"David! Ecko's hurt! I need help!" The world went dark again. Then she was lying on a hard surface and a strange man she had never seen before was standing over her. She turned her head away, frantically searching for a familiar face. All she could see was cabinets, a sink, a stove. Her eyes closed and she was lost in the darkness again. But there were things there, things with sharp teeth in the void surrounding her.

She came back awake screaming and thrashing. She heard a deep voice shout, "Hold her down!" Strong arms wrapped around her, pinning her to the table. She smelled the comforting scent of her father's cologne just before his face came into view. "Here, baby girl. I'm here. You must calm down and lie still and let us help you. You're going to be just fine now. I've got you, sweetheart."

She immediately relaxed. Her father would take care of her. He would take care of everything. A sharp needle stabbed into her arm, the overwhelming scent of alcohol, a stinging burning fire in her neck. Then she spiraled back down into the dark again, and this time she stayed down.

When Ecko woke hours later, she was on the couch in her own familiar living room with her head in her dad's lap. He was slumped over to the side, head back and mouth hanging wide open. Huge, gusting snores rumbled in and out of his chest. She couldn't help it; she giggled at the sight of him.

That small sound was enough to jar Dan wide awake. His eyes immediately locked onto his daughter, giggling up at him with her eyes wide open and watching him. Relief coursed through him like he'd never felt before. He loved this little girl so much, and that alone was enough to fill him with the need to keep her safe. But more importantly, if the secrets he had been entrusted with were true, (and he had no reason to doubt them at this point) Ecko *had* to be protected at all costs. A lot of lives depended on it.

Dan's heart swelled with gratitude; she was alive, and she would heal. "You scared the crap out of me, Kiddo," he murmured as he stroked her hair back out of her eyes.

She nodded. "Scared me too. It was Sigmund, that dumb teddy bear that Karen gave me. Somehow, he came to life and tried to eat me. I swear it, Dad. I'm not making it up and I'm *not* crazy! Please, please believe me!" She started crying softly.

He lifted her up and looked straight into her eyes. "Hey, none of that now. I will *always* believe you. No matter what. I have always believed everything you've ever told me and that will never change. I admit that I don't understand how something like that is possible. But strange things have always happened around you. I thought I saw something, well, not quite right about that bear when I first got to you. I thought it was just because it was out of place and covered in blood. I knew something crazy was going on, but there was no time to stop and figure out what was happening. I made your mother and sister lock themselves in the safe room because I didn't know what the threat was or if there was even still a threat at all."

Dan frowned fiercely and his face flushed with anger. "I am going to burn that bear to ashes. *After* I rip all of its parts off!"

Ecko giggled again and laid her head on his shoulder. "I love you, Dad," she whispered. "So, much." Rachael walked in at that moment and saw that Ecko was awake. A tiny whimper escaped, and then she started sobbing into her hands. Ecko tried to get up and go to her, but her legs felt like rubber and her vision started swimming.

"Whoa!" Dan cried out as he kept her from falling over. "Hold on there! You lost a lot of blood and you're going to be weak for a while. You have to take it easy!"

Rachael came over and sat on the couch next to them. "I th...th..th.. thought wh..wh..wh..we had llo..llossttt you. Th..there was sss..ss..so much blood!" she stuttered as she unsuccessfully tried to stifle her sobs. "I don't even understand what happened!" she wailed.

In that moment Ecko realized exactly how much she loved her, this woman that had always treated her as if she were her own daughter. She *had* to do everything she could to protect her, even if that meant lying in order to do so. She couldn't tell her the truth. No, not *that* truth. "It was glass," she finally said. "I accidentally knocked my lamp over and the light bulb hit the corner post on the bed. Then the lamp fell straight down on top of me and the glass cut my neck." As lies went, it was weak and highly unbelievable. But the mind will overlook the obvious, and believe the unbelievable, when it didn't want to acknowledge the truth behind the lies.

Rachael hugged her and cried, "You clumsy girl! You could have been electrocuted too! What are we going to do with you?!"

Ecko put her arms around her and hugged her tight. "I love you, Mom. Thank you for always loving me when I know that you didn't have to." The three of them had a good cry fest there on the couch, laughing and hugging and just basking in the relief that their family was still whole.

When they'd all calmed a bit, Ecko asked where Karen was. "Oh, she went to the movies with her friends," Rachael said with a dismissive wave of her hand. "She had to get out for a while after being locked in the safe room for so long. And honestly, I was glad that her friends called and asked if she could go. All that complaining on top of my worrying about what was happening with you was driving me nuts! I've never been so glad to see anyone as I was to see the two of you when you got back from the hospital, for more than one reason!"

"Hospital?" Ecko frowned as she tried to think back. She clearly remembered her dad catching her as she started to fall in her bedroom, but everything was blurry after that point. She remembered a man in pajamas and a stove, of all things. No matter how hard she tried, she couldn't remember anything about doctors or even a hospital. She tried to make sense of the memories that she had and the memories that were clearly missing.

"That man," she said to her dad. "The man in the pajamas. He helped me. His name was David, right?"

Dan shifted uncomfortably in his seat. "Um, yeah. I think that's what he said his name was." Her dad nervously cleared his throat. He widened his eyes and gave her a tiny, almost imperceptible shake of his head.

Rachael was busy fussing with the bandages on Ecko's neck, so she never noticed it.

"Yeah, there was a man in pajamas in the waiting room. He held the compress in place and kept pressure on your neck while I filled out your paperwork. By the way, Kiddo, I'm going to have to buy you some new sheets. I threw yours away at the hospital." Dan turned away, an uncomfortable, sheepish look on his face.

Ecko frowned. Her father was lying. There had been no waiting room, no paperwork, and no hospital. She was sure of it. But for some reason, he didn't want Rachael to know that they'd never made it to a hospital. He had taken her to a *house*, and he knew the man that lived there. Her father was keeping secrets from her mom. *Weird* secrets. But she didn't question him, and she kept her thoughts to herself. She didn't think less of him either. She knew he had to have his reasons. After all, didn't she have more than her fair share of secrets?

"Well, it's over, thank God, and you're home now," Rachael exclaimed as she pushed Ecko's hair back out of her face. "And I bet you're starving. I made some soup for lunch. I thought that would be easiest on your throat. Chewing and swallowing will probably be uncomfortable for a while. And besides, soup is always just the thing to make you feel better when you're not feeling your best."

She stood up and said, "You just stay right here; I won't have you tiring yourself out by walking to the kitchen. We can have lunch in here today. When we're done eating, I'll go up and clean the mess in your room so that you can get into your bed and be comfortable. I haven't had a chance to go up there yet."

She turned to leave but Dan quickly stopped her. "No, Rachael. I'll go up and clean the mess after lunch. If there's glass everywhere, I certainly don't want you getting hurt too."

Her mom frowned, but readily agreed. "Well, ok then. If you think that's best and you really don't mind doing it, Dan. I'm extremely tired anyway. I was too worried to sleep while you two were gone. If you're sure you won't need me, I think I'll lie down for a nap after we eat."

Dan and Ecko smiled conspiratorially at one other. "Perfect," Dan whispered. The two of them had a hot date with a teddy bear to attend. After they'd all eaten and Rachael was fast asleep, there was no one to question them about the strange, sacrificial ritual they performed in their backyard fire pit. Ecko had never enjoyed anything so much, or gained such satisfaction, as she did when she watched her dad dismember, disembowel, de-fluff, and then burn that furry little monster to ashes.

Ecko tossed her book down onto her bed in disgust. She was beginning to get moody and cranky. A whole week of lying around, being treated like an invalid was wearing on her nerves. She'd been confined to her bed to rest and heal. She'd read her books and watched movies until she just couldn't stand another minute of it.

She *had* to get out of her room, out of the house, before she lost her mind completely.

Thankfully, she only had to make it the rest of the day. The next day was Christmas tree day and there was no way she was missing that! While most people put up their Christmas trees after Thanksgiving, the Roberts family put theirs up and started their decorating on November 18th every year. It was something that Dan's family had done when he was a child and he had carried on the tradition with his own family.

His ladies didn't mind; they all loved Christmas as much as he did and wanted to celebrate it as long as possible. Ecko's parents had assured her that her confinement would be lifted and that she'd be allowed to help with the decorating, *if* she took it easy. She couldn't wait! Honestly, she didn't know if she was more excited about Christmas decorating or being released from her imprisonment.

Ecko knew that she was being overly dramatic. It really hadn't been *that* bad, just terribly boring. She knew that it could have been so much worse. To her immense relief, Samara had been absent for most of the week. The few times that she'd actually made an appearance, her face had looked drawn and haggard. She was obviously exhausted, and she didn't stick around for long.

Apparently trying to murder someone through magical means drained you of energy and power. Who knew? All Ecko knew was that she was extremely grateful for the reprieve. She still had no idea how to get rid of Samara, but it was imperative that she do something and soon. That girl was pure evil, and she was dangerous.

Ecko knew without a single doubt that Samara wanted to be over here, in this world and that she was doing everything in her power to get here. So far, for whatever reason, she'd been unable to break through. Maybe she didn't know how, or maybe she just didn't have enough power. Or maybe there really was no way for her to get through, although that didn't feel true to her somehow.

But Samara didn't even need to come through to cause problems and to wreak havoc. She could hurt Ecko or her family any time she chose, even from the other side of the glass. She'd proven that time and again.

Ecko had laid there in her bed, day after day of her recovery, trying to come up with a solution, *any* solution. There had to be something she could do to stop Samara. Maybe she *should* get rid of her mirror. Maybe she should get rid of every mirror in her house. If she told her dad, if she explained everything, he would help. He would understand and he would make sure that all the mirrors disappeared.

But then how would Karen put on her makeup every day? She would definitely be angry about it. Her sister already thought she was a freak. Banishing all mirrors would make Karen hate her even more.

Maybe she should just run away. If she was gone, if she were no longer here, would Samara leave her family alone? Or would her disappearance set Samara off? Would she then turn her anger on her loved ones? Ecko slammed her fists down onto the bed. She was just so frustrated, not to mention scared! She had no one to turn to, no one that could help. She threw the blankets off and swung her legs to the floor. She was making herself crazy, she had to do something besides lay there worrying. Maybe she could sneak outside for a bit, even if it was only for a few minutes. Her mom would be so mad if she caught her though. Worth it, she decided as she stood up and put on her robe.

She peeked out her door to make sure the coast was clear but immediately jerked her head back into the room. She couldn't believe it. *Of course,* her mom would be coming down the hall, now of all times. Ecko tugged her robe back off and jumped back into the bed. Three seconds later and her mom was pushing the door open with her foot.

She had rolls of wrapping paper under her arms and her hands were filled with shopping bags. She set the bags down and let the rolls of Christmas paper fall to the floor. "Hey baby," Rachael cheerfully called out. "I know how bored you've been, stuck in here by yourself for so long. I thought maybe you'd like to help me get started on some gift wrapping. I could really use the help and it would give you something to do. What do you say?"

Ecko grinned. "Oh yeah! I'm ready! Do I get to wrap my own gifts?" She jumped down off the bed and peeked into the bag closest to her.

Rachael laughed. "Nice try! I left all of yours downstairs. Go ahead and empty the bags and pile everything on the floor here, off to the side. We'll just sit right on the floor. That will be easiest, I think. Plenty of room for the both of us."

She did as she was told, taking the items out one by one. Of course, she had to inspect them all to see what everyone would be getting. "Don't you dare tell Dad and Karen anything. I don't care how much they beg!" Rachael ordered with a fake frown on her face.

"I would never! It's our secret," Ecko promised as she giggled at her mom's stern expression. She took the last box from the bag she'd been emptying. It was upside down, so she flipped it over to see what it was. There was nothing on this planet that she hated and feared more than porcelain dolls, and there was one staring up at her with its creepy little dead eyes. With a frightened little yelp, she dropped it and scrambled backwards. She tripped over boxes and landed hard on her butt.

"Oh my God! Ecko! What happened? What's wrong?" Ecko gasped for breath. "Doll," was all she managed to say as she got back up. Her heart was racing, and now her butt hurt. She felt incredibly stupid. She wasn't a baby anymore. She was 14 years old for crying out loud. Entirely too old to be squealing at the sight of a toy. She *knew* that. But she still backed as far away from it as she could get.

"Oh! Oh, Ecko. I'm so sorry. I forgot about that one. Here, I'll get it out of here right now. I'm sorry!" She sat on the bed and stared down at the floor as her mom picked the dreadful thing up off the floor.

"I'll be right back!" Rachael called out as she turned away. She felt terrible. She discreetly glanced at Ecko's reflection in the mirror as she passed by it to see if she was ok. Ecko was staring after her, watching her leave with a huge, creepy smile on her face. Her eyes looked strange, cruel almost. Rachel's heart skipped in fright as she spun back around, but Ecko was still staring at the floor, looking embarrassed.

When she turned back to the mirror, the reflection showed just that... Ecko looking down at the floor, her fingers fiddling with Sir Didymus's ears. She always did that when she needed comfort. "Trick of the light," Rachael whispered to herself as she carried the doll back downstairs to wrap later. "Yeah. Just a trick of the light and your own stupid imagination," she muttered to herself.

She put the doll away, then went back to her daughter's room and they got down to the serious business of wrapping gifts. After a while, Ecko got over her embarrassment. Rachael forgot the weirdness in the mirror, and they both just enjoyed spending time together.

Ecko, unfortunately, hadn't seen the incident between Samara and her mother. If she'd only known that Samara had been around at that moment, maybe there would have been some kind of warning. If she'd only known that Samara had witnessed her reaction, that she had learned of her fear of dolls, she would have known that the girl in the mirror had new ammunition to use against her. If Ecko had seen the excitement on Samara's face, and the way that she'd watched her mother, she would have known that something terrible was coming. She would have told her father everything, then and there, and together they would have worked it all out. If she'd only known, she could have stopped The Bad Thing from happening. But she'd been so focused on her shame and embarrassment that she'd been completely unaware that Samara and her mother had finally been 'introduced'. If Ecko had only known, maybe, just maybe, she could have saved them all.

Wish I Could Be Part of Your World

(Samara 14 years old)

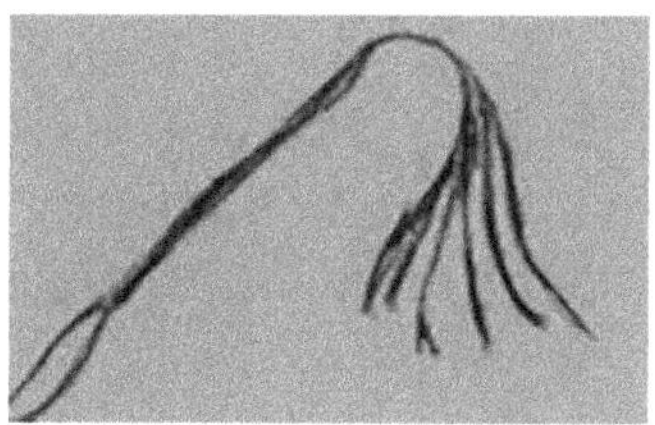

Father is pissed… and I am so deliciously happy about it. I thought it was a brilliant idea to have that fuzzy brown thing that Ecko is so afraid of try to tear her to pieces and gobble her up. The unequivocal fear in her eyes when she'd turned her head and saw it lying on the pillow next to her face was pure euphoria to me. It almost made up for the pain and misery that I'm currently experiencing.

Father had his men punish me...again. Even though it had been agony, I laughed the entire time they were ripping my fingernails out, because nothing pleases me more than tormenting my sister and defying my father. I *tried* to play it his way and do everything that he ordered me to do.

Dear old daddy has it all wrong though. He's got the wrong daughter if he wants blind obedience. I tried it his way, I really did. I tried to feign submission to give myself time to grow stronger. It sucked. And it lasted no more than a few weeks. I couldn't do it. It just isn't in me to play the meek, pathetic damsel in distress. I'm a fighter. I always have been, and I always will be. Father is doing his best to beat the fire out of me, to force me to bend to his will.

But what he doesn't seem to understand is that will *never* happen. He doesn't realize that I'm learning to enjoy the punishments that he doles out. The bite of the whip, the drip of the blood down my back, the way that my tongue continuously worries the cuts in my lips. I think about Krispin all the time now, especially when father is on a rampage and administering his abuses. I picture him in my mind and imagine that it's *him* behind me with the whip in his hand instead of my father's ugly minions. That makes everything better. Suddenly the pain is bearable, almost pleasurable even. The images in my mind make my heart beat faster as excitement fills me. I do believe I am beginning to crave Krispin's depraved attentions.

I lay across my filthy bed, on my stomach, because the whelps on my back are just beginning to heal. I watch Ecko healing from her own wounds. So. Damn. Boring. All she does is lie there in bed, same as me. But at least she has that magic box on. It's almost like watching the Otherlands, but better somehow.

It's so much more exciting to watch other people's lives through her magic box than it is to watch them through the mirror. It's like Ecko has the ability to skip all the boring stuff in the lives of the people that she's watching. It only shows the important and interesting parts, almost like a story being told. Sometimes she watches people for just a few minutes before it changes to someone new.

I'm pretty sure they're singing, but the things they do are so strange! Sometimes they dance and jump around, but none of it makes much sense to me. I wish I could hear into her world, as well as see into it. Especially that time she watched that group of people all kissing each other. Oh, the things I have learned about her world through that magic box! Once I even caught a glimpse of a woman dressed all in black beating a bound man with a riding crop! That was so very exciting. But unfortunately, my prissy, 'I'm such a goody goody girl' sister would never watch something so depraved as that. She switched it to a different place, to watch someone else. Ugh, why does she have to be so boring? I really wanted to see what was going to happen next. It's just not fair. Why did she get the best of everything? Why not me? I want what she has, all of it. I want it desperately, even more than I desire Krispin. I want it even more than my need for revenge on my father. I'm determined to have it too. My mind is made up. Somehow, someday, I *will* find a way to go through the mirror and into her world.

I roll over onto my back and feel the newly scabbed wounds reopen and the wetness of the blood soaking into the mattress beneath me. I writhe through the pain/pleasure and grin up at the ceiling as I picture myself taking Ecko's place. Oh, the joy that will bring me! I swear to myself that someday it will no longer be a fantasy. Someday I will make it happen, I *will* find the way.

Someday.

Merry Christmas

Thanksgiving Day came and went without incident and the Roberts family wholeheartedly threw themselves into the Christmas spirit. Rachael and Karen had been out shopping more than they were home, while Dan and Ecko preferred to purchase the majority of their gifts online. Amazon and eBay were their best friends during the holidays. They were both completely content to spend their days sitting in front of the fireplace, shopping and chatting away about everything.

Ecko's wound had finally healed enough so that most of the pain was gone and she no longer had to keep her entire neck covered in bandages. When it came time to take the stitches out, Dan decided to do it himself. He didn't say so, but Ecko knew that he was avoiding taking her to a doctor's office. In fact, she couldn't remember a single time that she'd been to see a doctor. She must have just forgotten. Surely, she had to have gone, at least when she was small. Hadn't she gotten shots and such? She just couldn't remember, and it seemed strange that her dad wanted to take the stitches out himself... and that he waited until Rachael and Karen were out on one of their shopping sprees before he suggested it.

She kept her thoughts to herself though and didn't question him about it. She knew that her father had secrets, lots of them, same as her. But she trusted him with all her heart, and she knew that he would do everything in his power to protect her. He had his reasons, and so she held her silence as she watched him gather a tiny pair of sewing scissors, tweezers, gauze and the rubbing alcohol.

Under the bright kitchen lights, he carefully removed the bandage and took a good look at the wound that he would soon be playing doctor on. It was the first time he'd set eyes on it since the night of the *accident*. Having no desire whatsoever to confront the damage and be reminded of how close he'd come to losing her, he'd gladly left the cleaning and care of the wound to Rachael.

He couldn't avoid the reminder any longer though. It was *terrible*. The wound began right above where her shoulder met her neck. That was the widest area of damage, as it was where the little monster had actually bitten her. That part was almost three inches wide. The rest of the wound had been made when Ecko tried to jerk the bear away. Its teeth had ripped off a strip of flesh an inch wide that wrapped around and ended on her larynx. The entire laceration was six inches long and it almost looked as if someone had tried to slice her throat.

Dan had swallowed hard, thinking to himself that he just might be sick. He really hadn't thought it through properly, and it was almost all over before it really even began. What *had* he been thinking? He was no doctor. But the stitches had to come out, and if he wanted to avoid taking her to an actual physician, well, he would just have to man up and do it himself. With hands shaking and stomach churning nauseatingly, he started on the first stitch.

Watching her father through the stitch removal process was almost comical to her. Before he'd even snipped the first stitch, his face turned a nasty green-gray color, and she was afraid that he was going to throw up on her. "You can do this, Dad. Just take it slow and get through the first one. The rest should be easier. Just please don't puke on me!" she'd cheerfully encouraged.

He had managed it somehow, stopping several times to wipe sweat off his brow. It was a lot harder to pull out those little strings than he thought it would be. They got caught in her skin and were sometimes stuck. The worst part was that he hadn't been prepared for it to be painful for her. The tugging *did* hurt a bit, but she assured him that it was bearable. But *he* just couldn't stand it. A tear fell down his face with every wince that his daughter made.

By the time her dad had removed all thirty-seven stitches, he was bawling, the tears streaming down his cheeks. When that last one was finally removed, he set the scissors down, closed his eyes and let out a deep, shaky breath. She laughed and told him to go make himself a 'grown up' drink while she cleaned up the mess, and that had been that. Ecko would always have a nasty scar, but she was alive, and she was grateful.

Even though Samara had been mostly absent since the teddy bear incident, Ecko dreaded being in her room more than ever and spent as little time in there as possible. The few times that Samara actually showed her face, she'd been suspiciously quiet and subdued. Ecko figured that the reprieve was due to one of two things. Either Samara still hadn't recovered from whatever plagued her. Presumably, she had overexerted herself in her murder-by-teddy bear attempt, or Samara was planning something new and was conserving her strength. Ecko hoped and prayed that wasn't the case, but deep down she was sure that something bad was on its way.

Only one small disturbance had occurred during those uneventful days, and thankfully no one had been hurt. Well, no one on Ecko's side of the mirror anyway. She wasn't so sure about whoever was on Samara's side.

One evening Dan had announced that he was taking everyone out to dinner, so Ecko had dashed into her room to grab her coat. As always, her eyes automatically darted to the mirror to assure herself that all was well. Samara had been standing there, grinning like a mad thing. Her right arm was raised up and blood covered her hand

and arm all the way up to her elbow. It dripped off her fingers, as she started to draw on her side of the glass.

Ecko watched in apprehension as she finger-painted one word. Just four little letters. Ecko. She pointed back at herself and then reached up and ran her fingers over her face, leaving streaks of blood behind. As vague as the message seemed, Ecko heard it loud and clear and understood it perfectly. Samara had grown up and left behind all pretenses and vestiges of innocence behind. No more kid games. She was upping the stakes and would now be playing for keeps.

Samara no longer wanted to be the Other girl in the mirror. She no longer wanted to be over there in that Otherworld, living that Other life. Samara wanted to be *her*. She wanted to come through the glass, take *her* place and live *her* life. For now, she was trapped, but she wouldn't be forever. She was coming, and she was pissed.

Ecko had never been so terrified in all her life, not even when Sigmund the demented teddy bear had tried to turn her into a kid's meal. She started draping a blanket over the mirror whenever she had to spend time in her room. She knew that it was a juvenile and desperate gesture. It was basically the equivalent of a child hiding its head under a blanket. If she couldn't see the bad thing, then the bad thing couldn't get her. Maybe if Samara couldn't see, she would be unable to inflict any damage.

As the days passed, Ecko often thought about Samara's 'message'. She just couldn't get the images out of her mind. Her hands coated in blood, the streaks on her face, the red letters dripping down the mirror. She wondered who had donated the 'paint' for that macabre art. What poor soul had been unfortunate enough to earn her wrath? What had Samara done to spill so much blood? She hoped that she *never* found out. There were some questions that just didn't need answering.

Time passed and it was soon Christmas Eve; it had finally, *finally* come! Ecko had always loved this day, even more than Christmas itself. Something about the anticipation, the hope, the absolute joy of the whole family gathered together, carrying out their own special traditions. This was always a fun filled day with games, movies, junk food, and eggnog... *so* much eggnog!

That morning, four alarms went off at exactly 6:00 a.m. Four eager people jumped out of their beds, threw off their pajamas, and raced to put on...a completely different pair of pajamas. This was the first and most important game of the day. It was a contest on who wore the craziest or ugliest pjs. Each contestant had a whole year to figure out what they wanted to wear, the crazier the better. The rules were simple. They could buy their pjs or make them themselves. Everyone got a vote, and they could not vote on themselves. The winner got to be the Christmas Goofball Queen...or King of Dorkville for the next two days. They got to wear the ugly old plastic crown that Dan had found years ago for just this purpose.

The king or queen got special treatment, and of course the bragging rights that came with the win. The best part was that the winner got their framed photo added to the Wall of Dorkdom. Every year, when they put up their Christmas tree, the wall behind it became the designated Wall of Dorkdom. There was a special place of honor for every single year's king or queen, with one spot left open right at the center for the current winner. The rest of the wall got covered with photos of the whole family wearing their ugly pajamas together.

Most years it had been a king that got crowned the winner. Dan really had a knack for finding outfits that made his ladies giggle. This year was no different. He had transformed himself into Princess Peach from the Mario Brothers video games. He wore a pink princess nightgown, a little golden crown and a long blond wig. He was even wearing the blue jewelry, pink lipstick, and super long fake eyelashes.

They didn't even have to take a vote. Dan won the contest instantly. His ladies took one look at him and had to bow down to his expert level of dorkiness. The combination of beard stubble and princess attire had been more than enough for him to score the win. But it was all over when they saw his unfortunate little mishap. They couldn't catch their breath as they howled out their laughter. Dan had accidentally glued one of his fake eyelashes to his eyebrow.

He had such a serious look on his face when he called out, "Go ahead and laugh. Hahahaha. But when you're done, can one of you girls please help your poor, old dad out? It's really stuck in there. I tried to pull it off, I really did. But it hurts! Why would you ladies willingly do this to yourselves?" It was another fifteen minutes before everyone stopped laughing long enough for Karen to wash away the glue and defeminize her poor father.

After they framed the new (and extremely hilarious) photos and added them to the wall with the others, they cooked and ate breakfast together. They watched A Charlie Brown Christmas, Rudolf the Red Nosed Reindeer, and Ecko's personal favorites, The Grinch and The Nightmare Before Christmas. They played games and ate junk food all day and danced crazily around the house.

When night fell, they all bundled up and went outside to make their yearly wishes on the North Star, another tradition that they followed every year. Dan always started the requests. "I wish for nothing more than another wonderful year of making my three ladies happy. I want to see nothing but smiles upon their beautiful faces," he said.

Rachael went next. "I wish for a year of peace and good health for my family. Please watch over us and keep us all safe." She glanced at her Ecko and silently added, 'Please no more craziness. Please!' But she kept that part of her wish to herself.

"Amen to that! What a great wish, honey" Dan praised as he wrapped his arms around his wife. Karen cleared her throat dramatically to get everyone's attention. "Everyone already knows *my* wish. I want the new Ford Mustang GT. A pink one. I've been begging all year and Daddy still hasn't bought it for me," she grumbled as she pouted.

Dan laughed and came back with, "I see that *my* wish won't be coming true. I guess there won't be many smiles from you, because I am *not* giving in on this one. I can't believe you just wasted your wish on *that* when I've told you no a thousand times already. I've said that I'll buy you a car next year for your 18th birthday, and it will be a very nice, dependable car. I'll even make it pink for you. But I am *not* buying you a brand-new car. And it probably won't be a Mustang either. I haven't decided on that part yet though."

Karen rolled her eyes, crossed her arms and turned away. Dan merely smiled and shrugged, then turned to Ecko. "How about it, Kiddo? What are you going to wish for this year?" Karen spun back around. "I don't know why you even bother asking her. We all know that she's going to wish for snow. She *always* asks for the same old boring thing."

Dan frowned. "Pay her no mind, honey. She's just mad at me and she's seriously working on convincing me that she doesn't deserve to have a car given to her at all. Go ahead, make your wish."

Ecko threw her arms out and spun in circles, laughing merrily. "She's right though. I *do* wish for snow! There's something so magical about a white Christmas. I wish we could move to New Hampshire! Don't you guys remember? That was the best vacation ever! It was so beautiful, and it snows there every winter too."

Dan and Rachael smiled at her exuberance and Karen rolled her eyes again. "Do you guys remember the last time it snowed here? It was five years ago. I was nine. We were opening our presents, when I looked out the window and saw the snowflakes falling everywhere. We all ran outside and threw ourselves down to make snow angels. Then I pelted Dad right on the side of his head with a snowball. Remember how he stood there all shocked for a second, with snow melting down his face? Then suddenly there were snowballs flying everywhere! That was so much fun! Oh! And then we all went back inside, and mom made hot cocoa to warm us up. I just *love* hot cocoa!"

Dan's heart swelled with happiness at seeing her so exuberant and full of joy. She was almost always guarded and reserved and quiet, so he loved any time she poked her head up out of her shell. He couldn't help but smile and hug her close before they all turned and made their way back into the house. They reminisced about years gone by and even Karen had to smile at some of their silly shenanigans.

Then everyone got to choose one gift to open. It was something they did every year, and everyone had their own way of deciding which one to open. Ecko always opened her smallest gift. Karen always opened her biggest. Dan and Rachael always chose one from each other. After the gifts were opened and the messes were all cleaned, everyone gathered back around the fire. Dan read aloud from a book of Christmas poems and ended the night with The Night before Christmas.

By that time, it was nearing midnight, and everyone was ready for sleep. They all said their goodnights and fell into their beds happy, exhausted, and with slightly upset tummies from all the junk they'd eaten. If they had only known that they would never celebrate another Christmas Eve together, they would have stayed awake and made it last all night. They would have laughed more, sang louder, read one more poem, and danced just one more dance. If they had only known, they would have loved each other just a little bit harder, for a little bit longer.

Ecko knew that she was dreaming. *She stands alone in front of a wall made entirely of mirrors, staring at her reflection. She's dressed in a shimmering, silver ball gown and jewels sparkled in her hair. A silver and black lace Colombina mask covers her face, accentuating the green of her eyes, the pout of her ruby red lips.*

She hears a violin begin to play behind her and turns to see a group of musicians all dressed as court jesters. Their long nosed Zanni masks and the smiles painted on their faces should have lent them a comical appearance. Instead, they exude an air of rancor and pure malice. The singer stands center stage, illuminated by a single spotlight. He's dressed as a Plague Doctor, wearing a long black tailcoat and a Medico Della Peste mask. His eyes travel the length of her, from the riot of red curls framing her face to her glittering silver heels.

She shivers with revulsion at the evil that's oozing off of him. Her distaste seems to amuse him, and he grins wickedly at her as he begins to sing. She turns away and desperately tries to wake herself up then. "Wake up! Wake up right now! You do not want to be here," she whispers as she pinches herself.

She'd always wanted to attend a masquerade ball, but now that she'd dreamt herself into one, she wanted nothing more than to escape. This wasn't what she'd had in mind. This was not a dream come true. This place was off somehow, the atmosphere forbidding and overwhelmingly sinister. The ballroom was dark, lit only by the tiny twinkling fairy lights cascading from the ceiling and the candles scattered throughout the room.

Shadow people are suddenly dancing all around her, their masks sparkling and glinting as they pass by. A giant of a man wearing a horned, black and gold mask appears out of the crowd. He takes her hand and elegantly bows, then wraps his arms around her. His touch fills her with the deepest apprehension, like she has a heart attack sleeping in her chest…and it was beginning to wake.

The man ignores her feeble attempts at pulling away and twirls her around, then pulls her back in closer. His piercing green eyes search her face, studying her so closely that it seems as if he's looking into her soul. Those eyes are so familiar to her, a memory she can't quite grasp, dancing just out of reach. They send waves of dread coursing through her, filling her with a deeply ingrained fear. She tries to pull away again, but he grips her tighter, his fingers digging into her flesh. He spins her faster and faster, round and round the dance floor. The other couples become little more than shadowy blurs whirling by.

As they pass by the mirrored wall, she's horrified to see that her reflection tells a different story from the reality that she's experiencing. Her mirror self is all alone, spinning around the empty dance floor by herself. Her arms are raised and she's smiling up at an invisible partner, her face frozen in a mask of adoration. She jerks her gaze away from the image in the mirror and focuses on the here and now right before her.

Everyone's spinning around her so quickly that they remind her of the spinning tops she used to play with as a child. Her partner spins her ever faster too, making everything blur together. Like water splashed on a painted canvas, the colors all bleed and then blend into one another. The only sure things she can make out are the masks and laughing mouths of the other dancers. And HIM. His masked face is all too clear.

Suddenly, Ecko feels a hand stroke her face, a caress on her shoulder, a tug on her hair. The other dancers all begin to reach for her as they twirl past. Each couple reaches out and touches some part of her.

"Don't touch me," she begs. "Please, please don't touch me!" But they don't stop. They won't stop! And oh, how they laugh! She feels more and more hands on her as her partner spins her round and round, and in a moment of sudden clarity she realizes…they're not just touching her.

They're ripping pieces off of her, giggling behind their masks at her fear.

All the while he grins down at her as he spins her in perpetual circles, round and round and round. He waltzes her over every inch of the dance floor, ensuring that each of his guests have a chance to take what they want from her. Their greedy hands steal more and more, peeling away her skin, tearing out muscle and pulling out organs. All the while, his smile grows wider and wider until it's bigger than his face and she finally recognizes him for who, and what he is...and she starts to scream. The Shadow Man.

He's found her at last, and she realizes that there's no escape for her now. The band slows the tempo and the song changes to a sad symphony, a haunting rendition of Come, Sweet Death, by J.S. Bach. The dancing is finally coming to an end and the Shadow man slows their manic spinning. He twirls her back to where they'd started, bringing her to a stop in front of the mirrored wall. Then he lets go of her and takes a step back.

The other dancers all crowd around him and hold up their stolen treasures, her blood dripping down their arms. She looks at her reflection and all she can do is scream, one long tortured cry after another. They've stolen her away, all of her. There's nothing left but bloody bones standing in front of the mirror, screaming from an empty skull. She can't stand the nightmare that she's become. She whirls back around so that she doesn't have to endure the sight of her gruesome reflection for another second, screaming all the while.

Suddenly, the other dancers all step aside and clear a path. They kneel down and bow their heads. Samara, wearing her own ball gown and mask, glides towards her through the path that the crowd had created.

Samara, here...on this side of the mirror. She must have escaped her world. Or maybe Ecko had somehow got pulled into hers. She doesn't know which to fear more; both options are equally terrifying. Samara stops beside Shadow Man; he takes her hand and carries it up to his lips for a devoted kiss. Then he puts his arm around her, and they both walk towards her, the living dead girl still screaming in horror. The two of them come to a stop in front of her and stand there, arm in arm and smiling cruelly, and still she screams. She can do nothing else.

Samara reaches out and gently caresses her bare skull, smiling that nasty little smile that she's come to recognize as a warning of wicked things to come. And then Samara shoves her backwards, straight at the mirror. Instead of smashing into the glass, she falls right through it and gets swallowed up in a terrible black void.

Ecko woke up to utter darkness with a scream on her lips, for a moment convinced that she was still trapped in the nightmare. She gasped for breath, desperately trying to get air into her oxygen starved lungs. She touched a hand to her face, relieved to feel skin and not bare bone. She's fine. It was just a dream and she's fine, lying in her bed, in her own room. She worked on getting her breathing under control as her heartbeat slowly returned to normal.

She tried to think of something, *anything* other than that horrifying dream. Her thoughts settled on her father dressed as Princess Peach, and she couldn't help but smile at the memory. Oh! It's Christmas! She turned her head to check the alarm clock, hoping that it would be time to wake the family up, so that they could open their gifts. Disappointment filled her when she realized that it was only 3:03 a.m. It was much too early to get up. She'd only been asleep for a couple hours, although it felt like she'd been trapped at that hellish masquerade ball for a lifetime. She settled back in, hoping she'd be able to fall back asleep...this time with no more dreams.

But her eyes popped back open when she heard rustling, thumping, and tiny pitter-pattering noises running across her floor. The sounds reminded her of Sigmund the Demon Teddy, and terror immediately consumed her. She began to hear whispers all around her, and she wasted no time in jumping up and clicking on her lamp.

Dolls! There were dolls *everywhere.* Karen's collection had grown considerably over the years until she had a veritable army of miniature, porcelain people. There were now over two hundred of them, *and every one of them was here, in her room.* Somehow, they were alive, crawling and climbing and running *everywhere.*

When the light clicked on, they froze in place and turned their little demon faces to look at her. As one, they all opened their mouths and issued a high pitched, chirping screech. "No!" she whispered in horrified disbelief. "No, no, no, no! This isn't happening. Not again!"

As if the sound of her voice was the signal they'd been waiting for, they all ran straight at her, giggling as they swarmed her. She started to scream as they crawled all over her, pinching, biting, yanking her hair, touching her with their tiny cold, dead hands. She howled as she started kicking and punching for all she was worth. She snatched up the little bodies and smashed their faces into the wall, quickly tossing them aside before reaching for the next one.

She didn't know how many she was able to stop before her family came running, but there was shattered porcelain everywhere. Shards and splinters littered the bed and the floor. Chunks of glassy body parts were embedded in the walls, resembling the shrapnel from a bomb. Blobs of hair and empty doll clothes were scattered across her dresser and writing desk. There was a tiny, dismembered hand on her blanket, the fingers clenching and unclenching, still trying to get to her.

Her family had come running to her rescue but were now stopped in the middle of the room, their eyes wide and mouths slack with shock. The door suddenly slammed shut behind them and it kicked Karen back into gear. She immediately turned around and raced back to the door, trying desperately to escape the madness. Shrieking hysterically, she pounded at the door, her hands uselessly clutching at the knob. No matter how hard she tried, she couldn't get the door to open. They were all trapped together in this nightmare.

The dolls attacked in earnest. A large portion of them swarmed Dan, probably because he was the biggest threat. He refused to panic, and he fought ferociously, like a momma bear protecting her cubs. He shattered several of their faces, just by squeezing their heads with his bare hands. While he was distracted, the rest of the fiends spread out and attacked the girls.

Rachael was the first to fall. An old bride doll, (much like the one that Ecko had accidentally shattered all those years ago) the one that she hated the most, crawled out from under the bed with half of another doll's face clutched in her tiny hands. She tried to get to her mom, before the bride could reach her. But her mom tripped, and they were on her the instant that she hit the floor. Bride grinned right at her, as she calmly and meticulously sliced Rachael's throat open.

Ecko cried out in horror as she continued to throw dolls off her in every direction. She scrambled through the broken glass, sobbing uncontrollably, until she reached her mother. By the time she got to her, the bride had disappeared, hidden somewhere out of sight. Ecko pressed her hands to her mother's throat, desperately trying to hold the blood in, but it continued to pour out from between her fingers. She was dying, and there was nothing she could do to stop it. The bride had killed her mother using another doll's broken face as a weapon. "Dad!" she screamed to be heard over the sounds of the fighting and the glass shattering. "Mom needs help!"

Dan threw his head back, howled in anguish, and slowly fell to his knees when he saw his wife bleeding out onto the floor. He crawled over to her, the dolls still attacking him from every direction. Ecko scrambled back as he pulled Rachael into his arms. She couldn't watch anymore. She couldn't bear anymore of the pain. She moved away from her parents so that she could try to help Karen instead.

She found her sister sitting on the floor, slumped up against the door. Her head was bent down, her hair completely covering her face. It looked for all the world as if she'd fallen asleep there, but Ecko knew better. Deep down, she just *knew*.

"Karen?" she whispered. She said it again, louder, when she got no response. "Karen? Are you ok?" She reached out and slowly brushed the tangled, brown hair aside. Her heart froze into a block of ice inside of her chest as she tried to swallow back her screams. Dismembered doll arms had been shoved through Karen's eyes and into her brain, shoved in so deep that only the hands protruded from her bloody, ruined sockets.

Horrified beyond all reasoning, Ecko slowly backed away. She felt her mind beginning to crack. She was swaying, teetering on the cusp of a complete mental breakdown, a shattering of the mind so great that the pieces would never fit back together correctly. Nothing made sense anymore. Her mother and her sister were gone, and there were broken doll parts strewn all over her bedroom.

There seemed to be only fifty or so dolls left that were whole enough to continue the fight and they were all gathered around her parents. Ecko began to cry in earnest when she saw that her father was still trying to protect the woman that he loved. He didn't realize that she was already gone. His mind hadn't caught up to what his eyes had shown him.

The few dolls that were crawling over Rachael weren't after her at all. She was just in their way of getting to him. Her father was fighting harder than ever, but there were just too many left. They swarmed him, overwhelming him with the sheer number of combatants still in the fight. He curled his body over his wife, his best friend and life partner, and he shielded her with all that he had left in him. The dolls didn't stop, they stabbed him over and over with the shards of their fallen sisters. But still he clung to his fallen love. They would have to get through him to get to her.

Ecko rushed in to help him, pulling the evil things off of him and smashing them onto the floor. She heard a squeal behind her, just before one of them jumped off the top of the shelf and landed square on her shoulders. It wrapped its arms and legs around her neck and squeezed… so tight! Her vision began to blur as her oxygen was cut off.

She reached up and grabbed onto it, but it wouldn't budge. It had latched on tight, and it held on in a death grip, laughing hysterically into her ears. Ecko slammed herself backwards into the wall, trying to dislodge it. It loosened its grip the tiniest fraction, so she moved forward to do it again. That was when she caught sight of what was transpiring in the mirror.

Samara was there… *of course* Samara was there, her mouth moving as if was speaking. The words didn't carry through the mirror, but Ecko heard them just the same. She was reciting some sort of spell or enchantment. Her hands were held out in front of her, palms facing the glass. Thick black fog, or smoke perhaps, flowed out of her hands and was coalescing on the surface of the mirror.

The thick black mass obscured the view, concealing whatever it was that Samara was trying to do. Ecko knew deep in her heart that she was trying to open a gateway into this world. She didn't know if it could be accomplished, but without a doubt, Samara was trying her best to cross over. *Right now.*

She didn't stop to think or question if she was doing the right thing. She acted on pure instinct, reaching up and snapping the arms right off of the creature clinging to her neck. It screamed furiously, its arms dangling uselessly inside its sleeves. The nasty little thing leaned down and bit a chunk right out of her hand in retaliation. Ecko yelped and snatched it off of her shoulders. Then she launched it as hard as she could, straight at the mirror.

Of course, it was the bride doll. She'd known *that* the minute that it had landed on her. The evil thing spun its head around backwards and snarled at her, even as it was sailing through the air towards its doom. It slammed into the mirror and just *exploded*. The porcelain shrapnel of her body flew through the air as her empty wedding dress fluttered to the floor.

The mirror fractured and spider webbed with a million cracks. In that instant, the girls' minds melded together; somehow, they were now linked. Samara grabbed her head and screamed in pain as her spell backlashed. She shrieked so loudly inside their shared consciousness that blood began to drip from Ecko's eyes and ears, and then burst from her nose like a geyser erupting.

Ecko dropped to her knees and wiped the bloody tears from her face, forcing herself past the pain. She had to see if she stopped Samara by breaking the mirror or if she had accomplished just the opposite and set her free instead. Thankfully, Samara was still trapped on her side and all of that dark smoke was recoiling backwards, off the glass like someone had hit rewind on a movie. It shot straight back into her, flinging her aside from the force of the backlash. The moment she disappeared from the mirror, the few remaining dolls reverted back to their inanimate state and fell to the floor. Without the puppeteer pulling on their strings, they were no longer demonic little killers. They were merely lifeless glass figurines once again.

Ecko knelt motionless on the floor, the sudden silence loud in her ears. She sucked in air as fast as her lungs would allow, her chest heaving with the effort. She heard her name whispered behind her and the breath caught in her throat. "Ecko," she heard again.

She turned to see her father lying on his stomach, trying to crawl to her. He was bleeding from a thousand tiny stab wounds. He was using one arm to slowly drag himself towards her and she saw that his wrist had been sliced from his hand up to his elbow. Blood pooled beneath him as he dragged himself along, leaving a gruesome snail trail behind in his wake. He had Sir Didymus, of all things, clutched in his other hand.

Ecko crawled the rest of the way to him and laid his head into her lap. She curled herself around him, her tears splashing down onto his face. "Don't die, Daddy. Not you. I can't lose you. Please, please don't leave me too. I need you," she sobbed.

He tried to speak but no sound came out. "Sshhhh. Don't talk. Save your strength." Ecko's eyes darted around wildly for help that was nowhere to be found.

"What do I do, Daddy? What do I do now?" He began to cough violently, a terrible, watery sound rattling in his throat. It went on forever, before a huge glob of blood spewed from his mouth and he was finally able to suck in a breath.

I have to hold on, Dan thinks to himself. *I have to tell her. There are things that she needs to know, things that I should have already told her.* Regret filled him as he realized that he's out of time. He's fading fast, his voice and the words that he'd always meant to say dying with him. Still, he had to give her something. He tried again to speak and this time his voice came out in a harsh, shaky whisper.

She leaned in closer, but she could only make out a few of his words. "Didymus......safe. Find......Maggie.... Hide." His eyes fluttered and closed.

Ecko whimpered. "I don't understand. Who's Maggie? I don't understand! Don't leave me. I don't know what to do!"

His eyes opened again as he lifted his hand up and pressed Sir Didymus into her arms. He smiled and lovingly stroked her face. "Keep. Safe," he repeated. His eyes became fierce, determined. "Have always. Loved you. Never forget. Not…crazy. Remember." Then his eyes closed once more, and they stay closed. His rattling breaths stopped, and his hand fell away from her face. Her daddy was gone, and she was all alone.

Ecko stayed right there on the floor, stroking his hair as she slowly rocked back and forth. So many different emotions well up inside of her, sadness, fear, regret and longing… And *Rage*. So. Much. Rage. It was too much to feel all at once. A storm cloud formed inside her head, gathering emotions instead of moisture, a thunderhead built by compressing and pressurizing her internal anguish. It grew exponentially as the feelings built and built and built up inside of her, feeding it until it became too large to contain within her. Thunder rumbled and boomed through her mind.

She was overwhelmed by the sheer magnitude of the storm that was brewing inside of her and she began to panic. Her eyes darted wildly around the room as her breath came faster and faster. She took in the devastation around her as the pressure in her head skyrocketed. She saw all the dismembered, broken doll parts. She saw all of the shattered glass and the blood splattered on everything. She saw all of the wreckage and carnage, the destruction of all the treasures that she'd cherished. They all suddenly seemed so childish and stupid now.

Janey-Bug the glow worm was lying across a headless doll's lap, smiling and glowing happily away at her. The camera her father had given her was smashed to pieces. Her bookshelves had all been broken, the books spilled into a heap on the floor. Her globe with the thumbtacks marking all those places she'd wanted to visit had been knocked loose from its stand. It had rolled to the other side of the room and now rested in a pool of her mother's blood.

Her mother…the woman that had accepted her and treated her like her own daughter. Gone. She couldn't look, so she turned her gaze to Karen instead. Her sister had fallen over, sliding the rest of the way down from her slumped position at the door. Ecko shivered and turned away yet again. The tiny hands reaching out of her sister's eye sockets made her think of a soul trying to escape its prison.

She glanced back down at her father, lying in her lap, and cried out in shock. His eyes were open, and they stared sightlessly up at her. That did her in, finally. It was all just too much for her to bear. The dark storm cloud inside of her evolved into a supercell storm, a dangerously unpredictable force that was unparalleled by any other. Lightning streaked across her mind and thunder crashed in its wake. Her hair whipped around her face from a purely psychological, raging wind. Her eardrums popped from the pressure, trickling more blood. And then the world stopped, becoming silent and still. It was the calm in the midst of the raging storm.

Ecko slowly raised her head and opened her eyes. Somehow, she was standing before her mirror, yet she had no memory of how she had gotten there. The surface was all jagged cracks, distorting her reflection. "Samara," she whispered as she pressed her hands to the glass. It was *her* fault. Everything was all her fault.

She said it again, louder this time, screamed it, in fact, dragging out each syllable. "Saa-Marr-Raaa!" The surface of the mirror started to ripple under her palms. The cracks disappeared as the glass turned to liquid, molten silver. Shapes and distorted images emerged from the depths of the flowing, silver pool. Then, suddenly, she was looking into a sparsely furnished bedroom.

It took her a moment, but then she understood. She was seeing Samara's room for the very first time. She had somehow managed to open up her side of the mirror so that she could see out, just as Samara had been doing all these years. She was looking into Samara's world, into her room… and then there she was, Samara.

The girl was sitting on a stained, bare mattress. Her hands were clutching at her head, and she was crying, moaning in pain as if she was suffering from a terrible headache. Rage tore through Ecko's mind and the storm cloud finally, *finally* burst. The air around her snapped and crackled like electricity from a live wire. A scream of pure, unadulterated fury ripped from her throat and Samara jerked her head up, her gaze darting straight to the mirror. Her eyes grew wide, and she recoiled back, before cowering down in fear.

Ecko's hands grew uncomfortably warm, then hot and hotter still, until a glowing blue light began to radiate from them. All those terrible emotions raged through her and formed into some sort of magical force, a strange supernatural power. Suddenly, blue bolts of deadly energy shot from her hands and struck Samara in the chest.

The force of it threw the Other girl back, slamming her back against the wall. She howled in agony as blue fire coursed through her body. Her eyes changed from green to electric blue, then flashed to silver, and finally turned them to black. She fell to the floor and crawled away, out of view and out of the line of fire.

But the raging power that was still coursing through Ecko had to go *somewhere* or surely, it would burn her up from the inside out. An anguished cry of rage and pain poured from her lips as she slammed her fists into the molten mirror. The images blanked out and the Otherworld disappeared. A rush of energy shot out of Ecko's hands and into the silver pool of glass, causing it to re-solidify under the onslaught. The electric blue force flowed over the surface, just as Samara's black smoke had on the opposite side. A loud crackling sound filled the air, just before the mirror exploded, shooting glass and balls of sizzling blue electricity all over her bedroom.

One of the bolts smashed into the light fixture on the ceiling and disappeared into the socket, following the electrical currents. It lit up the wiring as it traveled throughout the entire house's electrical system. Bolts of azure lightning shot out from every electrical outlet in every single room. Everything that the blue energy struck, instantly burst into flames until the entire house was burning around her. Her books, her collections, her furniture...even her family was on fire.

Everything was burning out of control. Unconsciously, Ecko reached out and snatched Sir Didymus up off the dresser where she'd dropped him and backed away as far as she could. Her back bumped into the wall, and she slowly slid down to the floor. She wrapped her arms around Sir Didymus and watched as the flames licked their way across the floor and up the walls, moving closer and closer towards her.

She had no concept of how much time had passed, but suddenly, she heard a man's voice shouting and then the sound of pounding and kicking on her door. Someone was trying to open it and they had no way of knowing that Karen's body was blocking it. Ecko watched dispassionately as the door thumped into her sister's body, over and over again, sliding her across the floor inch by inch.

The man finally managed to push the door open enough where he could fit inside and she realized that it was Old Man Charlie, the sweet old man that lived next door. He stood in the doorway and stared in shocked disbelief at the horror story he'd just entered. His face was red and tears streamed down his cheeks. He began to cough violently as the smoke billowed into his face.

He made his way over to her and said, "We gotta get you out of here. Come on, honey. Let me help you now." He bent down and gently scooped her up into his arms. "Cover your face now, girl. We have to get through a lot of smoke."

He turned to go but stopped suddenly when he spied a thick photo album lying on the floor. Something compelled him to pick it up, tuck it up between their bodies, and carry it out with them. Maybe it was just because subconsciously, he knew that she'd just lost everything else. He cradled her close as he worked his way out of the house as quickly as his old body could manage it. They were both coughing and choking by the time he got them to the safety of the yard. He stumbled as far from the flames as he could before he fell to the ground in exhaustion. They both just lay there in the grass trying to catch their breath as they listened to the sirens of the fire trucks and ambulances approaching.

Ecko was in a daze, floating in and out of awareness as the paramedics gave her oxygen, checked her vitals, and wiped away the blood, tears, and soot. They carried her from the front lawn to a waiting ambulance and wrapped her up in blankets. Police officers stood by, keeping all the neighbors dressed in their pajamas and robes from getting too close.

She heard bits of conversations around her, but none of it really penetrated. "Poor kid," and then, "The whole family." "Wonder what happened" "On Christmas, of all days." "Never saw a house burn so fast". The gossip went on and on and on, but Ecko barely heard any of it. Her eyes were locked on a red ball that rested in the grass, just a few feet away from her.

She realized that it was one of the ornaments from their Christmas tree. How did it get all the way out here? How had it not been shattered? That fragile glass bauble had miraculously survived the annihilation of its entire family and had somehow made its way out of the destruction zone. Ecko watched it obsessively, waiting for one of the many people that had been coming and going to step on it and shatter it, but somehow that never happened. She continued to stare at it in utter confusion, trying to understand how something so fragile was still whole when her entire life had been shattered.

The firefighters had no hope of saving the house, all they could do was spray it from the outside to contain the fire and keep it from spreading. Old Man Charlie rested on the back of another ambulance, periodically taking deep breaths through an oxygen mask. He'd finally gotten his coughing under control, but his lungs felt raw and burned.

A police detective walked over and asked him to give a verbal report. "Well, I woke to the sounds of screaming, things crashing around and breaking in there." Old Man Charlie shook his head. "I don't really know what I saw. Nothing makes any sense a'tall."

He sighed and pointed a gnarled, wrinkled finger towards his house. "My bedroom is up there." Then he waved his hand in the direction of the burning house. "Her room is directly across the way. And that's where all the commotion seemed to be coming from. I opened my window to try and see what was going on. It was madness. The whole family was in there, and at first it looked as if they were shadow boxing, fighting off imaginary attackers...or spiders maybe. You know how people do when they walk into a spiderweb? How they suddenly become Kung Fu fighters? Well, that's just what it looked like. *At first.*"

"Then I saw all these little...*things* jumping and crawling all over them and *that's* what they were fighting. I didn't have any idea what they were, but that family was screaming and throwing them things off of them left and right. I know this is gonna sound crazy to you, and I'm sure it was just my old eyes playing tricks on me, but just as I was turning away to go phone 911, I swear I saw a doll in a wedding gown grinning at me from that window. I don't care what you think. I know how it sounds. But that's what I saw. At least, that's what I *thought* I saw. Anyhow, I called the police and then ran back to the window. It had gotten really quiet over there and I couldn't see nothin' moving anymore."

"Then I heard a girl's voice," he nodded his head towards Ecko, "Hers, I believe. She screamed out a name, Mary, I think it was. It got quiet again and a few seconds later there was all this blue lightning streaking around inside that room. Then it was *all over* the house, lighting up the windows in all the other rooms. I saw that a fire had started in there, in the room where everything had gone down. And then in every window that I could see, things just burst into flames. I ran back and called 911 again and told them they was gonna need to send fire trucks too. Then I ran outside to wait for 'em to get here."

A coughing fit came over him again and it was several minutes before he was able to continue. "Well, I got out here and I knew right away that help couldn't possibly arrive in time. I knew that house was a goner, it was burning up too fast. I had to do something. I just *had* to help. That there girl is the sweetest little thing I've ever met. See, I lost my wife a few years back. We were married almost 54 years when the cancer took her from me. At the funeral, I just stood there staring down into that hole as everyone else walked away. I remember thinking that there was no way I could leave my love down there in the dark all by herself. Not my sweet Gretchen."

"And that's when I heard a sweet, tiny voice from behind me. "Sir? Mr. Charlie, sir?" I turn and see this beautiful little angel. I knew she was one of the little girls that lived next door to me. I'd seen her several times, though we'd never spoken to one another before. But at that moment when I turned towards her, the setting sun was shining behind her, and she was lit up with a hazy, unearthly glow. She looked just like an angel. She walked right up to me and placed a large envelope in my hands. I will never forget the words spoken in that small, quiet voice that day."

"I'm so sorry, Mr. Charlie," she'd said, "Mrs. Gretchen was a beautiful lady. And I'm sorry that you're so very sad." Then she turned and ran back to where her father was waiting. She took his hand and then they walked away. Such simple, heartfelt words. Such profound, soul- shattering words. Of all the condolences I received during that terrible time, that one from that small child comforted me the most. And it still does."

"Anyway, I opened the envelope after they'd walked away, and then I collapsed to my knees, right there in the grass beside my wife. It felt like a dam burst inside of me and I cried a river of tears when I saw that there were dozens of photographs of us, my wife and I. Photos that I'd had no idea existed. That little girl had taken them in secret, you see. And she had captured some of the most beautiful images of my wife.

"My Gretchen, working in her garden, a streak of dirt on her cheek and surrounded by her flowers. Feeding a tiny sparrow from her hand. Her face lit up, smiling that beautiful smile up at me as I opened the car door for her. There were several photos of one evening in particular. We were sitting hand in hand on the porch swing in the early evening light. The first picture in the set showed us smiling softly at each other. Another one showed our kiss. Then my lips pressed to her forehead."

He stopped talking and quickly swiped at his nose. Tears fell from his old eyes as he shook himself from the memories. "Oh, goodness me! I am so sorry. I tend to get carried away when I talk about my wife. Anyway, my point is, that girl needed saving and so I did it. I didn't even think about not being able to make it back out. It was just something that had to be done. For my Gretchen, you see. For the beauty that girl saw in my wife. I'm just sorry I was too late to help the rest of her family. But they were already gone by the time I got there. The girl was the only one left alive. I just picked her up and carried her out of there. Where will she go now? I can't bear the thought of her being in one of them foster places. How will her beautiful soul survive in that kind of environment?" Old Man Charlie lifted the mask back up to his face to try and hide his tears. But there was no disguising his shoulders shaking with his silent sobs.

The firefighters were unable to put out the flames and the house burned down to the ground in record time. They trudged back and forth through the ashes and poked through the rubble of the broken home. Eventually there was nothing left to do, and the responders started packing up to leave. It was Christmas morning, and everyone was anxious to leave the devastation and ruin behind and get back to their loved ones. They averted their eyes away from the withdrawn and dispirited girl and thanked God that their own families were safe.

Ecko dispassionately watched it all from the safety of the ambulance. She saw small white flakes drifting all around her, and at first, she believed them to be ashes from the fire. Her gaze fixated on one particularly large one as it fluttered down, down, down to land on her foot and melt away into nothing. A snowflake.

She shivered as she noticed that her foot was cold and bare. Only then did she realize that she had on only one fuzzy pink slipper. She looked all around her for its lost mate, but it was nowhere to be seen. She briefly thought about taking the remaining one off to match, but she didn't want that foot to get cold too, so she just left it alone. Another snowflake fell and landed on the end of her nose, and she glanced up at the sky. It's started to snow just as the sun began to peek out from behind the clouds. It was Christmas morning, and it was snowing. It looked like her wish had come true after all.

The lady from social services set her phone down on the back of the ambulance and turned away to speak to the detective. Ecko peeked down at it and saw that the time was 6:19 am. Three hours. Just three hours and sixteen minutes had passed since she woke from a dreamed nightmare and entered into a very real one. A mere one hundred and ninety-six minutes was all that it had taken for Samara to destroy everything that she loved.

The Roberts family was gone, wiped almost completely out of existence. Her family, her house, and all the memorabilia that had made up her life was nothing more than ashes in the wind now. Even the cars in the garage had been burned away, leaving nothing but their steel skeletons behind to smolder. The only things that survived the absolute destruction was Ecko herself, a photo album, a dirty, blood-soaked Sir Didymus, and miraculously, a red Christmas bauble.

The lady from social services came back and finally introduced herself as Renee Callahan. She sat down next to Ecko and explained what would have to happen next. The ambulance would take her to the hospital where she would be further examined and have her wounds treated. Renee would meet her there and at some point, a police officer would come and ask her some questions. Then they would figure out what to do with her and where she would go next.

Ecko stared at the ball in the grass and said nothing. Old Man Charlie had been watching her throughout all the chaos. It broke his old heart to see the lost look in her eyes. He stood back as the paramedics helped her to lie down and then strapped her to the gurney. She never once took her eyes off that bauble.

They wheeled her into the ambulance and started to shut the door. "Wait!" Charlie cried. He shuffled over and picked up the ornament, his sore, old body protesting every step. He carried it over to her and a single tear trickled down her face as he placed it in her hand. "I'm so sorry this happened to you, honey. So very sorry. I don't know what happens next, where you will go. I'll try to find out. If you ever need me, you find a way to get to me. I'll help you any way that I can. You find me, whatever it takes, you hear? You are good, and kind. Don't let this change you, sweet girl."

Tears poured down his face as he stepped back to let them shut the door. Ecko hugged her pitiful treasures to her chest and closed her eyes as the ambulance carried her away to a new life.

Doll Deaths ~ Samara

I wake slowly, painfully coming back to my senses. I'm standing outside, my arms wrapped around a thick post, hands bound in front of me. It's a position that I know well. Father is preparing to have me lashed. What I don't know is how I'd gotten here. My head is pounding, and there's a shrill, piercing ringing in my ears. Blood leaks from my eyes and nose.

My brow furrows as I try to think back, try to remember the events that led me to my current predicament. Ah yes, I remember now. The dolls. I had brought them to life and commanded them to kill Ecko's beloved family while I'd worked out my spell. But I don't understand what went wrong! I followed the instructions in my head precisely. I'm sure I did everything right. I've never had a plan go wrong before. When the instructions manifest in my mind, things always, *always* go according to the plan. So, what had happened this time? What caused it all to backfire?

Everything had been going great, just how I'd pictured it. I had the death dealing dolls busy making sure that Ecko stayed distracted, while I recited the spell to get the mirror to open to me. My Shadow magic flowed out to cover the surface of the mirror and I could *feel* that it was working. I was *finally* going to get through! But then my cursed sister realized what was happening and launched that doll straight at me. *That* was the precise moment the spell had misfired and gone all wrong, causing all that magic, all that power to suddenly backlash into me. And oh, how it *hurt*. I thought my head had been split open like an overripe fruit that's been dropped to the ground.

Then, the mirror really *was* open, but it wasn't my magic that had done it. I will never admit it out loud, but in that moment, I'd been scared, absolutely petrified. My sister had stood before me, with her eyes gone silver, screaming out my name. Her hair whipped all around her face and her hands were suddenly encased in a glowing blue light. The glow spread up her arms first, then flowed all around her until she was fully engulfed in the radiance of it. She looked deep into my eyes, searching for...I don't really know what she was searching for.

Then she'd lifted her hands up and blasted all that blue fire straight at me. Yeah, my father could learn a thing or two from my dear, sweet sister. I have never felt such pain in all my life. I don't even have words to describe it. I have never, ever wished for death until that very moment. I screamed and screamed and screamed, until I felt the inside of my throat tear and fill with blood. The absolute agony of it went on forever; it just wouldn't stop. It wouldn't ease up, not even a fraction. There seemed to be no end in sight, and I felt my mind beginning to crack under the strain of it. Finally, mercifully, my mind could bear it no longer and it shut itself down out of sheer self-preservation. I sank into blissful, peaceful darkness and knew no more.

Now all I can do is stand here and listen to my father rant at me, by way of his lackey's vocal cords. He may forever be trapped in his castle, cursed to never set foot outside its walls, but that has never protected me from his wrath. His Night Shades can go anywhere, just like smoke and shadows. When he sends his Night Shades to enter someone, he *sees* what they see, *hears* what they hear. He knows their thoughts and learns their every secret. He feels everything they feel and then he uses it all to his advantage as he controls them.

The unfortunate possessed ones are like inverted puppets, with their strings *inside* of them instead of on the outside of their bodies. My father is the puppet master. He gets inside and he pulls their strings from within, his hand on their very soul. They have no choice but to obey him. They go where he tells them to go, do whatever he commands them to do. They're completely at his mercy, and my father is not known for his kind, merciful ways. This time is no different.

"Why are you so disgustingly weak?" he snarls. "I cannot even begin to fathom how I begat such pathetic spawn as you. Will my disappointment in you never cease?"

I don't even turn my head in the direction of the deep, rumbling voice to see who my punisher will be this time. I don't need to. I already know which guard stands behind me. As usual, Father has sent his Night Shades into the largest, strongest body available. The more muscle they possess, the more severe the beating will be. They have the power to *really* get into the swing of things. The Drocknal that my father has chosen to inhabit this time is so huge, so threateningly massive that when it's his turn to guard me, he can only take up position outside my window. He doesn't even fit inside the house.

My ears detect the silent scream of the whip slicing through the air and my whole body tenses up in preparation. *Crack!* The very first bite of the whip cuts through my shirt and parts my skin as easily as a hot spoon dipped into Storver's lard bucket. The crop buries itself so deep that it momentarily gets stuck in my flesh, and he grunts as he mercilessly rips it free. The agony is unbearable, and it drops me to my knees.

The Drocknal/Father bends down beside me and whispers almost seductively in my ear. "Fight me." He stands and backs away, then doles out four more excruciating lashes in quick succession. The blows are delivered with so much force behind them that they threaten to break straight through my bones. The skin splits and the blood flows in rivulets down my back.

"Fight me!" he screams. "I know you have strength inside you. I've seen the things you can do. I've felt your magic." *Crack!* "Stop me!" *Crack!* Father makes the Droknal move in close behind me again, so close I can feel the heat of him. He strokes my hair in a nasty facsimile of a loving, caring father. His hand slowly trails down my back, fingers dipping into the wounds, slicking through the blood.

He bends down once more to softly, soothingly croon in my ear. "This can stop. It can all go away. *You* can make it go away." *Crack! Crack! Crack!*

"AAAARGH!" he roars as he tosses the whip away. "Why? Why are you like this? How can there be so much raw potential trapped inside such a wretchedly fragile creature such as yourself?" Father pulls his Night Shades out of the Drocknallian guard and sends them to me. They pour into my mouth and up through my nostrils, flowing through every part of me on a molecular level, in search of my every flaw.

Finding nothing that satisfies my father's suspicions, they pour back out and go to work searching the outside of my body. They spill beneath my torn and bloody clothes to slither over every inch of my body, leaving invisible trails of *ick* on my skin, like a slug leaving a slime trail behind itself. Suddenly all the Night Shades flow down my body and concentrate on my ankle, the one with the golden tattoo.

For some unfathomable reason, terror strikes my heart and I frantically begin struggling to free myself of my bonds. I don't know why. I don't even know where I'd gotten the tattoo, or what it means. All I know is that I've had it for as long as I can remember, *and it is mine*. There is nothing in this world that I can claim as my very own, nothing other than my mirror (I stole it, fair and square. Might equals Right is my motto), my name, and the tattoo of the golden chain threaded with a single blue strand that encircles my ankle.

For some reason, I don't want Father to know about it. And I certainly don't want him to study it. So, I become a wild thing, twisting and turning, jerking on the ropes that hold me in place. I care naught for the blood that spills from my wrists where the ropes cut into them. All I care about is escaping. The Night Shades rush back into the Drocknallian guard. He steps forward and bunches the back of my shirt and pants together in one fist, and with one powerful tug, he rips them from my body. I am stripped naked for all to see, and my hatred knows no bounds.

"What is this?" Father asks. He grabs my ankle and pulls it up, backwards, bringing it closer to his face so that he can inspect it. "WHAT. IS. THIS?" he roars once more. He studies it closely, turning it this way and that, uncaring of the pain that he's causing me as his grip threatens to tear my leg right off my body. "This is Laelynn's magic, Irredarrian filth! It's a protection spell."

He jerks my ankle up higher, as high as it can go, threatening to rip me in two. Then he bends down the rest of the way to sniff at it. He yanks his head back up and laughs. "Ha! Protection, with a binding spell woven into it as well. Very clever, Laelynn. Very clever indeed. Now, how to remove it without damaging the package?"

Panic fills me and makes me do something I have never done before, *swore* I would never do. I beg. I cry, and I beg, and I plead, all the while knowing that it's falling on deaf ears. Lips curled in disgust at my pathetic display, Father has the Drocknal pull the blade from the sheathe at his waist. Though I struggle and fight as hard as I can, he easily lifts my leg back into the air and slashes the blade across the tattoo.

But the knife miraculously inflicts no damage to my skin, none whatsoever. Golden light bursts out of the tattoo, and the blade suddenly flies out of his hand and impales itself deep into the Drocknallian's heart. He drops to the ground, dead as dead can be. The Night Shades instantly retreat from the lifeless body and flow into the closest available guard. Father is pissed, *beyond* pissed, but absolutely determined to remove the blight on what he considers his 'property'.

Hours later, I'm unceremoniously dumped onto my bed to recover from my ordeal. Father had tried everything he could think of to remove my mother's offensive taint from *his* heir. He'd ranted that I belonged to him, and she'd had no right to alter me in any way. (Might equals Right I wanted to tell him, but I didn't quite dare to be so defiant so soon). Eleven guards, three witches, a gnome, a FireFairy, a hobglin, and one cockatrice have (unwillingly) sacrificed their lives in my father's futile attempts at ridding me of that spelled tattoo.

Every single thing he'd tried had backfired. The magic of the spell instantly killed anyone and anything that tried to change it in any way. And try they *had*, in every way imaginable, slicing, burning, boiling, flaying, poisons, and magic. They even tried to cut my ankle off. When that hadn't worked, they tried to remove my whole leg. Everything they tried with the intent of removing, damaging, or altering it in any way was met with instant and deadly retribution.

But they found that the spell only protected the tattoo itself. Father could whip me and torture me all he wanted, just like he always has. He could hurt me in any way he chose, so long as it had nothing to do with that tattoo. He even had the tip of my pinky finger chopped off to test that theory. He set Leeches, Ribbitters, electric eels, and even one extremely deadly Slurpbat on me to see if their various specialties would inflict any damage to it. Every one of them became just one more casualty in his failed mission. Nothing had worked. None of it got Father his desired results, and eventually his rage got the better of him.

He went absolutely berserk for a while, slaughtering everyone that was unfortunate enough to fall within his sights. The bloodthirsty crowd that had gathered to watch my shame had scattered like Vika Vakooja roach-beetles before him. When finally, there was no one left to take his anger out on, Father commanded the meat suit that he was currently wearing to return me to my room and make sure that I was fed and that my wounds were tended. The guard choked and grunted as the Night Shades poured out of him and then disappeared, blending into the dark.

I'm unsure of what's to come next. Father's orders have me worried. Never has he been concerned about what happens to me after his punishments were meted out. Never has he cared if I was given food or even if I was denied it. He certainly never cared if the wounds that he'd inflicted were properly tended to. Until now. For him to suddenly show an interest in my recovery fills me with dread. What could he possibly be thinking in that diseased mind of his? What will he want of me next?

Lost and Alone

After The Bad Thing (Present day)

Journal 1

Entry # 1

I'm not sure how long I've been here. What day is it? Worse, what month is it? After having listened to the account of my entire life (starting with my father's affair and how he'd brought me home to his unsuspecting wife, to the night that I lost everything) the doctors had apparently thought it best to keep me medicated for the first several months of my confinement. *supposedly* to help me adjust to the loss of my family, my home, my life, and my freedom. I've been floundering, lost in a fog of grief and a chemically induced, altered state of awareness for what seems like years.

It's been like living at the bottom of a deep, dark lake. Sometimes I could see and hear the things going on around me, but it was all distorted and unintelligible. I could feel that my eyes were open and blinking, but I couldn't see anything. There was nothing, just a black void of *nothing!* I could hear voices but could never quite discern where they were coming from. Sensory deprivation. That was it. That's what it felt like, like I was suspended in a sensory deprivation tank. For months, years even.

But there were dream people in there with me sometimes. I remembered faces, but they all blurred together into one being, a monster creature with ever-changing features. I have memories of a woman with a soft voice washing my face with a warm, soothing cloth, of being lifted and carried, of lying on a bed and being rolled from side to side. I remember the sharp smell of too much cologne and hard fingers cruelly pinching my nipples. A brush gently combing through my hair, stinging, stabbing needle pricks, and rough invasive hands. I remember bright lights shined directly into my eyes, slaps and pinches, icy blue eyes, and cruel, heartless laughter. It was all so confusing. It was all I knew, everything that I was. I don't know what was real and what was imagined. And it's even worse now that the doctor is slowly weaning me off of the majority of the medications. I've spent the last thirty days detoxing and going through intense withdrawals. I almost wish I could go back to the sensory deprivation, because I have never felt so terrible in all my life. I would rather have my throat ripped out by Sigmund again.

My belly is constantly queasy. I sweat. I shiver and shake uncontrollably, and my heart suddenly races for no reason at all. I puke and then I sweat some more. Then there are the nightmares. I don't know if they're caused by my head finally clearing, letting me remember and allowing me to feel again, or if they're symptoms of the drug withdrawals. Perhaps it's both.

All I know is that the dreams are terrifying, unlike anything I have ever experienced before... And I know nightmares. They are no stranger to me. Those terrible dreams are part of the reason why I am now writing in this useless notebook. The doctor wants me to write all my thoughts and dreams down, then read over the notes later. To quote 'See if I can try to finally distinguish dream from reality' unquote.

She thinks that everything I've told her was just my imagination, possibly brought on by PTSD. She says that she's hoping that writing it all down will be beneficial to me, therapeutic even. She's sworn to me that the notebook will be kept private, that no one else will read the words I write in here. Not even her. But I don't believe that. *Nothing* is private in this place. They are bumptious and invasive, and I know that this is nothing more than a trick, just another tactic to try to get me to open up.

I've refused to talk to them anymore because they simply refuse to listen. They don't believe anything I say, and I'm just too tired, too *sick* to continue fighting them. So yes, just for the record.... I recognize this for the trap that it is, and I know that it's all a useless waste of time. But I just don't care anymore. If I have to keep these thoughts in my head any longer, I really *will* go as stark raving mad as they believe me to be. So, I'm just going to go along with it. After all, what have I got to lose when they do read it? It's not like they'll think I'm crazy and lock me up in a loony bin.

Entry #9

The best thing about this place, or more precisely, the ONLY good thing about this place is…there are no mirrors here. We're not allowed to have anything that we could potentially use to harm ourselves or others with. The powers that be are very strict with what items we're allowed to have. (I'm surprised that they even let me have a pen to write with.) Mirrors are glass, and glass is a very big no no around here.

I'm a teenage girl, but I function just fine without access to a mirror. No mirror means no Samara. I'm not ready to face her. As much as I want to, I just can't do it yet. I know that I'm not strong enough, and that I would lose should I go up against her. I also know that there will eventually come a day of reckoning and that I will avenge my family.

Samara is evil and she'll have to pay for her crimes. I WILL be the one to stop her and make sure she never hurts anyone else, ever again.

I now know that somehow, I have magic inside me too. I just don't know what it is or how to access it. There's so much that I have to figure out. I realize now that there's a big part of me that's missing, as if a critical piece of my puzzle got lost somewhere along the way of my life. Or a whole chapter of my life had somehow gotten erased before I had a chance to read it and learn exactly who I am meant to be and what I'm supposed to do. But... *Someone* out there knows me. Someone out there knows *something*. Maybe that David guy that my father took me to when Sigmund had tried to eat me. I just have to find that particular someone and then somehow convince them to tell me everything they know.

Entry #21

I've started dreaming of the Red Door again. In these dreams, I'm walking down a long, dimly lit, stone corridor that appears to be part of an old castle from a time gone by. Both sides of the passageway are lined with heavy wooden doors. I try to open each one as I pass by, but they're all locked, greedily withholding all of their secrets from me. They have intricate iron locks that I instinctively know will only open with skeleton keys.

Knowing that it's a useless gesture, I nevertheless pat my clothing down, hoping in vain that I'll have a ring of keys hidden within my pockets. Disappointed but not surprised, I come up empty handed. I *always* come up empty handed. I continue down the seemingly endless hall, unsuccessfully testing each door until at last, I come to a dead end. And there it is, that hateful Red Door.

Dread courses through me as I slowly, hesitantly approach. Standing all alone at the end of the corridor, it's unlike all the others that I'd passed by. Aside from the fact that it's painted rebellious, crimson red, it's also taller and not quite as wide as the others. There's no fancy craftsmanship, no ornate and elaborate lock, just a simple keyhole carved right into the wood. As much as I want to turn back, I know without a single doubt that *this* is why I'm here. I am meant to find a way past *this* particular door. The others had merely been a distraction. But try as I may, I can never, ever get through and I inevitably awaken, frustrated and full of sorrow. This night is no different. My eyes spring open and all I can do is lie there, staring up at the water-stained ceiling above my cot with tears on my cheeks and cries of desperation and despair on my lips. My mind replays the dream again and again when all I really want to do is forget it, roll over, and go back to sleep. But my mind is its own Hell and has apparently deemed me guilty and feels the need to torture me.

I close my eyes in exhausted defeat and immediately slip back into my troubled dreams, transported back to that stone corridor. This castle hallway may be a new aspect that I've never encountered before, but the Red Door, oh that Red Door is an old, life-long acquaintance.

When I was a small child, it made an appearance in nearly every single dream that I'd had. It could pop up at any time. If I dreamed that I was a tiny ant living in an ant hill with my ant family, my tunnels could at any moment suddenly become blocked by a miniature Red Door. If I dreamed that I was Alice in Wonderland, I was always a giant, and much too big to open a normal sized door, or the Red Door was huge, and I was too small. And there were *never* any magic mushrooms handy to shrink or grow me.

The Red Door could also appear in random, nonsensical places. If I was walking through a field of flowers, there it was, defying logic, without any kind of structure to hold it up. I once dreamed that I died and went to heaven, but I had to get through that infernal Red Door before I could enter. There were no pearly gates that I could see, and I had ultimately been forced to go back the other direction, to Hell, because I was unable to get through it. As a child, I had dreamed of that cursed door more than anything else.

As I got older, I saw less and less of it until one day I stopped dreaming about it altogether and completely forgot about it. But now, *now* I remember. It's been years since I've seen that terrible thing, and I wish with all of my heart that it had stayed in the past. Because now that the dream is back, the memories have resurfaced as well. I remember it all. I remember the tidal wave of emotions that washed through me every single time I saw it, desperation, fury, despair, hysteria, sorrow, longing, frustration. And pain, always so much pain.

All those feelings and so many more flooded every inch of my soul every time I'd dreamed of it. I didn't understand the dreams then and I still don't understand them today. I don't know what, or who, lies beyond it. I have never once been able to open it. No matter what I tried, it remained shut tight, forever keeping me out, or keeping someone in… and I *know* there's someone in there. I know it's a woman. I've heard her on several occasions. I've listened to the sounds of her screams, her cries, her unhinged, maniacal laughter. I've heard her whispers, her unintelligible mutterings, and her begging. I've heard the soft sounds of her footsteps shuffling past, pacing back and forth, back and forth. I have shed thousands of tears with her as I unwillingly listened to the sounds of slaps, of a whip cracking and striking flesh and her pleas for mercy. I was desperate, always so very desperate to open that door, to let her out, release her from the hell that she was trapped in.

In every single one of these dreams, I searched for a key that would unlock it. I've kicked and punched that door and I've thrown my whole body against it until I was bruised from head to toe. I've gouged deep furrows into the wood until my fingers bled from trying to claw it open as I listened to her bang upon it from the other side, begging to be let out.

I remember talking to her, trying to discover who she was, where she was, and how I could help her. Where was the key? Why was she locked inside, and who had locked her in there? Who was hurting her? Why? I never once received an answer. Not once. I finally realized that even though I could hear her loud and clear, she could not hear me in return. Just as I had never been able to get through the door, neither had my voice ever gotten past it either.

Seeing that dreadful Red Door, hearing the poor woman night after night had been traumatizing to the child I'd been. Thankfully the dreams had eventually stopped, and I'd somehow forgotten all about them. I cannot fathom *how* I could have ever forgotten something so abhorrent and yet so very familiar to me but forget them I did. And I'm *glad* that I did. I hate that door. I hate it with everything in me. But I think I understand why I've suddenly remembered and started to dream about it again.

The nightmares had stopped when I'd finally grown strong enough to *make* them stop, to block them out completely. It took me losing control over my own mind to get to a place where I could no longer block them out. The drug dependency and then the withdrawals had opened me up to all sorts of unpleasantries, and that Red Door was probably one of the worst things my mind could conjure up. Not THE worst thing, but a very close runner-up.

Entry #32

Virgil…I detest that name. I have never understood why those two syllables irritate me so intensely. I only know that it has always done so. I'd heard it for the first time when I was very young, perhaps only two or three years old. Although I can no longer remember who the name belonged to, what I do remember with perfect clarity is how it had made me feel, uncomfortable, anxious, confused. And every time I've heard it thereafter, the feelings of unpleasantness that it elicited grew stronger inside of me. I have never understood why. Until now.

Now I know that it was some sort of premonition, an internal warning for myself to beware the monster that I would one day encounter. And now I *have* met him, and he produces the same feelings in me that his name always had… a shuddering revulsion that prickles my skin into gooseflesh, an itchiness inside my brain, and a hard knot of fear twisting in my belly. He's a nurse's assistant here, and he makes my skin crawl every time he gets near me. Even before I discovered what his name was, his very presence set off warning bells inside my head, a stutter in my heart.

He has a very large nose, cold blue eyes, and that good old boy smile that screams 'Trust me. I'm here to help.' But I don't trust him. I *know* better. He's the only staff member that I studiously try to avoid. And I know that I've seen him before, I just can't remember where. I watch how everyone acts around him and I've discovered that none of the other patients like him either, especially the girls.

They're all terrified of him. They flinch and cower and try to scoot away from him any time he comes near. I don't blame them. There's a mean glint in his icy blue eyes and a cruel twist to his lips. He sneaks in sharp pinches and slaps and little jabs with his ink pens and toothpicks. He times these little tortures perfectly, when no one is near enough to see what he's doing. He watches every move I make sometimes, and I can feel his eyes lingering on parts of me that he has no business looking at. He is a nasty bully, a dangerous one. I know it, and so I avoid him at all costs, because I know that there's no one to help me here. No one will listen. No one will care. No one will even believe me if I were ever to make a complaint. I know this, and he knows it too.

Entry #38

The withdrawals are finally getting better. My body doesn't ache so badly anymore, and the fog is beginning to lift from my mind. The only problem is, now that I can feel again, I can also remember. I remember Rage.

Entry #49

Oh. My. God! I just realized that I'm 15! My birthday was March 21st; today is June 4th. I missed it! Not that it would have made any difference had I known. My doctor had me so drugged up that I hadn't even known my own name, much less what day it was. Besides, what did it really matter that I missed it? What do I have to celebrate anyway?

Spending my life alone, locked in here, year after year? Yeah, that's definitely cause for celebrating. But 15? *Really?* I just can't believe that it passed by without me even knowing.

Entry # 62

My head's clearer now. I have completely and successfully overcome the effects of the drugs. I'm 100% clean. Well, 100% except for the Zoloft to help with my anxiety from my PTSD and the Wellbutrin for the depression. Thank God, they took me off all that other stuff they'd said I needed in order to keep me from having my 'hallucinations'. Now that I'm clearheaded once more, I've learned how to compartmentalize my thoughts, my memories, and the sheer amount of overwhelming emotions that never cease to haunt me.

I've discovered that I can create mental boxes inside my head and when any unpleasantness begins to surface, I simply pack it all up and lock it away. I cram all my vexatious thoughts, offensive memories, troubled dreams, and fragile hopes up into boxes. I give them a name, label them, if you will, and then lock them all away where I don't have to deal with them.

Not very healthy, I know, but I have to make sure that Dr. Bradburn has no reason to put me back on those meds. I can't go back to that. I just can't. So, I will do what I must. On a positive note, writing in this journal actually seems to have helped me tremendously... with everything but the anger. I'm finding *that* increasingly difficult to suppress. It's like a living, breathing, and ever-growing monster inside me and I've named it Rage. It constantly threatens to consume me. I have it stuffed into a huge, purely mental box, a container much larger than all the others. It's strong and sturdy, made from solid steel and it's locked up tight, wrapped in chains and barricaded behind reinforced iron doors. And *still* it's barely able to contain the violence within its prison walls. For the moment, Rage is trapped. But it fights, always searching for a way to escape.

Rereading this entry, I'm thankful that no one else will read these words. So far, I don't think anyone has even tried. But then again, I really haven't given them the opportunity. I carry it with me at all times, so unless they literally snatch it from my hands, they won't ever get the chance.

On a side note here, now that I have started this whole compartmentalizing and locking nasty things into boxes and barricading them behind doors inside my mind, I've discovered that there's also a locked Red Door inside my head too. Of course, I haven't figured out how to get *it* open either. Has it always been here or is this new?

Entry #70

It's all my fault, that terrible thing that happened to my family, that whole inconceivable devastation. I know that now, despite what anyone says. Well, I suppose it wasn't *entirely* my fault. I wasn't the one that actually 'pulled the trigger' if you will. And I certainly never got blamed for it. But it was my doing all the same. If I hadn't done the things that I'd done, hadn't been the person I was, my family would still be here. And I wouldn't now be one of the lucky members of the prestigious Regal Falls Psychiatric Ward.

I spend all my time reflecting back on my childhood, and why not? What else am I to do? I have nothing *but* time. It's not like I'm going anywhere anyway. Might as well try to figure out where everything started to go wrong. I have replayed every single event of my life, big and small, over and over in my head. At least a thousand times. I placed my entire life on a loop, and I watch it in slow motion, examine it from every angle. Over and over and over, and still I can't isolate an exact incident that led up to me becoming a ward of this great state of Texas and a resident in Dr. Bradburn's institution for disturbed teens.

Maybe it all started going wrong on the very day that I was conceived. Or maybe it was the day that my dad brought me home, breaking my mother's heart in the process. Maybe it was all the decisions I'd made along the way. And maybe it all would have happened anyway, no matter what actions I'd chosen to take. If that's the case, then nothing I could have done differently would have changed the outcome. Perhaps it was always meant to happen the way that it did. Fated, set in stone or some such happy horse poop.

But I have no way of knowing if that's true. What I *do* know is that ultimately, I played a hand in the downfall and destruction of my family. *I* was the one that had given that *thing* that wore my face power over us. *I* was the one that made it possible for her to reach across worlds and unleash her unfathomable evil upon my loved ones. All those years of interacting with that Other girl in the mirror, I had unwittingly been helping her powers grow. I had innocently and unknowingly acquiesced to Samara's selfish demands for constant attention. I perpetually played her little games. I sought her out and spoke to her, day after day. The more notice I took, the more attention she received from me… *that* had been the very thing that she'd needed in order to strengthen herself.

The little spark of dark magic that lived inside of her had been just like a baby, an infant that needed constant care. It was a greedy thing. The incessant attention I lavished upon her was like mother's milk to that new, infantile bit of magic. Never once suspecting, or even comprehending what I was doing, I had fed it. I'd nurtured it. And like any good mother, I had encouraged it to grow. And so, it thrived under my constant, unwitting care. Samara's power had flourished and grown immensely, a dark and twisted thing. And it was *angry*.

Entry # 163

I had a visitor today! Old Man Charlie came to see me! It's Thanksgiving, and we're allowed to spend holidays with our

160

families. Since I have no family left, Dr. Bradburn made an exception for me. Because this was my first visit with anyone other than my case worker, we were isolated, and I was closely monitored. I don't care. I'm used to that now anyway. We had to stay locked in an observation room while we talked and ate our disgusting meal, turkey that was a slightly greenish color, thin, watery mashed potatoes, a pile of limp, unsalted green beans, and a dry, rock-hard roll. But there was pumpkin and pecan pie for dessert and *that* made up for it. We are very rarely allowed sweets in here. Charlie (I suppose I really should have stopped calling him Old Man Charlie before now) tells me that he had tried several times to visit me before now, but he'd been turned away every time. They'd told him that I was too unstable to see anyone from my past.

Suddenly, I feel Rage rattle the chains on his box inside my head, so I take a deep calming breath. I guess it was true though. I *did* act nuts when I first got here. It's just that I stay so angry all the time and I'd had so much trouble hiding it back then. Even the tiniest and most insignificant things filled me with fury and set me off into uncontrollable rages. I couldn't control it and I actually hurt some people.

There's a boy admitted here with schizoaffective disorder. Robert Walters. He's a very disturbed and disgusting bully and he deserved it, but I didn't mean to do it. I don't even know *how* I did it. He'd been harassing me for days. He'd started off acting charming and flirty, but he got really angry when I continued to show no interest in him. The day it happened, he'd taken a seat across from me in the cafeteria and started his usual spiel and I immediately tuned him out. I'm really good at that.

I got up to take my mostly untouched tray to the cleaning station and he came up behind me, whisper-yelling that I shouldn't be such a snooty tease. He'd grabbed my arm as he spoke, and my mind literally filled with the color red. Nothing else, no thoughts, no emotions. Just an empty crimson void. Just red, and red, and red.

The next thing I knew, I was lying on the floor with orderlies yelling and piled on top of me, holding me down and fighting to restrain me. I panicked. I don't like to be touched at the best of times and there they were, seemingly attacking me out of nowhere.

So, I fought back. Of course, I fought back. Who wouldn't? But I did not win that battle. I woke up from a drug-induced sleep with padded restraints on my wrists and ankles locking me down tight. When the sedatives had finally worn off, I found out that I'd hurt two orderlies pretty badly, before they managed to subdue me and get me back to my room. They informed me that I'd punched Robert in the chest so hard that he flew backwards and cracked his skull on the floor. They had to take him to the emergency room, where he spent the next week in intensive care, recovering from a cerebral contusion. He also had several cracked and bruised ribs on the right side of his body. When he came back, he told everyone that I had done it without even touching him, that I'd somehow done it with my *mind*. No one believed him, of course. Who's going to believe that something crazy happened to a crazy person in a crazy house?

We both got punished for the incident and had to do some time in 'observation' which is just a nicer way of saying solitary confinement. Me because I had acted out in violence and I hurt people, and him for putting his hands on me in the first place. They also wanted to monitor him because of his new 'hallucinations' and to give him time to adjust to his new (stronger) meds.

Dr. Bradburn threatened to put me back on some of my old medications too, but ultimately decided against it, thank you, sweet baby Jesus. I'm so grateful and I've resolved to keep a better hold on my emotions. It helps that Robert has left me alone since then. I think it's due more to the fact that the meds have reduced him to zombie mode than any real fear or remorse that he might feel towards me. But I'll take what I can get. I still don't know what happened, or how I hurt him. I don't remember anything.

So, yes, I was very angry and unstable for a while. I'd just lost my entire family. Who wouldn't be upset? I would have loved to see old man Charlie during that struggle. I think it would have really helped me adjust, but what do I know? I'm just a crazy person.

Seeing him today was amazing. It hurt at first and we both cried a lot. But it was *good*, like it was something that had needed to be done. I hope he comes back. I need someone to love. And I need someone to care about me, to care what happens to me. I feel so empty and alone all the time. This is not a happy place, and I honestly don't know if I will survive it. Charlie assures me that as long as I'm doing well and not 'acting out' he will be allowed to visit once a month. He promises that he'll be here. I'll try my best to fit in, do as I am told, and not draw any attention to myself. I'll convince them that I'm fine. I can do it. I've had plenty of practice already. After all, I've pretended to be just like everyone else my entire life.

Entry #174

Dr. Bradburn is a cruel and sadistic witch hiding behind a Psychology degree. I almost hope that she *does* find a way to sneak past me and read this journal. What she did was just cruel. Today, during our session she pulled a mirror out of her desk and held it up in front of my face. Just sudden-like, out of the blue and with no warning whatsoever.

I got one brief glimpse of my wide, startled eyes before fear and instinct took over. My right arm reflexively swung out to knock the mirror away. It swung out *hard* and fast and before she could stop it, the mirror crashed backwards, RIGHT INTO HER FACE. Cracked her right up under her left eye. I became aware of the fact that I was screaming, had in fact, been screaming since I'd first laid eyes on that small circle of glass. And then Dr. Bradburn was adding her own anguished howls to mine. Several orderlies burst into the room, two of which automatically tackled me to the ground and held me there.

They were hurting me! I was going to be pumped full of drugs again. I just knew it. I stopped screaming and started crying instead. Dr Bradburn surprised me by ordering them to let me up. She was holding a hand over her injured eye and tears leaked from her good one.

"Let her up," she ordered. "Let her go. This is all my fault. I am very sorry Adrina." She refuses to call me Ecko, says the name is unusual and disturbing, whatever *that's* supposed to mean. It's just a name, and I have actually always loved it.

"I'm so sorry Adrina. I shouldn't have sprung it on you like that. I should have given you some warning. I considered telling you at our session last week but decided against it because I didn't want you to have time to stress over it. I wanted to see what your reaction would be. Now, I know. But you do know that you'll have to get over this, right? Your fear of mirrors and of your reflection is a large part of your illness, and the only way to recover is to face those fears head on."

All I could do was take deep, shuddering breaths, in and out, in and out, until I was somewhat calmer, and my heart was no longer trying to beat its way out of my chest. "We will try this again, but we'll take it nice and slow next time. I won't spring it on you like I did today. You have my word. Now, are you okay? Are you calm or do you think you may need a mild sedative? I'm trusting you to let me know how you feel right now."

I quickly shook my head. Definitely not. I hate the drugs. I hate the helplessness that I feel when I'm that out of it. I will *never* willingly choose to take them. "I'm fine. I'm just sorry I hurt you. I didn't mean to do it," I muttered.

Dr. Bradburn turned her attention to the orderlies standing right up on me, just waiting for me to freak out again. "It's time for her to go to lunch. I think she'll be fine but keep a close watch on her to ensure that she really is okay. If there's any trouble at all, escort her to her room and give her an injection of Diazepam, .5 mg" she told them. Then she turned back to me and added, "It's okay. I know that you didn't mean to. I'll be just fine." She smiled reassuringly and lowered her hand, wiping the tears off her face. Her eye was already turning purple and was swelling shut. Her nasty little surprise for me had turned out to be a nasty surprise for her too. Bet she won't try that again.

Entry # 181

Our next session didn't go well either. I was in full panic mode before I ever even sat down in Dr. Bradburn's office. I was transfixed, my entire being focused on the mirror lying face down on her desk and suddenly I couldn't breathe. I began to hyperventilate, and she had to give me the dreaded sedative. I didn't really mind this time though. If she keeps the dose low enough, it's actually quite pleasant. I don't worry so much, and I can still function, which I guess is the whole point.

Dr. Bradburn told me to just relax. She said I won't have to look at the mirror yet, and that we can take it slow, one step at a time. She assured me that she'll leave the mirror lying face down on her desk for now. We'll build up to it. I did relax a bit after she told me that. I had no choice *but* to relax. The drugs made sure of it. But I still don't trust her. She has proven to be duplicitous and untrustworthy. I don't think she's above sneak attacking me again. She'll just be more careful next time. Also, her plan for me to 'begin my recovery' is stupid. Who cares if I don't like mirrors? Do I really need to be able to see myself in order to live a normal life? I don't think so. I really don't. I am more than willing to live out the rest of my life without ever looking into another mirror again. Happily. Is that odd?

165

Entry # 189

Today's session was better. Surprisingly, Dr. Bradburn was true to her word. She never once moved the mirror from her desk. I couldn't take my eyes off of it, though. I watched that thing like it was a snake that would strike the moment that I turned my attention away from it. But I got through it and that's what's important. I didn't panic and I hadn't needed a sedative. That's always a plus. Gold star for me. Dr. Bradburn has decided to put the mirror away for our next two sessions, because of the timing. She says that my first Christmas since The Bad Thing will be hard enough on me and she doesn't want to add any more stress. This is a welcome reprieve. I'll take what I can get.

Entry # 193

Christmas Day. Everyone's been so excited. They've gone on and on about it since Thanksgiving. I just can't figure out *why* they're so excited. This is going to be just another day in prison, but I guess they think that adding bread pudding to our lunch and dinner menu is cause for a celebration. It is *not*.

I'm in the sitting room waiting anxiously for Charlie to arrive. He said he would be here. He promised. I'm getting a nervous, restless feeling in the pit of my stomach and my heart keeps fluttering like the wings of a hummingbird. I get up and pace, then sit back down and write. I do *not* think about past Christmases. I especially don't think about *last* Christmas. I have those memories neatly packed away in their very own box. It's labeled The Bad Thing: Do Not Open. EVER. I avoid it like it's a Pandora's box, full of nightmares and dipped in the bubonic plague. Nope, not going there. Come on, Charlie. I need you. Please hurry.

It's December 28th and Christmas had been just as dreadful as I'd expected it would be. Charlie had finally arrived, and we sat and talked for a while. He could tell I was having a hard time keeping it together, but he never said a word about it. He just silently took my hand and patted it every once in a while. Good old Charlie. He never pries. Eventually, an orderly came to inform us that it was time for lunch and told us to calmly proceed to the cafeteria. "They always say that. Calmly proceed to the cafeteria... like we're gonna cause a stampede in our hurry to go in there and eat the world's worst meatloaf", I whispered to Charlie.

He had started to laugh, but quickly turned it into a cough when the orderly glared at him. As we walked into the cafeteria, he glanced down at me and bumped my shoulder with his elbow. We both started giggling and everyone turned to see why. I totally understood why they looked. There's not much laughter around this place and we're all drawn to any bit of happiness that we can find. Even if it belongs to someone else, we all want to be near the source of it.

I glanced around the lunchroom and suddenly my feet were rooted in place, right there in the doorway. I was holding up the line and the people behind me started grumbling. My smile disappeared in a heartbeat. Someone had thought that it would be a good gesture to put up a Christmas tree in the corner of the room. I'm sure that they were trying to boost morale and bring a bit of cheer to the patients, and it probably achieved just that for everyone but me.

The Bad Thing box had begun a steady thumping inside my head. *Whomp! Whomp! Whomp!* Rage was suddenly awake too, banging on the walls of his prison to be let out. I backed up until I bumped into the person behind me. My lungs were stuck, I couldn't breathe. I felt a scream beginning to form in my mind; it was right there on the tip of my tongue.

Then all I could see was Charlie's face. He had somehow figured out that I was going into freak out mode at the sight of the decorated tree, and he stepped in to block my view of it. He didn't touch me, and I am extremely grateful for it. Most people's first instinct is to reach out for someone in distress. It would have been all over if someone had touched me right then. But good old Charlie just looked into my eyes and talked me down with his soft, soothing voice. I don't even know what he said. All I know was that he had me focus on his eyes and the sound of his voice, and suddenly I could breathe again.

There were three orderlies crowding around us in case I got out of control. Charlie had his hands held up at them, warning them back. All the while he kept his eyes locked on mine. He motioned for the patients and their families in line behind us to carefully step around us and continue on their way until I got everything locked back up and under control again. Rage grudgingly went back to sleep, and The Bad Thing settled down to just a few sporadic bumps. My heart was still speeding out of control, but it seemed like the crisis had been averted. For the moment anyway. I just had to ignore the festively decorated monster in the corner of the room.

Charlie requested and got permission for us to eat in another room to make things easier on me. An orderly walked me back to the sitting room and hovered over me while Charlie got our food. I'm so thankful for him.

He is the only bright spot in my world, and I told him so as soon as he got back and set my tray in front of me. "I feel so ashamed," I whispered. "I'm so sorry I almost lost it back there. Are you going to stop coming to see me now? Please don't leave me. I need you. You're the only person in the whole world that cares about me. *Please!* I can't lose you too!"

I know that I'm pathetic, but I just can't help it. I could feel the panic returning and my voice steadily grew louder with each word until I was practically yelling, my chest heaving with the onslaught of my fear. Charlie's eyes filled with tears as he slowly reached across the table for my hand. He didn't take it though, he stopped and waited for me to take *his* hand. "Don't you know? I love you girlie. I love you like I would have loved my own child, if my Gretchen and I had been able to have kids. Nothing will keep me from coming to see you every chance I get. And don't be sorry. Don't you *ever* be sorry. None of this is your fault. Now, let's eat before this lovely meal gets cold and makes it even harder to choke down."

He grinned and wiped his eyes with his handkerchief, and I couldn't help but smile through my tears back at him. We ate our meal (as much of it as we could stand) and Charlie took our trays back to the cafeteria. Lunch hour ended and then it was time for our 'Christmas party.' An orderly acted as a photographer, and we were given the opportunity to take a photo with our families…if they were willing to pay the fee for one. Charlie insisted that we get in the waiting line.

"A photo will help both of us, Ecko my girl. I can take it out and look at it whenever I get impatient for visiting day to get here and you'll have a physical reminder that I love you and that I'm here for you." I couldn't argue with that, so I stepped into the line and looked away, so he wouldn't see how much his words had touched me. Charlie paid for two copies and then we posed with our arms around one another. It was a beautiful photo, even with the ugly, olive-green wall behind us.

"I love it, Charlie. Thank you." I whispered. Charlie wiped at his eyes again and said, "I wish my Gretchen was here for this. She would have loved you so much, honey."

The patients are allowed to receive two presents each. No more, but most of us are tremendously grateful for them. Our families had been allowed to bring us one, pre-approved gift and the hospital put together the other one. The families gave out their gifts first. Charlie handed me a box wrapped in paper that said Happy Birthday! on it. I smiled, because I immediately understood that he'd wrapped it in birthday paper because he doesn't want to throw Christmas in my face.

Blinking back my tears, I handed him the envelope with the poem that I had written for him and told him that I didn't want him to open it here. I wanted him to take it home and read it. I apologized that it wasn't much, but I had nothing else to give. Charlie agreed to wait and set it aside with his photo. He squirmed in his chair as he waited for me to open mine. His eyes were lit up with excitement like a small child's as he watched me slowly open my gift. I was careful not to tear the paper, it was just as precious to me as the gift was.

I opened the box and pulled back the tissue paper and Charlie could contain his elation no longer. "It's cashmere and it's the softest sweater I could find. My Gretchen used to just love cashmere, said there was nothing quite as lovely as the feel of it on her skin. I know that you're always cold in here. I see you shiver and rub your arms for warmth all the time. And I just *know* that the color is going to bring out the green of your eyes! You're going to look so beautiful in it. Don't you like it?"

I sat there staring down at it so long that I think he was beginning to get worried that I didn't like it. It was just the opposite, I loved it. It was beautiful and thoughtful too. I ran my hands over it in wonder, before I lifted it out. It was the softest thing I had ever felt in my whole life. I couldn't help but rub it onto my face. "It's beautiful. I know how expensive cashmere is and I want to say that you shouldn't have spent so much money on me. But I just can't make myself say it. This is amazing!"

I watched as Charlie's face lit back up in sheer pleasure. I realized in that moment exactly how much this man meant to me. I pulled the sweater on over my ugly pajama-like outfit. It was too large for me and swallowed me up, but I know that he did that on purpose too. He'd figured out that being swaddled is a comfort to me.

"I was right! You look more beautiful than ever. And it *does* emphasize the green of your eyes. I just knew it would!" Charlie exclaimed triumphantly. I wrapped my arms around myself and went on and on about his gift and his thoughtfulness. I was so tickled at the pride in his eyes. I hugged him and ran my sleeves over his old, wrinkled cheeks so that he could enjoy the soft too. He beamed down at me in pleasure, and I basked in the love I saw shining in his watery old eyes.

The orderlies interrupted our revelry then by passing out cookies. That was an unexpected treat. We ate our treats as they passed out their gifts for us. Everyone got pretty much the same thing, so there would be no feelings of unfairness and no fighting. It was a box of practical things like socks, deodorant, combs or brushes, toothpaste and toothbrushes. Things like that. I was grateful to be getting anything at all.

Everything would have been fine if they had just been a little more careful with the way things had been done. If more thought had gone into each individual patient and their personal cases. I mean, they *do* invade every aspect of our lives and have extensive files with every bit of information that pertains to us. They *know* that little things that would never bother other people could potentially set us off and cause us to break down into an emotional mess that could be dangerous. I understand that there are a lot of us in here and it's hard to keep track of all of our problem areas, our triggers. I know it was just an oversight on their part. But… Yeah, there is *always* a but.

This is a hospital for mentally troubled teens. More care should be taken with each patient's needs. I don't think they ever took into consideration my weird Christmas-themed phobias. I never got the chance to open my gift. An orderly stopped in front of me, and I looked up to see that it was Virgil. He towered over me, staring down at my chest as he tried to hand me the gift. It was wrapped in silver paper that was covered with *RED. CHRISTMAS. ORNAMENTS.*

My mind snapped like a dry twig, and I screamed and recoiled back so hard that my metal, folding chair overturned, spilling me backwards onto the floor. Virgil was shocked for a moment, but then he started laughing! He saw the panic on my face and his eyes lit up with excitement, just like a dog that senses fear. He stepped towards me, and I frantically scuttled backwards, trying to keep distance between me and the image of those red baubles. He noticed what my frightened eyes were focused on and realized that for whatever reason, I was terrified out of my mind by the gift he was holding.

He cruelly pushed it towards me, jabbing it at my face while all I could do was scream and cower. Suddenly, Charlie was standing between me and my tormentor. Then my seventy-eight-year-old hero balled up his fist, pulled back his arm and let it fly! There was a loud cracking sound as his knuckles met Virgil's overly large nose. Cartilage crunched, blood spurted like a geyser, and then there was a loud thud as his body hit the floor.

I felt a sudden sting in my arm. I had just been doped up. I could hear Charlie shouting my name as my eyelids got heavy and my head started to float. I couldn't find the strength to answer him. But I smiled as I listened to the sound of his voice, cursing and yelling as I was being lifted and carried away. "Merry Christmas, Charlie. I'm sorry. Love you," I managed to mumble just before my eyes rolled back and darkness claimed me.

Entry #199

Why am I still here? I don't have anything to live for anymore. I wish I could just die. Just go lie down and take a nap and never wake back up. Sounds like Heaven.

Entry # 200

Major setback. Why should I even try? Why do I even care? I hate everything. I hate this place. I hate Dr. Bradburn and all the orderlies. I hate the disgusting food I'm forced to eat. I hate Christmas. I hate perverted men that take advantage of their power over young, helpless girls. I hate olive green walls and old, yellowed linoleum floors. I hate all those people out there in the world taking their freedoms and their daily comforts for granted. I hate myself. And I hate my family for leaving me all alone. I hate my dad most of all. I loved him beyond reason; he was my hero. Well, here's a news flash.... HEROES DON'T DIE! I should just make a list of things that I *don't* hate. It would be a lot shorter. Empty page? Done. There's my list of things that I don't hate. Rage is angrier than ever, violent almost, and closer to escaping than ever before. It grows stronger every day.

And to top it all off, Dr Bradburn failed the test. I will never trust her again. Also, the mirror will remain face down on the desk during my sessions for a while. I am too 'out of control'. Yippee for me.

Entry # 213

Dr Bradburn had to change my meds and raise the doses. She said that my anger was getting out of control. I feel more like myself now, but all that really got accomplished was that the new meds had put Rage back to sleep. It's not gone. No. Never gone, as the good doctor believes. It's most definitely still there. Sometimes I can feel it stirring, fighting the effects of the drugs. One day it's going to wake back up, and when it does, oh man is it going to be pissed. I do *not* want to know what happens when you piss off a monster named Rage. I really don't. But I know that it's coming.

Entry # 215

Positive thought for the day: there's been an investigation on Virgil, the big nosed creep. Charlie raised all kinds of hell until they'd decided they had better look into things. Plus, Virgil's own actions on Christmas had brought some negative attention to himself, and now it's all being dragged out into the light. None of the patients would say anything against him though and I can't blame them for it. Because, what if they *did* tell and he still wasn't fired? Things would be even worse for them then.

But apparently one of the janitors came forward and testified that he had witnessed an 'unpleasant incident.' He told the committee, "I had just got done mopping up an accident and was wheeling my mop bucket back to the janitor's closet. I come around the corner and he had a girl pinned up against the wall and she was crying. She was scared and she was crying, and her eyes were begging me for help.

When he realized I was there, he got mad. I mean UGLY mad. That man has a nasty temper, let me tell you. Yes siree. His face turned bright red, and it looked like the hell fires were burning in his eyes. Spittle flew from his lips when he snarled out, "What are you looking at? Keep moving, idiot."

I just stood there. I was scared, 'prolly just as scared as that poor little girl. I'm old. What could I do? I knew I couldn't fight him off if he came at me. But her eyes were begging me, see? I couldn't leave her, I just couldn't. So, I stood there and just looked at him, waiting. Hoping and praying for him to give up and leave and not come after me instead.

He finally turned back to the girl and screamed, "GET BACK TO YOUR ROOM" right in her face. Poor girl 'bout jumped outta her skin, before she ran like a scared little rabbit, wiping the spit off her face as she passed by me. HE just pointed at me and grinned before he turned and left. He actually *whistled* as he walked away! Scared me half to death. This all happened 'bout two weeks ago and I've been watching my back ever since. If he don't get let go, I'm turning in my resignation right here and right now. Because if he *is* allowed to stay, he'll eventually get his revenge on me. Guys like him always do." I guess that was enough to convince the powers that be to get rid of him because he no longer works here.

Finally, something good has happened in this horrid place. Everyone sing it with me now. Ding dong, Virgil the huge honker man is gone.

Entry # 233

February 28

I did it. I reached over and picked up the mirror today. I didn't think about it, I just *did* it. I picked it up and turned it over and looked at myself for the first time in more than a year. My reflection stared back at me, exactly like it was supposed to. Thankfully, it was just me. No Samara. I looked different. Older. Sorrowful and hopeless. Lost. Dr. Bradburn was very pleased and went on and on about my 'progress'. I didn't tell her that it wasn't progress. It was just me not caring about what happens anymore.

Entry # 247

March 21, 2011

Another birthday has come and gone in this place. I'm 16 years old and still stuck in a mental ward. I do not belong here. I know the difference between dreams and reality. I'm not crazy. I know I'm not. I know that the things I've seen have *all* been real, just as real as I am. The only problem is, no one else knows it.

Except for Charlie. He believes me. He saw parts of The Bad Thing that happened to my family. But we can't talk about it. Not here. It would just make things worse for me. I keep it all bottled up inside of me. I can't tell my story. I can't speak truthfully without Dr. Bradburn wanting to change my meds or up the doses, and then deliver the whole 'your mind is protecting you' spiel.

"Now Adrina, we've discussed this," she always says. "You know that someone broke into your house on Christmas Eve and murdered your family. You know that they tried to hurt you too. The mind is an extremely complex thing, and it will try to shield us from events that we find frightening or abhorrent. Your mind created a scene that makes the trauma that you faced easier for you to deal with. It's blocked the memory of the killer from you and replaced it with one of your biggest fears... Porcelain dolls. It's merely a defense mechanism. That's all."

Bah. I don't know how she could even think that my mind would accept killer dolls easier than a real human killer anyway. What I think is that she needs some of those meds that she keeps pushing off on me.

Hopes and Dreams, Plans and Schemes

Time crawls by, the minutes passing slowly, torturously creeping into hours. Weeks flow seamlessly into months and still I'm here, forced to live in this hell. I've lost her, Father's precious Ecko. In the time since the doll war, as I like to think of it, I've searched thousands, *hundreds of thousands* of mirrors on her world. But there are just too many to check. How can one world have so very many when the world I live in has only the one that I'd stolen for myself all those years ago? Father doesn't care. He will keep me locked in this room filled with one torture after another until I find her. How could I have been so stupid? Why don't I ever think things through? I never once considered that my spell would backfire and my sister would be lost to me, never once thought of the resulting punishments that Father would visit upon me should I ever lose track of her.

I've been thinking on something else though. My tattoo. I fear that I have become almost as obsessed with it as Father has. He still hasn't made any headway at having it removed, and although I suffer his constant displeasure, there's no denying the joy that I feel at each one of his failures. I don't even care how bad it hurts. He's running out of ideas, finally. Then I wonder... Father has had no success at removing it by force, but has he ever entertained the possibility of it being removed *willingly*. What if *I* were the one to try to remove it? Surely it wouldn't kill *me*, I'm the one it was made to protect. If I can remove it myself, I would no longer have my mother's protection... not that it's done me much good anyway. My life thus far has been full of unpleasantries, bloody wounds and scars.

But what is the binding spell for? What exactly does it bind? Maybe, just maybe, my wonderful, loving mother had my magic bound and restricted to limit me... to *flaw* me. I'm thinking that's exactly what she did. What other reason is there to add a binding to a protection spell? Is this the reason that my spell failed me during the doll war? Is this why I can't escape my Father? Had I purposefully been kept weak and pathetic, my magic stunted and confined? Could this be the answer to all my problems?

The thought of it fills me with rage, but at the same time, a stubborn determination too. The idea that I have needlessly been held back for so long by a woman who had abandoned me to this fate makes up my mind for me. I *will* try to remove the tattoo. I'll attempt to cut my mother's so- called 'protection' from my skin. But I'm scared. I don't want to die. So far, I have just been existing, surviving. I haven't even begun to live yet.

But this is a chance that I have to take. It may just be the key to freeing myself of my father's dominance, his eternal abuses... and *that*'s what decides it for me. I just have to wait for the right time. They watch me so closely now. But I'll be patient and bide my time until the perfect moment arises. If I'm right, it will all be worth it. Besides, I really have nothing more to lose, but oh, so much to gain.

My eyes are stubbornly drawn to the window again. I have more and more trouble looking in the mirror for my sister, because I spend so much time looking out there for Krispin. I thought I saw him there once, staring in at me. I can't be sure because it was really just a glimpse of a movement that shouldn't have been there. But it *could* have been him, and that gives me hope. If he's watching me, I know that he'll help me escape when the time finally comes. But what if it wasn't him and he's forgotten all about me? What if he's found someone new? The thought fills me with such intense rage that I almost foil my whole escape plan by being dumb and careless and trying to fight my way out of here. I calm myself with thoughts of what I'll do to Krispin when I finally get free if he has dared to stray. Oh, how the blood will flow....

Fake It 'till You Make It

Notebook #2

April 3, 2011

I knew that eventually they'd snoop and read my journal. Nothing is private here. That's what the 'test' was for, the test that they failed when they had me drugged after my 'Christmas incident.' I keep the corners of certain pages folded in. I know exactly which ones are folded and *how* they're folded. It's my journal, after all. Three of those folds had been straightened out. It's not a mistake either. I am very meticulous about my little snoop traps, and I check to ensure that they're just right every day. Paranoid much? Absolutely. But at least I'm in the right place for it, am I right? And can it *really* be considered paranoia if it actually comes true? They read my journal the very first chance they got. Dr. Bradburn had given me her word that they wouldn't do that. I knew that she was a liar, I just knew it. So, now I'll be keeping two notebooks. One for my eyes only and a phony one that I WANT them to read. I've been here a long time now and I have found the perfect place to hide the real one. They won't find it. From here on out, Dr. Bradburn will only know what I want her to know. I tried to do things her way. Not my fault she failed the test and proved that she's not to be trusted.

April 4

It happened. It took five weeks, but it happened just like I knew it eventually would. Today during my session, I was staring into the mirror pretending to look at myself, but I was secretly watching the Otherlands instead. I've missed them more than I realized. I was watching two of the strangest little creatures I had ever seen, and that's really saying something because I have seen some crazy stuff. They looked for all the world like tiny people. Well, mostly. Their bodies looked completely human, just miniature sized. Maybe a foot tall, but no more.

It was a male and a female, and they were clearly a couple. The only way I could tell them apart was that he was bigger, broader, and his bare chest and legs were muscled and hairy...obviously male. The female was smaller and wore no shirt, her tiny breasts swinging free as she moved. They both wore skirts made out of leaves, and their legs and feet were bare. But their heads…those were definitely not humanoid. They were just skulls, bird skulls with long bony beaks and holes for their nostrils and their eyes. There was a tiny glowing light set deep inside each of their empty eye sockets, yellow for his and red for hers. They weren't blind. It was obvious that they could see one another and the world around them, so I assume those lights were their optical systems.

I was so entranced with those two bird-people walking hand in hand down a dirt path that I almost missed it. I just barely caught the movement out of the corner of my eye. A movement from my reflection that I, myself did not make. My eyes automatically followed the motion and there she was, smiling that nasty, smug smile of hers. Samara. Her voice whispered through my mind. "There you are. I've found you at last. Father will be *so* pleased." I calmly placed the mirror back on the desk and kept my mouth shut. I didn't say a single word about it to Dr. Bradburn. If the good doctor noticed my trembling hands, well, she kept her mouth shut too.

April 13

Renee, my caseworker came today. She's required to come check on me once every month. She tries not to show it but she hates it here, hates having to come to this depressing place. Same, lady. Same. This time she didn't act so nervous and repulsed by the everyday unpleasantries that we're forced to live with in here. She actually had a smile on her face as she sat across from me at the table for two that I spend most of my time sitting at. It's situated beside a small window, and I like to look out over the grounds and to the busy street beyond.

"I have some good news for you today," Renee cheerfully announced. I was immediately suspicious, and my body automatically tensed up. "There's a very good chance that you'll one day be released from this place." I sat quietly waiting for her to continue, as a small seed of hope started to sprout in my heart. "This is a hospital strictly for teenagers. They don't treat adults here. When a patient becomes an adult, they get reevaluated and sent somewhere else. The ones that need further care and treatment go to other facilities that work with adults. But" she pauses here to smile at me again and I feel that sprout growing bigger, preparing to bloom. She continued, her eyes sparkling with excitement. "The patients that have been successfully rehabilitated and get a clean bill of health, well, they get to go home! Isn't that wonderful news?"

And there it was. Just like that, my little sprout died and shriveled up. A single tear rolled down my cheek before I turned my face away to continue my silent vigil of the world beyond the window. "What's wrong, Ecko? I just told you that you could be released, that you could go home when…oh. Oh, I see. I'm so sorry sweetie. I didn't mean to be insensitive." Yeah, it took her a minute, but she'd finally caught up. Renee had just realized that my family was gone, and my house had burned down. I *have* no home and there was nowhere for me to go. I wouldn't be able to support myself out there on my own. I wouldn't know how to. Renee's eyes got a little teary, but she quickly blinked them back.

"I guess no one's told you this yet, but all of your family's assets will belong to you when you turn 18. Do you know what that means? It means that everything your parents owned, everything that they had invested in will be yours. Their will stated that you and your sister split the estate equally, but since Karen has passed away along with them, it all goes to you. Your father was smart and extremely frugal with his money and investments. He bought huge amounts of stock, invested in real estate and property. Did you even know that he owned land all across the United States? Lots of it. His assets are all just sitting there, gaining interest until you, as his sole beneficiary, comes of age to claim it."

I'd been staring out the window, but I was listening to everything she had to say. I turned to look at her as she rushed on. "Your parents had over 10 million dollars in their savings accounts, 5 million in their checking account. Over 25 million dollars in stocks and properties. You and Karen both have savings accounts with 5 million dollars in them. All of it goes to you, when you turn 18." Renee reached across the table to take my hand. I was too shocked to pull away.

"Do you understand what I'm saying? You'll be able to go anywhere, do anything you want to do. You'll be able to get as far from this place as you want to. Your parents loved you and they provided you with a great future. They made sure that you'd be taken care of, even if they couldn't be here. All you have to do is get out of here first." By that point I was bawling, crying like I haven't let myself cry the entire time I've been here. I missed my dad. I missed my mom. I even missed my mean sister. I laid my head down on the table and cried and cried for what seemed like hours.

I was vaguely aware of people talking, hushed voices murmuring around me. I heard Dr. Bradburn say, "No, this is good. She needs to cry. She needs to feel. She's held everything in for so long. She needs to let this all out. This is a positive step forward. Let her cry," she repeated as she walked away.

I eventually got control of myself, and Renee passed me a handful of tissues so that I could dry my face. I sat up straight, squared my shoulders and asked, "What do I need to do to get out of here?" Renee smiled at the determination on my face.

"First, you need to get into a school program. Finishing high school and getting your diploma will be a big step towards normalcy. That's where we'll start. I'll be back in a week or so and we can go over everything that you'll need to do. But the main thing is, you're going to have to pass all your medical and psych evaluations. You have to prove that you are mentally capable of living on your own. Now, I don't know what really happened to you and your family. I've heard your statement and I've also heard Dr. Bradburn's assessment. I am in no way judging you. I can't even imagine going through anything like what you have had to endure.

But I am telling you right now, getting out of here is going to be *hard*. You have a lot of work ahead of you." Renee leaned in close to me and whispered urgently in my ear, "As long as you stick by your original statement, you will *never* get released with a clean bill of health. You won't pass the evaluations. You didn't hear this from me...but you need to do anything and everything in your power to convince them that you now realize that it was all in your mind, and that you are getting better. *Make* them believe it. Lie if you must. You are very smart. Figure out what it's going to take and then go for it. Do you understand what I am telling you? *Fake it until you make it.* Then you go and take it! Take back control of your life! Get out of this hellhole, move on, and don't you ever look back."

Then she nonchalantly sat back and continued in her normal voice, "Think about everything I've told you and when I return, we'll go over what you will need to accomplish between now and your 18th birthday. You have two years and I think that will be plenty of time to prepare, to get you back into shape. We're going to work hard on getting you healthy." Two years. Now that I know there's a chance that I'll be getting out of here, two years seems like a lifetime away. Now that I know it's possible, I *will* 'get better.' I will one day walk away from this place a free woman and I will never look back. Bet.

May 23

I've been given daily access to a huge, ancient computer to do my schoolwork on each day. I nicknamed her Big Bertha. She's old and cranky and frustratingly slow, but I guess she gets the job done. I can even send (monitored) emails, if I had someone to send them to, that is. I'm going to teach Charlie about computers and try to talk him into getting one for himself. That way we can talk every day and not just once a month on visitation day.

June 1

Today is my first day 'back to school' with my online high school program. I took the placement exams and found out that I wouldn't have to make up the 10th grade, the year I missed. I'm advanced enough to skip it altogether. I've been placed straight into the 11th grade. I'm also now enrolled in four basic, beginner's college courses that I can take along with my regular classes. It seems like a lot to take on all at once, but it's a work-at-your-own-pace program. Plus, I have nothing but time. I can handle it. Having something besides my anger to focus upon will be a good thing.

June 11

Everything's going smoothly. I have found that my schoolwork is still relatively easy for me and I'm breezing right through it. Even the college courses haven't been a challenge, yet. Getting back into school, having a positive end game to work towards has made all the difference. I don't feel like a complete loser and failure anymore. I'm actually excelling at this. I never would have thought that I'd enjoy school this much. I'd hated it before. Part of it was that I just didn't fit in at public school. Everyone had always treated me like a freak. Another part is that I was always so very bored. Learning has always come easily to me. So easy that I get bored if I have to go over and over the same material. This program is really working for me though. It lets me learn at my own pace and then move on as soon as I'm ready. I can't believe I'm saying this, but I do believe that school is going to make this place bearable.

August 22

I am no longer on the 'high risk' watch! They have moved me from the Sub-Acute level to the 'assisted' Board and Care level. Basically, what that means is that I have gone from having my every move monitored and examined while living in a locked, padded cell to a more casual observation, group therapy, and a slightly larger room that I can lock from the inside if I want. Of course, the powers that be have the master keys and can get in any time they choose, but it's still nice to have that tiny bit of (illusive) control. And the best news of all…I get a day-pass Every. Single. Month!!! I get to leave the grounds for eight whole hours, once every month, as long as I have a responsible adult to 'look after me.' All these privileges can and will be revoked if I don't strictly follow all the rules, or if Dr. Bradburn thinks that I'm showing signs of stress or relapse. Not gonna happen. I am going to follow every single instruction to the T.

September 3

Renee has helped me get access to my bank accounts. I've actually been allowed to buy a few things, with Dr. Bradburn's approval of each purchase, of course. I bought two iPads, one for myself and one for Charlie. I'd already set up an email account for him and taught him how to use it, but he didn't have a computer at home. Now, we will always be able to contact one another. I'm very restricted on access to it, though. I only get to use it for schoolwork and to email Charlie. No social media whatsoever, no YouTube, no movies, no online shopping, and it has to stay in the computer room at all times. But I have access to it as long as the computer room is open, which is usually Monday to Friday, from 9:00 a.m. to 5:00 p.m. There's a log in/out sheet that the orderly in charge makes me sign any time I use it. Being so restricted is sometimes annoying, but I'm also very, very grateful.

The only other thing that I asked permission to buy is a globe for my room. Now that I have some real hope of getting out of here, I've found that I still want to travel. I used to dream of traveling all over, exploring everything that this world has to offer. There are so many wonders out there. I do *not* want to be trapped inside the same walls my whole life, even more so now that I've been trapped in this hospital for so long.

I used to have a globe, back before the Bad Thing, and every time I'd found a new place that I wanted to see, I would mark the spot with a thumbtack. Dr. Bradburn did not approve my request to purchase the globe. She said that the metal parts on it could potentially be used as a weapon. But she suggested that I buy a world map instead and tape it to my wall. I can't have any tacks. I am not allowed to have sharp, stabby things. I use little gold star stickers instead. I want to see everything! My map is already covered with glittering, golden stars. Looking at it gives me hope, and I am that much more determined to get 'well' and get out of here. I *will* see the world. One day soon.

September 18th

Oh my Gosh! I am so excited! *Finally!* The day that I get to escape this place for eight whole, magically wonderful hours. Charlie's here, signing me out *right now*, and I am just so excited that I can't stand still. It's the same for Charlie. He's bouncing around, trying to hurry through the checkout process, and we're both grinning and laughing like idiots. Time to go! I'll check back in later, after our adventure!

Today has been the BEST DAY EVER! Charlie and I exited the hospital with our arms wrapped around one another. He even opened the passenger door on his car and bowed for me like I was some kind of princess. It sent us both into another fit of laughter. We had already discussed what we wanted to do, how we would be spending this first day of freedom. Charlie headed straight to his favorite little cafe. I used my debit card for the very first time and I bought one of every single thing on that breakfast menu. We each took a bite of everything, more from the dishes that were too tempting to stop at just one taste. Charlie brought a camera with him, and he snapped photos of us both chowing down and enjoying every single bite.

I have been desperate for some real food, for *enough* food. The hospital provides us the bare minimum on our dietary needs. But even more than good food, I wanted coffee. I miss coffee so much. We're not allowed to have sugar or caffeine, no stimulants that may make us nervous or excitable. I drank a large cappuccino with our meal and ordered another one to go, for later. We eventually got done stuffing ourselves and I carefully packed up the leftovers.

On the drive to the cafe, I'd noticed a young, homeless woman standing on the corner of the busy street, begging for food. My heart hurt for her, and for the two small children sitting at her feet watching the cars go by with their hungry, bleak eyes. We delivered the boxes of food, and I pressed the money that I'd pulled from an atm into the sobbing young woman's hands. Since losing my family, I have felt the relentless, unforgiving bite of hunger. I wouldn't wish it on anyone, especially not innocent children.

Then we were off to our next destination! We'd decided to go to the Houston butterfly exhibit. I've been there a few times before and loved it, but Charlie's never been. He had suggested going to the zoo, but I begged him to take me anywhere but there. I hate it. Always have. It makes me cry to see the animals trapped and miserable. It would be even worse now that I know exactly how they feel. So, we went to the butterfly exhibit instead and Charlie enjoyed it just as much as I did.

Strangely, the butterflies seemed drawn to me. They followed me everywhere and landed on me whenever I stood still. Charlie and I both took loads of pictures, and we looked through them as we walked back to the car. My favorite one is of him with a huge black and blue swallowtail perched on the tip of his nose. He'd been trying to focus on it and his eyes were crossed. He looked so funny, and we both laughed uproariously at that one.

We only had two hours left by the time we made it out of the exhibit, so we decided to go pick up a pizza for dinner and eat it in a nearby park. After we ate all that we could stomach, we sat quietly swinging until it was time to go back. We were both fighting the sorrow descending over us as the day came to an end.

A car pulled up, just as we left the swings and made our way back to the parking lot. Something made me stop, some strange feeling… an instinct almost, had me looking into that car to see…*something*. I don't know what. I just knew that I had to look. I had no idea what was going on or what I'd find when I got there, but I walked over, opened the passenger door and sat down next to the woman behind the wheel.

She didn't even respond to the fact that a total stranger had just gotten into her car. She reached over and turned the volume up on the radio, then leaned back and stared at me with silent tears streaming down her face. I sat there and listened to that song with her. I have never heard anything so heartfelt and terrible and beautiful in all my life. I've never related to anything more than I did to that song and to the stranger I was listening to it with in that car.

When she restarted it and played it again, we both reached out and clasped hands, just held onto one another as our tears fell like raindrops. We both cried for our own personal reasons, but also from the shared empathy, the mutual pain that we felt in each other.

Poor Charlie stood right outside the door, wringing his hands, not knowing what to do. Before I got out and walked away, I told that woman not to do what she was thinking of doing to herself. I assured her that there were people who loved her and that her story was not meant to end there, not like that. I hope she listened to me. I hope that she felt my words, as much as I felt her pain, as much as I felt the pain behind the words of that song. I hope I helped her as much as she helped me.

Listening to that song with her made me realize how much I had missed music. I used to love music, all kinds. I loved how a song could just take me away and make me *feel*. Once upon a time, in another life it seems, I'd adored singing and dancing. I want that back. I want to *feel*. I want to live again. Somehow, I will find a way to put the music back into my soul. I'll convince Dr. Bradburn that it will help in my recovery.

When Charlie and I got back to the hospital, I immediately felt the weight of despair settling back down on my shoulders, but I refused to cry. I was absolutely determined not to cry. But Charlie sobbed as if his heart was breaking. He just couldn't bear bringing me back here. *I* had to comfort *him*. It wouldn't be forever, I told him.

Dr. Bradburn interviewed me and seemed pleased with my answers and my overall mood. She asked if I had trouble making myself come back. I considered my response for a moment, carefully deciding how much to reveal.

"Honestly, I thought about running away and never returning," I said, "I even worked it all out in my head. How much cash I would be able to get and how far it would take me. I thought very seriously about disappearing. But in the end, what made me come back was that I WANT to get better. I want to do things right and I want to be normal. I'm going to get my diploma and my driver's license. My goal is to have my Associates of Art degree when I get out of here too. I am getting better, stronger every single day. If I ran away, I would be giving up. And I will *not* do that. My father would be so disappointed in me if I just rolled over and gave up." Dr. Bradburn was very pleased with my answer.

October 1

Music! Oh, how have I survived without it for so long? Because I've been doing everything exactly as I should and because I've been making so much progress, Dr. Bradburn has granted my wish and allowed me access to YouTube and iTunes. I am also allowed to keep my iPad in my room with me now. No more having to keep it in the media room. The only rules are that I have to keep it locked inside my room or in the media room at all times. I can't bring it out into the common areas. Another stipulation is that I must continue going out into the common areas. I can't stay locked up inside my room watching YouTube all day and night.

Dr. Bradburn reasons that if everything continues to go as well as it is right now, I'll only be here for just over one more year anyway. And she realizes that I needed more exposure to the outside world to properly prepare me for my release. Do you hear what I'm saying? *Prepare me for my release in one year!!!* Even Dr. Bradburn now believes that I won't be here forever. This is the best news! I can't wait to tell Charlie.

But back to the music! The first song I put on my playlist was that one I first experienced with the stranger in the park. I'd had to type in the lyrics and do a search, but I found out the title and also the band that sings it. The 21st, by Blue October. Isn't that such a lovely name? Blue October. I've become completely obsessed with them. I've downloaded every one of their songs that I can find, and I love them all. I can totally relate to their story that they share with the world, the depression, the anger, the tears, the feelings of loneliness and of never being good enough. I understand the hospitalizations and addictions and the recovery. Everything they've been through and the road that they are on now, the road back to happiness gives me hope for myself. Their music has such a strong message and they've been a huge help to me. A band-aid on my wounds and a balm to my soul. Music really IS therapeutic. But I have already learned that music can have such a strong effect on me that I have to change up what I listen to quite often, in order to maintain a balance.

I can't listen to more than a couple of sad songs before I am a crying mess. I can't listen to more than a few heavy, angry songs before I feel Rage perking up his ears and stirring in his sleep. I do NOT want to wake him up. Never that. I can't listen to too many happy songs…well, just because too much of that can make me sad too. Do normal people really feel that much joy and happiness? Every day? I listen to anything and everything and I already have more than a thousand songs on my playlist. Aahhhh! That was such a normal thing to say… *I have a playlist!* I am no longer just some freak in a mental ward with no life. I may still be a freak, but I am forging the beginnings of a life. Most importantly, it is *my* life and I'm determined to make the best of it.

October 17

Things are still going very well. I'm already halfway through my school curriculum and I've completed my first two college math classes. My sessions with Dr. Bradburn are still (always) frustrating, but I try not to show it. She is pleased with my progress, but at the same time she's also worried that I may be pushing myself too hard. She worries that I am focusing so hard on my schooling that I am not addressing any of my other issues.

I have assured her that I'm still very angry, but that I'm working on it. I let her know that I am still writing in my notebook every day. I've even offered to let her read it, which pleases her to no end. I handed her the fake journal that I always carry to my sessions and to the common rooms. That notebook is nothing more than a make-believe fantasy, so full of sappy, crappy bull poop that it makes me want to gag. I hate writing all that nonsense, but I want out of here. I want my freedom and so I have to manipulate the system any way I can.

I told Dr. Bradburn that although I still don't remember the killer's face, I now know that there WAS someone else there that night. I told her that for some reason, when I woke up that morning I was in Karen's room. I don't remember why I was in there, but when I opened my eyes, all I saw was those dolls surrounding me. Then, I ran to my room and my mom and sister were already on the floor, all bloody. Daddy was fighting a tall man. I couldn't see his face. The man started stabbing him and then there was fire everywhere and the man ran away. Then Charlie was there, and he carried me outside, to the front yard. Dr Bradburn cautions me to not to push too hard to remember everything all at once and assures me that it will all come back to me in time. Or not at all, in which case I will have to find a way to cope with the lost memories. I just nod and tell her that I am trying to be patient. Is it bad that I don't even feel guilty about lying to her anymore?

November 12

Last night I dreamed of our vacation in New Hampshire. It was this same time of year, back in 2006. I was 11 years old. I remember that Daddy had some business in New York but first he wanted to show me what Autumn looked like 'up North.' For two wonderful weeks we stayed in a little log cabin up on a mountain. The view from that cabin was breath-taking. It overlooked a wooded valley down below. I'd never seen anything so beautiful in all my life. The trees were a riot of bright, vivid colors. They were simply magnificent, and I'd been thoroughly enchanted.

Karen complained the whole time that she was bored and there was nothing to do in these 'Godforsaken woods'. But I loved every moment of it. To this day, I can close my eyes and still see the brilliance of that valley, smell the crisp Fall air. I had cried genuine tears when it was time to leave. For some reason, I'd felt like I was leaving a piece of myself behind. Autumn has always made me a bit wistful. It's always made me yearn for something, something that I just *knew* was missing from my life. I had never felt that as keenly as I did there at that cabin in the mountains.

When we got to New York, I found that I didn't like it half as much as I'd liked New Hampshire. But there was beauty there too, and I did love the fact that it snowed the entire time that we were there. My mom and Karen had adored New York, naturally. They got to do some serious shopping that year. I remember that we had a hard time getting all the stuff that they'd bought back home. Oh, how Daddy had just laughed and laughed and laughed about it.

I have tears pouring down my face as I write this now. This is the first time that I have really let myself reminisce on my life before the Bad Thing. And oh, how it hurts.

November 24 Thanksgiving Day

I get to spend this Thanksgiving with Charlie, at his house. We have both been looking forward to it all month. But the closer the time came, the more apprehensive I became. Now here it is. Today is the day. I clutch my notebook in my hands to keep them from shaking while Charlie checks me out of the hospital. I decided to bring the journal with me on this trip to help keep me calm. It's become a comfort, and I can distract myself with writing until I get there.

Charlie wrapped his arm around me as we walked to his car. He understands me so well. He knows how anxious I am, but he doesn't pry or try to make me talk about it. He knows that if and when I'm ready, I'll eventually tell him what's bothering me. We're both silent and somber during the drive. I'm nervous and tense and so very conflicted.

On one hand, I'm excited about getting away from the hospital for a while. Any time I get to leave is cause for celebration. Any time I get to eat food that doesn't come from a hospital cafeteria is absolute nirvana to me. Any time I get to see Charlie is a blessing. I'm so thankful to have him in my life. I don't think I would have made it this far without him. In fact, without Charlie I probably would have sat right there in my bedroom and burned up in that fire with my family. I owe him everything. But on the other hand, we are going to be at his home. his home that is right next door to where I used to live. I don't know if I'm ready for this. Will I be able to handle seeing the burned-out shell of the house that I'd once called home? Where all the terrible memories live now, so much horror that they overshadow all the good that once lived there?

Where I lost my family and apparently my sanity? I don't know if I can do this. I really, really don't want to do this anymore. But I know that I have to face it all sooner or later, so ready or not, here I come, I guess. I'm going to put my notebook away and try my best to remain calm during the drive home. Hopefully, nothing drastic happens and I'll be back later to recount it all.

I found myself holding my breath as we drew closer and closer to my old neighborhood, but then Charlie turned left where he should have made a right, and I raised questioning eyes to search his face. What was he up to? Where were we going? Charlie felt my eyes on him, sensing the spike in my anxiety level. He reached over and patted my hand to calm me. "Relax, girlie. We'll go home soon enough. I just have something that I want you to see first. It should only take a moment and then we can be on our way again."

I trust him explicitly, so I just turned back to stare out my window at the people we pass. They all continued going about their own affairs, doing whatever it is that they were doing. Busy little bees, worrying only about what goes on in their own small worlds. They minded their own business and hastily turned their eyes away from the naked hurt that they saw in mine. Other people's pain is always so easy to ignore, especially that of a stranger.

At last, the car came to a stop, and I looked out the windshield to see where we were. We'd stopped at the gates of a cemetery, the car idling as Charlie nervously fiddled with his seat belt, his window, the buttons on the radio. anything to keep his hands busy as his eyes started to tear up and he searched for the words to explain why he's brought me here. I guess there was no easy way to say it, no sugarcoating to add to make the words taste better on his tongue. So, he sucked in a deep breath and then just blurted it all out as quick as he could.

"After you got admitted to the hospital, I spoke to your caseworker and your dad's lawyers and the police and so many other people to find out what was to be done with your family's remains. The lawyer revealed that your father had already taken care of all those things. He had already bought a family plot in a cemetery, this cemetery. But as you know, there wasn't much left to bury. The fire just about destroyed everything. There just wasn't much left behind when it was done burning. The morgue was going to just incinerate it all, since there was no one to come forward and claim them. But I couldn't stand the thought of them just tossing your family out as if they had never existed. I was fairly certain you wouldn't want that either. I wanted to ask you, but that dad-blasted Dr. Bradburn locked you away for so long and then refused to let me see you."

"So, I made the decision for you, and I pray to God that I did the right thing. I claimed your family's remains for you. I had the morgue cremate what little was left after they'd gotten done analyzing it all, or whatever it is that they do in that type of situation. I bought a lovely, silver urn and had them put the ashes into it for you, for when you got out of that hospital. They're safe, at my home. Then I had headstones put up for them, here in the little section that your father had picked out. I did it so that you would have a place to go, to visit, or pray, or remember, or talk to them...whatever it is that you need to do. We can go in now, or we can come back another time. Or we can never come back at all. It's completely up to you. Please, please don't be angry with me. I just wanted you to have *something*."

I looked out the window at the rows of markers, the flowers, the marble headstones and angels and the little black fences sectioning off individual families. I wondered where my own family was, which one of the stones marked my family's final resting places. I am so thankful that Charlie has taken care of these things, made this all possible for me.

But I wasn't ready to face them just yet. The hurt was still too fresh, the guilt still too strong. I leaned over and kissed him on the cheek to assure him that all was well and whispered, "Not yet". Charlie nodded his head once and immediately turned the car around and put us back on the path home. No other words were needed. He knew that I was grateful for all that he had done, I just couldn't talk about it yet.

We turned onto our street, Charlie driving so slowly he could pass for a snail. "You ready, hon? We can always turn around and go somewhere else." I managed to squeak out a tiny "yes" that I wasn't sure he could even hear, so I nodded my head too. I stared down at my hands until he pulled in his driveway and came to a stop. He turned off the car and waited quietly while I took several deep, fortifying breaths.

My heart was racing but I knew that I could put it off no longer. I slowly raised my head and looked over to the left of Charlie's house. I'd been mentally preparing myself to see the black, burned-out husk of my old home as it had looked the last time I'd seen it, on the night of The Bad Thing. But I don't see that at all. I don't see anything, just a big empty space where the house once stood.

I got out and walked over to get a better look. Charlie walked along with me, right there beside me as always. There was nothing left to show that tragedy had once struck there. No burned-out home with its broken, burnt boards sticking up and jutting every which way like old, rotten teeth inside a diseased mouth. There was no burned-out garage or metal car skeletons, no burned trees or dead, empty flower beds. There was no debris or even any scorched earth.

All that remained from before was the pool, covered over and secured with a new chain length fence and the tree house my dad and I had built. I couldn't believe it, the old fort that my father and I had defended from so many enemies and strange creatures still stood strong. I couldn't help but smile as I thought back on all the amazing adventures we'd had within those walls. I turned to look at Charlie with my eyes full of tears and questions.

He gave me a sad little smile and murmured, "I had it all torn down and cleaned up last year. I was going to tear the treehouse down too, but something stopped me. It just felt wrong, so I left it. I'm sorry if, once again, it wasn't my place to interfere. I just couldn't stand the thought of you coming home and seeing it that way. I wanted to make things easier on you. It's not fair, all the bad that's happened to you." He quickly looked away and I knew that he was trying to hide his tears.

I wrapped my arms around him and laid my forehead against his chest. He smelled of peppermint oil. He ALWAYS smells like that. I think that even if I live to be a hundred years old, that scent will forever be a comfort to me. "Why are you so good to me?" I softly whispered. "Of course, I'm not mad. I'm not mad about any of it. How could I be? You are amazing and wonderful and always so very thoughtful. You have no idea how the thoughts of what had become of my family has tormented me. I will forever be in your debt for taking care of them when I couldn't. And I am so grateful that I don't have to see the house that way again, broken and burned and ruined. I honestly don't know if I could have handled it. I love you, Charlie. You really are the best thing that has ever happened to me…My very own guardian angel."

I laughed when Charlie blushed bright red and mumbled, "Oh, go on with you now!" But he was smiling from ear to ear, tickled pink by my words. I turned my attention back to the treehouse, my old safe haven, and my smile faded. Charlie followed my gaze and whispered, "Do you *have* to?"

I reluctantly nodded my head and whispered back, just as quietly, "Yes. I'm afraid that I must. Go on inside now Charlie. I have to do this. I won't be long." I felt his worried eyes tracking me the whole way.

I stopped at the ladder and looked up. The distance to the entrance seemed so much closer than it used to. I climbed up those six rungs fastened to the tree and paused to knock, our old secret code. If you didn't know the secret knock, you weren't allowed to enter… Only my dad and I knew it. I pushed open the trap door on the floor and climbed inside. It was so much smaller than I remembered! I guess everything seems bigger when you're a kid. I walked around, touching everything as I thought back on all the adventures my father and I had in this tiny room. I remembered the comfort that I had found here any time that I was upset. I heard a child's laughter echo through my mind. I heard her cries. I recalled her dreams. That room will forever be haunted with all of my childish hopes and dreams and fears. I slowly sank to my knees on the floor and sobbed. I have cried a million tears over the loss of my family. That time, for the first and only time, I cried for the lost and broken little girl that got left behind. I cried for a long, long time and when I was done, I was surprised to feel better. Cleansed. When I finally exhausted all my tears, I knew that I would never cry for my lost innocence again. I was moving on, at last.

Maybe, just maybe, on my next outing I would be ready to face the cemetery. I said my final goodbyes to my childhood and turned to leave. I took one last glance around and my eyes came to rest on a framed photo of the little stream in the woods that I used to love so much. Then I remembered! I rushed over and took the picture down to reveal the little hidden compartment behind it.

I held my breath as I pulled out the Ziplock bag containing the map that my dad and I had hidden in there. I opened it up and unfolded the map and I couldn't help but laugh out loud. It's the funniest thing ever. Hand drawn by the both of us, it's a mixture of my childish drawings and my dad's neat handwriting. I was immediately bombarded by the memories, the two of us making our time-capsule, searching for the perfect spot to hide it, drawing out the map and then burying our secret treasure. And I remembered our vow.

We had made a promise to one another that in ten years, when I turned 18, we would follow the map, dig up the time-capsule and add more items to it before reburying it once more. We promised that no matter where we were in our lives, we would come back every ten years and repeat the ritual. My heart broke all over again, we never even made it to the first ten-year mark. I gathered up the picture of the stream and the map and hugged them to my chest. I'll ask Charlie to hold onto them and keep them safe for me until I get released from the hospital and can come back and fulfill my vow. I WILL keep my promise.

I took my last look around then climbed down the ladder and firmly shut the door, leaving the ghosts to continue the fight to defend the old homestead. I gave my treasures to Charlie, and he carefully placed them into his safety box. He'll keep them there, safe, until I can come back for them.

The rest of the day was amazing. Charlie and I had a fantastic Thanksgiving together. We ate until we were stuffed, and then we ate even more, because we just couldn't stop ourselves. It was all so delicious!

Afterwards, I turned on my iPad and played some of my favorite songs for him. Some new ones, but also some of my old favorites from before the Bad Thing. I handed the iPad to Charlie and told him to pick a song while I used his guest bathroom. My heart melted when I walked into the restroom and saw that he had placed a sheet over the mirror for me. He's always so kind and thoughtful. I stared at that sheet the whole time I was taking care of my business. I stared at it while I washed my hands. Then I stared at it some more as I washed my hands a second time.

Something was nagging at the edges of my mind, calling to my soul, and tugging at my heartstrings. I really, *really* wanted to rip that sheet away and look. I just knew that I would see something special, something that my heart had been searching for my entire life. My trembling hand reached up on its own accord, but I quickly stepped back until I bumped against the door.

I would not look. I couldn't. I refused to bring any more danger to Charlie. Samara had vowed to take away everything I love, and she'd already taken enough from me. She cannot have Charlie too. I firmly believe the only reason she hasn't gone after my dear friend is because she simply doesn't know about him. I resolved to keep it that way. He's already at risk just because I know him and care for him so much. I refuse to add to it.

When I returned to the living room, Charlie had his eyes closed and his feet were tapping in time with the Elvis song that he'd chosen. I sat down beside him on the sofa and his lips lifted in a sweet, wistful smile as he said, "My Gretchen always loved to dance. When I listen to this song, I always close my eyes because then I can still see her as she was back when I'd first met her. Young and beautiful and so full of life. All the guys wanted to be her boyfriend. But she chose me, can you believe that? I was the luckiest old fool for that. Oh, how I miss her. She'd adored Elvis, bought every record he ever made. I still have them. One day I would love to play them for you... Seeing as how you seem to be a big Elvis fan too."

I hugged him, just because he was a little bit sad, and I told him that I would love to listen to them any time he wanted. "I've always loved Elvis, lots of the older music too. I've always wanted to learn all those old swing dances. They look like so much fun! My dad always said that we would go take lessons together." I paused to swallow the sudden lump in my throat. "Well. Maybe I can still learn, somewhere down the road. I'll just have to learn it on my own, that's all."

Charlie let out a loud laugh and told me that my lessons would begin on our next day out. I was obviously confused. "What?" I asked. "What do you mean?"

Charlie answered with a pleased grin, "I know every old dance there ever was. I learned them all to keep my Gretchen happy throughout the years. You don't need to go looking for an instructor. You have one right here! I can teach you any dance you want to learn, so long as it's the OLD dances. None of this newfangled nonsense they do nowadays. That ain't even dancin'! Oohhh, this is gonna be great fun!"

Charlie's joy and eagerness in that moment shot an arrow straight into my heart. I felt warmth, hope, and a happiness inside that I haven't felt in such a long time, had never thought to feel again. I loved seeing the twinkle in his old, watery eyes. Teaching me to dance would obviously bring him great joy. Refusing him because my dad was no longer here to dance with me would be selfish. So, even though he misses his wife and I miss my dad, we'll both dance and hope that somehow, somewhere, they are watching us…and that they're happy.

Twisted Things and Dirty Dreams

I'm dreaming. I know I'm dreaming. But this is real too. I don't dream very often, but when I do, this is how it always goes. Everything that I see in my dreams is actually happening, even as the events play out in my mind, behind my closed eyes. Right now, I see Krispin lying on the roof of an old, abandoned house across from mine. He's watching my window, waiting for his chance to help me escape my guards. If I hadn't been in Dreamworld, as I call my little dreaming escapades, I never would have seen him climb up there.

I guarantee no one else was able to detect him either. He's in camouflage mode, naked as the day he was born, his skin blended perfectly with what is left of the slate grey roof beneath him. He is the most beautiful thing I've ever seen, and I want him. Badly. My eyes travel the length of him, over his broad shoulders, narrow waist, perfectly rounded buttocks, and long powerful legs then back up again. I find myself wishing he would roll over onto his back so that I may see the other side as well. I want to reach out and touch him, stroke my hands all over that smooth blue-grey skin.

But that's not how the Dreaming works. I'm a silent spectator, a ghost floating along watching as events unfold, unable to speak or touch or feel anything at all. I can look all I want, but I can never touch. That's always frustrating, but never more so than it is right at this moment. I've never wanted anything as much as I want *him*. I lie down next to him and watch him trying to get a glimpse of me through my window. A low, continuous growl of frustration rumbles in his chest and I know he wants me just as desperately.

For an hour, I lay there beside him on that rooftop, listening to him growl and snarl and curse. Even as fascinating as I find him, I'm beginning to grow bored with it all. Is he going to stay up here forever? Will he never get up so I can see the rest of him? I sigh in disappointment as I sit up and prepare to leave. I don't know how long I have until I'll wake up and get ejected from Dreamworld.

I want to go around town and snoop, learn everyone's dirty little secrets. Last time I was in the Dreaming, I came across a man and two women rolling around naked in the old blacksmith shop. The things I saw them do with their hands and mouths…I've never been able to get it out of my mind. I think about it all the time. The man hadn't been impressive to look at, but that doesn't even matter now. I don't remember what he looked like anyway, because all I can see is Krispin there instead. Krispin naked and hard and doing all those deliciously naughty things. But then I get mad, absolutely *livid* at the thought of him doing those things to those women. How dare he kiss them, touch them, do *that* with them. I have to constantly remind myself that Krispin had never really been there. It wasn't him I'd seen, thankfully, so I won't have to kill him.

Suddenly Krispin groans and rolls onto his back, and I'm left staring dumbfounded down at him. I thank my darkest little stars that he can't see me right now, because I know my mouth has dropped wide open. He. Is. Magnificent. So much more than I ever imagined. I'm looking down at that huge, hard part of him that I want to explore so badly, when I hear him whisper my name.

My eyes fly up to his face, thinking that somehow, some way, he can see me. But no. He's just thinking of me, the same way I always imagine him. Heat pools low in my body and my heart speeds up, but there's nothing I can do about it. There is absolutely no relief in the Dreaming. Ever. No respite from hunger, fatigue, lust. I suffer until I awaken. And then I suffer even more because I'm a prisoner in the waking world as much as I am a ghost here. I'm not free to fulfill my own basic needs in either world.

But right now, right before my very eyes, Krispin runs his hands down his body and takes all that maleness into his hands and pleasures himself. With every stroke, he whispers my name until he is breathless, and his chest is heaving. His hips lift up off the roof, pumping to thrust himself into his own hands. Faster and faster, until he suddenly lifts one fist up to his mouth and bites down, hard, onto his knuckles to hold the roar inside as he spills himself onto his belly. "I *will* have you, Samara. Soon," he whispers as his hands drop away and his body relaxes.

Standing there on weak, trembling legs, all I can do is swallow hard and try to remember how to breathe again. My legs give out and I plop back down onto my butt beside him. Holy. Hot. Hell. I don't think I'll ever get my body cooled down and back under control. Not after witnessing that.

When Krispin has caught his breath, he leaves the roof, crawls straight down the wall, like a lizard, until he's back on the ground. He reaches into a broken window to retrieve his clothes and quickly slips them back on. His skin lightens from the slate grey color of the roof and returns to his normal pale blue. It's getting late now, the shadows deepening, becoming more efficient hiding places.

Krispin slinks from one building to the next, always blending precisely into the gloom around him. I follow behind him, I want to learn all *his* secrets. I want to know where he goes. I want to know who he spends his time with. I want to see more of who he is when he thinks no one's looking. I wish I could listen to his heart beating from the inside. I wish I could peel his skull back and read his thoughts. I want to know him, *really* know him.

He stops abruptly and peeks into the kitchen of The Chopping Block Eatery. The door is usually kept open to let the heat out, and apparently, he sometimes uses Storver's laxity to garner free meals for himself. I stick so close to him I can hear the grumble of hunger from his belly, the angry protest at its emptiness. Mine rumbles in response. I loathe being hungry, in Dreamworld even more than in the waking world. In Dreamworld I'm able to see the food, smell it, watch others eat, but I can never even taste it. At least in my tiny prison room, I'm not subjected to the torment of having it right in front of me but denied the pleasure of consuming it.

Well, not typically. Sometimes the guards like to flaunt their meals at me, just to see if I'll beg. I won't. Not ever again. But oh, how I want to sometimes, like right now. The delicious smells wafting out of that kitchen are pure torture, especially to a bodiless soul that's incapable of consuming any form of sustenance. But even if I were to cry out, beg for mercy, there is no one to hear my pleas. Not in Dreamworld. I am alone here in the Dreaming, just like always.

The low, ferocious snarl from Krispin snaps me out of my pity party for one. He is starving too, just as desperate for nourishment as I am. His eyes track every move that Storver makes, his stomach growling so loudly that I'm terrified he'll give himself away and get caught. But Storver's completely oblivious to what's taking place behind him, too busy stirring the contents of the huge pot on the stove. Suddenly, Krispin disappears from beside me. He's just gone, and so is the tray of skin-wrap burritos, just taken from the oven and set out on the cooling rack.

Krispin had moved so incredibly fast that there was never any chance of him getting caught. But he can't escape from me quite so easily, not while I'm in this form. I spin around and my eyes immediately pick him out of the surrounding shadows. He's halfway down the street, crouched down with his back against the wall, so that he can watch anything and anyone that may be coming at him.

He shoves half of a burrito into his mouth, chews twice and then swallows before shoveling the other half in right behind it. Soft, incessant grunts and growls issue from his throat as he fills his belly. I'm forced to look away after just a few moments. I can't watch anymore. My desperate need for food wars with my hunger for him. It's terrible and overwhelming, and I honestly don't think that I have ever felt worse than I do right at this instant. I would rather have Father rip all of my fingernails off again than live one more second with this gnawing hunger in my belly and the aching fire burning down lower. And even though I turn my back on him, I cannot unsee him enjoying his pilfered meal any more than I can forget the sight of him back on that rooftop. I'm powerless to hold back my own desperate snarls, but they're silent to his deaf ears anyway. Dreamworld makes everyone deaf, dumb, and blind to me. There are no exceptions.

Finally, mercifully, the agony of listening to him eat comes to an end, but my empty belly refuses to shut the hell up about it. I turn back and see that he's consumed all but one of the burritos. He picks it up, drops the tray to the ground, and sneaks off into the dark once more. *Now* where is he going and what, exactly, is he up to?

Krispin leads me to the old, abandoned orphanage where he'd once lived as a small child, before they'd condemned the building and kicked all the children out onto the streets. The glass in the windows is all gone and most of the roof has fallen in. The walls seem about to fall down any minute now too, but that doesn't deter him. He walks right through the door anyway.

I follow him deep into the deserted building, only to find that it's not as empty as I had thought it to be. People are living here, probably the very ones that had survived being tossed out of these halls years ago. There are so many of them, so many people with nowhere else to go… kids even. I gag at the stench of them, at the filth of their disgusting unwashed and diseased bodies.

Why, oh why is the ability to smell permissible in Dreamworld but nothing else is? I press a hand over my nose and mouth as I angrily curse the fates responsible for making up the rules. There are too many people crowded into the room, making it difficult for my eyes to focus on any one individual. They take up every bit of free space, some lying on thin blankets or old, moldy straw pallets. Others sit propped up against the walls. A large group passes a bowl of what looks like yellow berries amongst themselves. They each take one and pop them into their mouths and quickly swallow them down. Thirty seconds later they all fall to the floor giggling hysterically.

Krispin ignores them and walks on by. A filthy woman looks up and grins with half of her teeth missing, the other half black and rotten. "Hey there, Handsome. You got some suga' fo' Momma?" Krispin never turns his head to look at her, not even when she screams at his retreating backside to, "Git back ova' heeya and give me some suga!" He obviously has one destination in mind and will allow no distractions to slow him down. He doesn't even care about the naked couple in the corner, fornicating right there against the wall for all to see.

He does not slow down. He does not look at anything or anyone around him. He steps around, or over, all that lies in his path until he finally comes to a stop at a small pallet in a dark corner. There's a woman sitting there, a pretty woman with wild red curls framing her face. Hair much like mine. She's much older than him, and age is beginning to erase the pretty right off her face.

Krispin pinches a lock of her hair, rubbing it between his fingers briefly before releasing it. He silently holds out his hand to her, but she ignores it and pouts up at him. "What took you so long to come back? It's been forever. I won't just sit here and wait for you to show up. I have needs too, ya know." Krispin grunts and stubbornly keeps his hand out for her to take.

She folds her arms against her chest and mutters, "I'm not sure I want to go with you again anyway. You were too rough last time. You left bruises and I could barely walk afterwards." Krispin flashes the skin- wrap burrito at her and I watch her eyes grow wide and fill with greedy anticipation. "Get up, or I'll find someone else that's hungrier than you are." Krispin's growling voice sends shivers down my spine.

The woman licks at her lips, then reaches up and snatches his hand. "There is *no one* hungrier than I am," she snaps as he pulls her to her feet and leads her from the room. He's moving fast, fairly dragging her along behind him. "What the hell are you doing Krispin?" I murmur as I follow them up a rickety flight of stairs that's barely clinging to its original purpose. He *better* not be up to what I think he's up to. He just better not be. But he is. I know he is, and I have never felt so furious and hot and hungry and crazy as this. Ever. If I were here in the waking world instead of trapped in the Dreaming, I would kill them both. After I played with them for an hour or ten, of course.

The woman pulls back at the last moment, hesitant to follow him those last few steps into the small, private room, away from prying eyes. Well, from all eyes but mine, but they don't know I'm here, do they? When he turns to glare at her, she whispers, "The same as last time, right? Nothing more?" Krispin sets the burrito down on the windowsill and gives her a brief, curt nod of his head.

She takes one more glance at the meal awaiting her and tells him, "Just try not to break me this time. You gotta save some for later, ya know?" And then the little slut drops to her knees, takes down his pants, and goes to work on *my* man with her mouth. He buries his hands in hair, then throws his head back and grits his teeth up at the ceiling. My vision begins to grow dark as the rage overtakes me. She. Is. Playing. With. My. Toy. I want to rip out her throat. I hate this. I hate watching him with another woman, but there's no way I'll leave either. I will see this through to the bitter end. I swear to all the dark gods that ever existed that I will make him suffer for this. I make this solemn vow to myself, right here and now. I will play with him too. I'll take my fill of him, work him out of my system, and *then* I'll make him pay.

Krispin's frustrated snarl brings me back from the edge of darkness. My eyes dart back up, just as he pulls himself out of her mouth and pushes her to her hands and knees. He rips his shirt off over his head, positions himself behind her, and fiercely thrusts into her. Fast. Hard. She cries out, and I'm not sure if it's from pleasure or pain. Probably both, and I am so mad, so insanely jealous that if I ever see her while I'm in the waking world, I will immediately, no questions asked, no explanations given, squish her insides out. Slowly, so that it hurts forever before she dies.

I grin at the mental image of her guts splattered upon the walls of this room. But then I'm snapped out of my bloody fantasy when Krispin roars out my name. *My* name! I don't know if I'm more flattered or pissed at him for pretending that she's me. Oh, who am I kidding? I. Am. Furious. How *dare* he pretend that pitiful old hag is anything like me. Next time I see him, I am going to bite pieces of him off, dip them in scree sauce, and then force feed them to his little bitch. We'll see how much he likes putting his body parts in her mouth *then*.

"Oh, thank every god in the Overneath! Get it out of me!" the woman cries. Krispin slips himself free, throws his clothes back on, and without a word, turns and leaves her there on the floor. "Freak," she mumbles after him, then jumps up and snatches her cold meal off the windowsill.

The room suddenly starts shaking and rumbling around me and I know that I'm about to be spit out of Dreamworld. Someone back in the waking world is shaking me, trying to wake me up. For a moment, I almost feel sorry for the poor hapless fool, because as angry as I am right now in the Dreaming, I know that the rage will be doubled once I'm actually awake. Oh, how the heads will roll and the guts will squish. "Oh, do hurry and get on with the waking up, Samara," I tell myself, as anticipation fills my dark little heart. *Somebody* needs to pay for the things that I've just witnessed. Might as well be a guard or two that I detest anyway.

I'll feel better after I let some of this rage out. After all, if I were to go after Krispin straight away, I would just kill him in a jealous fit, and I most certainly don't want that. I would regret it forever if I were to kill him now. I must play with him first, taste him, feel how it feels to have him moving inside *me*. Oh, I *will* kill him, but I want to have some fun with him first. I have some games of my own that I've been aching to teach him.

Learning to Live Again: Notebook #3

November 28

I've done the unthinkable. I asked Dr. Bradburn to put up a small Christmas tree in her office to help ease me into the Christmas holiday. I assured her that I don't want to cause any trouble this year and since her mirror therapy had worked so well, I was hoping that the same treatment would work again. After all, if I'm ever to live a normal life outside the hospital walls, I can't freak out over the sight of Christmas ornaments. That's what I *told* her, but really, it's just strategy on my part.

My Christmas trauma is just one more thing that I know she'll make me deal with before she'll declare me mentally competent and soundly sane. Even though it was my plan, I have no doubt that this is going to be *hard*. I really don't know how I'll find the strength and the courage necessary to fake my way through this particular test. I want to throw up every time I even think about Christmas and all the lavish decorations that go along with it. Those stupid red balls. And it'll be much worse when I'm closed in with them inside Dr Bradburn's small office.

A small part of me has hope that this plan to surround myself with holiday cheer will actually work. Oh, not that I believe Christmas will ever bring me happiness again. That will never happen. I know that. My only hope is to subject myself to so many of the holiday's decorations that I eventually overcome my fears. Or at least hide them well enough that they won't show on the outside. Who cares if I'm screaming on the inside? No one else will hear it but me. I just have to make it *look* good. I have to convince Dr

Bradburn that I'm healing and moving on in every way. Just like I did with the mirror. *Fake it till you make it*. I will *never* admit that when I look into the mirror, a monster sometimes stares back at me. I'll never admit that I still see everything that I've always seen, but I can look at that mirror now and fake it even better than I had ever done while I was growing up. So much more is at stake now. My freedom, my very life depends on my hiding and acting skills. As I'd known she would, Dr. Bradburn readily agreed to my plan to set up a small Christmas tree in her office. She's pleased with my progress and proud of her… I mean, *my* success with the treatment plan that she'd engineered. Today is my first session since I'd made the request for my 'Christmas tree therapy'. Wish me luck!

That went a lot smoother than I expected, but when I walked into the office, I didn't see a tree. What I saw was a box on the floor, propped up beside my chair. Dr. Bradburn leaned forward and announced, "I thought this might be a good idea for you to try. You can put the tree together and decorate it yourself. It's just a tiny one, only two feet tall, and you can set it up right on the corner of my desk. I will be here with you the whole time and if at any point you get too overwhelmed, we can just stop the session. We won't do anything that you're uncomfortable with."

I giggled a little at that, but only on the inside. Apparently, she's remembering the black eye that she'd sported for an entire month after she'd introduced her 'mirror therapy' plan. The good doctor didn't want me to beat her up again! Then I thought about the upcoming ordeal and the laughter shriveled up inside of me. I took a deep breath and nodded my head. I could do this. I *had* to do this.

I opened the box and unloaded all the parts. Aside from the tree itself, there were also several plastic bags of miniature decorations included. The tree was separated into three pieces, the base with the stand, the middle, and the treetop. I snapped them together with no problem and quickly moved on to decorating it. As expected, this part was more difficult for me, but I got through it. I added the string of lights and then the beads. Then I hung the ornaments, tiny, disturbing, *loathsome* balls the size of marbles. I placed the little star on top and the tiny, wrapped gifts beneath it. I even sprinkled it with the white Styrofoam and glittered 'snow'.

Dr. Bradburn plugged the lights in, and I sat back in my chair, a pleased smile on my face. That wasn't so bad. It really wasn't! The tree was actually really cute. "Well done, Adrina!" (I hate that she still refuses to call me Ecko.) "Well done! I'd hoped that this would make things easier on you! We'll leave the tree right there for you to look at and become more comfortable with."

I plastered my empty-headed, all is well smile on my face as I praised her thoughtfulness. "Thank you. It was a brilliant idea. I'm not uncomfortable at all. I think the fact that everything is miniature sized helps also. I've always loved minis. I used to have a collection of them, in fact. Thank you for this, Dr. Bradburn." I asked her if it was at all possible that I be allowed to have the red Christmas ball from THAT day, the one that was brought in with me.

My few belongings had been placed into the hospital's storage room, to be given back at the time of my release…standard procedure. I wanted to keep *that* particular Christmas ball in my room with me. It was all part of my plan. Hopefully the prolonged exposure to it will lessen the effect it has on me. Or at least numb me so that I can fake the appropriate reactions.

Dr. Bradburn agreed and I hastily asked if we could wait until after Christmas before we try it out. I don't want to push myself too far, too fast. The Christmas holiday is already an extremely stressful time for me, and I want to get through it without incident. "I think that is a very wise and well thought out plan. Every day I'm amazed at how well you're doing and how far you have come. You keep doing this admirably and you'll be out of here in no time."

I smiled and hid the palm of my left hand against my leg. I couldn't let her see the bloody marks that my fingernails dug while my right hand was busy hanging those tiny ornaments onto the tree. What she doesn't know won't hurt her, and more importantly... won't hurt me.

December   25

Christmas Day

I made it through the day just fine! Not a single melt down or freak out. I stayed as far away from the full-size tree in the cafeteria as I could get, and the staff made sure that they gave me a gift wrapped in cute little animal paper. (No repeats of last year please.) Charlie bought me a dancing outfit complete with a poodle skirt, Bobby socks and saddle shoes. There was even a scarf for me to wear around my neck or as a headband.

I laughed as I handed him my gift to him. He couldn't hold back his own laughter because I'd gotten him the same thing…Well, not a poodle skirt, but the equivalent in men's clothing. Only I couldn't decide which look I wanted to deck him out in so I went with two different styles. For the greaser look, I bought him dark blue Levi's jeans, a white t-shirt, and a black leather jacket. For the more sophisticated style, there was a grey jacket and pants, vest, striped button up shirt, tie, Oxford spectator shoes and a black fedora hat.

We promised each other that as soon as I busted out of here for good, we would celebrate by getting all decked out in our outfits and finding a club where we could swing dance the night away in. I told him he was going to be the most handsome man there and that I just knew I'd have to beat all the ladies off of him with a stick. He blushed to the roots of his hair and that made me laugh even harder. Now we're both super excited and can't wait for my lessons!

January 22, 2012

Dr. Bradburn brought the red Christmas ball to my room yesterday. She held it out and waited for me to take it from her hand. I stared at it with complete and absolute loathing. "I can't yet. I'm sorry, but I just can't make myself touch that thing," I miserably tell her.

She walked over and placed it on top of my dresser instead and said "That's fine Adrina. Don't be discouraged. You might not be able to today, but maybe tomorrow you will. Don't take this as a setback. It is not. It may not seem like it, but you're actually taking a big step forward. You're doing remarkably well. If having this in here gets to be too much for you, just let one of the staff members know. I've instructed them to remove it upon your request."

I sat up all night staring at that cursed ball, thinking and remembering, hurting and hating. But this is a test that I will need to pass. Soon I'll have to hold that ball in my hand and completely hide my revulsion. I'll have to convince Dr. Bradburn that it no longer holds any power over me. It will probably take all of my acting abilities because there is no way I will ever be ok with that thing, no way. It just hurts too much.

January 29

The Christmas ball has been in my room for a week now. I watch it like it's a snake (or a stuffed teddy bear) about to bite. I wake up each morning and there it is. I go to sleep each night and it's still there in the same spot. It hasn't moved a bit. I feel myself beginning to relax and forget about it being there, so I've decided on a plan of action. I'll turn on my favorite songs, blare my happiest music, and place one finger onto it every time I pass by it. Just one single finger at first, and gradually I'll build up my courage until I can actually pick it up. This will work. I'll *make* it work.

February 11

I received my high school diploma today! I have also begun my second year of college classes. School is the easiest of all the things I am trying to accomplish. In fact, I wish everything could be so easy. I still haven't been able to pick up the dreaded ornament, although I can place my whole hand onto it now. I try to be patient with myself. As Confucius said, "It does not matter how slowly you go so long as you don't stop." Forward is forward, even if I'm moving at a snail's pace.

My first dance lesson was so much fun. I can't believe what an amazing dancer Charlie is! On my day out, we drove out to the park (the one we had gone to on our very first outing.) We moved all the picnic tables to the side of one of the pavilions, connected my tablet to my new Bluetooth speaker, cranked up the volume, and blasted Elvis Presley's Jailhouse Rock. Charlie showed me all the basic foot moves that I would need to know to dance the Jitterbug.

We both had such a blast! I almost bit the dust a couple of times, but Charlie never once let me fall. All in all, I caught on fast and I think I did pretty good. Every night in my room I practice everything that he showed me. I can't wait to show him my moves.

March 2

Dr. Bradburn has sprung some news on me. I guess I'll start with the good stuff. I am no longer restricted to one day-pass per month. As of this weekend, I'll be allowed to go out every…single... Saturday! I can't wait to tell Charlie, coffees and movie theaters and good food and dance lessons galore!

I want to go to Galveston and walk on the beach. I want to go to a dog park and pet puppies. I want to feed the ducks and go on nature hikes. I want to go on a motorboat ride and paddle a canoe and a paddle boat and a kayak. I want to swim in a pool and buy meals for homeless people. I want to climb to the top of a tall hill, lie down in the grass, and roll down it. I want to go roller-skating and work in a soup kitchen. I want to buy rubber duckies, a whole *army* of rubber duckies. I want to write my name and phone number on them and then release them out into the wild… in streams and rivers and public fountains. I want the joy of having some random person call me up out of the blue to tell me that they found one of my duckies. I want to crash a wedding and surprise the bride and groom with an amazing, extravagant gift. I want to hug the father of the bride and assure him that the beautiful bride is still his little girl, and she always will be. I want to somehow make Charlie feel like he is the most special person in the world, because he is, and he deserves it.

There are so many things I want to do. I'm going to have Charlie make a bucket list with me. Yeah! That's a great idea! But I'm getting carried away. Moving on. I'll be 17 in a few short weeks, so I'll be starting my driver's education classes on April 1st. Pretty soon I'll be driving Charlie around! I wonder how he's going to feel about that. Knowing Charlie, he'll be all smiles and encouragement, even if he's terrified.

Now the not so good news. Dr. Bradburn says that I need to learn to do 'normal' things that 'normal' teenagers do every day. She says that I need to learn how to apply makeup and style my hair. She insists that these are standard, typical things that I should learn how to do. She's going to bring a beautician in to teach me all that I need to know. She says that I would have already learned this stuff on my own by now, if I'd had normal teenage years.

I hate that word, normal. I've always hated it, because I have never *been* normal. But whatever. That's not even important. What *is* important is the fact that learning how to apply makeup requires being able to look into the mirror without my 'reflection' trying to kill me. Yeah. I have no idea how I'm going to pull this off either.

March 22, 2012

Dr. Bradburn let me have a sleepover at Charlie's house yesterday for my birthday! It was meant to be a reward for my hard work, but it was also a test. She wanted to see how I would do away from the hospital overnight. I knew I would be fine. I knew it would be fun to stay the night with Charlie. It would also be a huge relief to not have to hide and playact 24/7. That gets exhausting.

As far as Dr. Bradburn knows, I have not seen anything but what I'm supposed to see in the mirrors. I will never admit to her that her therapy is crap and doesn't work. Nothing at all had changed. I still see the same monsters and Otherworlds that I have always seen. I've just learned to hide it better.

Spending the night at Charlie's, I'd only been worried about one thing. I was afraid that I wouldn't be able to resist the temptation to look in the mirror in Charlie's guest bathroom. When I was there for Thanksgiving, I'd nearly given in. This time may be even harder and it's not like I can just avoid the bathroom. But I needn't have worried at all. Sweet, old Charlie always knows exactly what I need and what to do to make things easier on me. When he came to pick me up, he leaned down and whispered in my ear, "I hired someone to come in and take the mirror out of your bathroom at the house. You're the only one that even goes in there. No one else ever comes to visit me and it's important to me that you're comfortable." I love this sweet man with everything in me.

When we left the hospital, Charlie drove me to the mall and bought me a nice dress and some warm fuzzy pajamas and slippers and the necessary toiletries. Then he took me out to a very nice, very fancy restaurant for dinner. It was all so sweet. Later, when we were back at his house, we made popcorn and watched movies until we passed out. I had a wonderful time, just being able to do the simple things that most people take for granted every day.

But now I'm back in this gross place and I'm not allowed to do any of the five million and twenty-three things that I long to do. I can't go to any of the places I want to see. Now, don't get me wrong. I am extremely grateful for my time away, but I'm also resentful at the same time. I should *not* be stuck in this place. But I'm 17 now and one step closer to the beginning of my life of freedom. When I finally get out of here, no one will ever have control over me again. No one, but me. When I finally bust out of here, there'll be no holding me back. Just wait and see.

April 14

Charlie and I have fans! On my days out, we grab some takeout food and drive over to the park for my dance lessons. People have started to take notice of what we're doing and now they show up every Saturday to cheer us on and encourage us. Some of them have even begged Charlie for lessons too!

Today I sat watching from the swings while I pretended to take a break, so that others could enjoy dancing with 'the teacher', as I call him when we're out there. It makes his face flush with pleasure, and I can never resist making him feel good. There was quite a crowd today. All the tables were full and there was nowhere left to sit, so I walked over to the swings.

There was only one other person swinging, a woman that appeared to be in her early forties. We swung quietly, companionably while watching Charlie and all his groupies. After a while, I got up to leave. Charlie needed to rest for a bit. I always have to force him to take breaks. He'll dance until he drops if I don't interfere, and that's just not acceptable.

So, I hop down from the swing and I'm walking away when it happens again. That strange, silent voice in my head, whispering for me to do *something*. I got the urge to turn around and walk back to the woman. She had stopped swinging and was watching me with wide, questioning eyes. I stepped up beside her and just *looked* at her. Looked *into* her, somehow, into her mind. I see things. I see the woman's mother, a sweet little old lady named Susan. She had recently been forced to give up living on her own and had moved into her daughter's house to be looked after. She's overwhelmed with feelings of sadness and loss and guilt, and she's begun to feel like she's nothing more than a burden.

The woman on the swing had done everything that she could think of to make her mother feel better, but no matter what she said, Susan couldn't seem to find her way back from her depression. The woman on the swing felt a terrible weight in her heart because she was watching the light slowly leave her mother's eyes right in front of her. She had started coming out here every day to swing in the park while the home health nurse was with her mother. To think, and to pray, perhaps.

I saw all this in her mind in an instant. Then I saw an image of Susan, there in the park, watching me and Charlie dance. I saw her face light up in an instant. I saw Charlie and Susan dancing together, there in the park with everyone watching. Then I saw them there, alone and dancing in the dark with nothing but the stars watching. Charlie's arms wrapped around her as he slowly twirled her around. Susan was staring up at him with love shining in her eyes.

My heart filled with so much happiness and relief. I knew then that Charlie would be fine. No matter what happens to me, I knew that Charlie wouldn't be alone. I smiled as I felt a huge weight lift from my shoulders. My hands reached out and grasped onto the woman's hands. We held on tightly for a moment and I whispered, "We're out here every weekend. Come back Saturday. Bring Susan. I promise that you won't regret it." I smiled as her eyes filled up with wonder and hope. I felt her watching me as I went to collect Charlie. I couldn't help but laugh as the crowd good naturedly boo'd me when I told them that I was taking him to rest. Everyone loves

Charlie. I don't think there's a single person who can resist his charm. I'm positive that Susan won't be able to resist him either!

April 21

Susan turned out to be just as lovely as I knew she'd be. What I didn't expect was for her to be such a firecracker! Charlie and I were already out on the 'dance floor' doing our thing, crowd clapping and cheering us on when she arrived. I saw her sit down at one of the tables to watch, but Charlie didn't notice. He's always such a gentleman. When he dances, he gives his partner every bit of his attention.

I waited until someone cut in and took my place, then I sat down to watch. I wanted to see what was going to happen, though I didn't know exactly what to expect. The song ended and another one began. I didn't get discouraged when Susan just continued to sit there on that bench and frown at Charlie. I knew that something beautiful was about to happen. I'd seen it.

Susan kept her face scrunched up in thought throughout that whole song and into the next one. I witnessed the exact moment that things changed, and recognition dawned. It was like a curtain got pulled aside, revealing the answer that had been alluding her. Her frown suddenly disappeared, and her eyes lit up with recognition and wonder. I could see tears glistening in her eyes. When the song ended, I paused the music.

Susan stood up and called out, "I see that you're still quite the charmer, Charlie Monroe. And it looks like you still have some half decent moves. But I'm just not convinced that you can handle all *this*. Get on over here and dance with me. Let's see what you've got, Old Timer." She held her arms out and waited for him to catch up.

Charlie spun around to look at her and it only took him a moment. His eyes lit up like candles in the night. "Susan? Susan

Browning? Is it really you? It *is* you! Oh, this is amazing!" He rushed over and picked her up, then he spun her around in circles. When he stopped spinning, he pulled her in close for a hug, then stepped back to get a better look at her. "My God, the last time I saw you was at prom, back in 1955. Wow, what a night *that* was, do you remember? How is it that you're still just as lovely as you were back then? How've you been? *Where* have you been?"

Susan giggled, actually giggled like a schoolgirl. "There will be time for all that gossip later. Right now, I want to *dance*! What do you say, Charlie, my boy? Want to show these youngsters how it's *really* done?"

Charlie threw his head back and roared with laughter. "I can think of nothing I'd like more," he answered in a deep, flirty voice. Then, remembering the onlookers, he glanced around and told the crowd, "Y'all better stand back now. We got a loaded pistol here!" I grinned from ear to ear as I restarted the music and turned the volume up.

Everyone stepped back to give them room as 'Come on Baby. Let's do the twist' blared out of the speaker. *Wow* is all I can say. Those two sure could dance! There was no awkwardness, not an ounce of shyness. They moved as if they'd danced a thousand times together. Who knows? Maybe they had. All I know is they twisted up a storm today and everybody loved it.

The crowd clapped and whistled and cheered them on. When that song ended and Chris Montez's 'Let's Dance' began, everyone crowded back onto the 'dance floor' and monopolized the two of them. All the ladies just had to dance with Charlie, while the guys took turns swinging Susan around, as well. The men were extra careful with her because she's such a tiny old gal, but they made sure to give Susan a day that she wouldn't forget.

They passed her around and played a hilarious game of keep away with Charlie. If I didn't know better, I would say that they'd had it all planned. Every time Susan and Charlie got close enough to each other to partner back up, some guy would cut in and whisk her away from him. Charlie would jokingly shake his fists after them. Susan could only shrug her shoulders at him and let herself be swept away, her peals of laughter ringing out behind her. I couldn't make myself stop smiling like a crazy person. I loved this so very much. I knew without a doubt that neither one of them would ever feel alone again.

Finally, the crowd took pity on them and stepped off the floor as 'In the Still of the Night' began to play. We all watched as they slowly danced all around that concrete platform. Nora, the woman from the swing sat down beside me. "Thank you for this," she told me. "I was watching my momma waste away day by day. There was nothing I could do about it and it was breaking my heart. But she's going to be just fine, right? They're going to be together now, aren't they?" I could hear the hope in her voice, and I nodded my head as I continued to watch them slowly swaying together. Nora reached over and squeezed my hand. She said, "Thank you so much for this. For sharing your magic. You saved her life. I just know it."

I squeezed back and murmured, "Nah, it's not my magic. Look at them. They make their own magic. Charlie is the best of the best. He'll take care of her, when that time comes. And she'll take care of him. But they have to realize that they belong together first. You have a couple months of her acting like a lovesick schoolgirl before that happens." Nora smiled and said she couldn't wait to see that.

A cute, young man walked over at that moment and asked if I would dance with him. My eyes darted over to Charlie in complete panic mode. He merely grinned and nodded at me. I was terrified as the man took my hand and pulled me to my feet. I have never danced with anyone other than Charlie, and my dad, when I was young. I was a bit clumsy at first, but he was very patient, and we ended up dancing together for two more songs. It was actually sort of… *nice*. And he was really handsome.

Charlie didn't even tease me about it on the ride back to the hospital like I thought he would. I guess he was lost somewhere back in the 50's, his mind full of memories of his Gretchen and of Susan. I wasn't going to pry. I knew that he would share when he got his thoughts all straightened out in his head. But I smiled to myself as I thought back on their phone number exchange, and then the soft kiss he had placed on Susan's cheek as we were leaving. So. Freaking. Sweet.

May 9

Ok, so I suck at driving. No big deal. Lots of people are bad drivers. I live in Houston, Texas. I'll fit right in with everyone else! Charlie showed up today for my driving lessons wearing a crash helmet and a roll of bubble wrap around his body. I threw my hands on my hips and glared at him as the hospital staff got a good laugh at my expense.

"Ha ha. Very funny, Charlie. You know I'm not THAT bad at driving." He nodded solemnly at me then draped his arm around my shoulder, as we walked to his car and said, "You're right, baby girl. You do just fine. You've got this!" I actually felt a tiny bit better until I realized that he did not take off any of his protective gear before he got in and strapped himself into the passenger seat. Oh well. I haven't run over anyone yet… and I'm sure I'll get better. Eventually.

June 1

My first makeup lesson was a complete and utter disaster. Tara, my instructor, told me to try it on my own the first time. I told her that I really didn't want to and please don't make me. She insisted and it was just as terrible as I'd assured her it would be.

I broke lipsticks and dug deep gouges in the eyeshadow. I smeared such a thick, gloppy layer of gunk on my face that I was afraid it would never wash off. I ended up with black circles all around my eyes and thick, bright pink circles painted on the middle of my cheeks. Tara could only shake her head and watch the train wreck in progress before her.

"Haven't you ever put on makeup before? Never? Not even to play dress up as a little girl?" she questioned; an expression of disbelief clearly stamped on her face. I just shrugged and told her that I had never been a girly girl. The only dressing up I played at involved body armor and swords to fight off monsters. Tara sighed heavily and had me scrub all the mess away, before showing me what everything was and how to use it. I was a bit surprised when she was finished and had me look in the mirror. I actually looked ok...kind of pretty even. And if my reflection was grinning back at me with blood in her teeth, well...what of it? No one else could see it, so no big deal, right? Just smile and ignore it and move on the next thing. Yeah, I have no idea how I'll be able to pull this makeup thing off either.

June 11

Susan is now a permanent member of our little pack. We bring her with us every time we go out. Charlie had been unsure of things at first, and he struggled with a few issues. First and foremost was his guilt.

He came clean and explained to me that he and Susan had been a couple, briefly, back before he'd met his Gretchen. But Susan had fallen for a guy named John and had tearfully broken up with him. She'd never wanted to hurt him, but she knew that John was it for her.

A year later Charlie had met Gretchen, and it was all over for him too. He immediately knew that she was the one for him, as well. Gretchen had been the love of his life and now he felt like he was dishonoring her by having feelings for Susan.

Susan didn't feel the same, and she soon set him straight. She told him they'd both lived full, happy lives and had loved other people. She had already known her soul mate, same as him. Caring about each other now, did not, *could not*, take away from what came before. Having already known great love once before didn't mean they couldn't find happiness again elsewhere. It wouldn't be the same, but who wanted it to be? It would be an all new and completely different adventure.

Susan assured him that she still had plenty of life and love left inside of her and that she wasn't quite ready to throw in the towel just yet. She felt that he shouldn't be either. When Charlie told me all this, I just nodded and told him that nobody wants to feel alone and unloved. I told him that he should greedily grab any scraps of love and happiness that he could find and that he needed to make the most of the time that he's been given. Life is so very fleeting. Live it, love it, and do not look back with regrets of what could have been.

Another thing that Charlie was also unsure of was what to tell Susan about me. He didn't know if he should explain. He didn't know *how* to explain. He didn't know how comfortable I would be with sharing details of my life with her. I told him that unless he was planning on dumping one of us, he would need to tell her everything. If she was going to be part of our lives from now on, she would need to know the truth. She would also need to make up her own mind if she even *wanted* to take on the risk of associating with me, a mental patient that all sorts of bizarre things tend to happen to.

So, he'd taken her out to dinner (ooh la la!) and confessed everything. Of course, it all came as quite a shock to her. She had just assumed that I was Charlie's granddaughter. I was in a mental hospital and had been there for years? Magic? Mirror people and death dealing dolls? It all sounded crazy, but somehow, she heard, *felt* the truth in his words. It was hard to imagine, but she'd immediately believed it all. She'd merely reached across the table and taken his hand in hers. "I'm in. Just you try to get rid of me now." It was that simple.

Charlie said he'd gotten goosebumps all over his body when she'd repeated the same exact words that I had said to him. "Nobody should feel alone and unloved." Charlie showed up the next Saturday with Susan by his side and she's been there ever since. We even initiated her into our little herd by letting her sit in the passenger seat for my driving lessons. Her face was pale, and she was breathing hard when I parked the car and turned it off, but she smiled gamely and groaned, "You, my dear, are a frightfully dreadful driver. We're definitely going to have to work on that. Can't have you out there adding to the 'women driver' stereotypes."

I heard Charlie snickering from the back seat. "Woman, if her driving skills didn't scare you away, nothing will. Welcome to our little family, Susan." I shot him a dirty look.

"But did you die, Charlie? Did you? No. You still have enough breath to dis my driving skills, so you must be fine. Sheesh. You old people are just mean!" We were all laughing as they walked me back inside the hospital. Now we're known as The Terrible Threesome instead of Double Trouble. That's what the hospital staff calls us. "Look out, everyone. The Terrible Threesome is back in the house!"

July 1

I hate makeup. I hate that I have lessons twice a week to learn to use the stuff. It always makes me look like a clown, even when Tara (the stylist) helps me. Wearing cosmetics is just one more thing that

I will *never* do once I get out of here. I would just rather go without it, and I don't see what's so wrong with that. What's wrong with the clean, natural look? I *like* just running a brush through my hair or putting it up in a simple ponytail. There really is no taming all my wild, red curls anyway. I don't want to spend an hour in front of the mirror. Who wants to waste their life away like that? I ain't got no time for that!

Oh, who am I kidding? This is my 'personal' notebook, not the fake one that I leave on my dresser for all to see. I don't like the makeup lessons because of Samara. I think that now that she's found me again, she's even more determined to get my attention. I know that ignoring her won't make her go away, but I refuse to acknowledge her. Not now, not here, in this place. I try my best to act as if I don't even see her, that I only see my own reflection. I can never let myself slip up or all will be lost. Everything I have been through, everything that I have worked so hard for these past few years, will have been for nothing.

Dr. Bradburn will drug me up, lock me down, and throw away the key so fast I won't even have time to blink. And then, I'll never be free. I can't let that happen. I *won't*. But it's all so hard! I'm so very tired of pretending and hiding. Why can't I just be who I am? Sure, I am not like everyone else, but so what? That is not a crime. I have goals and hopes and dreams just like everyone else, and I would *never* hurt anyone. Shouldn't that be the most important thing?

I guess if I'm honest with myself (and I try to always be) I don't really hate the makeup lessons. I just hate having to see Samara. I absolutely refuse to give her one single thing more than I already have. I will not help my family's murderer gain even the slightest bit more power. So, like a child, I am reduced to playing the 'I can't see you' game. I know that sometimes I don't hide it very well and that I don't always fool her.

But there have been several times that I know I've convinced her that I somehow have her blocked. I can tell by the confusion in her eyes and the anger on her face. Those times fill my heart with joy. Our day of reckoning is coming, but I can't confront her yet. Not here. I have to get out of this hospital and go somewhere far away from other people. I can't let anyone else get hurt and I *will not* take the risk of being locked back up. So, until then, until we are in a proper place to have our showdown, I'll take what petty little pleasures I can get.

When the time comes to have it out with Samara, how will I tell Charlie? How can I tell him that I have to leave him, after all that he's done for me? How can I break his heart like that…and my own? I can't think about it now. I just can't bear it. I've been shoving it all into the box in my head that's labeled 'Unpleasant Things to Worry About Later'. But that box is beginning to overflow…and later is approaching faster than I expected.

July 19

Dr. Bradburn asked me today what I thought I would do the next time I see a porcelain doll. I stare down at my hands in my lap and think about it for a minute before I can answer her. "Honestly, if you were to set one in front of me right now, I think I would be ok. If you were to surprise me with one, like if you were to walk up to me and suddenly pull one from behind your back and shove it in my face, I might react badly. I'm pretty sure I would scream, at the very least."

I looked up at her, dreading the judgement I would see on her face. "I hope that was not the wrong answer, because it was the honest one. I'm really hoping that you didn't expect me to say that I am magically cured of my fear of porcelain dolls. *That* particular phobia didn't start with the trauma I suffered. I have had an irrational fear of them my entire life. But" I hurried to add, "there are millions of people that have weird phobias. That doesn't make them crazy."

Dr. Bradburn smiled and assured me that there were no wrong or right answers. Yeah, right. I know better. There are answers that will get me released from this hellhole...those are the right answers…and then there are the ones that will keep me locked up forever and that definitely makes them wrong in my book. I've been here a long time. I have learned how to cheat the system…mostly. As I was leaving, I couldn't help but ask, "So.. Uumm...you're not gonna, right? You're not gonna shove a doll in my face or have them popping out at me, are you?" She smiled gently and assured me that she wouldn't do that to me and that any doll viewing events will be completely out in the open, no surprises. God, I really hope she was telling the truth. I've come too far to mess up now.

August 22

I have been practicing *everything*...and I mean everything, driving, applying makeup, dance lessons, and holding that stupid red Christmas ball. Yes, I can hold it and carry it around now. Repetition, that's the key, even if it makes my skin crawl. Fake it 'till you make it. I force myself to hold it in my hands every single day, because I know that Dr. Bradburn will be testing me, testing me *intensely,* before she'll allow me to be released from here. I'm certain that she'll spring all sorts of nasty little surprises at me, so I'm trying my hardest to be prepared for anything. I grit my teeth and I get through it all, and I promise myself that on my release day, I will crush that little red ball into a fine, crimson powder.

September 29

Charlie and Susan got married today!!! They wanted to surprise me, so they picked me up and took me to an undisclosed, 'secret' location. When we got to the church, I had to laugh because they seemed disappointed that I wasn't shocked. I'd already guessed exactly what was going on, as well as what they were planning. They were just too cute, all lovie-dovie and giggly.

Nora helped Susan with her dress and put the tiny pink flowers into her silver hair. I helped Charlie straighten his tie and collar. I smiled up at him, this man that meant so much to me. I wanted to tell him so many things, things that I would never be able to express with words. He just pulled me to him without a single word spoken between us and hugged me tight until the preacher said it was time to begin.

It was a very small, sweet wedding. There were only ten guests, and it only took thirty minutes from beginning to end. Nora sat beside me, and we both giggled and bawled the entire time. Afterward, we all went to Charlie and Susan's favorite restaurant for their reception party. Their little cake was the cutest thing ever. The bride and groom cake topper was a little old couple with a walker and a cane. I made sure to take lots of photos of the sweetest moments. I'm going to make them a wedding photo album. I am so very happy that they have found each other and that they're no longer alone. Today was a very good day. I seem to be having more and more of those.

October 16

I can't believe it. I passed my driving test! Charlie congratulated me and then assured me that he would now be adding all the other Houstonian drivers to his prayer list. I stuck my tongue out at him as Susan reached over and smacked him on the shoulder for me.

November 23

I spent Thanksgiving at Charlie and Susan's house yesterday. I even got to stay the night. It was such a lovely, peaceful time. I always love to leave the hospital. I don't even care where I go, as long as it's away from here. But going to Charlie's house is always great fun. Charlie and Susan dropped me back off here at ten a.m. After they were gone, I slowly walked back to my room with my spirits drastically, dangerously low.

Like always, I hated coming back. But somehow it was even worse today. And to top it all off, I guess Dr. Bradburn decided that today would be the day to begin 'testing' me to see if I am "all better'. There were red Christmas balls placed randomly throughout the hospital. I guess she thought that would freak me out? But it's all good. Really.

I've been practicing so much that I am pretty much numb to the sight of them now. I can carry my personal one around all day long if I have to. I certainly don't want to, but I *can* do it. I have already convinced the good doctor that my mirror hallucinations are over with for good. I put makeup on every single day now. Minimal amounts, just the basics really, but it has been enough to convince her that all is well when I look into the mirror. Jokes on her though. I've taught myself how to put makeup on without seeing my reflection.

December 3

I'm done with school! I have finished my last courses, passed all my finals exams, and successfully earned an Associates of Art degree…and I am *done*. No more schooling for me, at least not for the time being. I will (probably…maybe) eventually go back and continue my education, but for now I just want to focus on being free, free to do whatever I want and go wherever I want. Freedom, such a wonderful thing. I can't wait for the day when I can actually say it and mean it. It's getting closer every day.

December 17

I had to make a show of putting my makeup on for Dr. Bradburn. I guess I didn't have her quite as convinced as I thought I did. I only tried to stab my own eye out once, so that's a plus. I have a daily routine that I can get through in seven minutes, tops. I was at the six-minute mark, when I tried to impale my right eyeball onto a mascara wand.

I'd just started to relax, because I was so close to being done. In fact, I'd already finished my left eye and was putting the mascara on my right, when Samara decided to show up and scare the daylights out of me. Ever watch a horror movie where the scary thing suddenly jumps out at you with a scream from hell? Yep. That's exactly what she did. Only, this isn't a movie. It's my life.

One second it was just me in the mirror and the next second, she was there, filling my vision with the horror of her. She was covered, absolutely drenched, in blood and gore. There were even chunks of.... *things* in her hair and sliding down her face. At the very moment that she appeared, her blood curdling scream also somehow ripped through my mind. The sudden viciousness startled me enough to make my hand jerk and jab the mascara wand into my eye.

I was expecting her to show up and try something, but not *this*. I somehow managed not to scream at the fear or the pain, so I just tried to play the incident off as if nothing had happened. I pretended that I'd poked myself in the eye simply because I got the wand too close.

"I'm ok. Happens all the time, no big deal," I muttered as I wiped the tears and smudges away. When my eye finally stopped watering, I looked back into that mirror at Samara's nasty, bloody smile. With my heart threatening to explode out of my chest, I leaned in close, pretended that I saw my own face, and calmly finished putting on my makeup.

Even though she was clearly suspicious of the wand in the eye mishap, I think my cover up performance has *finally* convinced Dr. Bradburn that my 'mirror hallucinations' are gone. If not, I just don't know what else it will take. I think I deserve an award for my acting skills today.

Christmas

December 25

Christmas sucked so bad. This year, Dr. Bradburn wanted me to stay here, where she could observe me. She refused to let me go to Charlie and Susan's house and she wouldn't let them come here either. (Not that I would have let them. It's their first Christmas together. It wouldn't be fair to ask them to spend it here in this disgusting place.)

Dr. Bradburn's reasoning was that she needed to see how I would react to being alone on Christmas, without having my anchor (Charlie) there to keep me grounded. It's just another challenge in a long list of tests. I *know* that she thought I was going to flip out. But I didn't! I got through every nasty little aspect of this dreadful holiday all on my own.

If I'm being reasonable, I can kind of understand where Dr. Bradburn's coming from. She's just trying to cover her own A-double-S. She has to be extremely careful and overly critical. She would be held responsible for any damage I may cause once I get released from here. But I don't feel very reasonable right now. I feel angry, so very angry. I am so sick of feeling like a bug under a microscope or a rat in a maze. "Let's see what we can do today to make Ecko freak out."

I feel Rage begin to stir and drowsily roll over in his sleep, so I put my headphones on, turn the volume up loud, and play my 'Calm-yourself-down-now-or-you-will-regret-it-forever-Do-you-want-them-to-lock- you-up-and-throw-away-the-key' playlist. I fill my head with someone else's love, hate, happiness, sadness, desire, hopes, and dreams and I dance around my room. I sing and I dance for *hours*. I sing and dance until the storms in my head subside, my heart slows back to normal, and the monsters sleep quietly again… until I finally fall into my bed in exhaustion.

I really need to do something about all these 'boxes' inside my head. Things can't go on like this forever. I *know* that. But I have to get away from people, as far away from people as I can get. Then, I will take each monster out, one by one and figure out what to do with them, permanently. I need a real solution, instead of just locking them all away and avoiding them. If I don't, one day, one of my monsters is going to break loose. With my luck, it would bust the rest of its friends out of their prison cells too. I have to be far away from here if/when that happens, because I think a whole lot of bad is going to happen when Rage gets out. I don't want to hurt anyone, well, except Samara. I hope I can hold Rage back until I meet up with her. When that day finally comes, I will happily unlock the chains and swing the cell door open wide…and I'll invite him to come out and play.

December 26

I am in total, complete shock. I don't even know what just happened. I'm in the back seat of Charlie's car with my small box of belongings beside me. I'm writing this all down, because it helps me work things out in my head. I am just going to write it all out so maybe when I go back and read it, it will all finally make sense to me.

I woke up to a knock on my door this morning at exactly 8:00. One of the morning nurses informed me that Dr. Bradburn wanted to see me in her office. My heart instantly froze up inside my chest. This had never happened before, so I was immediately on my guard.

Heck with that...I was petrified. I got dressed slowly, dragging it out as long as possible. While I shuffled my way down the hall to her office (at a snail's pace and dragging my feet), my mind ran through so many scenarios, some very likely and some outright ridiculous. It didn't matter even the slightest bit that most of them made no sense. They were still terrifying.

Had Dr. Bradburn lied to me? Was she going to have a doll in there with her? More than one? Were there teddy bears involved...or a bouncy house full of red Christmas balls that she would want me to jump into to show that I was 'rehabilitated'? Then the most horrifying image popped into my head, a porcelain doll with red Christmas balls for eyes, just like Coraline's Other family with their button eyes.

If I walked in and saw that, it would have been game over, instantly. They would have to lock me up tight with no possibility for parole. It was such a disturbing image that I almost couldn't make myself knock on the door. But eventually I managed to muster up the nerve to force one tiny rap of my knuckles against the door.

Dr. Bradburn brusquely instructed me to come inside. My hand trembled on the doorknob, and I had to take several deep breaths to calm myself. It didn't work, but I turned the knob and pushed the door open anyway. I did get a surprise, but not an unpleasant one...just a puzzling one.

Dr. Bradburn was seated in her usual spot behind the desk. But four chairs had been set across from her and three of them were occupied. Charlie, Susan, and Renee all turned to look at me as I cautiously stepped into the room. My eyes darted all around, frantically searching for any hidden threats. When I determined that I was safe for the moment, I turned my attention to Dr. Bradburn. "What is this? What's going on?"

Charlie could see that I was in panic mode. He was quick to reassure me. "Good things Ecko, my girl. All good things! Breathe.

Relax. We have some news for you, that's all. Come sit next to me." I released the breath that I hadn't realized I had trapped inside and nodded my head.

I looked up at Charlie with questions in my eyes as I sat in the chair next to him. He just patted me on the shoulder and turned his attention back to Dr. Bradburn. Susan reached across him and took my hand, and I clutched it like it was a lifeline.

"Adrina, I have decided to put you into a new program…." I didn't give the doctor a chance to finish.

"But why?" I desperately burst out. "I have done everything you wanted me to do. I've followed every single rule! I am finally doing good!" My stupid eyes welled up with foolish tears. I can't go backwards. I just can't. I will run away and never look back. I braced myself for a fight and for flight. I shot a quick glance at the door over my shoulder. I'm a goner if she tries to take away a single privilege.

Dr. Bradburn smiled reassuringly, but what she didn't realize was that her smile has never put me at ease. Not once. "Calm down, Adrina and hear me out please. You're going to like this program. You'll be 18 in three months and at that time you will be released and no longer under my care. You have made so much progress. I firmly believe that you still suffer many effects from the trauma you faced, but that is to be expected. You will probably always have a few issues, but that is completely normal and to be expected. Everyone has issues that they have to deal with in their lives. I think that you've learned how to deal with yours and that you are now able to work through any problems that may arise. So long as you take your medications, I'm positive that you can easily keep it all under control."

"Well, this new program… " she continued, "If you're willing, I'm going to release you on a temporary, trial basis. You will live with Charlie and Susan for the three months between now and your birthday. You'll still have to come in for your sessions twice a week, mostly just to check in and assure me that you are doing as well as I think that you'll do. If all goes as planned and there have been no major setbacks in your recovery, I will sign your release papers, your REAL release papers, on your birthday. So, Adrina, what do you think of my new program *now?*" Dr. Bradburn laughed at the dumbfounded look that I'm sure was on my face. I couldn't process what she'd told me. I glanced over at Renee. She smiled and said, "Congratulations Ecko. *You made it.* I'm so very happy for you. You deserve this." I looked over at Charlie in desperation, hoping that he could make sense of it all for me.

He had tears just pouring down his face. "You did it, my girl. You've worked so hard; you've come so far. It's finally time for you to be done with this place and come home…where you belong." He reached for his handkerchief and wiped his old eyes.

My eyes dumbly followed every move his hands made. I was so shocked that I couldn't even think straight. "You would let me live with you? Even knowing how crazy I am? Susan? You're ok with this too?"

Charlie's eyes flashed and his face flushed with a sudden, intense anger. "Don't you ever let me hear you say that again. You know damn well that you're not crazy. You have *never* been crazy. Just terribly wounded. And of course, I want you to finally come home and live with us. Susan is fine with it too. She *wants* you there with us."

Wow. Just *wow.* I had seen Charlie mad a few times before, but it had never been directed at me. "I'm sorry!" I cried out. "Please don't be mad at me. I'm just scared that I'll let you down. I don't want you to ever regret getting involved in me."

Charlie's eyes softened and he relaxed his clenched jaw. "Don't you know by now, girl? I love you. I couldn't love you anymore if you were my own daughter," he whispered as he wrapped his arms around me. I couldn't help it. I couldn't hold it back any longer. Tears ran down my face like tiny, rapid-flowing rivers.

Susan leaned over and wrapped me up in her arms too. We sat there like that, all of us crying for a long time. Even Renee had to conspicuously wipe her eyes a time or two. I couldn't seem to stop bawling long enough to regain control and pull myself together.

Finally, though, Charlie let out a gruff laugh and untangled himself from our embrace. He said that we had paperwork to sign before he could spring me from the joint and that we had better get to it. We had celebrating to do! He said that he'd already made dinner reservations *and* found us a club that we could go swing dancing at.

Now here we are, on our way to Charlie's...I mean *our* house (What? How crazy is that!) from the hospital and I'm functioning in a weird state of shock. I can't wrap my head around the fact that I won't have to spend another night in that place, not ever again. *That* is the fact that I keep coming back to.

More than anything else, I just can't imagine being able to sleep at night in peace and without fear, no fear of being drugged or strapped down for days at a time, no fear of things being done to me without my consent, completely against my will. I would no longer have to fear the other patients, the ones with the unpredictable, violent natures, or perverted old men with giant noses that have the power to do terrible things to people that can't protect themselves. I would have no fear of being locked away and forgotten, of being deprived of food until I slowly starve to death. I have lived with all these uncertainties, and so many more, for years. I can't even imagine what it's going to feel like to be able to sleep soundly, secure in the knowledge that I am finally safe. I guess I'll find out tonight. But first, I have a dancing date to attend.

December 27

We had so much fun on our dance date! It turned out to be even better than I'd hoped for. Charlie had somehow gotten everyone in on it. All of our dancing friends that had been joining us in the park every weekend for lessons were there at the club to dance the night away with us. During a break (I don't know how those old folks do it. I *had* to take a breather!) I stood aside and watched Charlie and Susan dancing the Watusi.

Nora was out there on the dance floor too, dancing with a man that she'd met at our lessons in the park. I watched all of our new friends, these happy people just out having a great time. *All* of this was because of Charlie. None of these people, myself included, had known any of these old dances until he took the time to teach us. I'm so lucky that he decided to care about me and be a part of my life. I hope I'm worth it. I hope he never has reason to regret it.

I couldn't help but laugh when he boogied his way over to me and pulled me back onto the dance floor. He leaned down and yelled in my ear, "Resting is for the weak. You got no business taking a break! Get back out here and dance, girl!" He let out a loud whoop when the next song started playing, "Hound Dog", by Elvis Presley. He absolutely loves dancing to Elvis songs and this one was his favorite.

All I could do was roll my eyes and dance along with him. There was no way I was going to disappoint that man. Not even with a tiny thing like sitting out for a dance to catch a breather. I would dance until my feet fell off if that's what he wanted from me, which actually almost happened. We danced until the club closed down and they threw us all out!

We didn't get home until 3:00 in the morning. My feet hurt so badly, and I was so utterly exhausted that I didn't even brush my teeth or change out of my poodle skirt. I stumbled straight into my room and fell face first onto my bed and didn't move again for 10 hours. There was no time for me to lay in bed and think up things to be afraid of.

Charlie probably planned it that way, the sly, thoughtful old dog. It would be just like him to find a way to make the first night in my new bed easier to handle. He knows me so well. He knew that I would lie awake worrying about everything and that I would come up with all sorts of stuff to frighten myself. He probably wanted to distract me from all that, so I would actually be able to sleep. He succeeded brilliantly. I was snoring the instant that my face landed on my pillow.

March 1

This will be my last entry in these notebooks. Writing in these journals has really helped me get through these past few years, but I'm done with all of that now. I don't want to remember my time in the hospital. I just want to forget. I want to move on with my life. I have so much living to do, so much lost time to make up for.

We only ever get one life to live, with just a few short handfuls of years to live it. And I want to live. *Really* live. I want to do it all, see it all. So, tomorrow morning I will take a shovel and follow that old map that my dad and I drew all those years ago. I will keep my promise to dig up our time-capsule and then I'm going to add these journals to it. I will lay these books in the ground and bury them, and I will hope that I can put aside those troubled years just as easily. I don't know if I will continue the ritual every ten years, but I have to honor this first anniversary. The journals are the perfect (and only) thing I have to offer. I have nothing else. Maybe that will change when this is all done.

I plan to get my own apartment as soon as I am completely free. I have less than a month of sessions left with Dr. Bradburn, and I'm no longer worried at all about 'failing' and being sent back. Everything is going perfectly. But even if they weren't, I'm not going back. I will never go back. I have felt freedom. I have remembered the taste of it on my tongue. Even if it somehow all goes to hell, they won't take me back there alive. I won't allow it.

Signed,
Adrina Ecko Roberts

Come Out and Play

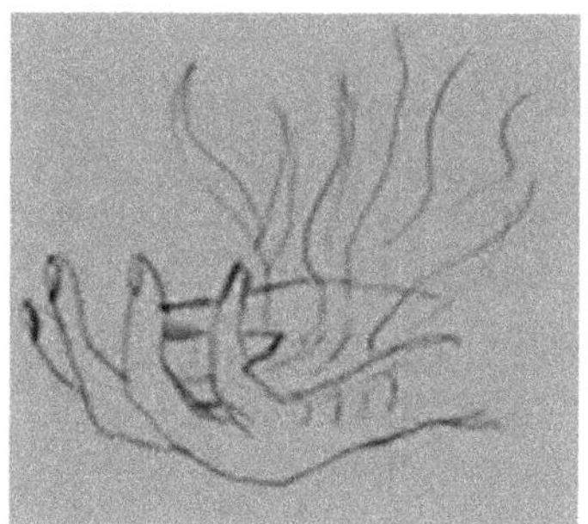

It's time. I will not spend one more second as my father's puppet, his scapegoat, his perpetual whipping girl. I've spent my entire life searching for my sister. Don't get me wrong. I *want* to find her. I want to make her pay for every single misery she has caused me, every wrong ever done to me, all in the name of getting her back to our father. I *will* find her and make her sorry she'd ever dared to share a womb with me. And then I'll set myself up in her world, far from my father's reach.

But I have priorities. I have to remove this binding spell first and get out of here, escape from this house and my father's unlimited supply of goons. And then I want some play time. I need it. I *deserve* it…and I will have it, one way or another. Oh yes, I'm coming for you Krispin.

I wait for my next bathroom break to make my move. Thankfully this guard has grown careless. He's gotten too used to my total cooperation and my quick obedience to his commands. Sadly, for him, he does not pay me enough attention now and I'm able to slip my chunk of mirror into my clothes and smuggle it out of the room with me.

There's no other way out of the privy room and no lock on the door to prevent them from entering whenever they wish, so I'm usually allowed a bit of privacy to do my business. Sometimes, I'm forced to deal with the perverted guards that like to watch, but this particular man isn't one of those. I knew he wouldn't be tempted in coming in to watch me. Thankfully, I don't have the right equipment to interest him. Now, had I been the boy that my father had expected me to be, that would have been a different story. He probably wouldn't have granted me the privacy to pee in peaceful solitude.

I close the bathroom door behind me and immediately drop to the floor. I prop my back against the door and push my feet against the wall opposite me to hold it shut. The guards are much stronger than me and I won't be able to hold them back for more than a few seconds, if they become suspicious, but maybe it'll buy me just enough time to get the job done.

I remove my smuggled mirror from my clothing and position the sharpest point directly above the golden tattoo that surrounds my ankle. My hand shakes with undeniable terror and I take a deep breath to try and calm myself. It doesn't work, but I plunge the sharp glass down anyway, a half inch above the tattoo.

I bite my lip to hold back the cry of pain, as I slice a furrow all the way around my leg. Then I do the same a half inch below it, until the tattoo is sandwiched in between the two bleeding cuts.

So far so good, nothing has gone wrong yet. But I haven't actually tried to cut the tattoo itself yet, just the skin around it. There's a hard thump on the door behind me and the guard yells, "Hurry up in there!" I am so focused on my task that his shouted command through the door startles me, causing me to jerk my hand back. The mirror, slick with blood, slips right out of my hand and clunks loudly to the floor.

"Time's up!" he shouts just before he tries to barge in and retrieve me. The door slams against my back and shoves my feet against the wall. My strategic position works just how I'd intended, it buys me a few precious seconds to finish what I've started. I snatch the mirror back up and with no time left for doubt, I slice a vertical line that connects the top wound to the bottom one. The mirror cuts right through the tattoo with no resistance whatsoever.

I release the breath I had been unaware of holding inside me with a relieved hiss through my clenched teeth. It worked! I'm still alive! But not for long if I don't hurry it up. The guard is shouting now and pushing against the door with all his weight. The strain of trying to hold him back is threatening to buckle my legs, to shatter them at the knees.

I slip my fingers up underneath the wound that I'd just cut through the tattoo, working them in until I can get a grip on the resulting flap of skin. Screaming in sheer agony, I slowly rip the loosened swatch of skin that contains the spelled tattoo right up off my leg. It makes a horridly wet, tearing sound as it rips free. I hold it up in front of my face and watch in awe as the tattoo begins to burn, turning the once golden threads to black ash that sprinkles down to land in my lap. I'm left holding up a bloody patch of skin that shows no evidence of ever having been tattooed.

The moment, the very *instant,* that it's free of my body and incinerated to ash, I feel the magic flare to life. I feel the completeness, the insertion of a missing link snapping into place inside me. This is it. *This* is what I've been missing my entire life. Power surges inside me, much too big for my body to contain. It shoots out of me, out of my eyes, my nose and ears. It explodes out of my fingertips like invisible flames, out of my very pores even. All I can do is scream as all my senses are completely overloaded, scrambled, reorganized, and then put back together; scream until it all finally settles in place inside me.

I slowly lift my head and grin. I know that had anyone been in here to see it, they would have fled in terror, immediately and as fast and far away as they could manage. Oh, but I feel *good*. I feel powerful. I feel *nasty*. Briefly, I wonder if this is how Ecko had felt when she'd aimed all that blue energy at me, but then I push all thoughts of *her* from my mind. There will be time for my dear, sweet sister later.

It's time to focus on me for a change. Right now, I want to find out what revenge tastes like. I want to surround myself with my enemies' heads, slather myself with their blood, lick it from my fingertips. And I want to find Krispin and see if he tastes as good as I've imagined. There's so much I want to do, all at once. Yes, Ecko will just have to wait for her turn while I go out and play.

The pounding on the door has ceased and I open it to find the guard embedded into the wall across the hallway. He is badly burnt, charred and blackened, with smoke pouring out of the holes in his face. He no longer has a nose, ears or eyeballs, just bloody, burnt out cavities that belch out smoke. He'd been standing entirely too close when the power surged through me. It struck him with such force that he was instantly crispy fried and flung backwards to become a permanent wall ornament.

His fists are clenched and raised above his head, forever locked in the upraised position of banging upon the door. The other three guards back away as I walk through the house. I laugh maniacally when the two old fools back themselves into their bedroom and slam the door shut. As if that would stop me, had I wanted to pursue them. I didn't, not yet anyway. I have better toys to play with right now. I sit down on the wobbly, wooden chair in the living room, as regally as if it were a golden throne and I it's queen. The guards watch me with wary, suspicious eyes, and who could blame them? They *knew* that terrible things were headed their way. They also knew that they deserved whatever punishment I decided to serve them.

I raise my hands and my Shadows, stronger than ever, pour out for the terrified guards to breathe into themselves, like breathing in the smoke from a lit thistle-root cigar. They cough and choke and sputter on my Shadows, clawing desperately at their throats in an effort to rid themselves of the invasive, cloying mass filling them full of dread. But there's no escape. They stop fighting and go motionless, as the light fades from their eyes.

My heart pounds at the thought of all the wicked things I could do to them, what I can make *them* do to each other. I stand up and go to them, circling round and round them as I think up and disregard ideas. "I've got it!" I yell into the silence. I lean in and whisper, "Eat." Then I go back to my throne to watch.

The three unfortunate guards give a single simultaneous whimper as they turn to face one another. Then they open their mouths wide and begin to bite huge chunks of flesh out of one another. They chew and swallow, then repeat. Bite, chew and swallow, over and over again, their eyes wide with pain and fear and horror until I can contain my giddiness no longer. I throw my head back and scream peals of delighted laughter up at the rooftop. The guards eat and eat and eat until their bellies are hugely, grossly distended. Large pits have been hollowed out of their bodies and entire limbs are missing completely.

The first one finally drops, dead or close to it, and the remaining two fall upon him, burying their faces into his soft, opened belly. The next one drops and twitches on the floor for a few moments before going still and quiet. Finally, the third one is all done with his last meal. I think *his* belly blew up from the massive dinner he'd just consumed.

As I stand up to leave, I turn my head and look towards the old geezer's door. All I see are two pairs of eyes, opened wide and shocked, peeping out at me through the crack. When my eyes meet theirs, the door slams shut so fast that the old man's nose gets pinched in it. My peals of laughter join his howls of pain and make a most beautiful duet.

"I'm coming Krispin," I whisper, as I step outside. I sure hope he wants to come out and play. If he doesn't, he will be very, *very* sorry. Either way, I'm bound to have the time of my life!

Jinkies! I Found a Clue, Scooby Doo

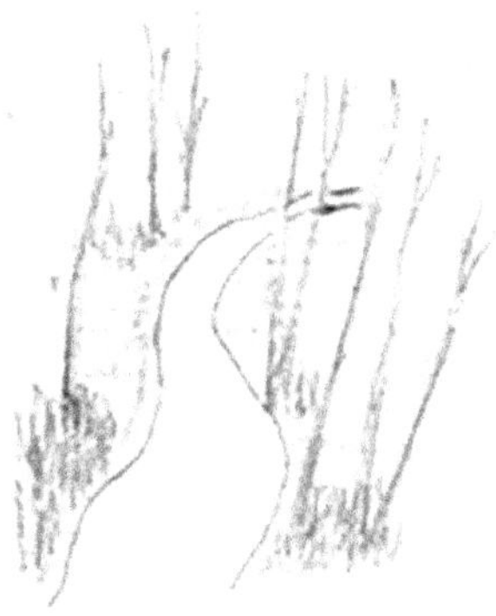

Ecko set out on her mission bright and early that morning to avoid another confrontation with Charlie. When he'd learned of her plans to dig up her old time-capsule, he tried his best to talk her into allowing him to come along. He didn't want her to face that all alone. He'd felt that he needed to be there. It took a while, but she'd finally convinced him that this was something she had to do alone. But she still made sure she was gone before he woke up anyway, just in case. She didn't want to upset him or go against his wishes, but if she was going to start living and making a life for herself, she had to do things on her own. Now was as good a time to start as any. She couldn't be coddled and babied forever.

Melancholy descends upon her the moment that she enters the woods. The memories, haunting and poignant, rush in and take her back in time. They threaten to drown her in sorrow as she steps onto the familiar path. She doesn't need the map for this part of her journey; she remembers it as if she'd been here just yesterday. Her feet know exactly where to go. To distract herself from falling further into despondency, she searches for all her old favorite landmarks as she walks along. She's surprised to see that everything is mostly the same. Not much had changed in the time that she'd been away. That seems so unreal to her.

So much had happened in her life since she'd last walked this trail. It's unsettling to find that things here had not changed right along with her. She feels as if she's gone back in time. She briefly entertains the idea of spinning around and running back to see if her house still stood, if everything had all been just a bad dream. But no. The notebooks clutched in her hand tell the truth of the past. If she were to go back and look, it would still be just an empty lot with a lonely, abandoned treehouse. As much as she may wish otherwise, this is her reality, her life…and it is bitterly disappointing. No matter what happens to her, what trials she may face, these woods will continue on as they always had.

While she's comforted by the fact that at least one part of her childhood remains intact, she also feels a bit resentful. How is it possible that this place shows no signs of devastation when *she* had suffered so much? How had it been left completely untouched and unscathed? At this very moment, Ecko is learning a very hard truth, the same one that millions of others before her had been taught. Even though her whole life had been ripped apart, the world just kept right on turning. Mother Nature will always, always do her own thing. She does not care what happens in the small lives of small girls. It's a hard pill for her to swallow. But swallow it she must, as she makes her way to the little stream, coughing and choking on that harsh truth pill the entire time.

X marks the spot, and she digs until she unearths her buried treasure. Tears drip off her chin as she sits on the sandy stream bank to open the large, plastic box. She misses her father more than ever as memories assail her. She remembers them picking out this box, their time-capsule.

They'd needed a container that would be big enough to hold years of memories, and it had needed to be weatherproof to protect all of their secrets. They'd found this one at a Goodwill thrift shop and had immediately deemed it to be perfect. They'd brought it home, put their 'treasures' inside it and carried it all the way through the woods and buried it here by the stream. Afterwards, sweaty and exhausted but well- pleased with themselves, they'd sat down and drawn out their treasure map together.

Now, Ecko feels her heart breaking with each item that she takes out to inspect. There are several little trinkets that would never be worth anything to anyone, but her and her father, dried flowers, friendship bracelets, hand drawn pictures they'd given to one another, the cheap plastic ring that she had given to her dad when she was four years old… and the book of Wishes! She had forgotten all about this one!

The book of Wishes was created before she could even write down her own hopes and dreams. Dan had written them down for her, all those old childish dreams. The very first one was a wish from her. "If I have to get married someday, I only want to be married to my Daddy."

The next entry was from Dan. "If Ecko CHOOSES to get married someday, I hope it's to someone that treasures her just as much as I do." The Wish Book is only about halfway filled. They'd left plenty of room to add new hopes and dreams. Ecko has only one to add now. "I wish you were here, Daddy." It is the wish of all wishes. She swipes at her tears as she sets the book aside. She intuitively knows that she will never add another wish.

There are several photos to look through, for which she is eternally grateful for. The Bad Thing had taken most of her photos right along with her family. (Which reminds her...she has to ask Dr. Bradburn about the rest of her belongings that had been brought to the hospital with her. One of her photo albums had made it through the fire and she wants it back.) She is so grateful that her dad had decided to add these pictures to their time-capsule. There are a few family photos, a hand sketched cartoonish portrait of the whole family from one of their trips to Kemah, and a whole stack of photos of just the two of them. She sobs uncontrollably as she looks through them. What she wouldn't give to have him back.

The last thing in the time-capsule is a book, and it's a book that definitely shouldn't be in there. It's her hand drawn, handmade book of fairies, the one that she had absolutely adored. She pauses and stares down at it in confusion. They did *not* put this book in here, she's absolutely positive about that. It had been one of her most treasured possessions and there was no way she could have willingly parted with it.

She gently lifts it out of the box and runs her hands over it in wonder. She can't believe that it's here, safe in her hands. She thought it had been taken by the fire, along with everything else she had ever loved. But how? How can this be? She opens the cover and there it is, the answer. It's a letter from her father.

He explained that years after they had buried their capsule, he'd woken up in the middle of the night from a horrible nightmare. He had dreamed that Ecko was trapped in the dark, locked inside a room behind a terrible red door. He couldn't remember much else about it, just ghastly bits and pieces. The images were all mixed up and made no sense in his waking mind. Flashes of shadows, cruel smiling lips that dripped blood, a wall of flames and pools of bright red blood, a gravestone with his name on it, and finally, her beloved book of fairies.

He'd had terrible nightmares before, many of them since she had come into his life. But this was different. *This* one had the sinister feel of promise, or fate perhaps, a premonition of things to come. He'd been shaken to the core, inexplicably horrified. Dan went on to tell of how he had quietly gotten out of bed, snuck into her room, and taken her book. He'd climbed up into the treehouse, quickly scratched out this note, retrieved the map, and then ran all the way to the stream to bury it where it would be safe.

He went on to explain that he had no idea *why* he had to put the book of fairies in the time-capsule. He was not sure if it was the book or his next words that needed protecting, but it was probably both.

Ecko flips the paper over to read the message on the back.

'If you are reading this, then something has happened to me, and I was not able to reveal the truths that I was instructed to share with you. I was supposed to tell you who you are and where you came from…to the best of my ability, for there are so many things that I don't know. I was to tell you all that I DO know and explain exactly why things had to be so complicated, so secretive. And why it all has to *remain* secret.

I was also instructed to give you something. Two things, actually. I have already given you one of them, though you are not aware of it. I pray to God that you still have it because you will never find the second without it. And it is all so very important. YOU are so very important, and *you have no idea.* I always meant to tell you the truth, but the time never seemed right. Or maybe I just kept putting it off. Maybe I didn't want you to look at me differently. I hope that wasn't the case. I truly hope I wasn't that selfish.

But I guess the reasons why I didn't have 'the talk' with you don't even matter now, not really. And I'm sorry. I can't actually tell you anything in this note either. I have to protect you, even if I'm not physically there to do so anymore, even if it's from my grave. Your safety means everything to me. If anything were to happen to you, because of me, because I wasn't careful enough.... All the hiding, the cover ups, the lies, all the hurt I caused will have been for nothing if I were to get careless and something happens to you now. I can't even think about it. It's just too horrible to consider.

I'm sorry, sweet Ecko. I know I sound like a crazy person. None of this will make any sense to you right now, but it will. I promise that at least some of it will finally make sense. But you HAVE to find the clue I left for you. The truth lies in Didymus. Find it and follow it and everything will be explained to you, every bit of the truth that I know.

But I also have to warn you. You *will* get some answers, but knowing the truth is going to bring about even more questions. Of that I'm certain. I, myself have lived the whole of your life plagued with questions, doubts, uncertainties, and fear. So much fear, all the time.

I am so scared for you, Kiddo, of what lies ahead for you. I'm afraid of what may happen to us all. I'm terrified that I didn't do the right things, that I didn't make the right choices. Did I do right by keeping the secrets locked up inside of me all these years? Could I have told part of the truth and soothed some troubled minds, bandaged some wounded hearts? Would it have even helped? Or made things worse? I just don't know. I don't know the answers and I guess I never will, because I'm even more afraid of what may happen if I *don't* keep the secrets buried. So, I will remain silent, at least for now. Hopefully, the time will come when I can finally be done with the secrets and the lies, and then I will make things right. But I had to write all this down and put it where I knew that only you would find it. Just in case.

I can only imagine how frustrated and confused you are. I'm sorry for that, more than you will ever know. I'm sorry for so very many things. But I want you to know that I love you. I want you to hear my voice in your mind as you read these words. I love you, no matter what. You are my daughter and I love you. *And I would do it all again.* Love you always and forever, Dad.'

Ecko doesn't know what to think or how to feel. There is so much chaos and confusion swirling around inside her mind that even Rage begins to stir inside of his box. Not so much from being fed her anger, but from the sheer force of emotions that are currently bombarding her. She imagines that it's almost as if someone had taken her life and cut it up into a thousand puzzle pieces. Then they tossed them up into the air and let them fall wherever they may. Now she's left to scramble around and search for all her pieces to put herself back together. But there are so many pieces missing, too many.

She begins to question everything, especially her sanity. Had she even left the hospital at all? Is she really here right now, in these woods, reading a letter from her dead father? Or is she still strapped down on a gurney, drugged out of her mind and living out a strange, make-believe reality? Had she actually died in the fire along with her family? Is this some sort of sadistic purgatory? She drops to the ground, tucks her head between her knees and takes slow, deep breaths. In and out. In and out. Be calm. Breathe.

She manages to talk herself through the panic attack. It takes a while, but she finally wrestles her fear back into its proper compartment. But even though she's considerably calmer, her hands still shake as she places everything back into the time-capsule. Everything but the letter.

She even returns the fairy book. She considered taking it with her. She wants to, but it just doesn't feel right. There must have be a reason for why her father had felt compelled to bury it here.

Besides, she tells herself, she could always come back and retrieve it whenever she wanted. She hastily adds the three journals, seals the time-capsule back up, and then reburies it. She stands over the mound of dirt for a moment, just trying to catch her breath and gather her chaotic thoughts. She decides to say a few words, as if she were attending a funeral, which, in a way, she really was. She was trying her best to lay her troubled past to rest.

"Well Dad," she whispered. "I made it. Our first ten-year anniversary. I wish you were here. I miss you so much. I am so confused! My head is always so messed up and crazy. And now, on top of everything else, I have to figure out what your weird, cryptic letter means. Find clues? Where do I even start looking for clues? And clues to what? I don't know what to do! I just want all this madness to stop!" She listens to the deafening silence all around her.

She takes one final look around and realizes that she'll find no answers here. So, she swipes at the tears in her eyes and heads back to the trail. The tears blur her vision, causing her to stumble a bit on the walk back to Charlie's. But that's nothing new. It feels as if she's been stumbling along her entire life. Every time she gains confidence and feels steady enough to take a step forward, her world shifts beneath her feet again and she's right back to bumbling along.

Charlie, as expected, is waiting for her on the porch when she finally makes it back. He sighs with heartfelt relief when he sees her, but then frowns as he gets a better look. She's covered in dirt, and she has bits of leaves and grass in her hair. She looks exhausted, and she's been crying. Her face is red, and her eyes are puffy and swollen. He knew that he should have gone with her!

She sits down beside him on the swing and lays her head on his shoulder. He just wraps his arms around her and waits. She's quiet now, but he knows that she'll eventually open up. He doesn't have to wait long. The whole story erupts from her, like a swollen river bursting through its dam… and he can't understand a word of it. She's crying and half yelling, her words coming out so fast that they all blur together. There's an overabundance of tears, snot, and hiccups involved. Her hands are everywhere, gesturing and pointing back towards the trail in the woods. Then she pulls out a piece of paper and thrusts it at him, "See?"

Charlie takes the paper from her and sets it aside. Then he takes her hands in his and calmly looks her in the eye. "I want you to go inside and take a nice, hot bath. It's cold out here and your hands feel like ice. Relax. Wash away all this dirt. Try not to think about anything, but how nice the bath feels. Calm your heart. Calm your mind. Susan and I will go make us all some lunch while you're in the bath. You'll feel better when you're clean and have some food in you. And then the three of us will work all this out. Together. You are *not* alone. We'll figure it out."

Ecko lays her forehead against his chest for a long moment and takes slow, deep breaths. The familiar scent of his peppermint oil comforts and calms her enough so that she can get a handle on her emotions. Finally, she nods and whispers, "Love you so much, Charlie."

She's enormously comforted by his gruff response. "I love you too, my girl. Go on with you now. Get yourself into the bath." As she heads inside to do as she's told, she hears him conspicuously trying to clear his throat and hold his tears at bay. As the door closes behind her, Charlie picks up the letter and frowns as he reads it. *Now* what's happening to his poor girl, he wonders, and how much more can she possibly take?

Later, after she had taken a very relaxing and healing bath, Susan serves up bowls of hot, comforting cheddar and broccoli soup, along with thick slices of fresh bread, slathered with butter. "Thank you for lunch, Susan. The soup was amazing. It was just what I needed," Ecko compliments as she leans back in her chair. Charlie was right. She does feel much better now that she's clean and her belly is full. She's had time to calm down and she's thinking a bit more clearly now. The three of them are sitting at the table sipping their coffees, puzzling over the letter lying in front of them like it's written in some sort of alien dialect. No matter how many times they read it, they just can't make sense of it.

Even Charlie's beginning to get frustrated though. "Why does it all have to be so secretive? Why can't your father just come out and say what he needs to say. How could he possibly think that leaving a crazy, cryptic letter for you to find and then keeping you in the dark is protecting you? What's he protecting you from? And where could he have possibly left clues? Clues to what?! This is all so frustrating!"

She feels guilty for bringing more stress into his life and she starts to get teary again. Sniffling, she apologizes with a soft, regretful tone of voice. "I'm sorry that it's always one thing after another with me. I'm sorry that I'm so crazy and my life is so unstable. I'm sorry that craziness follows me everywhere I go."

Charlie grunts at her. "I keep telling you. you are not crazy! Yes, strange things happen to you, but that doesn't make you crazy. And I wouldn't care even if you *were* crazy. You could lick the windows, eat crayons, wear a helmet, run into walls, and occasionally pee on yourself and I would still love you. You are special, Girl. You mean the world to me."

Susan covers her mouth to hide the grin on her face. She just loves watching these two together. It's hard to believe that they'd only known each other for a few short years. They act as though they'd known each other their whole lives. "I agree with Charlie. You are definitely not crazy, but it *does* seem to surround you. This letter is proof of that." She glances down at the letter, points at a line and mutters, "I keep coming back to this line right here. This, more than any other thing that your father wrote, makes no sense to me. 'The truth lies in Didymus'. What in the world could he possibly mean by that? What, or where, is Didymus? Maybe we should look for clues in that old treehouse. Perhaps we'll find some answers there."

Susan continues rambling on, but Ecko no longer hears her. Her thoughts are whirling all over the place, as if her head is filled with hurricane strength winds that are blowing and tossing them about. Didymus. The answer lies in Didymus…hhmmm.

"My favorite movie of all time is The Labyrinth. I absolutely adored it when I was a kid. I watched it all the time, so much so that I had every line memorized. I can still recite the entire movie today.

It was creative and imaginative, full of magic, hobglins, and odd fae creatures. One of those creatures was a little guardian dog with an eye patch, a tiny fierce protector. He was such a funny little…" She stops and frowns in thought.

Then her eyes light up and she grins up at Charlie and Susan. "Oh my God!" she suddenly shouts as she thumps her fist down onto the table. "I know where the clue is! It's in Didymus!" Then she starts laughing hysterically, complete with little snorts and shoulders shaking. The confused looks on her old friends' faces just sets her off more. She laughs and laughs until she realizes that even though she now understands where the clue is hidden, there might just be a problem with getting a hold of it. That sobers her back up and her laughter subsides.

"The dog, the little dog protector from the movie, his name was Sir Didymus. I used to have terrible nightmares and so my dad bought me a stuffed Sir Didymus plushie to protect me from my night terrors. I loved that little guy so much. He and I went through all sorts of adventures together. Don't you see? The clue must have something to do with my old toy!"

Susan shakes her head sadly and murmurs, "I guess that's that then. I can't believe it. I just can't believe we finally figured out *where* it was hidden, but we'll never know *what* the clue is. We'll never know what in the world your father was going on about in his letter. And all because he couldn't hide a dumb clue properly. If only he'd hidden it somewhere else, somewhere outside the house. I'm so sorry, honey. It sure is a shame that the clue got burned up in the fire with your old toy."

She stops speaking when she notices Ecko and Charlie grinning conspiratorially at one another. "*What?* What are you two idiots laughing about now?" She looks from one to the other, her frustration growing from being left in the dark.

"It didn't," Ecko replies. "It didn't burn in the fire."

Susan stares blankly at her, waiting for the punchline. "But I thought everything was destroyed in the fire...?"

Ecko grins over at Charlie with so much love in her eyes. "Everything *was* destroyed in the fire, everything but what Charlie was able to carry out of it. When he saved me that night, he also managed to save one of my photo albums and the stuffed animal I had clutched in my hands...Sir Didymus."

Charlie is tickled pink. He laughs and slaps his hands down on the table. "If that don't beat all! The clue is locked up tight in the Regal Falls Psychiatric Ward's storage room. Now all we have to do is get Dr. Bradburn to release Ecko's belongings. That shouldn't be a problem. She's no longer a ward there, so we should be able to just go sign her things out. Besides, there's less than three weeks left until she turns 18 and is permanently released from that hellhole. Yep. They're gonna give my girl her stuff back. *Today.* Come on, ladies. Let's go spring Sir Didymus from the slammer and find out what secrets he's been hiding."

Dr. Bradburn reluctantly agrees to let her have her things a bit early. with a stipulation. She's to come back immediately for an extra session if she feels the slightest bit out of control. Dr. Bradburn says that she'd planned on presenting her the box of her belongings during one of next week's sessions so that she could closely monitor her reactions. Charlie, the old smooth talker, basically charms her into letting them take the box now so that she can go through it in the comfort of her own home. He reminds the doctor of how well she's been doing since she's come home to live with him, and he assures her that he'll keep a close watch on her.

In the end, Dr. Bradburn can find no real reason to deny their request and they walk out with Ecko clutching the box tightly to her chest. Charlie is quite disgusted with Dr. Bradburn for some reason. He has *never* liked her, but he seems to like her less and less the closer they get to her final release day. He mumbles under his breath the whole way home. "Have to make sure she's stable... Blah. That dumb heifer. If all those terrible things that Ecko had to live through had happened to *her* instead, she wouldn't be so high and mighty. I bet she wouldn't have handled things even half as well as my girl did." Mumble grumble mumble. Ecko and Susan can only smile at each other and let the old guy rant and get it all out of his system.

When they arrive back home, Charlie and Susan gallantly offer to leave her alone to go through her things in private and she giggles at their sourpuss expressions. They respect her and want her to do whatever is the most comfortable for her, but at the same time, they're practically bursting with curiosity. They're dying to find out if the clue is there and what it is.

She can't blame them; the suspense is driving her nuts too. It would be cruel to cut them out of the picture now. "Together," she simply says as she sets the box on the table. When she opens it up, a lingering acrid smell of smoke permeates the air. They all lean forward to look inside, a photo album, a small pair of pajamas, a single fuzzy pink slipper… and her old friend, Sir Didymus. Ragged and singed from the fire and covered in the stains of her family's blood.

Someone had obviously taken the time to wash him, but they hadn't done a good job of it. They'd most likely just tossed him into a washing machine and called it good. Ecko's breath catches in her throat and tears flood her eyes. She's not sure that she'll be able to touch him, not like that, not with her family's blood stained into his fur.

Susan is immediately horrified, and Charlie is pissed, again. Absolutely livid. He's so mad that he has to get up and walk away. He silently stands up from his chair, walks out onto the porch, then softly, quietly closes the door behind him. Then he starts cursing and yelling…actually *cursing*.

Ecko and Susan stare at one another in disbelief. The shock of hearing Charlie throwing a fit, (and cursing!) causes the tears in their eyes to dry up completely. The fact that he'd gone outside so that they wouldn't hear his foul language, but he was shouting it so loudly that they heard every last word anyway, was priceless. They both burst out laughing, they can't help it. They howl with laughter while Charlie curses and kicks things all over the porch.

"You...you..you better go get..get the old fool before he hu, hu, hurts himself!" Susan finally manages to stutter between her snorts of laughter. Ecko nods and tries to stop her giggling. She doesn't want to hurt Charlie's feelings by letting him know that she's laughing at him.

She finally manages to calm herself and goes to fetch him. She drags him back inside and they all sit back down at the table with Charlie glaring down at Sir Didymus like he's the spawn of Satan. It takes every bit of self-control that she has to keep herself in check and to not start laughing at his sullen expression again. She makes sure to *never* glance over at Susan. If their eyes were to meet, it would all be over. There would be no stopping the hysterics.

Reaching into the box to pick up her old friend sobers her back up, but thanks to Charlie's tantrum, it's not quite as horrifying as it would have been. At least most of the blood had been washed away.

Ecko takes off Sir Didymus's hat, eye patch, and boots. Then she removes the rest of his clothes. "Sorry Sir Didymus. I know this is just not dignified," she murmurs to the naked dog. She hands all the clothing to Susan for her to look over, as well.

When they don't immediately find anything that could possibly be considered a clue, Charlie starts grumbling again, "Well, what do you know. No damn clue anywhere on it!"

Ecko remains quiet. She turns Didymus this way and that way, searching. Her eyes catch sight of a tiny blue string just barely poking out of the fur on his back. She looks closer and sees the blue stitches hidden underneath the fur. She grins up at Charlie. "Not *on* Sir Didymus. *In* him. The truth lies *in* Sir Didymus."

She uses a sharp knife to carefully cut the seam stitched into his back. She presses her fingers inside and feels plastic. "There's something in here!" She grips it with her fingers and tugs it out to find that it's a Ziplock baggie. Inside the plastic bag is a scrap of paper and a necklace with an intricate flower pendant that appears to be made out of a combination of glass and metal.

It's a long-stemmed rose, about two inches in size from top to bottom. The stem is pure silver but the flower itself appears to be glass, crystal clear glass. It's not a rose in full bloom, but instead a tightly closed, translucent bud. She opens the bag and reaches inside to take it out and get a better look. It's strange and beautiful and oddly familiar to her.

As soon as her hand wraps around it, she feels a sudden sharp stab on her pointer finger. She cries out, more from shock than pain, so she lifts the rose out to see what had happened. The stem sports a single, dull thorn, and balanced on the tip of that thorn is now a large drop of her blood.

All three of them watch in complete and utter bafflement as the drop of blood gets sucked down into the thorn, travels up the hollow stem, and into the bud. Then something's happening, something magical! The blood starts filling the bud from the bottom up, turning it purple *and it starts to grow*. The petals grow and unfurl until a fully bloomed rose rests in the palm of her hand. The petals are now a deep amethyst-purple color, and they shine just like a jewel.

"Uummm, what exactly did we just see? What just happened?" This from Susan, her voice shaky and high pitched with equal parts fear and awe.

"Yeah. Welcome to the freak show that I call my life," Ecko whispers.

Charlie simply holds out his hand.

"May I?" he asks, and she passes the rose to him. He holds it close to his face and examines every part of it. He mumbles the entire time as he scrutinizes it. "How in the world did…how is this possible? How did it draw blood? It's not even sharp!" He runs his fingers over the thorn every which way but it's dull, too dull to cut through his skin and draw blood.

"Look Charlie!" Susan exclaims. "Look at the tips of the petals. Are they losing their color again?" Sure enough, the tips of the petals are completely translucent again. He holds the pendant out and they all watch as the purple color fades away, almost draining out of it. When the top half of the blossom is clear again, the petals begin to move once again. The process goes in reverse this time, with the bloom closing back up into a bud. The last bit of purple tint disappears completely as the rose returns to its original state.

The trio is completely flabbergasted. How had that happened? And why? It was absolutely beautiful and magical and breathtaking, but what was the purpose of it? Charlie's still stumped, going on and on about how that dull thorn managed to draw blood in the first place. He runs his fingers over it again and again, even presses it into his skin. It just isn't sharp enough to pierce the skin. Susan takes it from him and examines it also. She searches for a 'made in' sticker to see where it had been made, but she's not surprised when she can't find one. She agrees that the thorn isn't sharp, and she feels no jagged edges on the rest of it that could cause a wound. Ecko takes it back and feels the thorn for herself. "Ouch!" she yelps. "It darn sure *is* sharp enough to cut. You two must have thick skin made of leather!" Another drop of blood sits on the tip of the thorn. They all watch as the process repeats itself, exactly as it had before.

When it's over, the transformation finished and the rose is back in its bud form, Charlie says, "It's meant only for you, Ecko. Somehow, and I have no idea how, it only works for you. But what could it possibly mean? And where did something like that come from? I've never seen anything like it in all my years."

Susan silently nods her head in agreement. Ecko glances down at the table in confusion and notices the scrap of paper left in the Ziplock bag. She'd been so distracted by the rose that she'd forgotten all about it. She takes it out of the plastic and reads it aloud. "Maggie Reynolds. 14321 Briarwood Road. Go alone. That's all it says. And it's my father's handwriting," she says as she holds out the note for them to see.

"Well now, who the heck is Maggie?" Susan exclaims in frustration. At the same time Charlie's yelling, "Over my dead body are you going alone! What foolishness! What absolute *lunacy!* One minute he's all secretive and protective and the next he is *still* secretive, but he wants to send you only God knows where...*all alone!* Well, I won't have it, you hear me, young lady? Don't you even *think* about it!"

Charlie's face is red and he's breathing hard and fast. She's terrified that he's about to have a heart attack. "Calm down, Charlie! I won't go alone! But let's think about this. Why would my dad tell me to go alone?"

Charlie stands up and huffs. "I really don't care about the whys of it. You are *not* going by yourself. We have no idea what kind of craziness is waiting there for you. We're all going. That's my final say on the matter. Let's go, gang, we've got a mystery to solve. Everyone, go get your coats." And that was that. Charlie had laid down the law, so they gathered their things, slipped on their coats, and followed him outside.

Once they're all settled in the car, Charlie asks, "You still got that tiny map inside your phone, Ecko? That one is so much easier to use than a regular paper map. Isn't technology amazing?" He's rambling. He *always* does that when he's worried or nervous.

"Yes, Charlie. All cellphones have GPS now. Yours does too." She programs the address in and informs them that their destination is nearly an hour away before directing him where to go.

The traffic is heavy, and it takes closer to two hours than the suggested one to get to where they're going. The tension in the car is almost unbearable as they finally arrive at a small, well-kept house with a very pretty yard. There are plants and vines and flowers growing everywhere.

The three of them sit inside the car (conspicuously parked on the opposite side of the street) and watch to see if anything strange happens. After ten minutes of silent observation, Ecko exclaims, "This is ridiculous!" The sudden outburst just about scares the old ones right out of their skins. Charlie jumps so high off his seat that he bangs his head on the roof of the car and Susan lets out a loud, startled squeak.

Ecko would laugh if she weren't so scared. "Sorry. But we can't just sit here all evening waiting for monsters to appear. The mystery is not going to solve itself, while I sit out here hiding in the car. You guys don't have to come with me. Just wait here. I'll be fine. I'll just go ring the doorbell. This Maggie person may not even be home."

She climbs out of the car and Charlie and Susan scramble out after her. Charlie catches up and glares down at her. "I don't think so, Missy. We do this together." He wraps a protective arm around both his ladies as they all stop at the door. Ecko takes a deep breath and rings the bell with a shaking hand.

"Oh darn. She's not here. We can come back another time," Susan whispers in a small, terrified voice. But no one turns to leave. They can all clearly hear someone inside approaching and then disengaging the locks. The door finally swings open and reveals a pretty, gracefully aging woman.

Everyone is completely silent. They all just stand there, quietly sizing each other up. The woman seems oddly familiar to Ecko. She can't shake the feeling that she's met her before. Her suspicions are confirmed when the woman sighs, smiles a sad little smile, and says, "*Finally.* Hello, Ecko. It's been a long time. Come on inside. I've been waiting for you."

She steps back to let them enter. The three of them look questioningly at one another and then simultaneously shrug their shoulders. As the man and protector of their little family, Charlie makes sure he goes in first. But the ladies are right on his heels, clinging tightly to his coat. They move together as if they're one entity, a weird blob creature with six legs and three heads. They take exactly five steps into the entryway before the sound of the door slamming shut behind them and the locks clicking back into place have them crying out and spinning back around to make a run for it.

The woman, Maggie presumably, laughs and says, "Boy, you guys sure are jumpy!" Charlie steps forward, his fist raised up in the air. "You let us out of here right now! Or else!"

The smile vanishes off her face in an instant. She moves out of the way so that she's no longer blocking the exit. She looks straight at Ecko and says, "Relax. You can all leave at any time. I always lock my doors. It's a habit. This is a rough neighborhood and I have things...secrets to protect." She examines each of them, noting their pinched, frightened faces. "Really. No harm will come to you here in my home. Come, follow me." She turns and walks away, leaving them to follow her into a very pink, very feminine dining room. Charlie stops in the doorway and looks around, scoping the place out, searching for any and all dangers. He immediately spots the framed mirror on the wall. Without a word of explanation, he walks over, nonchalantly takes it down, and turns it around before setting it on the floor in the corner of the room. Then, cool as can be, he turns and glares at Maggie with his eyebrows raised high, daring her to say a single word in protest.

Maggie is obviously confused, but she lets the incident slide without commenting on his odd behavior. Besides, she figures that before it's all said and done, she would find out exactly what purpose that action served. Ecko focuses her attention on the floor in front of her and covers her mouth with her hand to hide her grin. Charlie is always her old knight in rusty, ancient armor and she loves him so.

She collects herself and glances all around the room as she steps inside. There are framed photos everywhere, hanging on every wall and perched on every available surface. She stops to study one of a pretty young woman smiling down at the two children in her arms. It is beautiful. The photographer had captured the love on the woman's face perfectly.

She has always been enthralled with photographs, perhaps because they tell the stories of other people's lives, and this one is a prime example of that fact. Maggie smiles softly and touches the face of the woman in the photo that Ecko has paused to look at. "That's my daughter and my grandchildren. Aren't they just a lovely bunch? Here, have a seat and make yourselves comfortable. We'll have a nice little chat. But first I'm going to make us all some tea, or coffee, if you like. I, myself, prefer tea. My grandmother came from England, you see. She was always very formal and proper, so I grew up on teatime. Oh, I'll just make both! Tea *and* coffee. And scones, I think. Yes, scones with strawberries and clotted cream. It will only take a few moments to whip up some refreshments for you. Be back in a jiffy!" she calls over her shoulder, as she rushes from the room.

The three of them are left staring after her. "Wow. She sure is a chipper one." Susan remarks as she takes off her coat and lays it over the back of a chair. Ecko sits down at the table that's covered with a frilly pink tablecloth and adorned with a vase of beautiful, cut flowers. "Relax Charlie. I think we're safe. Somehow, I just don't think this Maggie is the vicious, serial killer type."

Charlie gives one last suspicious glance around the room as he takes off his own coat and hat. "Looks can be deceiving, young lady," he grumbles as he takes a seat too. He does *not* relax.

The woman returns and sets the table with a delicate, China tea set, complete with ceramic kettles of tea and coffee, cream and sugar bowls, and matching cups and saucers and stirring spoons. She lays it all out, goes back the way she came, then returns once more with a service tray piled with cookies and scones, bowls of cream and fruit preserves, and fresh sliced strawberries.

She seats herself and exclaims, "There! Isn't this lovely? Everyone, help yourselves to whatever you prefer while we make our introductions. My name is Maggie, as I'm sure you all know. And no introduction is needed for this beautiful young lady," she says with a smile as Ecko pours herself some coffee. "You're Daniel's little girl, Ecko. Although, you aren't so little anymore, are you? You are all grown up now."

Maggie stirs her tea and sighs. "I miss him, your father. He was a very dear friend of mine, although I hadn't seen him for years before he passed on." A moment of silence passes and then she claps her hands briskly. "Right! Introductions! I nearly forgot." Then "Stay on task, Maggie!" she mutters to herself. "Who, may I ask, are these lovely companions of yours?"

She leans back and sips her tea, her eyes focused on Charlie and Susan. As they introduce themselves, Ecko watches every move that Maggie makes. As Charlie and Susan begin to relax and exchange pleasantries with their host, her own guard goes up higher. She realizes that for some reason, Maggie is putting on a show. She's pretending to be nothing more than a sweet, slightly aging airhead.

But Ecko knows people and can usually read them pretty well. She's been a people watcher, a silent spectator, for years. She knows how to spot voice changes and weird gestures and body language. Being trapped in a mental hospital had only enhanced her ability to read into what others try to hide. All she had been allowed to do in there, for years, was watch other people. A sort of mental alarm goes through her head any time things aren't what they seem to be. The bigger the lie, (*threat!*) the louder the alarm rings, and right now, that alarm is sounding inside her head. Not loudly, not incessantly but softly. Just enough to let her know that all is not what it seems to be.

Maggie's sweet, innocent act isn't matching up with her shrewd, watchful eyes. "Stop the act, Maggie," she suddenly demands, causing everyone to stop talking and turn to her in surprise. Charlie is immediately back to being wary and suspicious. He places his cup back down on the table and sits back in his chair to frown at their host.

"I don't know what game you're playing, or why you feel the need to act sweet and clueless when you are clearly very intelligent and well informed. My father sent me to you for answers. Can we please be done with all the pretenses and just get on with it? I really don't know how many more games and riddles I can stand." She's ashamed of the tears that fill her eyes, but she determinedly refuses to look away.

"Please," Susan softly insists. "Maggie, please just tell us what you know. She's been through so much. If you only knew all the things this sweet girl has had to go through..."

"I do know," Maggie whispers in return with sudden tears in her own eyes. "At least some of it. I know it's been terrible. And I *am* sorry for all the subterfuge, I really am. But I made a promise to your father years ago to protect his secrets. to protect *you*. I've been prepared all these years to turn it all over to you when you came looking for it. But I promised to give it to you, and *only* you. When you showed up with other people, it threw me off. I didn't know what to do, so I've been trying to stall while I decide if your companions are 'safe'. I know it sounds strange."

"But your father was very cloak and dagger about it all. He said that it was imperative to keep it all hidden, that it would be very dangerous if it all fell into the wrong hands. I don't even know what it is!" Maggie exclaims. "All these years, I have kept it hidden here without so much as a clue as to what it could be. It could be a bomb, for all I know! I *do* know that it's dangerous though, or at least having it is dangerous. That much Dan made very clear to me. I didn't even want it in my house. But I owe him, you see? I owe him so very much." Maggie covers her face and begins to sob, leaving the trio to stare helplessly at one another.

Susan, ever the softie of the group, gets up and goes to her. She hugs her and murmurs that she's done a wonderful job in carrying out Dan's wishes and that the whole ordeal was almost over, and she would soon be able to put it all behind her. They wait patiently while Maggie collects herself and then profusely apologizes for momentarily falling apart.

"It's ok," Charlie, ever the diplomat, assures her as he awkwardly pats her shoulder. "You're doing great. Just take it slow and start at the beginning."

It's All Fun and Games

Samara

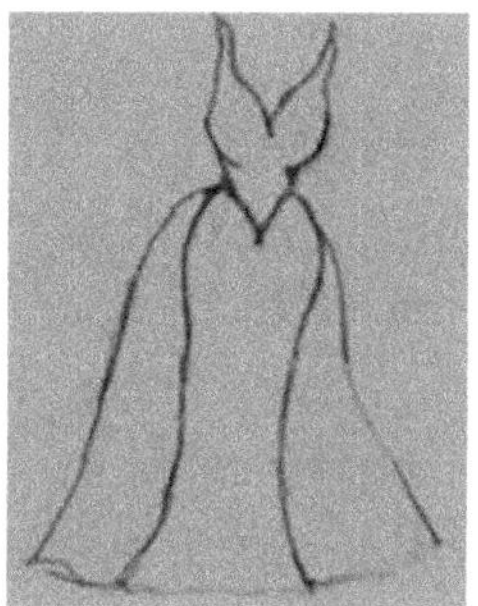

I open my eyes and grin up at the crumbling, water-stained ceiling above me. Languidly stretching out my entire body, I revel in the lingering remnants of pleasure that still thrums through me.

Krispin has proved to be a most wonderful lover, just as I knew he would, and he's quickly become my most favoritest plaything ever. Three months…I've had three delicious months to enjoy dallying with him, but I had started to grow bored. Until now, that is.

I turn my head to watch him lying naked on the bed beside me, softly, sexily snoring into the pillow. My poor baby. He just can't seem to keep up with my appetites and he's exhausted himself again. I trail my fingers through the still oozing whelps on his back, the bloody teeth imprints that cover him from head to toe, and he doesn't even stir. Our last romp had been mind-boggling, body-breakingly, amazing. He always knows just what I need, and he *never* fails to give it to me.

He knows when my anger gets too big for me and all I want is a whipping boy, he allows me to hurt him without fighting back. He recognizes when it is *I* that needs to be punished, and then he makes me do the bleeding. But this last time, oh, this last time wasn't like that. It was raw and desperate and fierce, a mutually violent mating. I'm not even sure what brought it on, or why.

One minute he was showing me how to open up the hard rockslugs that we had 'convinced' an old man to give to us (after he'd spent hours collecting them all for his own dinner.) We'd cracked them open and put them to our lips to suck out the slimy little things and swallow them down. Then our eyes met, and mealtime was suddenly over. Seems we'd lost our appetites for rockslugs, but we were still hungry, ravenous in fact.

In the time it took us to go from one breath to the next, our bodies were drawn together, and we were locked in a desperate battle of desire. We were instantly, brutally all over one another. We slammed into walls and rolled across the floors. We tore into each other with claws and teeth, our lips and tongues greedily stroking across every inch of the other's skin. It was wild and savage and incredibly beautiful. When it was over, when we were finally, (momentarily) sated and gasping for breath, a terrible rage suddenly took root and began to grow inside of me.

For one brief, disgusting moment, while my senses had been overwhelmed by his clever hands and his teasing tongue, I'd felt myself begin to fall under his spell. He's such a master at this game that I was almost suckered. For a moment, I *almost* thought that I could love him. But I do *not* love. I never have. I'm not sure if it's even a real thing.

Personally, I think love is just something that miserable people made up in a last-ditch effort to make themselves feel happy, to bring some sort of meaningfulness to their pathetic lives. But if it *is* true, if love is truly real, am I even capable of feeling it? I don't know, but I intend to never find out. Love is a weakness that only fools can afford, and I will never be weak and helpless and pathetic again…*never* again. Especially not for something as trite as love and happy-ever-afters.

Krispin knew better than to say what he'd said. He *knew* better. He knew what it would earn him, and still he let those words leave his lips. Lying there after it was all over, still all tangled up in one another, hearts pounding and chests heaving, I'd felt the spark of anger flare to life inside me. The more I thought about it, the hotter the fire inside me burned. How *dare* he? How dare he make me feel anything other than the mutually satisfying pleasure that we are so very good at?

Weeks ago, when he had confessed his love to me, I thought I'd made it clear that I would never reciprocate. I would never care for him, could never love him back. He was just a plaything, a pleasure toy to distract me until I can finally locate my sister again and somehow make it to her world, leaving this one behind forever. I assumed that he'd accepted my answer. He hadn't said another word about it, even though he'd sometimes silently said it with his eyes instead. And it pissed me off, every…single...time.

But this time, oh, this time, right as he'd found his release within my body is when he made his terrible mistake. As he poured himself into me, the "I love you" simultaneously poured itself out of his mouth. The rage that took over me then had been a terrifying thing to behold, even to myself. I lost all coherent thought and every vestige of self-control that I possessed…and darkness consumed me for a time.

Without having to mentally form a single command, my Shadows had taken it upon themselves to come out and play. They'd poured out of me to wrap around Krispin and bind him in place. A resigned sigh escaped his lips, and he lowered his head in compliance. He knew what was coming and he willingly accepted his fate. I reached out and jerked his face back up, so that I could watch his eyes and *that's* when I lost myself for a while.

When I came back to my senses, hours later, Krispin was chained from the ceiling in our playroom. Naked, legs and arms spread wide, he stood staring defiantly down at me as his blood ran in rivulets to pool on the floor. My arm was aching from overuse, and blood dripped from the riding crop clutched in my hand. I dropped it to the floor and walked slow circles around him so that I could get a good look at every part of him. I wanted to see how much damage I'd done, wanted to ensure that his punishment fit his crime.

I trailed my hands all over his body, smearing through the blood, loving the feel of the muscles bunched up tight beneath his skin. In the years since I'd first met him, he'd grown to be a truly magnificent male, the best this town had to offer, and he was all mine to do with whatever I wished. The sight of him, bound and bleeding before me had made my heart pound. I stepped in close and pressed my body to his backside. "Do you *still* love me?" I whispered into his ear just before I took it between my teeth and gave it a sharp, stinging bite.

I circled back in front of him, and clamped my teeth onto his perfectly pert, blue nipple. His gasp of pain excited me and so I did it again, harder this time, to the other one. "Do you love me?" I asked again, as my hands played over the muscles of his shoulders, slicked through the blood on his chest, and then lower. His body was beginning to grow hard with his own eagerness and the sight of it had mine responding in kind.

He grunted, as I dropped to my knees and buried my teeth into his belly. I glanced up at him then, and his eyes were filled with equal parts of anticipation and fear at the sight of my mouth so dangerously close to that male part of him that he cherishes so much. He was afraid but he still wanted it oh, so badly. I laughed at his growl of frustration as I denied him what he so desperately craved. I wanted him to take it back. I wanted him to rescind his declaration of love, undeclare his unwanted show of affection.

I spent the next four hours punishing him, trying to make him take his filthy words back. But he didn't break. He refused to even bend. In the end, it was I that had to cry mercy. My cursed body betrayed me, made me need the sweet release that only he could bring me. During his punishment, I had tried to do it on my own, had tried to ease the gnawing ache inside me. The sight of me pleasuring myself had Krispin bucking and straining at his bonds, desperate to get free and tear into me. It hadn't been enough, though, not nearly good enough to satisfy my needs. What I had needed, I couldn't give to myself.

I was eventually forced to release him and take my pleasure from his body. He was on me the very instant that I cut him loose, a starving wild animal, snarling with the fierceness of his need. I don't think *anything* will be able to top the wicked and lascivious attentions that I received after this latest little punishment session. I never did get him to take back his repulsive, "I love you", but I enjoyed every second of the attempt… immensely. Somewhere in all that pleasure and pain and blood, the flames of my burning rage had been doused, drowned out by my overpowering need, and eventually died down to smoldering embers.

Now, lying here in bed beside him, I revel in the aches, the delicious soreness of my well-used body. Krispin's blood has painted me crimson, and I can still taste his skin in my teeth. Poor toy, I think I may have finally broken him. Despite the pain I'm feeling, I find myself wanting to lean over and run my tongue over his lips. I want to taste him again, use my teeth to reopen the wounds that I'd given him. His eyes open, as if he can feel my stare upon his face. I watch his lips turn up slightly at the corners and his knowing eyes flash with a wicked mirth. My heart does a nasty little flip flop at the slow, sexy wink he gives me. He chuckles delightedly, as my breath gets caught in my throat at the sheer sexiness he exudes. The blue bastard knows *exactly* what he does to me.

I sit up quickly and swing my legs off the bed to the floor. I could easily be persuaded to go another round, but I haven't the time for it. I have *so* been looking forward to the upcoming festivities and I can't afford the distraction that Krispin's body offers me. I am *finally* able to attend the Mourning's End Festival. Every year, Joodin (a very small, very oddish little man…creature) brings his traveling band of gypsies to town for a week-long celebration. There are acrobats and performers, salesmen with their trinkets and treasures, magicians with their potions and spells.

They bring excitement with them, a welcome break in the dull and mundane lives of the ordinary. The townspeople prepare all year for them to show up, then they spend the entire week in a drunken stupor, squandering every coin they'd managed to save up. The level of rowdiness and drunken mischief increases exponentially as the week passes, ending with the last several hours of the Fair being loud and boisterous and wildly out of control. It's the whole town's favorite time of year. Not mine. I have never been allowed to join in the fun, although I did manage to sneak away and watch the festivities for an hour or so when I was seven years old.

But now I get to finally experience it for myself. I'll not be denied this year and I'm going to make sure that I see every single performance. I am going to play the games; tastes every kind of food they have to offer. And then I'm going to dance. I, myself, have never tried it, but I have seen it done. The people of Ecko's world are great fans of dancing. They have many different types to choose from, too. It doesn't appear to be too difficult so I'm sure I'll be good at it. And if I'm not, who would dare to mention it?

Krispin pumps the water from the cleanser-recycler that he'd somehow acquired (stolen) for me and then heats it for us to have a bath. We're both in serious need of washing up. We usually bathe together, but this time I make him wait until I'm done, no distractions. While he's busy cleaning himself up, I slip on the tight red dress that I Shadow-forced a seamstress to make for me.

I had never felt spiddersilk, much less owned a dress made from it. It slides deliciously against my skin, and I run my hands over my body, absolutely adoring the feel of it. I turn and see Krispin in the doorway, naked and dripping wet. He's been watching me, and his eyes are heavy lidded with renewed desire, his nostrils flared wide to catch my scent. He's full and hard, eager to go another round. I laugh in sheer delight at the effect I have on him.

"Later," I say, and he brusquely nods his head once to acknowledge my promise. He turns away to get into his own clothing, but suddenly spins back to face me. And then he's on me again, has me pushed up against the wall, his mouth mated to mine with his hand up under my dress. In less than three minutes, I'm screaming out my pleasure, my nails dug into his back, teeth tearing into his shoulder. He drags it out as long as he can, making my pleasure last for a small eternity.

When he's swallowed the last cry from my lips, drawn the last shudder from my body, he slips his fingers free and growls into my ear, "To hold you over." He steps back, and watching me all the while with his smoldering, needful eyes, he slowly licks me from his fingers. Holy… Hot...Hell, I guess I didn't break him, after all.

With no more time to spare, Krispin and I make our grand appearance like the royalty we are, right into the thick of it all. But for some reason our subjects don't seem happy to see us. I guess we'd killed too many people that had displeased us, tortured too many others to force them into giving us the things we wanted. Apparently, we had terrorized the town so thoroughly in the past few months that everyone is now too afraid to be near us.

The music screeches to a halt and everything becomes eerily silent. They all back away as we pass them, fear and resentment clearly etched on their faces. It makes me throw my head back and laugh up at the sky. Krispin's arm tightens around me and he grins wickedly, before he suddenly starts spinning me, dancing me around and around right there through the frightened crowd.

He cares naught that the musicians are no longer playing. He moves us to his own beat. Everyone turns away, intent on putting as much space between them and us as they possibly can. "I will kill anyone that leaves," I call out in a happy, singsong voice. "This is my time, *finally,* my time to shine, and I won't let you people ruin it for me. You will stay, you will do whatever I tell you to do, we will all have a fabulous time. Won't we?"

Shockingly, no one will meet my eyes, but they all become very interested in what they'd previously been doing. Krispin growls and I feel his claws come out and press into my back. "You heard my lady. Start the music back up. Eat…Dance…Play….Or don't, Samara will have just as much fun bathing in your blood and playing in your entrails as she will have dancing and watching the shows."

I pull my lover's head down and reward his loyalty with a deep, promising kiss that has his body instantly hardening against mine. His breath comes out fast and harsh when I finally pull away. I reach up and smooth out the mess I'd inadvertently made of his long hair that he's tied back in a futile effort to keep it out of his eyes. My naughty companion snatches an Octobeast leg right out of an overly fat woman's hand as we walk past her.

She gives a startled little pig grunt and then falls down in a dead faint. Her poor, bony husband, who must have starved in order to feed her, unfortunately tries to catch her before she hits the dirt. It does *not* end well, especially for the husband. Krispin ignores them both and bows at me, before offering me his pilfered Octobeast leg and I giggle as I curtsy back and accept his gift. We take turns tearing chunks of meat off with our teeth as we move on to enjoy the rest of the festivities. But I certainly do hope that poor man is alright.

By the time darkness falls, everyone has drunk themselves into a stupor and (mostly) forgotten that they're supposed to keep their distance from me. I have danced with every man around, and some of the women too. Krispin watches me from the shadows, eyes full of rage and lust and possessiveness as I seductively rub myself against my dance partners. I throw my head back and laugh when I hear the low growl of frustration rumbling in his throat. Silly boy, he's so adorable in his jealousy.

The band starts up a rousing, fast-paced song and the dance floor fills to overflowing with laughing, stomping, twirling people. Before I know what's happening, the men all spin away, switching partners in mid dance. My partner twirls me around and disappears, the man beside us stepping in to take his place. After a few moments, he passes me to the next man, and then the next and the next. The song continuously speeds up too, so we're all forced to spin faster and faster until everyone becomes just a blur of laughing faces.

The song finally comes to an end, and I glance up to see who I'm now partnered with this time. I have to look up and up, and I realize that my partner is a man, a very large man that I have never seen before. My, he is *huge*…and beautiful. And he smells oh, so very delicious.

I feel my body stir to life as he grins and winks at me, obviously sensing the desire that he's stirring to life inside me. He carries my hand up to his lips briefly, his tongue quickly darting out to taste me. "My name's Rommal. Come find me when you're ready." Then he bows and backs away to disappear into the crowd of laughing drunken revelers.

Suddenly Krispin is there, pressed up against my back, snarling and growling low in his throat with his overflowing anger. He feels my desire, smells it on me, and he is *pissed*, barely managing to keep himself in check. But he also cannot resist the scent of my hunger, my need.   even if it's someone else that's awakened it in me. He sniffs along my neck, sinks his teeth into my shoulder. My breath catches, as he wraps his arms around me and rubs his arousal against my buttocks. Looks like play time at the fair is over. It's time to go home and play some more satisfying games.

Our next few excursions to the festival basically repeat the events of the first one. Krispin and I show up at the fair. People scream. We punish them, laugh hysterically, and then move on to other fun. We play the games, eat the food, and dance to the music. And all the while I search incessantly for Rommal, who seems to have annoyingly vanished. Something must have happened to him or else he's playing his own game with me, in which case I will make him suffer. If he ever comes out of hiding, that is. He'd told me to find him when I was ready. Well, I've *been* ready.

I've been ready since I first laid eyes on him. He'd created an itch inside me, one that I can't reach and even Krispin fails to scratch.

But Krispin knows exactly what I'm about. He knows that when my eyes stray, I'm looking for *him*. I can feel the rage steadily brewing, churning inside of him and it thrills me at the same time that it enrages me. He has no right to be so possessive. "Might equals Right," he leans down and growls into my ear. I shiver because I have never said those words to him. He is so in tune with me, can see into me so deeply that sometimes he can actually read my thoughts.

I know I should put up a fight over his words, his possessive actions, but ugh, I'm tired. Who knew that fun would be so draining? So exhausting? I keep finding myself slowing down. I've been sleeping longer and losing interest in the things that please me faster than usual. I sink down onto the ground beside the fire to rest and warm myself by its flames. I'm stuffed full of face pies and scrambled rodent brains, candied spidders and pickled basilisk eggs and I can't possibly take another bite of anything, but I find that I'm incredibly thirsty for some chilled sour mead.

I watch the dancers spin around the wooden dance platform, while Krispin goes to fetch our drinks. Suddenly there's someone standing directly in front of me, blocking my view. I'm irritated by the blatant lack of respect for me and the things I can and *will* do. I'm just about to send my Shadows out to punish his rudeness, but when I raise my eyes to confront him, I find that it's Rommal standing before me. *Finally*. He watches me with eyes full of greed and lust, and I feel my body instantly heat with desire.

He holds out his hand, silently inviting me to come with him. My own hand rises, seemingly of its own accord, and he takes it and pulls me to my feet. His eyes never leave mine as he backs up, leading me towards the shadows of a nearby building. My heart thuds in my chest and my breath comes faster as desire pools low in my belly. But then there's a sudden, lightning-fast blur behind him and I watch his eyes go wide with disbelief and shock. Krispin growls softly, dangerously, then he pulls his deadly claws free of Rommal's neck and lets him fall to the ground to bleed out into the dirt.

"I wanted to play with him!" is all I can manage before my emotions choke off my voice. Equal parts rage and lust wash through my body and I feel the storm build within me. My blood begins to boil in my veins and my eyes go black with the overload to my senses. Forcing a calm that I certainly don't feel, I raise my eyes up to meet his. He's glaring back down at me and a lesser woman would have trembled at the fury in his eyes.

But I am *not* a lesser woman, and his anger does not frighten me. It excites me instead. I let my eyes rove over every inch of him, and I feel my body responding, growing wet with desire. Krispin's jaw is jutted out at a stubborn angle and his chest heaves with his every breath. He tries to clench his hands into tight, angry fists at his side, but he's too furious to make his claws retract and he ends up stabbing them into himself instead. Not that he cares.

He doesn't say a single word, just stands there, feet braced wide while he waits for my retaliation. And he has no doubt that retaliation is coming. But I'm just as turned on by his brutal jealousy as I am furious about it. I don't know which one I want more, to punish him or to fuck him. Both, I decide as I lick my lips in anticipation.

My body is in such sensory overload that I can't even speak. I spin on my heels and push my way through the nosy looky-loos gathered to watch the show we've been putting on. They scatter like the Vika-Vakooja roach-beetles do when they see me coming. Krispin falls in beside me, just as I knew he would. I feel the anger and the lust radiating off him and I unconsciously pick up the speed in an effort to get to Krispin's home even faster.

My nipples are like tiny, hard stones and the silk of my dress rubs deliciously against them. I am wet, so very wet, impossibly hot and swollen. I press my hand against myself *there* in a desperate attempt to ease the ache. Krispin follows my every move with his eyes. He is suddenly just as fiercely desperate as I am, and he mimics my actions. His hand drops down low and he rubs and squeezes himself and I suddenly know that I won't make it to the house. He realizes it too, and he jerks me up into his arms, spinning me around in midair so that I'm facing him. He pulls me in close and grinds himself against me, the pleasure of it causing me to throw my head back and scream.

He slams his mouth against mine, his tongue delving deep inside, reaching for my soul. I swallow him down and I can't breathe, and I don't care. My legs automatically wrap around him, my claws bury themselves into his back. I greedily suck at his tongue, desperately biting at his lips causing him to groan with frustration into my open mouth. And then he's running, his long, powerful legs eating up the distance.

My hands fumble frantically at the buttons on his pants, until I finally just tear them open enough to get to that part of him that I'm aching for. His breath hisses out as I reach in and free him, my hands running over and over him, just the way he loves me to. He tugs my dress up, his hands grasp my bare bottom and I'm biting his neck with the agony of waiting for it. He makes it to his porch, stumbles up the steps and kicks the door open so hard that it's knocked right off the hinges.

Then we're falling and he's in me before we even hit the floor. Hours, weeks, years later...I don't know and can't really be bothered to care, we finally reach a place where we must stop and rest. We lay quiet in each other's arms, the sweat and the blood and the other fluids drying on our skin. I hurt so bad. I feel so good. I don't ever want to leave here, and I want to run as fast and as far as I can get. I want to hurt him for making me want him like I do, but I don't want him to ever stop wanting me. I want to end this, and I want to keep doing this forever.

My exhaustion overtakes me and finally, mercifully, my mind grows quiet. I'm almost asleep, my head resting on Krispin's chest when he suddenly speaks, the words rumbling into my ear. "He belonged to your father, that man you wanted so badly to play with. The Lokskell sent him after you and he was filled with a magic that would have allowed him to take control of you. I smelled it in his blood, I smelled *you* in his blood. He already had a hold on you somehow, and he was about to take even more of you. And you would have just let him! I won't pretend that I wasn't jealous, and I'm not sorry that I broke your new toy before you got to play with it. You're mine Samara. I will not allow anyone else to fuck you. I'll kill anyone that tries. I don't share. I don't care how much you hate it. I don't care how much you deny it or how much you punish me for it. You *are* mine, just as I will forever belong to you. You'll have to kill me to be rid of me." My eyes are closed and I'm already half asleep, drifting out into the blessed, dark nothingness.

"Maybe tomorrow," I whisper and the laughter that rumbles his chest beneath me is the last thing I hear as sleep takes me to wherever we all go when we sleep.

Oh, the Tales that Dead People Tell

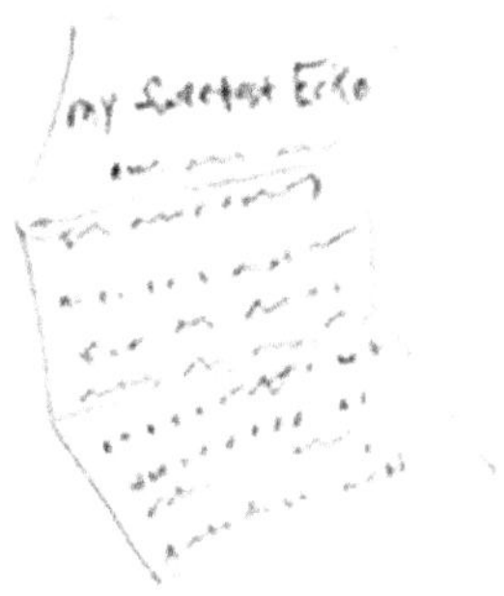

Maggie fiddles with her pecan shortbread cookie, frowning in thought as she breaks it into little pieces. When it's nothing more than crumbles on her plate, she nods firmly and takes a deep, fortifying breath. "The beginning. Yes, I suppose that is the logical place to start. Ok, let's see. It was 1995, one of the worst years of my life. And also, one of the best. That was the year I found out that chemotherapy alone wouldn't be enough to save my daughter. She would need to be placed on a waiting list for a bone marrow transplant too.

My Ally had leukemia, you see, and we had been fighting it for over a year. I was a single mother, and I'd needed a second job to help make ends meet. So, I started working the morning shift as a waitress at a little cafe called Momma May's. And that's where I met your father, on my very first day on the job." Maggie smiles gently at the memory.

"I was certainly no waitress. I had never even worked as a server during my teen years. I was unbelievably clumsy! I knocked his water glass over as soon as I placed it in front of him, and it spilled right onto his lap. It was terrible. I was so embarrassed, but also terrified that I was going to lose my job so soon. I *needed* that job. Dan, bless his kind heart, took one look at my tears and saw the fear clearly written on my face and he covered for me. He called out to my boss, the owner of the cafe, 'Momma May, I need some towels over here. I guess I decided that I needed another bath this morning. a cold one! I've managed to spill my drink all over myself. Thank God it was the water and not the coffee, right?' And then he winked at me and that was that."

"He turned what could have been a disastrous event for me into one that was no big deal. Such a sweet and thoughtful man. Anyway, I found out that he was a regular there and had been for a couple of years and that he came in every Tuesday and Thursday. We ended up becoming close friends over the next year or so."

Maggie stops talking and laughs at Charlie's frown and his disapproving 'harrumph!' "Close *friends*, Charlie. Nothing more, nothing less. The only man I ever loved ran out on me when he found out I was pregnant with his child, and I never wanted anything more to do with men again. And Dan was head over heels in love with his family anyway. He even brought his wife and baby daughter in several times to show them off. He was always so proud of his ladies, as he called them. That's why I could never understand about you, Ecko. There was no way that Dan had been unfaithful to his wife. *No way*. But there you were."

"Oh, but I'm getting ahead of myself. Anyway, we got close, and we talked about everything. We mostly bragged about our families, but I never told him that Ally was sick. I don't know why. Maybe I just didn't want his pity, but honestly, I'm not really sure why. All I do know is that I never told him. But Momma May confessed it all one day when I had to miss my shift, because Ally was back in the hospital. Momma May never admitted it, but I know she told him. He started leaving me outrageous tips. He also started sneaking me money by putting tips on other customers' tables! I caught him doing it."

Maggie pauses to wipe her eyes and blow her nose. "Oh, that man was something else. I never called him out on it, mostly because he could afford it and I knew that he really wanted to help. He *wanted* to help without making me feel bad for needing the help, understand? Judge me harshly if you must, but you don't know...*can't* know the sheer terror of watching your child suffer, the unmitigated helplessness of watching your baby slowly die right before your eyes, knowing there is absolutely nothing that you can do to stop it. You just don't know the sheer amount of guilt I felt for not having the money to stop it."

"So, yes, I said nothing because I needed the help desperately. I was in over my head. Ally was getting worse, and the bills just kept piling up. Then, one morning, it was a Tuesday, Dan came in acting so strange. He was nervous and jumpy, not his usual carefree self at all. He didn't have much to say and he left quickly. And then he didn't show up on Thursday at all. I was very worried about him at that point."

"But on Sunday, after my shift at the cafe, he showed up at my apartment...carrying *you* in his arms. I wasn't even aware that he knew where I lived, or that Sunday was my day off from my other job. I remember being so embarrassed as I let him into my tiny, rundown apartment. I'd sold my house and everything of any value that I had owned in order to pay for Ally's treatments. He never even noticed how shabby everything was."

"He gave me this wild story about having an affair and fathering the child he'd brought with him. He said that he was not free to discuss the details, but that the mother was gone and that he had sole custody of the baby girl. He never came out and said it, not in so many words, but he made it sound as if there were some very bad people searching for the child.   for *you*, Ecko. He told me that he had to hide something, an extremely important *something*. It was imperative that it be kept safe...and secret. He had to hide it far away from himself, so that even if someone were to locate it, they still would not know where to look for the infant."

Maggie stops when she realizes that her cup is empty and pours herself some more tea. "It was all very cryptic and confusing. I was already overwhelmed with my own problems, and then he dropped all of his problems in my lap too. I know I wasn't thinking very clearly. I glanced down at you lying quietly there in Dan's arms. You were watching me with those unusual green eyes, and I remember wanting to hold you so badly. I held out my arms and asked, 'May I?' I watched Dan pull you in tighter for a moment, closer to his body, as if he thought that he needed to protect you from *me* even."

"But then he reluctantly handed you to me. You were so tiny and fragile and so unbelievably beautiful. You were perfect in every way. I remember wishing for the strangest thing then. I wished that Dan had asked me to take *you* instead of some mysterious object that he wanted to hide. Such an odd thing to wish for, especially since I was in no position to take in a baby. But wish for it I did. I wanted you more than I had any right to."

"Dan watched me closely and I could tell that he wanted to take you back, but he allowed me to continue holding you. He said that he'd been struggling for days with the problem of where to hide it, of who he could trust it with. And then the answer had just popped into his head, and he knew without a doubt that I was the only one that he could entrust it to. He knew I would keep my word, if I gave it, to keep it safe and secret... always."

"He made sure to warn me that there was a slight risk of danger involved. He couldn't tell me what kind of danger though. I had already made up my mind that I wasn't going to do it, not if it meant putting my daughter in the slightest bit of danger. I had enough problems and worries without adding his to the pile."

"But he didn't give me a chance to deny him. He didn't play fair. He promised me that if I agreed to do this thing for him, he would pay all of my daughter's hospital bills...*all* of them, and that he would buy us a house. He said that moving us into our own home would serve two purposes. We would be safer and more comfortable, and that there would be less chance of *it* falling into the wrong hands. It was at this point that I asked him what *it* was. What could possibly be so important that it called for that level of protection, that he would go to such lengths and pay so much money to have it kept secret? He reached into the diaper bag that he'd brought with him and took out a cloth wrapped bundle."

"He carefully unwrapped it then and showed it to me. It was a beautiful purple and silver box, like a tiny jewelry box. He just shook his head at me when I asked him what was inside of it. He couldn't, or wouldn't, answer those questions. Then he quickly and nervously rewrapped the box and placed it back into the diaper bag. He assured me that he didn't expect me to make a decision right away. He told me to take my time and think about it very carefully and that he would be at Momma May's on Tuesday to hear my answer.

"But he'd already known my answer. How could he not? He knew that he'd offered me the one thing I couldn't refuse. He'd offered me hope. I was a mother, a desperate mother, and I would do anything to save my little girl. He knew and understood that fact because he too, was desperate to protect his daughter."

"But why?!" Ecko burst out. "I don't understand. I don't understand *any* of this! What was he protecting me from?"

Maggie stares down into her teacup, as if she'll find the answers there. But there *are* no answers written in the tea leaves and she shakes her head sadly. "I'm sorry, Ecko. I just don't know. I'm afraid that my knowledge of the whole situation doesn't really go much further than what I've already told you. Your father came into the cafe on Tuesday, and I agreed to his terms. He promised to keep it all very hush hush. He was a lawyer, you know, and a very good one at that. For the safety and privacy of everyone involved, he wanted to keep his name out of all our financial dealings. So, he hired one of his trusted lawyer friends, Mr. Murphy, to oversee everything. The two of them met with me at my apartment the very next day to set things into motion. Dan stayed behind to hand over the box in private, after the other man had gone. It was the one detail that he withheld from Mr. Murphy. As far as I know, Dan and I are the only ones that even knew about the box, and now you three, of course."

"But back to that Saturday, Dan solemnly placed the cloth-wrapped box into my hands. Again, he stressed how important it was that I hide it away, conceal it where it would never be found, and then never speak of it again. Not until either himself or his daughter came to collect it. I swore to him that I would uphold my end of the bargain; I would protect his secrets with my life. Then he hugged me tight, kissed my cheek, and walked away."

"That was the last time I ever saw him. He had reluctantly decided that we would have to go our separate ways to protect everyone involved. I also quit my job at the cafe. He didn't want anyone to be able to tie the two of us together in any way. Even more precautions, but I didn't mind that particular one. The only reason I'd gotten the job in the first place was to help pay for the medical bills, and he had taken care of those for me."

"Plus, it gave me so much more time to just be with my daughter. Within a month, Ally and I had moved into this house and all our bills were paid up, even the outrageously high hospital bills. Dan did everything that he'd promised to do, and so much more. I never saw him again, but he kept track of us, and he took care of us. When the doctors told me that Ally needed a bone marrow transplant, Dan somehow knew about it."

"He sent me one of those 'with great sympathy' cards. The message written inside of it had said, 'Don't worry about a thing.

It's already taken care of.' It was signed simply with a D, but it could have only come from him, and then somehow, miraculously, a donor... a perfect match for my Ally, showed up for the procedure. He paid for that too. Thanks to your father, my Ally made a full recovery. She grew up healthy and went on to college."

"Your father even paid for her college education. She has a wonderful life now, with a husband that adores her and two babies of her own." Maggie reaches across the table and takes Ecko's hands, then smiles with tears glistening in her eyes. "Best of all, my little girl has been cancer free for 16 years, and it's all thanks to Dan. I want you to know that your father was the greatest, kindest man I have ever had the honor of knowing."

"It broke my heart when Mr. Murphy informed me of the fire that took his life, and that of your stepmother and sister. I also learned that you were the only survivor. I couldn't help but wonder if whatever Dan had been running from had finally caught up to him, and if whoever, or whatever, he'd been hiding you from had found you."

Maggie stares out the window for a moment, seemingly lost in thought. Then she sighs forlornly and continues her tale. "I had Mr. Murphy look into things and found out that you'd been sent to that terrible hospital. I wanted to do something to help you so badly, but what could I possibly do? I couldn't just show up out of the blue and try to have you released into my custody, although that is exactly what I wanted to do."

"I even showed up there one day, prepared to try. I marched right in and asked to see you. The lady at the front desk looked your name up on her computer and then contemptuously informed me that you were on the no visitors list. I asked her why you weren't allowed to have visitors, but she didn't know. I demanded to talk to someone that *did* know. Snooty front desk lady made a phone call, then told me to have a seat and that someone would be there momentarily to speak with me."

"So, I sat down and waited. But God forgive me, I got up and left before anyone ever showed up. I knew in my heart that you were miserable, that you were possibly being mistreated even, and I got up and walked off, anyway. I cried the whole way home, but I still left you there and I am so very sorry for it."

"But as I was sitting there waiting, something strange happened. Someone spoke to me…*inside my head.* Some strange voice kept whispering to me to leave. She whispered over and over that I was making a terrible mistake, that it was not safe to bring you home with me. I didn't know what to do, but in the end, I listened to that voice, and I left, and I felt absolutely horrible about it. I *still* feel horrible."

"But I couldn't risk putting you in danger, not after everything that your father had gone through to keep you safe. I had Mr. Murphy keep tabs on you, that was the best I could do. I promised myself that if you were still in that hospital when you turned 18, I would bring the box to you there…somehow."

"I would sneak it in if I had to. Or I would find a way to bust you out. Whatever I had to do, I would do it. I owed that much, and so much more, to Dan. But then a few weeks ago, Mr. Murphy informed me that you'd been released and were living with your old neighbor. I've been waiting anxiously for you to come to me every day since. I was going to show up at your door on your birthday if you hadn't come before then. I am so very sorry for everything you've suffered. Please forgive me if I made the wrong choice in leaving you alone to fend for yourself in that place."

Ecko gently squeezes Maggie's hands as she begins to cry again and does what she can to comfort her. "There's nothing to forgive. I'm sure you did the right thing by listening to that voice and leaving me there, and it probably wouldn't have done any good had you stayed anyway. Like you said, there's no way they would have released me to a total stranger."

"I'll be perfectly honest with you. It WAS horrible, especially that first year. I don't even want to remember it. But you're wrong about me being alone to fend for myself. I was never alone, even though it felt that way for the longest time."

She glances over at Charlie with all the love she feels for him shining in her eyes. "Charlie was there for me, was *always* there for me. Dr. Bradburn refused to let him visit me for several months, but he just kept coming back. He finally got in her face and told her that the only reason to keep denying me visitation rights was because I was being mistreated. He said that if she turned him away one more time he would go to the police, and then to all the news channels. He assured her that he would sing like a canary in every single news reporter's ear until something was done. She'd had no choice but to finally give in and let him visit. He never stopped coming to see me after that. He's always right here beside me, any time I need him. Charlie has saved me so many times. I honestly believe that he's my guardian angel."

The three ladies turn as one to get a good look at what a guardian angel looks like. They burst out laughing as his face blazes red with embarrassment. He waves a dismissive hand at them and sputters, "Yeah, yeah. I'm a regular old knight in shining armor. Let's stay on track here, shall we ladies. What in tarnation was Dan up to, Maggie?"

She shrugs her shoulders and sadly shakes her head once more. "That's just it. I don't know. I've never known what he was up to, who he was hiding the box, and Ecko, from. I've told you everything that I know. The only thing left is the box itself. And now, I'm going to need everyone's help. It's going to take all of us to retrieve it."

She stands up and tells them to wait just a moment while she gets something out of the kitchen. When she comes back just seconds later, she's carrying a hammer in her hand. "Come, follow me. The box is hidden in my bedroom."

For just a moment, they regard one another with silent questions and wary concerns in their eyes, but then they all get up and follow her. When they're all crowded into her room, Maggie points to a huge, solid oak cabinet. "It's there," is all she says.

"Oh, that's a beautiful armoire. You have it hidden in there?" Susan asks with hope in her voice, hope that retrieving the box will be as simple as opening the wardrobe's doors. But nothing is *ever* that simple and straight forward when Ecko is involved.

"Not in it," Ecko whispers as chills rush over her body. *"Behind* it. I can feel it there, somehow."

Charlie steps forward and calls back to them, "Well, what are we waiting for, ladies? Let's get to it then." They all heave and ho, pull and tug, then push and shove that heavy armoire until they're wheezing and out of breath and they've created just enough space for Maggie to squeeze in between it and the wall.

She reaches up and rips the wallpaper off the section of wall that they had just exposed. Maggie draws the hammer back as far as she can in that tight space, swings it forward, and smashes a hole right in the middle of the wall. Then she goes to work widening the cavity with the hammer until she estimates that it's the right size. "Dan asked me to hide this very carefully, where no one would ever find it. This is the best I could manage and still keep it here where I could be sure of its whereabouts."

Out of breath from all of the exertion, Maggie falls silent as she reaches inside and pulls out a cloth wrapped bundle. "Let's take it back to the dining room so you can unwrap it comfortably," she manages to gasp out between her panting and puffing.

They all troop back to the table, but Charlie is frowning by the time they get there. "Maybe we should wait, Ecko. I mean, should you open it up here? Isn't there still a risk of danger involved?"

He turns his attention to their host and gently murmurs, "I would hate for something to happen to you because of us, Maggie."

But the stubborn woman's already shaking her head before he finishes that sentence. "I don't care. I really don't. I have kept that box hidden away for eighteen years now. You can't even imagine how crazy it's made me. Eighteen years of having that thing right there under my nose and never knowing what it was or what it contained. Eighteen years of wondering, trying to guess what secrets it was hiding. what secrets *I've* been hiding. Please don't shut me out now. I must know, finally, after all this time. I have to see this through to the end. Please," she begs.

Ecko understands her frustration completely. Hadn't she felt the exact same way all her life, too? Her eyes soften and she nods her head at Charlie. His shoulders slump and he sighs in defeat. He understands the frustration too, but he sure hopes that they're not tempting the fates.

They all gather back around the table and Maggie passes the bundle to Ecko. Her eyes are lit with excitement and eagerness at the thought of finally getting some answers. Ecko stares down at it for a long time, studying it, *feeling* it. She can actually feel the presence of that box. She can't properly describe it, but it's almost like a pulse, or a heartbeat that she can feel, thrumming inside of her.

When finally, she raises her eyes back up, she sees that everyone's sitting on the edge of their seats, trying to contain themselves and be patient for her sake. She would have laughed if the air hadn't been so thick with tension. She could barely breathe through it, much less laugh. "Here goes nothing," she mumbles as she unwraps the protective cloth from around it.

The first thing she uncovers is the envelope, sitting atop the box. Her eyes fill up with tears as she reads the words, 'To my dearest daughter Ecko' written in her father's handwriting. Maggie whispers, "You have no idea how many times I considered opening that letter and reading it. I wanted to do it so badly. There were times when I was sure that I wouldn't be able to resist it. But I could never actually go through with it. It was just too dishonest, and as I've said, I owed Dan too much to dishonor him like that."

With trembling hands, Ecko opens the envelope and silently begins to read the last words she will ever receive from her father.

My sweetest Ecko,

I am unsure of how things have turned out for us all, but if you're reading this, I fear the worst has happened and I am no longer here to explain things to you in person. But before I begin, I want you to know that at this very moment, as I'm writing this letter, I have you lovingly cradled in my arms. And I *do* love you, so very much. You have been here in my life for less than two weeks, and I love you like I have never loved any other thing in my entire life. That's not an easy thing for me to admit, because I love Rachael and Karen dearly.

But I was lost the instant that I laid eyes on you. Completely captivated and unconditionally devoted. I already possessed a father's fierce need to protect his family, but I took one look at you and that need suddenly intensified a hundredfold. I knew that I would do whatever it took, anything at all, to keep you safe. And for something so tiny and fragile, you sure did cause a lot of trouble. But no matter how things have ended up, I want you to know that I wouldn't have done things any differently. If I had it to do all over again, I would stand by the choices I've made. I need you to believe that, if you believe nothing else.

I have decided that I will not lie to you any more than I absolutely have to, so you already know that Rachael is not your biological mother. What you may or may not know at this point is…I'm not your biological father, either. I claim you as mine in every other way possible, just not by blood. Honestly, I have no idea *who* you are. It's as simple as that… and as complicated.

You came to me on the most anomalous day of my entire life. Things had been peculiar from the moment I opened my eyes that morning. I remember waking up terrified and covered in freezing cold sweat. I'd obviously had a nightmare, but I couldn't remember it, not even the remnant bits and pieces that usually got left behind for me to puzzle over upon waking. There was nothing but overwhelming feelings of fear and dread, and I was honestly glad that I couldn't remember what I'd seen in those dreams. Anything that was so horrifying that the feelings it evoked followed me around the rest of the day was certainly not anything I wanted to study too closely.

I felt *off* all morning. I was nervous and jittery, but I didn't know why. I assumed it was just some weird result of not sleeping well. But the feelings persisted, and my unease continued to grow stronger. I finally figured it out, as I was having breakfast at Momma May's. I was being watched.

Somehow, for some unknown reason, someone was watching me. Somebody, or something, had me locked in their sights. I knew it with everything in me, I just couldn't prove it or even explain it. My mind argued with itself that no one would have been able to watch me every place I had been that day. No one in that cafe was paying me any attention. There'd been no one in the car with me, and there certainly hadn't been anyone hiding in my bedroom watching me, for God's sake. Even if it had been possible, *why* would they have wanted to spy on me anyway? It made no sense whatsoever.

But I couldn't shake the feeling, and as I went about my day, I grew more and more certain of it. I tried everything I could to spot my stalker, but to no avail. Whomever it was, they were very cunningly sneaky, and I grew even more apprehensive as the day progressed. I was a nervous wreck and it showed.

Somehow, I made it through my day, even though I left everyone I came in contact with wondering what was wrong with me. Maggie, my coworkers, and especially Rachael, who knows me better than anyone else, were all worried about me. I was worried about myself too! I thought that I was going crazy. And then things went from strange to outlandishly bizarre.

That evening, as I was eating dinner with Rachael and Karen, I suddenly, crazily started hearing a voice whispering inside my head. A woman's voice, saying my name. Over and over and over again, calling me to her. I ignored it as long as I could, but then she screamed out my name one last time. Screamed it so loudly that I expected my eardrums to shatter from the force of it reverberating inside my skull. A sudden deep desire, an unignorable compulsion, took hold of me then and all I wanted to do was jump to my feet and run to *her*... whoever she was.

But I tried to stay calm and collected, at least outwardly, for Rachael and Karen's sakes. I knew there was no way I could explain what was happening. I didn't even *know* what was happening. So, I kept quiet. I knew that if I opened my mouth, nothing but gibberish would spew forth, confusing them further. I calmly stood up and left without saying a word. Just walked away without a single explanation. I simply got in my car and drove away.

I eventually ended up at the park, the one there by my office that I sometimes eat lunch at when the weathers nice. But I have no memory of the drive at all. One minute I was at home, walking out of the house and getting into the car, and the next I was sitting on a bench in the park.... with you on the seat next to me. You were lying there, all swaddled up in rags and you were crying your heart out.

But not normal, infant crying. You never made a sound, just stared up at me with your broken heart reflected in your eyes and silent tears streaming down your face. Then the strangest thing occurred. I felt my own heart simultaneously break and fill with love, all in the very same moment. I had no idea that my heart was capable of feeling such extreme opposites, all at the same time. I looked all around, searched everywhere for the person that you belonged to, even as everything in me illogically screamed that you belonged to *me*. There was no one else in the park with us though. No one at all. I had no clue where you had come from.

My head filled with questions, and I started to panic. Had I done this to you? Had I somehow stolen you and brought you there for some reason? Was *I* the reason for your tears? In my right mind I would never hurt anyone, and I certainly would never kidnap a baby. But I wasn't in my right mind, was I? I couldn't even remember how I'd gotten there. I had no idea what I'd done on my way to the park. But the sight of your anguish positively slayed me, so I reached over and picked you up, intent on soothing you. And it worked, very well, in fact. But it also soothed me at the same time. Your tears stopped as soon as I pulled you close, and I suddenly felt all my doubts vanish. I didn't know how, or why, or where you had come from. But you were mine. And oh, how I loved you!

I had no awareness of how much time had passed, how long I sat there just smiling down at you as I rocked you in my arms, kissing your tiny fingers. I eventually became aware of a woman sitting next to me, watching the two of us bond. I have tried, *extensively* but unsuccessfully to recall what she looked like so that when the time came, I would be able to describe her to you. But all I really remember about her is that she was beautiful, she was tremendously exhausted, and she had that same broken heart shining from her eyes that you had.

I remember thinking that someone or something had wounded her beyond repair. Somehow, I could feel the debilitating despair pulling the strength right out of her. Looking at her *hurt*. I could almost see her broken soul inside of her. And I could feel her panic. I knew that she didn't have much time, although how I knew all those things was beyond me.

I can recall one last thing. She had the most unusual eyes, eyes that weren't natural. They were purple with shining silver streaks. I thought for a moment that they were some weird contacts, but then I saw those silver streaks begin to sparkle and move, swirling through the purple. They were breathtakingly beautiful, but also very disturbing, mesmerizing even. I think I got lost for a moment, staring into them.

Then, while I was almost hypnotized by the lightning show in her eyes, she reached out and placed her fingers onto my forehead. Images flashed through my mind, so fast that I wasn't able to process them all. Some of it made no sense whatsoever. Some of it, I forgot instantly. Even more of it fades as the days go by. (When she touched me, I also remembered my nightmare from the night before, the one that I'd awakened from drenched in cold sweat. The one that had jump started this whole bizarre situation.)

It turns out, every bit of that dream was true and had actually happened...to *her*. SHE was the one that had been watching me. SHE had sent the dream to me, to illustrate some of the horrors that she'd gone through. (I wrote the whole, terrible dream down as soon as I was able to do so, just to ensure that I wouldn't forget it again. I'll include it at the end of this letter for you.) Along with the influx of images pouring into my mind came knowledge. She flooded my mind with all the information that she thought I would need to know. Without her speaking a word, I knew that her name was Laelynn. I knew that she was your mother. And I knew that *she was not from this world*. And neither are you. Trust me. I know how that sounds, but it's true, nonetheless.

I'm sorry to say that is all I ever really found out about her. Your mother may have given you up and entrusted you to me, but it destroyed her to do it. I know that without a single doubt. I *felt* it when she was mind-sharing with me. She told me that you were special, a gift. And that you had a very important role to play in saving worlds. Not just her world or my world…but multiple worlds. That perhaps the fate of *all* worlds would one day rely upon you. She told me that out of all the millions of people on Earth, I was the one that she'd chosen to entrust this gift to.

She said that she knew she had chosen well, she could sense how much I loved you already. I will never forget her next words. "Her name is Adrina Ecko Zyanya. On my world it means Love Repeats Forever. You must take her. You must promise to raise her as your own, to love her and protect her from all harm. There are those who seek to capture her and use her for evil purposes; others who would kill her on sight. They may come looking for her. *They must never find her.* Do you understand? It is highly unlikely that they'll be able to get to her, here on this world, but it is not impossible. There are ways, so you *must* hide her. Disguise her as your own human child and tell no one any differently. No one else can know the truth, it's too dangerous. Not just dangerous for her, but also for everyone around her. There are those who will stop at nothing to possess her. They will not think twice about killing you or anyone else to get to her. You must keep the truth hidden, even from her, at least until she is old enough to hear it. You will know when she is ready.

This childling will be very different from your human children. She will have…abilities. Magic, if you will. I have suppressed these abilities as well as I could manage, but some may still leak through. And when she turns eighteen, she will receive the full force of her powers. It will be extremely daunting and overwhelming for her, so you *must* prepare her before that time comes. Take her far away from other humans and just be with her when her time comes. Help her work through it so that she doesn't hurt anyone.

I am sorrier than you will ever know. I hope one day you will forgive me for thrusting you into this situation. Believe me when I tell you that there is no other way. Giving her to you will quite literally mean the death of me. But it is the only way that I can protect her. And now you must do it for me. You *must* protect her. Even though doing so will cost you dearly. You will have to lie to everyone that you love. It may not seem like it at times, but I promise you that it's worth it. It's worth all the pain and unpleasantness that you will have to face in the days and years ahead. *She* is worth it, worth *everything*. Just know that all of our love, all our hopes and dreams are with you. Our Everything is lying there in your arms. If evil finds her, our entire race will fall into darkness." And then she was gone. Just like that. Disappeared as if she were never there at all.

But in her place on the bench where she'd vanished from was a box and a necklace. I heard her voice whisper through my mind one last time. She told me that only you had the ability to use the key to unlock the box. She urged me to hide them away until you were ready for them. She said that I needed to take special care in where I hid the box. If someone, or something was able to track the magic in it, it would lead them straight to you.

I sat there staring down at that box for a long time, not even really seeing it at all. My mind was focused on one thing, the stupidest thing really. After everything I'd heard, everything I had learned that night, all I could think of right then was, 'Where am I going to hide these things. Where could I possibly hide something so important?' Now, looking back on it, I realize how ridiculous that was.

How absurd was it that my biggest concern was worrying about where to hide those things? Not the fact that I suddenly had a new baby. Not how I was going to *explain* having a new baby. Not how I was supposed to 'disguise' said baby as a human child, whatever that meant. And definitely not how I was going to go home and lie to my wife, and completely break her heart. Possibly have her leave and take Karen away from me.

No. I just sat there, thinking up and then rejecting hiding places until it finally dawned on me that Laelynn had said that only you would be able to use the key. Key? *There was no key.* I frantically searched everywhere for it. It wasn't with the box and necklace on the bench or in the grass beneath. I even searched in the rags wrapped around you, hoping that she'd hidden it there. But it wasn't there. It was nowhere to be found. It had either been lost before she'd arrived, or I had simply misunderstood her words. Either way, there was nothing I could do about it.

Hopefully you'll be able to figure out how to open the box. perhaps when your magic kicks in. And that was yet another worry. I have no idea how old you are or when your birthday is. Laelynn never told me that. I did the best I could to estimate how old you were, but that's all it was... a guess. I had no concept of how time works on the world you come from. How could I? And then the lawyer in me reared its head. I would have to make up a birthday. You would have to have paperwork, a birth certificate and social security card and shot records. I'm a well-known lawyer and I have connections to all sorts of people. I'm an honest man and I won't like doing it, but I can find someone to produce perfectly forged documents, for the right price. That wouldn't be problematic for me. But how am I supposed to get you away from everyone when you turn 18 if I don't know when your real birthday is? Hopefully you're reading this letter before that day comes around. Hopefully your magic hasn't awakened yet.

You'd fallen asleep, snuggled in my arms and all I could do was watch you. I sat right there on that bench rocking you and thinking of all the problems that I would need to work out. More and more of them kept arising, there was just no end in sight. Finally, I glanced at my watch and was shocked to see that it was close to midnight. I knew that Rachael would be frantic; I'd been gone for hours by that time. I gathered you up and gently strapped you into the passenger seat of my car as best as I could. I locked the things that your mother had left for you into the trunk of my car and drove straight to the nearest Walmart.

Babies need things. Lots of things, and all you had was some rags, a box, and a necklace. You didn't even have a diaper on. I bought everything that I thought you would need for the next few days, just the basics. Formula, bottles, diapers, wipes, clothes and a car seat. I got some strange looks from the cashier, let me tell you. I'm lucky she didn't call the police. But I made it out without incident, got everything loaded into the car, and strapped you securely into your new car seat.

Then, I just sat there beside you, trying to come up with a cover story. That didn't work out so well. I mean, really what *could* I say? I had been forbidden from telling the truth, so what else was there? Any story that I came up with that didn't make me look like a villain could get you taken away from me. Any attention, any kind of investigation would result in me losing all legal claim to you. That meant that I could potentially lose you and that just couldn't happen. So, I did the only thing I *could* do, and that was pretend that I'd been unfaithful to my wife and that you were legitimately mine. And *because* you were mine, no one would be able to take you away from me.

But oh, how it hurt to break Rachael's heart like that. And then to keep everything vague and not answer any of her questions, to watch the light in her eyes die. To see her cry every day and feel the distance growing between us...well, I freely admit that it unmanned me. I have cried a million tears, right along with her. I've begged and pleaded with her to stay, to give me another chance. I think if anything can convince her to stay, it will be you. The fact that you're just a tiny, helpless baby with no one else in the world to love you brings out her maternal instincts.

My Rachael is a beautiful, loving, and caring mother. I admittedly counted on that fact and shamelessly exploited it. I knew that she wouldn't be able to resist nurturing a baby. And no, I'm not ashamed that I played that card. I would do anything to keep my family, to have the chance to heal the hurt that I've caused them. Rachael says that she wants to try to work this out. I'm not sure that she can, but I have hope. As of today, she is still here. One day at a time, I guess. I promise that I'm doing the very best that I can do. This is harder than anyone will ever know.

Well, that's it. The rest, whatever happens after this, Maggie will have already explained to you. But oh, how I wish things had turned out differently and that I was there with you to help you along your path. I hope with all my heart that we had enough time to get to know one another. I hope I was able to show you how much I love and cherish you, and I pray that it was enough. What I wouldn't give to know how things all turn out. But I guess if you're reading this letter without me, it just wasn't written in the cards for me.

Well, Kiddo. Go save the worlds. I believe in you with all my heart and soul. And I wouldn't have changed a thing, I swear it on everything that I hold dear. Love always, Dad.

The sheets of paper fall from Ecko's violently trembling hands to lie atop the box that she's forgotten all about. She stares blankly at the wall, her face pale and expressionless. After a moment, Charlie feels a terrible fear creep into his heart. "Sweetheart?" he whispers. "What is it? What did you find out?"

She turns to look at him with shocked, disillusioned eyes. "It's all been a lie. My whole life...one huge, continuous lie." She hands the letter to Charlie, stands up and cries, "I'm sorry. I need to be alone. I need some time to think." Then she walks out the front door, leaving them to read what her 'father' had to say.

She walks blindly, lost in thought for the next hour. She thinks of all the lies and the secrets, and the absurd idea that she supposedly wasn't from this world, was in fact, not even human. But when it came right down to it, when she searches deep inside of herself...she finds that she really isn't that shocked at all. Hadn't she always known, deep down, that she didn't belong? That she was different? No, she wasn't really surprised, at all. But she *was* hurt. Hurt that she'd been lied to her whole life, about everything. That it came from her father, the one person that she'd had absolute faith in that had done the lying was the biggest betrayal of all.

Her emotions swell and churn inside of her, waking and rousing all the monsters inside her head. She knows she has to calm herself, knows that she has to quiet the noise in her head and lull them back to sleep before they start to riot.

She thinks of her father's letter. She thinks of how strong his arms were as they wrapped around her and held her close when she'd needed comfort. She remembers his hands, lifting her up off the ground any time that she fell. She thinks of his voice, always so encouraging and full of love, and his face, smiling and proud of her every little accomplishment. Her heart calms the moment that she pictures his face.

No matter what, she knows that the man she calls Daddy had loved her and had done everything he could to protect her. He had literally torn his entire life apart, rearranged it all and risked everything...for her. He'd been everything a father should be, and so much more. Daniel Lee Roberts *was* her father, blood or not...end of story. Now that she'd worked that out and her mind had remembered what her heart had never forgotten, she would be able to process everything else. As long as she could draw on the strength of her father, that lived on inside of her, everything else would fall into place, somehow.

Dan's Dream: A Glimpse into a Nightmare Reality

"Run! You have no more time. This is the only chance you will get. Do it now!" the woman tells herself. She glances down at the dead guard lying in the doorway of her prison cell. The burned-out eyes glare at her from its inhuman face, and a small tendril of smoke rises from its left nostril.

"Don't think about it," she scolds herself as she carefully steps over him. She doesn't understand what just happened, but she doesn't have time to dwell on it. HE would be coming for her. The Lokskell, the Shadow Lord, desperately wanted the magics that resides inside of her. He'd searched for a thousand years, and she was the only one he'd found that could give him what he desired.

She must escape. She must get as far away from him as she possibly can. Her hands cradle her hugely distended belly to steady it as she clumsily runs down the dark halls. He would soon know that she was on the run, if he hadn't already been alerted. His brand on her back that links her to him would make sure of that.

When his Droknallian creatures had captured and brought her to this castle, he'd known immediately that he'd better not underestimate her. The tattoo he'd given her was an extra precaution to the locked cell and armed creatures that guarded her day and night. That very first night that he'd come to her, he'd tied her down and gone to work inking her back. He'd added his own essence to the ink; blood from his human form and dark, misty shades from his shadow form. As he'd labored over her, he'd explained that the tattoo worked as a tracker. He'd said that even if she somehow managed to escape her cell, he would always be able to find her.

She didn't know what image he'd inked into her back, but it must have been extremely large and intricate. The pain was excruciating, and the procedure had lasted all night and most of the next day. The very second that he'd completed his mark and set the inking quill aside, she'd felt the spell snap into place and settle into her skin. She never doubted for a second that it would work just how he'd promised it would.

Now she feels it burning and writhing, as if it were a living thing that had been asleep beneath her skin but was now waking, alerting him of her escape. Yes, he would be coming for her, but hopefully not right away. After all, he believed that there was no way out for her, so perhaps he would take his time in retrieving her.

Anyone could enter this place, but they soon regretted it if they did. It was spelled to imprison all who were foolish enough to enter. There was no known way out. Even HE was trapped in this castle, a prisoner cursed to remain until his death or the end of time, whichever came first. He'd been stuck here for more than a thousand years.

She remembered how he'd told her that she belonged to him now and how he bragged that there was no escape for any of the lovely ladies that he kept here. He said that even if one of them somehow managed to get outside the castle walls, which was impossible, the land was harsh, cruel, and unforgiving. There was nothing left on this world beyond the fiercest of predators. Only the strongest, vilest, most perverted creatures survive.

Despite the fear coursing through her, the woman smiles as she rushes through the dark passageways. He'd known better than to underestimate her, and yet he'd done so anyway. She's special. There is no other in existence like her. She's the only living

Wandelaar, the one and only Mirror Walker. That's why he wants her. All she requires is a mirror and she could, at any time, travel wherever she desired. It was for this very reason that he'd had all the mirrors in his castle broken and ground to dust upon her arrival.

Unbeknownst to him, she wouldn't need a mirror to escape; there was another way out for her, hidden right under his nose within his own castle. The magic inside of her, what made her a Wandelaar, didn't stop at mirror traveling. There's so much more to it than that. For one, it allowed her to see what no one else can see, hear what no one else can hear. She can feel the secrets that this place keeps hidden away, they whisper in her ear, always.

This castle is one of the seven EverRealms, and each one of those magical places has a secret chamber that contains multiple enchanted portals, mystical doorways to other worlds concealed within them. There are very few beings who know about these secret chambers and the exits that they contain, and even fewer that had any hope of locating them. But she would always be able to find the hidden chambers of the EverRealms.

She can hear this one humming in her head, calling for her. It pulses as if it's a heartbeat. The entire time she'd been locked away she had listened to it, felt it calling to her. All she has to do now is get to it, and she must. The Shadow Lord cannot be allowed access to the power held within her.

She darts down one dark corridor after another, listening to the hum resonating within her. It grows louder and clearer the farther down into the bowels of the castle that she descends. Fear of being recaptured spurs her onward and lends her strength. Something inside of her, a buried instinct, guides her and urges her on. There!

The thrumming was coming out from behind a seemingly solid stone wall. She quickly sketches a small sigil onto the barrier, a Reveal Rune. The wall shimmers briefly and then disappears to reveal a vast, cavernous chamber. The instant that she steps inside, the wall solidifies once more, behind her, and all sound recedes. That persistent humming has finally been silenced. She turns back to look behind her to discover that the wall on this side is covered with its own runes and wards. She had never seen such magnificent rune-work before. It's beautiful, ancient, and extremely complex.

The mark on her back suddenly roils around and begins to burn like liquid fire. She must hurry! She doesn't know if the magic that's protecting this room will prove to be stronger than the tracking magic of his brand. She can't let him recapture her, but he can NEVER be allowed access to this room. The fate of not just this world, but countless others depended on it remaining hidden. If he tracks her to this chamber and the wards can't protect these secrets, then all will be lost anyway. Escaping will no longer matter.

The tattoo squirms and writhes beneath her skin. She hastily steps into the exact center of the chamber and opens up that part of her mind that allows her to see what others could not. She trembles with excitement as a bright white light flashes, brilliantly lighting up the room before quickly fading away to nothing.

This is it. This is what's been calling to her for months, and it is magnificent. The air throughout the room is suddenly full of long, jagged gashes. Bright, shimmering light shines inside each one. It looks as if countless bolts of lightning had struck all over the room and shiny silver- white scars were left behind to shimmer in the air. The air had been sliced and torn in a thousand different places, and the wounds were bleeding silver light.

These were called the Rips, or tears in reality, portals to other worlds. This room that exists, here, in this reality simultaneously exists in every other world too. She now has access to every single existing world. She can go anywhere she chooses, even without a mirror. But there's only one place she longs to be. She makes her way around the room, focusing on each Rip to determine which land they open up to.

She's looking for the entrance to one very specific world. She wants to go home. HE will never be able to have her recaptured if she can just make it home to her beloved Irredarr. If there be any creatures on her world that are willing to follow his bidding, they'll not fare well. Irredarrians are made of color and light and white magic. They will defeat any legion of darkness HE sends after her. Light will always beat back the Dark.

All of a sudden, the pain that's coming from his brand on her back becomes so intense that she cries out and falls to her knees on the cold, stone floor. The tattoo twists and churns angrily under her skin. She cries out as a rush of warm liquid pours from her body and the first sharp contraction rips through her swollen belly.

"No, no, no, no. Not now!" she moans. She cannot give birth here! The mark on her back grows hotter and hotter until it seems to catch fire, a blazing inferno excruciatingly burning inside her skin. A strange, high-pitched screeching begins to emanate from behind her. She feels her flesh stretching and extending outwards, painfully pulling away from her body as his brand endlessly twitches and writhes. It feels as if the skin of her back is being ripped right off of her bones.

The spelled tattoo has somehow become a living entity and it is now tearing itself out of her skin, shrieking all the while. She screams aloud as another agonizing contraction seizes her. She can't endure this, the combined pain of it all is unbearable. But the fear that instantly overtakes her when she hears HIM roaring out her name outweighs the agony. A wave of absolute terror crashes over her as she feels HIM closing in, threatening to drown her in the depths of her panic. In unimaginable pain and leaving a trail of blood and fluids smeared behind her, she crawls to the closest Rip. Without hesitation, she slips through the opening. The sounds of HIS rage thunder and reverberate throughout the entire castle as he feels her suddenly blink out of existence.

The Rip spits her out and she lands heavily upon her knees, in the dirt, right in the middle of a dark, black forest. Then the Rip disappears, leaving no evidence of its existence behind. The instant that it's gone, the tattoo finally finishes extracting itself from her skin. It's magically morphed into a flying, shadowy entity about the size of a small house cat. The creature vaguely resembles some sort of evilly twisted, miniature dragon. It flies around her head three times, screeching and shrieking, the blood from her torn skin dripping from its wings. Then it falls to the ground and disintegrates into a pile of black ash, screaming the entire time.

The screeching is mercifully silenced when a sudden wind lifts the ashes and scatters all trace of the Lokskell's filthy magic away. Apparently, the spell that animated it had been unable to survive the journey through the Rip.

For the moment, she's free of the Lokskell, but her troubles are far from finished. She's still all alone on an unknown world, about to give birth in the middle of a dark and sinister forest. The contractions come faster and faster, threatening to tear her apart. She cries out for someone to help her, but there's no one to be found. The forest is not a welcoming place. The Rip she had crawled through had led to a land that's almost as unforgiving as the one she'd just escaped. HIS dark influence reaches far beyond his own land to many others. This is one of the worlds that he holds a tight grip on, and it's dying.

Hours after her escape, the woman sobs in pain and exhaustion. Cold and alone, she lay bleeding into the dirt beneath a shriveled, stunted tree that's dripping with black moss. She focuses on her newborn daughter for strength. She wants to give up, oh, how she wants to give up. But she has to finish this...for all of their sakes.

She sits up and takes a couple of deep breaths, steels herself, and then bears down. With one final and tremendous push, the new life slips free of her body. She collapses back down to the ground and cries out a heartbroken wail of despair. She can't do it. She knows that she can't.

Even though she'd had several months to mentally prepare herself, she'd never truly believed that she could kill HIS son. The boy was a part of her too, it's not his fault that his father is evil. The moment she hears the babe cry confirms it. She cannot keep him, but neither can she kill him.

With tears streaming down her face, she sits back up to get a look at him. Her heart stops and her breath catches in her throat. She stares in shocked disbelief at the squalling infant she'd just given birth to. Another girl? How can this be? It's not possible! This childling should be a male. Always, in all the history of Irredarr, there is a daughter born to take after the mother and a son for the father to pass his powers on to. That is ever how it's been. But alas, here it is, and there are two girl-childlings instead.

The woman's eyes turned a shiny metallic silvery color, mirror-like as she uses her waning magic to study each girl. HER daughter, the one to inherit her own, Irredarrian magic will indeed become the next Wandelaar, with all the magic and abilities that comes with being a Mirror Walker. She'd also been gifted with extra abilities, powers unknown and undefined as of yet. Within her tiny, innocent body resides a tremendous amount of wild, undetermined magic. Only time will tell what those magics will become. They'll grow as the child grows. The aura surrounding this childling is bright and beautiful with a myriad of rainbow lights sparkling within it. It is everything expected of a Wandelaar heiress, but oh, so much more. And it's the most beautiful thing she has ever seen. But as she watches, she notices that there are three tiny, black blemishes mixed into the radiance of her daughter's aura, a darkness apparently passed on from the father. The new mother can only pray that the blights won't grow and spread like a cancer, but that it will disappear over time. Light defeating the Dark. She can only hope that her daughter will always use her abilities for good. She gently lifts the babe into her arms and holds her close.

She then turns her attention to the other childling, this daughter that should have been a son for the Lokskell, the Shadow Lord's heir. Although the girls look exactly alike on the outside, this one is the polar opposite of her sister on the inside, where no one could see. She too has a vast amount of magic churning inside of her, but it's dark and twisted and foreboding. A black, shadowy aura with three small flecks of silver light clings to her. The potential to do good is there, but the odds are monumentally against it.

The woman wishes that she could see into the future, but that's not an ability that she possesses. Even so, she knows that this childling is capable of great evil, but as long as those silver Irredarrian flecks remain inside of her, there's a small chance that the girl can be saved. The new mother picks the infant up and cuddles her close, too. She can only hope and pray for the best, because she cannot, will not destroy her. Dangerous as this daughter may be, she loves her anyway.

The woman travels for two days, cradling her babies in her arms, as she stumbles along, searching for signs of life. She grows weaker with each step that she takes, but she never loses hope. She will save her girls, even if that means forfeiting her own life.

When she finally comes upon the small town, she sobs with heartfelt relief. It's a run-down and dilapidated place, the inhabitants rough, rowdy, and distrustful. But it'll have to do. She's in desperate need of food and rest, but finding a safe place to lay low has to be her first priority. Then, after she recovers a bit, she'll find someone worthy to raise and protect her daughters.

Curiouser and Curiouser

Three worried faces greet Ecko when she knocks on Maggie's front door. Thankfully her phone had still been in her pocket when she'd run out earlier. GPS was the only reason she was able to find her way back, because her mind certainly hadn't been on watching her surroundings.

Charlie immediately grabs her and hugs her so hard that she can't breathe. Eventually he turns her loose and steps back so that he can look her in the eyes. "I'm fine, Charlie. Really," she tells him. "I just needed time to process everything. Did you read it? Did you believe it? Who *am* I, Charlie? Where did I come from?"

Charlie's watery old eyes fill with even more tears, and his chin starts trembling, but he quickly gets ahold of himself. "I don't know where you came from, sweetheart. And I don't care. You are still the same person you were yesterday. You're the most considerate and caring young lady that I know. And you are the strongest, bravest person that I have ever met. You've overcome so very much, and you haven't let any of it break you. *Nothing* you find out today will change that. You will still be Dan's daughter. And you will still be the daughter of my heart."

Ecko and Charlie turn as one when they hear sniffling behind them. "Oh great," Charlie exclaims. "Now we've gone and done it.

The womenfolk are leaking. Bah! Now everyone's going to want hugs. Durned softies," he mutters as he wipes tears off his own face.

"Ummm, Charlie? I really have to pee…" Ecko apologetically interrupts.

"Oh! Of course! Sorry, love," Charlie replied, "Maggie, have you got a blanket that I can borrow right quick?" She's obviously confused but retrieves the requested blanket and hands it to him. He goes into the restroom and covers the mirror, then comes out and gives her the 'All clear'. Susan quickly and quietly explains to Maggie that they cover every mirror that Ecko has to be exposed to and why they do it. Maggie, of course, has no idea what to say about that.

The sun is beginning to disappear behind the trees and the air is growing cooler. Night is quickly moving in, and there was still so much to discuss. Maggie, using a no nonsense, 'don't even think about arguing with me' voice, informs the trio that they will be spending the night there, as her guests. "It's getting late, and it's going to be a lot later when we get done talking. I have a guest room already made up and I have a couch that pulls out into a bed. I've slept on it myself and believe it or not, it's surprisingly comfy. I have extra toothbrushes and I can come up with some sort of sleepwear for everyone. Maybe some sweatpants for Charlie? No arguments now. I won't take no for an answer. The matter is already settled. Now, what does everyone want for dinner? I don't know about you guys, but I am absolutely famished. I simply *have* to refuel. Tea and scones only go so far, you know."

Maggie disappears into the kitchen and then returns with a stack of paper menus from local diners that make deliveries. She slaps them down on the table and orders, "Choose!" Then she's off again, back into the kitchen. The three of them look at one another and shrug. Not a one of them is willing to argue with the obviously determined Maggie.

"I guess we're having a sleepover," Susan tells them with a girlish little giggle.

Charlie gets a twinkle in his eyes then, and admits, "I've never been to a sleepover with a bunch of girls. Can we have a pillow fight?"

Ecko can only smile as she thinks to herself, 'What would I do without these two old kids in my life?' She knows that she wouldn't have even made it out of the crazy house if she hadn't had them to support her. She wraps an arm around them both and tells them how much she adores them.

Then they get down to the serious business of choosing what's for dinner. They all agree on a Chinese buffet and Maggie calls in and places everyone's orders. They gather back around the table where Ecko reads the rest of the papers that had been in the envelope.... the dream that her 'mother' had somehow sent to her dad. It sounded like some sort of make-believe story, a twisted fairytale that some author had dreamed up and put to pen and paper. But it was all true. She believes with her whole heart that every word of it was true. She has Charlie read it aloud to the rest of the group while they wait for their food to arrive.

She fiddles with the box while they discuss everything that they've learned. She concentrates on the magic that she feels inside it. It thrums and pulses in her hands, but only in *her* hands. The others have said that they can't hear or feel anything. The box is extremely well made, with no discernible way to open it. It's basically just a cube, albeit a beautifully decorated one, with no lid to lift or hinges to swing open. There's a rather large, odd-looking keyhole to unlock it, but *how* it opens has been cleverly disguised.

It really is a thing of beauty through, absolutely mesmerizing. It's made of silver, decorated with shining (purple?) jewels. They look like a cross between rubies and amethysts, but much, much darker than either of those. Ecko instinctively knows that there are no jewels like these on Earth. She even pulls out her phone and Googles different jewels and also all the shades of purple and red. She can find nothing like them online.

She tries to come up with exactly what color they are, but there just isn't a word for it. The overall appearance when she'd first set eyes on them was a dark purple color. But they are actually multi-faceted, seemingly made up of several different colors. She sees purple, red, black, and even blue; and those are just the ones that she can identify. She also catches glimpses of shimmering silver mixed in there too. The colors change depending on the way she turns the box.

Ecko looks up at the group when she realizes how quiet it's become. Apparently, she'd gotten too lost in her own thoughts to realize that Charlie had asked her a question. "I'm sorry, Charlie. I wasn't trying to ignore you. I was just trying to figure out what kind of jewels these are. Can you repeat the question?"

Charlie smiles and hurries to reassure her. "Quite alright, Sweetheart. I just asked what your thoughts were on coming up with a key to open that thing. Maybe we could take it to a locksmith, but I'm not entirely sure that's a good idea. It's supposed to remain a secret; no one's supposed to know of it. And also, there is the fact that others may try to steal it. It has to be priceless. Those are no ordinary jewels."

The doorbell suddenly rings, startling them all. They laugh as Maggie and Charlie get up to collect their food, where they promptly get into a small spat over who was going to pay the delivery man. Charlie, ever the gentleman, won that round. There was no way in hell he was going to make a woman pay for his meal. Ever. He was old school and extremely proud of it.

Susan giggles and whispers conspiringly to Ecko "Well, I guess the score is even now, 1 and 1. Maggie got her way about spending the night, Charlie got his way about paying for dinner. You want to take bets on who'll come out on top by the time we leave here? My bet's on Maggie!"

Ecko grins back and says she'll take that bet. "You're on! I've got a twenty-dollar bill that says Charlie's the more stubborn of the two!" They laugh and shake on it as Charlie and Maggie come back in carrying the bags of food.

"What's going on in here? What are you two giggling like schoolgirls about now?" Charlie demands, causing them both to crack up.

"We'll never tell!" Susan answers in a singsong voice as she helps set the table.

Everyone's just about done eating when Ecko becomes aware of the fact that her hip is on fire. Not *literally* on fire, but the skin there was really, really hot. Uncomfortably so. She frowns and reaches down to rub it and feels the lump in the pocket of her jeans. "The rose!" she shouts out, startling the rest of the group.

Back at Charlie's house, she had wrapped a cloth around it, before stuffing it into her pocket so that the thorn wouldn't jab her. Now she pulls it out and unwraps the cloth from around it, careful to avoid the thorn. The pendant has started making that same thrumming sound that the box has been making. They're evidently reacting to being in such close proximity to one another. In fact, they're both humming and vibrating so violently that the others can actually feel it now also.

"The rose is the key!" Ecko excitedly tells them.

Charlie thumps his fist down on the table and shouts back, "*Yes!* Why didn't I see it before? I knew there was something strange about that keyhole. It was just too big, too rounded for a regular key to fit into. But I think you're right, my girl. The rose will be a perfect fit!"

Maggie lurches up out of her chair and shouts, "What rose? Great! Now we're all yelling. I don't know why we're all yelling but I can't seem to stop myself! No one told me anything about a rose! Where did THAT come from?"

Susan quickly explains about the time-capsule, Sir Didymus, the clue with her name and address written on it, and finally the necklace. "Oh! I had forgotten all about that!" Maggie exclaims. "Your dad mentioned a necklace when he gave me the box, but I never actually saw it. Oh." Her shoulders slump as she gets a closer look at the size of the rose bud pendant.

"I'm sorry. I don't think that's going to work. It's still too small to be the key. Look at the size of that keyhole… What? What are you idiots grinning about?"

Charlie just laughs. "Watch this!" Ecko runs her finger over the thorn, gasps at the little pinprick, and watches as the drop of blood begins the transformation.

"Oh my God!" Maggie shouts when it's done and the rose is in full, magnificent bloom. She slaps a hand to her chest and shakes her head in astonishment. "That was incredible, absolutely *magical!* It really is the key; it *has* to be! *That's* why everyone's yelling! That's why *I'm* yelling! Oh, mercy me! My heart's just-a racing!"

Susan nods in agreement as she tells her, "Crazy thing is, it only draws the one drop of blood, no more. And there isn't any blood residue or even a mark left on her finger afterwards. Also, what Laelynn told Dan was absolutely, 100% correct. The key *only* works for Ecko. No matter how hard we pressed our fingers to it, it never once drew blood from either of us."

Ecko's having second thoughts, doubts about the entire situation. She'd been desperate for answers just a few short hours ago, but now she's actually considering forgetting about the whole thing, or trying to forget it, anyway. Maybe, if she begged her to,

Maggie would put the box back into the wall, board it back up, and forget that she'd ever come here. Her father had been right. The more she learned, the more she questioned, and the more she learned, the more afraid she became.

There *had* to have been a mistake. There was no way she was some sort of hero, destined to save the world. She was just the crazy girl, the one that talked to herself and saw things that weren't there. The one that spent years locked in a mental institute. The one just stumbling through life, barely functioning. Her heart suddenly starts thumping in her chest and panic begins to build in her mind.

She hears Charlie talking to her, but his voice sounds far away. Her internal ears pick up the sounds of rustling and thumping. Her old friend Fear, who'd kept her company for so many years before she'd learned how to cage her monsters, is starting to wake back up. Her breath comes faster and faster and she looks to Charlie, her rock and anchor, with fear and desperation in her eyes.

He immediately recognizes the signs of her panic and rushes over to squat down in front of her. He holds her hands and speaks slowly and softly, steadily as he looks into her eyes. "Deep breath in, now slowly let it out. Let it all go. Again. Breathe in..." Charlie works with her, calms and comforts her, until she's steady once more.

"Ecko honey, do you want to call it a night? Today's been very stressful for you. You've had to deal with some extraordinarily shocking news. That box has waited all this time, it can wait one more day. There's nothing that says you have to open that thing right now," Susan says with worry evident in her voice.

Ecko quickly shakes her head. "No. I want to get it over with. I have to know. I'll never be able to sleep tonight if we put it off. I'm ok, now, I promise," she assures them. The rose key had reverted back to its original state while she'd had her mental breakdown, so she pays it another drop of blood. They all watched in awe as it blooms again, just as mesmerized now as they were the first time they'd witnessed the magic of it.

She takes one more deep, steadying breath, then gently inserts the blossom into the keyhole. Of course, it fits perfectly. She knows the instant that the box's magic is triggered. There's a small click as the lock springs open and then the jewels begin glowing and shining. It looks as if there's pure white light emanating from within, almost as if there's a tiny sun trapped inside of it.

She quickly sets the box back on the table as purple and silver light shoots out of the jewels in every direction, filling the room with an otherworldly glow. She hears the others gasp, then ooh and aah in wonder, but she never takes her eyes off the box. She watches as it unfolds itself, opening up from the inside. The walls all fold outwards, revealing the wonders that reside inside.

There's a ring, unlike any she has ever seen before, a magnificent, rainbow hued, jewel circled by tiny, silver pearls marbled with pink streaks. It is absolutely stunning. Ecko reaches out for it, but a woman's face suddenly appears in the space above the jewel before she can take it, an image of an elegantly beautiful woman with pale hair and swirling shades of purple and magenta-colored eyes. It's some sort of holograph, magically projecting out of the ring.

Then she begins to speak, and it's a voice that Ecko has been hearing in her dreams for her entire life…the voice behind the red door. A sudden chill sweeps through her. She breaks out in goosebumps and every tiny hair on her body stands straight up. She'd always hated the saying, 'Someone just walked over my grave', had never really comprehended the meaning of it. She understands now. She feels haunted, somehow as she listens to her mother speak. She knows, irrefutably that this is her mother. Her heart had recognized her immediately.

"Hello my sweet Ecko. Oh, how I wish I could be there with you to watch you grow. To teach you, guide you, comfort you. love you. There is so much that you need to know, so very much that won't fit into this message. I don't have much time left, or strength. My magic is dying. It is leaving me before its time, and it's taking every bit of power I can spare to create this message for you. I must use every precious second that I have left to tell you who you are, where you come from, and to prepare you as best as I can for what comes next."

"As you've learned by now, you are not the Earthling that you've been led to believe you are. We come from a world very far from the one I've left you on. My home world is called Irredarr, which in *words* loosely translates to Iridescent Dreams. But it's so much more than that. It is the most wondrous land you could ever imagine, beautiful beyond comparison, full of light and color and life."

But perhaps you've seen it? Caught glimpses of it in the Earth mirrors? Was my spell strong enough to suppress all of your magic? Or, as I suspect, has some of it spilled over and leaked through the protection spell I gave you? The gold and silver strands of the tattoo wrapped around your ankle is the spell that protects you. The single purple strand woven into them is the spell I added to suppress your magic. It will disappear when you're old enough and you reach your full potential. By my best estimation, that will be when you turn 18 Earth years.

"Time is different on Irredarr, it moves much slower there than on Earth. It makes it difficult to know the exact timelines, but you will know it when it happens. I'm afraid that it will hit you all at once, with little to no warning at all beforehand. There will be a massive power surge inside of you, and unfortunately, there is no way of knowing what else may happen, or how you will react when it hits. It's different for us all and you, my precious girl, will be unlike any other Wandelaar in Irredarrian history. Your magic is immense, wild, and unpredictable."

"It would be wise for you to not be in close proximity to any other Earthlings when that time comes. I will instruct the human named Daniel to care for you, to nurture you as if you are his own flesh and blood. I know that he will love you and be good to you. His heart is very pure, especially for an Earthian, and a male one at that. That's what drew me to him. It's what made me choose him. I saw his light shining through the mirror and I knew he was the one. He will give you a good life, since I cannot do so."

"I am a Wandelaar, a Mirror Walker, and I am the only one in existence. There is only ever one at any given time. The current Wandelaar must give up her magic to her heiress. YOU are that heiress. YOU will be the universe's next Mirror Walker. The magic will leave me, and you will inherit it when you come of age. There are many powers, magics, and abilities that come with being the Wandelaar...and many burdens."

"But the main thing, the *best* thing is that you'll be able to travel to other lands through the mirrors. You will also be able to open the way for others to travel with you, if you so choose. Thousands of years ago, our people used this ability to explore the Otherlands. We wanted to see everything, learn all there was to know about the worlds around us. Every new discovery, every new species was a fascination to us. We forged alliances and made many friends on nearly every world that we visited."

"The hostile or inhospitable lands we stayed clear of. We are, for the most part, a peaceful people, friends, not war-makers. We're wanderers, explorers, scientists, and archivists. Every land that we explore, we try to leave it better than how we found it. Trade stations were set up on those welcoming worlds and the inhabitants would come from all around, travel hundreds of miles to see the wonders that the other worlds had to offer."

"We rendered aid to many other races during their times of need. Sometimes, we'd come across a dying species and were able to save it by bringing it to our own world to be protected. No matter what, we tried to always do good wherever we went, to share what we could and give aid where it was needed. Everything was perfect, peaceful for many, many years and all the lands in our trade system flourished."

"But all that tranquility came to a sudden end a thousand years ago. A terrible fate befell our people. Our Wandelaar, Lamora Deidra was viciously, ruthlessly murdered. She'd taken a large group out on a scouting expedition to a world that had been mostly unexplored. She'd heard rumors of a towering, magical tree that grew deep in one of the forests, hidden away and almost impossible to find. The rumors told of its beauty, that thousands of different kinds of flowers bloomed from its branches. It supposedly bore hundreds of different types of fruit and berries."

"It was called Mother Tree and it was said to be the origin of every single flower, fruit, and berry that had ever existed. The natives had insisted that it was the only one of its kind, and that it held a single seed inside of it. They'd said that it would only surrender its seed to the one it found worthy."

"Our people are great lovers of beauty. We adore anything colorful, glittery, shiny or magical. We cannot resist the allure of anything that we find beauteous or mysterious. Lamora Deidra was no different. She could not resist the temptation and she'd quickly become obsessed with it. She *had* to find that tree, to see it for herself."

"So, she gathered her group of explorers and they all left Irredarr with high hopes of discovering something new and wondrous. But they found tragedy instead. Unbeknownst to them, a terrible evil had come to that land that they were visiting. It sensed our Wandelaar's power, and it coveted it. It wanted that magic for itself. It killed her for it. Not only did it take her away from us, it did so before she'd had an heiress to pass her magic on to. Her death meant the end of all mirror travel, amongst the many other things that we lost on that fateful day."

"It also meant that the group of explorers, all 324 souls, got trapped on that world with the evil one. The Shadow Lord, or Lokskell, as he came to be known, was a creature of darkness and shadows, a lover of carnal pain and dark pleasures. He was capable of great evil, thriving on filth and absolute depravity. He tried to steal our Wandelaar's ability to travel to the Otherlands, killing her in the process. There'd been a fierce battle, and Deidra had bravely fought against him with every bit of magic she'd possessed."

"She'd almost beaten him too and had been preparing to end him when he hit her with a last desperate wave of his own magic. Deidra realized that she had no hope of defeating the evil creature, for he was no mere flesh and blood man, but was made up of shadows... foul, murky mist and inky, black darkness itself. She recognized too, that she wouldn't even survive the encounter. But even though her life would be forfeit, she had to find a way to stop him, stop his evil from spreading."

"So, with the last of her strength, she'd called on her Wandelaar magic one last time. Unfortunately, it hadn't been enough to end him, but there'd been just enough left inside of her to banish him to the nearest of the seven EverRealms, Sheol Castle. She'd cursed him to live out the rest of his unnatural life as a prisoner, forever trapped within its halls. And there he has remained for over a thousand years, and with every passing day his fury grows stronger, sending him further and further into madness."

"That ill-fated world and all of its inhabitants have since suffered many atrocities, such unthinkable evil and terror, for although the Lokskell remains imprisoned for all eternity, that is not so for his Shadows. They are free to roam wherever their master sends them, for how does one imprison a sliver of darkness? With his foul presence untethered as it was, he was able to send his evil intent out into the world, to rape and ravage and ruin. Over the course of time, the once beautiful land eventually became a barren wasteland where only the worst of the worst has managed to survive."

"Our world suffered a great loss as well, although outwardly you'd never have known it. Irredarr fell into a deep despair unlike anything it had ever experienced before. Our entire way of life had ended. We were lost, adrift in a sea of sadness and loss and endless tears. It took years for us to find our way again. But finally, we did."

"Our hope was restored when one of our Seers had a vision of the future and The Prophecy was foretold. It spoke of a new kind of Mirror Walker that would one day be born to them, one with original and wondrous magics to offer. It would be a very long time before the prophecy was fulfilled, but finally it came to pass. After a thousand years of waiting, a new Mirror Walker was born to Irredarr."

"I was recognized the instant that my mother bore me. I'd been born with solid silver eyes, the distinguishing feature that belongs exclusively to Wandelaars. Despite all my years of training and preparing, it had still been exceedingly hard on me when I came into my magic. It took a long time for me to get used to the immense power I held inside of me, and even longer for me to learn to control it."

"By the time the magic settled in, and I'd grown comfortable with it, we'd already figured out that the Prophecy still hadn't been fulfilled. A new Wandelaar *had* been born, but I was not the one that the Prophecy spoke of. *You,* who'd also been born with the Mirror Walker's silver eyes are the fulfiller of the Prophecy. *You* are the extraordinary Wandelaar with the new, mysterious powers to offer. I can't even tell you what to expect as your magic is completely unknown and unlike any that's come before you. I can only imagine how difficult it will be for you when your time comes, and the magic takes you. I am sorrier for that than you will ever know."

"After I came into my own magic and learned to control it, I spent many years traveling and exploring the Otherlands. I discovered that many worlds had become infected with the poison of the Lokskell. His Night Shades and Slivers had taken root and made themselves at home on those ill-fated lands. Eager to do his bidding, they'd quickly multiplied and spread like wildfire. They corrupted everything they came in contact with, creating more and more evil beings to help with the destruction of these once beautiful paradises."

"On some worlds, I discovered only faint traces of the Shadow Lord's filth. On others, it had spread like a cancer. The world in which the Lokskell remains trapped, the world that Lamora Deidra tragically lost her life, is one such place. He's had a thousand years to work at transforming it into the kind of place where evil things like him thrive."

"The land has fallen into darkness, full of rot and filth and decay. It is dying. Very little of its previous beauty and goodness has survived. I'd been told all my life how beautiful it was there, but I never got to experience that beauty for myself. A thousand years is a long time for a wound to fester, and that's exactly what the Lokskell's corrosive foulness had become to that wounded and dying land. It's a terrible, wasted world now, full of despair and hopelessness and corruption."

"I renamed it the Shadowlands, for that's exactly what it was now, and I avoided it at all costs. Not even the temptation of finding the Mother Tree could sway me. There was absolutely nothing that would make me choose to go the same way as my predecessor, especially as my own heiress hadn't been born to me yet either. Until something *did* make me change my mind. I discovered that our people, the ones that had been left behind in the Shadowlands all those years ago, were slowly and meticulously being slaughtered, one by one while they slept in their stasis forms."

"I know that you don't understand, and I can't take the time to explain. It's complicated and would take up too much time, but think of it as sort of like hibernation. They were being killed in their sleep, a magical sleep where they should have been safe. I couldn't just sit back and ignore their deaths. Not when I felt everything they felt, their pain, their fear, their hopelessness. I heard their voices as they cried and begged for help that would not, could not come for them."

"I found that I couldn't ignore them. I couldn't silence those voices and pleas for help. I had to at least try. I wouldn't have been able to live with myself if I'd done nothing. So, I'd gathered a small, *very* small, group to accompany me on my quest. Hunters and fighters mostly, I didn't want to put any more of my people at risk than I absolutely had to. I forbid my lover, Aruune, from coming with me."

"I wanted to, *needed* to keep him safe. I told him that when I returned, I would finally wed him, and we would have our heirs. I told him that I loved him, and I kissed him goodbye. I went to that terrible world to save my people, but I got trapped there too. The Lokskell, the Shadow Lord, felt my presence the moment I stepped through the mirror, and he sent his creatures after us. They killed my men and eventually captured me."

"I was his prisoner for six years, six long, torturous nightmare years, before he was finally able to force me to bear my heiress...you. The Lokskell had long ago discovered that he was unable to steal fully mature magic. He can only pilfer magic when it is brand new, wild and undeveloped. In other words, he has to steal magic from infants and children *before* they get a chance to grow up and their magic settles in, *before* they get a chance to be all they are meant to become, *before* they can use their abilities to fight back and save themselves."

"He cares naught for what happens to the children after he takes what he wants from them. Most die. The rest are left broken and given to Lamashtu to play with, like old, discarded toys. I pray you never meet *her*. She is horrifying beyond all words, but she is no threat to anyone other than infants, young children, and expectant mothers. She is the Lokskell's favorite servant, and he rewards her with the children that survive his abuses and thievery."

"But he does not care one way or the other what happens to any of the children, once he's gotten what he needs from them. All he cares about is gaining more power. He's desperate to free himself from his captivity, and that's why he wants you. He hopes to steal your magic from you. And if he can't take it, he will keep you and use you for his own purposes, the same way that he has used me. But I promise you, I'm doing all that I can to ensure that never happens. I escaped and ran from him long enough to find you a protector, far from his reach."

The image of the woman flickers like a candle flame in the wind. She turns her phantom head for a moment to look at something behind her. Then she hastily turns back around and there's panic evident in her eyes as she continues in a hushed, hurried voice. "My time grows short. He has found me and is even now on his way here to take back what he claims as his. *This* is the reason why I'm sending you away from me. I *must* keep you safe. You will never belong to him, not as long as I have breath left in my body. But his anger at my defiance will be enormous. I will not survive it. I don't have enough magic left in me to fight him. I'm afraid this has to be goodbye, little one, my beloved daughter."

"There is one last thing that I must tell you. You have a twin sister. I don't know how it happened, or why. It is unheard of. When you learn more about Irredarrians you will know just how impossible it is, how impossible SHE is. But I need you to listen to me now, and you *hear* me. She may look just like you, but she is your exact opposite. *She is not good.* You are made of love and light while her heart is a dark, twisted thing. She will be as dangerous as the Lokskell, and you must avoid her at all costs. I know that I should have snuffed out her life as soon as she left my womb. I was supposed to. Forgive me, but I just couldn't do it. A mother's love is unlike anything I have ever felt."

"You are my heiress and I love you with everything in me, but I can't help but love her too. She has a tiny bit of me inside of her, even though she is HIS heiress. I know that she probably cannot be saved. I know that she will most likely take after her father and grow up to do terrible things. I know I have complicated things immensely for you and I am so very, very sorry for that. I just didn't have it in me to harm her. Please, please forgive me. I hope one day you understand. But for now, I need you to be strong. You *must* be strong. You have a wonderful, terrible destiny to fulfill. You are the Chosen."

"Irredarr's very last Prophecy was written about you. I don't have time to recite it word for word, but it basically states that there is a delicate balance between Light and Dark. Neither one must ever be completely banished. Both must always coexist, or all shall be lost into Chaos. The Shadow Lord has spent a thousand years working on putting out the light. The scales are now tipped dangerously close to the Darkness. YOU are the only one who can right it, rebalance the scales, and even the forces. YOU are the only one that can put an end to the Shadow Lord's reign of terror. The fate of our world, and many others, lies with you. You must make things right. It is a terrible burden to bear. I know that your life has probably been exceedingly turbulent, and it will get even more tempestuous the closer you get to fulfilling the Prophecy. Waves of fear and hopelessness and despair will sometimes crash over you, overwhelming you at times and threaten to drag you under. You may feel that you cannot go on. But you must. You must give everything you have inside of you, and then you will be asked to give even more. You must bear it all and ride out the hurricane. But always, *always* remember, your purpose is greater than the Storm.

I love you, my darling girl, more than you can ever know. I wish I could be there to help you along your way. But know that I will always be there in spirit. You carry all my love and hope inside you." Tears cascade down the woman's face, as if a dam had been opened up and the waters would no longer be contained. "Take the ring," she continues. "It was a gift from my beloved Aruune. He gave it to me in hopes that I would one day be his wife. I want you to have it. When you find your way back home to Irredarr, please tell him that I am so sorry. Tell him that I loved him and wish with all my heart that I could have been the one to make his dreams come true. Goodbye, my sweet Adrina, my brave little Ecko. May we meet again in the EverLands."

The image of the woman flickers and then goes out completely. The group is silent, trying to process everything they'd just learned. Ecko only now realizes that she's been crying, and that her face is soaked with tears. Silently, she takes the ring and slips it on her finger. She folds the box back up, lining the sides up until the lock snicks back into place.

She wraps the rose necklace back up in the cloth. Still she is disturbingly quiet.

Charlie, Susan, and Maggie look at each other in helpless indecision. What should they say? What *could* they say? "Ecko..." Charlie begins but stops when she looks up at him. There's so much hurt and confusion in her eyes, such naked pain. It breaks his old heart to see it. "Oh, Sweetheart. Come here."

He gets up, pulls her out of her chair and wraps her up in his arms. She immediately starts sobbing. The old man slowly inches them towards the couch and eases them down onto the cushions. Ecko doesn't seem to notice, she just burrows in closer. Then she's talking, babbling really, and most of her words are unintelligible. "I saw my mother for the first time today. Then I lost her. My dad is not my father. My father is some terrible Shadow man that wants to kidnap me and use me for evil. I have a twin sister. Other me, Mirror me, is my twin, not just a reflection of me. Samara, she's been there the whole time, right there in front of me. I already know *she's* evil. Prophecies and magic and mirror walking."

Charlie croons softly to her and runs his hands over and over her hair. She finally goes quiet and just lies there, breath hitching and sniffling. Exhausted and emotionally wrung out, she closes her eyes and falls asleep. Charlie covers her with a blanket and quietly tiptoes back to the table. "Some slumber party," he grumbles to himself. "This is no fun for my girl at all."

The next morning, Ecko opens her eyes and all the events from the day before rush back into her mind. It's very early morning, still dark outside and no one else is awake yet. She has time to herself to just lie there and think about everything she has learned.

What a mess, she thinks. What a complete, crazy mess her life has turned out to be, had always been, actually. She yawns and does a full body stretch. She'd slept surprisingly well, and she can't believe how good she feels this morning. Better than she had in a long time actually, which is a complete enigma to her. She hadn't needed any chemical help to fall asleep and no nightmares had infiltrated her sleep to disturb her rest. She feels rejuvenated and energized and ready for whatever the day may bring.

Even the fact that she has to go check in with Dr. Bradburn today doesn't faze her. She's about to sit up and go see about finding herself some coffee when she hears a noise, a quiet little snort. She knows that sound. Charlie is sleeping somewhere nearby.

Warmth fills her heart, and a smile comes to rest on her face. The old goat had refused to leave her alone, just in case she woke up and needed him. She sits up to look for him and her eyes come to rest on the woman lying curled up in the recliner, piled under a mountain of blankets. Maggie. Her eyes are open, and she smiles sweetly when

Ecko takes notice of her. She presses her finger to her lips in the universal sign for quiet and points to the floor.

Charlie has dragged a mattress into the room, right up next to the couch where she'd been sleeping, and him and Susan are cuddled up and snoring away… her faithful, fearless guardians. Her heart practically melts. She smiles back at Maggie, then stands up and quietly makes her way to the restroom for her morning business.

She takes a quick shower, letting the hot water wash away all the stains of yesterday. There's a gentle knock at the door while she's brushing her teeth with one of the toothbrushes that Maggie has laid out for them. She opens the door just a crack and Maggie hands her a stack of clothes to choose from.

"If you pass me your dirties, I'll throw them into the wash for you," she says. Clean and dressed in her borrowed clothing, Ecko follows the tantalizing aromas and sounds of coffee percolating and meets Maggie in the kitchen.

"How are you this morning, Dear?" Maggie asks as she pours herself some tea and some coffee for her guest.

"Thank you, Maggie. I feel amazing, actually. I'm surprised at how well I slept. Nights are usually hard for me. I think I had just reached my limit. Yesterday was a very long and crazy day. I was so overwhelmed and exhausted that I was at my breaking point. My mind must have turned itself off and shut my body down so that I could recharge, I guess."

Maggie smiles and tells her, "Good thing, too. You needed the rest. And you look like you're feeling much better. You're handling things so much more bravely than I would be. Gracious me, what an outlandish tale!"

The two of them talk quietly, companionably for the next hour or so. "I've made a decision on what to do about my birthday and the whole 'coming into my powers' issue. I know what I have to do.

I know where I must go. Charlie's going to be so angry about it though. He's going to fight me, but I can't let him change my mind," Ecko confides. "I only have a couple of weeks left before I turn 18... Well, before my fictitious 18th birthday anyway. I have to stay close by, until then, I have no other choice in the matter. I need to meet with my father's lawyers on that day to go over his will and my inheritance. I also have to check in with my doctor twice a week until then. But after that, I'll be free to go wherever I choose, do anything I wish to do. I can only hope that this 'magic' doesn't hit until after that day. I've decided that if nothing *has* happened by then, I'll go away. There's a cabin that my family vacationed at when I was young. It is secluded, deep in the wilderness. I'm sure it will be far enough away from other people for whatever may occur. I'll just go there and wait it out."

Maggie agrees that it is probably the best plan of action, but she tries to talk Ecko into taking Charlie and Susan along, or herself even. But Ecko holds firm and refuses to compromise. She will not willingly put any of her loved ones in more danger than she already has. Maggie gets all teary eyed and stops arguing about going with her to the cabin when Ecko informs her that *she* has now been added to the very short list of loved ones and that she refuses to risk her safety as well. Besides, Maggie is positive that Charlie will be giving her enough hell when he finds out what she plans to do.

Charlie's not angry. He's pissed, absolutely livid. The two of them argue for the next three weeks, up until the very day before her fictional birthday. Their house had become a battlefield and the only thing that poor Susan could do was try to avoid getting caught in the crossfire. She's tried to stay out of it, because she sees both sides. They both just want to protect the other.

But she has come up with a compromise and both of the combatants have reluctantly, grudgingly agreed to it. They will *all* be going to New Hampshire, but they won't stay in the same cabin. Charlie and Susan would stay in cabin #9 and Ecko would stay in cabin #10. It should be fine, Susan had reasoned. There are ten cabins available, and they each have miles of wilderness in every direction surrounding them. That should be plenty of room for 'anything strange' to happen.

Ecko grudgingly reserves their cabins and makes their travel arrangements. Charlie opens his mouth to argue when he finds out that she's paying for the whole trip, but Susan quickly elbows him in the ribs to shush him. He shushes, but he looks like he's sucking on the world's most bitter lemon while he does it. They each go to their respective corners and spend the rest of the day packing. Now, they just have to get through tomorrow.

The dawn finds Ecko up and eager to get things done, so that she can close this chapter of her life. Today is her 'human' birthday, but there won't be any celebrating. There's entirely too much to do. They have appointments, necessary appointments to attend before she can sequester herself out in the wilderness to await her true birthday.

She rushes through breakfast, hurrying the grumbling old couple along. Then they're in the car, speeding her along towards her freedom.

They pull into the parking lot, and she looks up at the dismal walls of the Regal Falls Psychiatric Ward. She silently thanks the powers that be for allowing her to finally escape this hellish prison.

Dr. Bradburn's waiting for her at the receptionist's desk. She has all the paperwork ready and all that's needed now is their signatures. Ecko's given a copy of her file and all her release forms proving that she is a completely sane, competent adult. Then Dr. Bradburn surprises her with a gift.

"It's a bucket list journal," Dr. Bradburn tells her. "A scrapbook for you to document all the awesome things you'll get to see and do.

Now, get out of here. Go. See it all. Do it all. *Really* live your life to the fullest."

Ecko smiles and says, "Don't take this the wrong way, Dr. Bradburn, but I hope I never, ever see you again. Here, Charlie. Will you carry my things for me? I need my hands free." She passes the journal and paperwork to him, then gives him a wink. She hits play on her iPod and Missio starts singing about throwing Middle Fingers in the Air. She puts up her own middle fingers and flies those birds high as she walks out of those hated doors for the very last time. She grins from ear to ear as Susan's "Oh my!" and Charlie's howling laughter rings throughout the lobby behind her.

The next appointment is with Mr. Peterson, her father's, well, her lawyer now. For the next three torturous hours, they go over her father's will, her bank accounts and all of her assets, the stocks and bonds, the properties and realty, and the staggering amount of money. Ecko is shocked (and ecstatic) to learn that she had unnecessarily paid for their stay at the cabins in New Hampshire. She *owns* the resort! Apparently, her father had purchased it for her when he realized how much she'd loved it there.

Mr. Peterson and Ecko discuss the things she wants to change and what she wants to keep in place. She assures him that she is happy with his services and that she would like for him to continue working for her.

If her father had trusted him, then so would she. Mr. Peterson accompanies her to the First Commerce Bank where a great deal of her money is entrusted. They meet with the bank's president, Mr. Davidson, where she quickly settles all of her accounts and signs the mountain of paperwork.

When the meeting is concluded and they're walking back out to their cars, Ecko informs Mr. Peterson that she'll be heading out of town and not to worry if he doesn't hear from her for a while. She would be unreachable, but she would check in with him from time to time.

Mr. Peterson shakes her hand and tells her that it's a pleasure working for her, just as it had been to work for her father. He wishes her luck and safe travels and then they part ways. Now there's just one more stop to make and then she'll be free to leave Texas behind. She wants to, *needs* to finally visit her family. She cannot leave without saying goodbye. She needs to let her father know that she forgives him for all the secrets and the lies. She has to say the words out loud.

The thirty-minute drive from the bank to the cemetery is quiet and somber. Ecko settles herself into the back seat and immediately plugs her earbuds into her ears and cranks her music up, a very clear sign that she needs some space. Charlie and Susan leave her to her thoughts, but they're obviously worried about her. They exchange silent, anxious glances throughout the drive, right up until they pull through the cemetery gates.

The car comes to a stop and Ecko turns her music off. They all get out and make their way to the small family plot. Three graves filled, one empty and waiting. Charlie and Susan place the flowers that they've brought onto the three graves and quietly pay their respects.

"I'll watch over her, Dan. I promise," Charlie murmurs. Then he turns and tells Ecko, "We'll give you some time alone, honey. Susan and I are gonna go say hello to my Gretchen while we're here, should you need us." Charlie looks down at his girl and feels his heart breaking inside his chest. She looks so lost, so alone. His eyes tear up and his chin starts that terrible, unmanly wobbling thing so he quickly turns and walks away.

Ecko watches them leave before she hesitantly steps forward and lays the single pink rose down for her sister, who wasn't really her sister, after all. It was a pretty, pastel colored rose for Karen's inner princess and her love of all things pink. "I know that we were never close. You always thought I was such a freak. Turns out you were right all along," she murmurs with a sad little smile. "I wish things had turned out differently. I wish you were here. It's all my fault, everything that happened. I know that. I'll have to live with it until the day I join you. I'm so sorry, Karen."

She moves over and bends down to prop the red rose against her stepmother's headstone. "Thank you for accepting me and loving me when I know that it broke your heart to do it. I can't even imagine the pain that you lived with all those years, having to look at me all the while believing that Dad had been unfaithful to you. I know he hurt you. And so did I, just by existing. But he adored you, always. And even though I have always known that you weren't mine biologically, I always thought of you as my mother. I love you, and I'm so very sorry, Momma."

Ecko moves on and sits down next to her father's grave. She leans forward and places the bundle of lilies onto her hero's final resting place, stalling a bit by arranging and then rearranging them until they look perfect. They were his favorite flowers, he'd told her once. They reminded him of his lovely wife. He'd said that she always smelled just like a lily.

How he had laughed when the five-year-old Ecko had run and sniffed Rachael's leg to see for herself. Her breath hitches sharply, just once. That's all the warning she gets before the pressure inside of her becomes too much to bear. The dam bursts and the flood of tears overflow their banks in her eyes and course like miniature, raging rivers down her face.

"I was listening to music on the ride here and a song came on Pandora that hit me so hard. I *thought* that I wanted to come here to tell you that I forgive you for all the lies and the secrets. I wanted to tell you that I understand why you did it all."

"But listening to that song made me think, *really* consider all that you had to go through, everything that you had to endure…just because you loved me. You were given a terrible, impossible burden to bear. And you did it so bravely. You lost your friends; you nearly lost your wife and your real daughter. You lived with the shame of everyone believing the very worst of you, when in all reality you were more of a hero than anyone would ever know. A silent hero. And then, not only did you lose your life, you had to watch your family die right in front of you first."

"You gave me everything, forfeited your entire life for me. And I had the nerve, the unmitigated *gall*, to believe, even for one second, that you needed my forgiveness for the lies you told. Every single thing you've ever done was for the sake of your family. My existence was a huge burden on you, and yet you loved me anyway. I know without a doubt that you loved me completely, unselfishly and unconditionally. So, now here I am, begging *you* for forgiveness for all that you had to endure on my behalf. Begging you to forgive me for my part in your death, for the deaths of our loved ones. I hope there really is a Heaven and that you're looking down on me now."

She wipes the tears from her face and turns on her iPad. "I'm going to play this song for you before I go. I'll be leaving town for a while, but I promise I'll come back to visit you after I stop Samara. I swear with everything in me, I will not stop until I put an end to the one that took you away from me."

She locates the song and hits play. Madonna starts singing about how a man could tell a thousand lies and how the secrets burn inside of her. Ecko quietly sings along with her, her voice soft and hauntingly beautiful. When it's over she stands up and lovingly runs her hands over her father's headstone one last time. "I love you, more than I can ever say. I *will* come back when it's all over, I promise. Goodbye Daddy," she whispers as she walks away with one last lonely tear trailing down her cheek.

Hours later, flying 35,000 feet in the air, Susan turns to Ecko with a sad, thoughtful expression. "I'm so sorry we didn't get a chance to celebrate your birthday today. You had to sit through all those boring meetings and now you're stuck on an airplane. No cake, no gifts... It's just not right."

Charlie takes her hand and says, "Now Susan, don't you be sad. Our girl may not have had a party or got to have any fun, but she did get a gift. And it's the one that she's been wanting desperately for years now. She has her freedom. And besides, who says we can't have a late birthday party once we get where we're going?"

Ecko just smiles and nods. Charlie understands. Charlie gets it. She's finally away from that terrible hospital and she's free to choose her own path. But then she remembers the 'destiny' that her mother spoke of. *Was* she free to choose her own path? Was she truly? Or had her path been chosen for her long ago?

A frown replaces her smile as she realizes that she's *still* doing what others have dictated that she do. She doesn't want to hurt anyone when these 'powers' arrive and so she'll do as her mother suggested. But after that, her life is her own. What she does with her abilities will be up to *her*, and no one else. Until then, she'll take things one day at a time and just be grateful that she's no longer locked away. Everything is going to be so much better now. Life is going to be good from here on out. She'll make sure of it. She watches the clouds drift past the window and listens to Charlie snore beside her for the rest of the flight.

The Blood Never Bothered Me Anyway

Something's wrong. I don't feel right. I don't feel like me at all. I think something, *someone* has gotten inside of me somehow and is slowly taking control. My anger is failing me. I don't know how, or why even. It has always been a part of me, almost like an extra organ. I don't know how to function without it burning away inside me. Rage is an essential ingredient for making my abilities work at their full potential. My fury seems to be dying a slow, disinterested death. The fire doesn't burn as hot as it used to, it has died down to a slow smolder. The magic inside me is weakening along with the flames, taking longer to respond to my commands than they ever have. My Shadows have become slow and sluggish, barely managing to rouse themselves into being when I call to them.

At first, I blamed Krispin and his tiresome, disgusting feelings for me. I believed that it was his claims of love and commitment that was doing the damage to me, to who I am. Changing me, somehow. But now I know otherwise.

I woke up this morning feeling tired, drained of energy and passion, and lacking my usual desire to cause mischief. I think back on all that Krispin had said, how Rommal had somehow gotten a hold on me, how he could smell me in his blood. I don't know how, but I know that it's Rommal who's responsible for how terrible I feel today. I think he infected me with something, something that's weakening me. But I was just too tired to think on it too hard. I promised myself that I would try to figure it all out later, after the fun at the fair has ended.

I didn't want to miss a single second of the Mourning's End festival. I've already missed out on enough in my life. I refuse to just lie in bed and miss out on one single thing more. Even though I didn't feel like my normal, angry self, I was bound and determined to enjoy myself to the fullest. As I readied myself for the evening's festivities, I sensed Krispin's eyes lingering on me, felt his worried, questioning stare. He knew something was wrong. He'd said he could smell it in me, like a sickness had spread throughout my body. I merely shrugged it off, shrugged *him* off. I knew I should be alarmed, but I just couldn't be bothered to care at that moment.

When we arrived at the center of town, everyone tried to act normal, like we were one of them and that they weren't scared out of their minds of us. They knew better than to run away though, knew better than to try and leave. Krispin and I had made sure of that. This past week of celebrating had been amazing, for the two of us anyway. Not so much for the imbeciles around us. But then I'd begun to falter, and I really just didn't care to hear their screams anymore....

Seriously? I absolutely *adore* hearing the screams of my victims and tormentees. That's when I knew for sure something was bad wrong with me. I just didn't know what it was or how to fix it, so I ignored the problem and hoped it would go away. It didn't.

Now, as Krispin and I wander through town from show to show, I get the feeling that someone's watching me. Not Krispin, his eyes never leave me for long, so I'm used to his stare. Not the townspeople either, because they stare after me with such naked fear and loathing that it permeates the air around them with fear-stink. No, this perusal of me is focused, possessive and controlling, and oh, so very angry. The weight of it settles over me like a cloyingly, malicious cloud made of want and greed and hate.

Ah, now I recognize it, and I don't know how I failed to do so before. Father is at last making his move to reclaim me. I knew he would eventually. Apparently, he must feel threatened by my new level of power because he's chosen to send some real magic after me, not just muscle. I should have known he would hide behind the most dangerous goon he could find. I can feel it now. The sheer magnitude of power that I'm sensing is overwhelming and actually quite daunting. I do not scare easily; I haven't found much in this life that *can* frighten me. With a father like mine, there's not much room left to fear anything else.

But whatever this is, whoever Father has sent after me now fills me with an almost paralyzing terror. I stop in the middle of the street and look around me, searching all over for my stalker. Krispin moves in even closer to me, instantly put on high alert by the vibes and the scents that he's getting from me.

Then a man steps out of the shadows and stands before us, confidently and without a single trace of fear. He is fairly small and underwhelming, positively nondescript in every way. Except for the waves of power radiating from him, that is. What I'm seeing totally contradicts what I'm feeling, and it throws me off, confuses me for a moment. I'm not sure what action I want to take. Fight or flight?

I feel Krispin's entire body tense up beside me in preparation of the mauling he's about to deliver, but something inside me is screaming that's the wrong decision. I take myself very seriously. After all, I've kept myself alive thus far, hadn't I? Flight it is. I grab onto Krispin's arm to still him, to hold him back.

He glances down at me questioningly and I shake my head no. This man is trouble. He's dangerous. Although it goes against everything in me, I whisper, "Run," just before I turn and flee. But it's not in Krispin to back down either and the damn fool stands there a moment longer than is good for him.

I feel a surge of magic behind me, an intense crackle of energy. It feels like the worst case of static electricity imaginable. Every hair on my head stands up and I run even faster when I hear Krispin's roar of anger. I turn back in time to see him on the ground surrounded by a slew of my father's men. He appears to be struggling against some sort of net that's wrapped around him. I grin and turn away once more, intent on nothing more than escaping.

Krispin's on his own. He'll be free of that trap in mere moments anyway. Nets can't hold him for long, not with those razor-sharp claws of his. Now, if he can get away from the mystery man and the other twenty or so hooligans is a whole other story altogether. If he *does* manage to escape them, he will meet me at our safe spot. That's where I'm headed, just as soon as I can be sure that I've eluded my father's men. My feet pound on the ground, my legs pumping so fast that they've become a blur of motion.

I round an old, dilapidated building, stopping to press my back up against the crumbling wall so that my backside is protected against anyone wanting to sneak up on me. Then, I wait, and I watch. I stand still and quiet for ten minutes. Then, I wait ten more. I breathe a sigh of relief and keeping as close to the buildings and their concealing shadows as I can, I begin to make my way to the outskirts of town. I creep through the empty streets, past the last of the deserted houses and suddenly the man is there again, standing just before me. I never even saw him coming.

One moment my freedom is right there within my grasp and the next he's blocking the path and I have no choice but to try and find another escape route. I turn to run back the way I came but find that the path behind me is now blocked by more of my father's men. I call upon my Shadows for help, but they're disturbingly apathetic and slow to respond.

The man grins smugly, like he knows just what I'm attempting, and failing to do. Perhaps he does, because when he opens his mouth and speaks, it's my father's voice that comes out. "Hello Daughter. Have you enjoyed your little vacation? Was it pleasant? I certainly hope so. I hope it was all worth it, because I think you've had enough time to yourself. Your little play date is over. It's time to come back home to Daddy."

And then that unremarkable little man does something I never would have expected. He takes a palm sized, silver disk out of his breast pocket and he flings it right at me like he's throwing a kylie, or a boomerang at a Octobeast during rut season. The air is suddenly full of that terrible static again, the energy snapping and crackling around me so strong that it's created an invisible electric shield.

I'm trapped inside of it, completely immobilized. I'm powerless to stop it or even move out of the projectile's path. All I can do is watch it spin ever closer. It strikes me directly in the center of my chest and immediately explodes upon contact. It bursts open, the delicate, gossamer spidder-silk strands spilling out. They unfold themselves from their packed, compressed state and then they spread, exactly replicating a spidder web in the making.

It starts out small, but steadily grows until it has become a glimmering, silver net that's large enough to encompass and ensnare me within it. I want to laugh at such thin, seemingly weak strands. But I don't, because I know better. Father wouldn't have bothered with this particular undertaking if he hadn't been sure of his success. I reach up to pluck at one delicate, ultra-fine strand and find that it is indeed stronger than bands of steel. I also discover another nasty little built-in surprise. That single, tiny string that I was trying so hard to sever begins to glow between my fingertips.

I watch as the glow spreads down that one particular strand and when it's lit up in its entirety, it sends a shock through me everywhere that it touches my skin. It's dreadfully unpleasant and I can't even imagine how horrible it would feel if *all* the other hundreds of strands were activated simultaneously.

I shudder. Poor Krispin. I have no doubt that my defiantly ambitious lover has felt the agony of it. He would have immediately tried to use his claws to sever as many strands as possible. I drop my hands down by my sides and wait for what's next as Father mentally commands the little man he's currently possessing to throw his head back and laugh. "Good girl", is all he says as his men close in on me and drag me away.

Now I'm back in this repulsive house that I have hated my whole life away in, hated the old folks, my mother and my father, my sister, these walls, babies and flowers, the town and all the people in it, flutterbutterby's... and myself. Mustn't forget myself, because none of this would be happening right now if I weren't the pathetic weakling my father has always labeled me. My father's men had hauled me back to my room where I'd unceremoniously been tossed onto my filthy old bed, magic net and all.

Father knows better than to have it removed. He's taking no chances. A Wartallian and a Hobglin enter the room carrying cages, and the screeching coming from within them tells me everything I need to know. I am about to have my energy stolen, leeched out by

Ribbitters. The Hobglin sets the cages on the bed next to me and opens the latch.

The nasty little beasties hop out and make a beeline straight for me. I shudder uncontrollably at the feel of their slimy, yet somehow sticky tongues, as they start slurping my magic up and out of me. The Wartallian guard stands over me, watching with narrowed, wart encrusted eyes and I know that this is who my father has chosen to inhabit for the time being.

He seems to favor this particular Wartal because of his skills at removing the skin from his victims, whole and completely intact. He's very good at what he does, and the finished product never fails to please my father immensely. I once witnessed a man step into one of his flawlessly removed skins like it was a one-piece suit. By the time he'd gotten all settled inside it and had the back sewn up, I never would have known that he was wearing a person-suit had I not watched with my own eyes as he'd slipped it on. Yes, this is one of my father's most favorite henchmen. He loves to watch this man work, which does not bode well for me and my current predicament.

Before I become too weak to do it, I ask him, "Why the Ribbitters, Father? You already have me. There's no way I can escape this net."

My father laughs using the Wartal's lumpy, disgusting lips to do so. He turns to the Hobglin and orders, "Bring him in and set him up over there, in front of the window." Then he turns back to me and evades my question by asking his own. "Did you know that if you eat Ribbitters you gain their power-draining abilities? No? Well neither did I, not until I encountered Rommal, the man that your plaything rudely slaughtered in the street. Now *he* was something special."

Father watches as his guards drag a glaring, angrily defiant Krispin into the room. They chain him from hooks in the ceiling and the floor, arms and legs spread wide apart. Father has him put in that particular spot so that I can watch every atrocity that he decides to inflict upon my lover. And so that *he* can see me in return. Krispin's eyes never leave me as the guards lock him down tight. I'm beginning to get sleepy now. My eyelids are growing heavy, but I manage to keep my focus for a bit longer. I need to know exactly what my father is up to. "Ribbitters are poisonous. They are not for eating," I insist.

Father snorts from his borrowed, hideously bulbous nose. "True, my daughter. And that is just what *I'd* said when Rommal told me about his abilities. Come to find out, it's only Ribbitter *skin* that is poisonous. They apparently secrete some sort of venom from their pores. Remove the skin, and they are perfectly safe for consumption. Rommal ate the Ribbitters and then he received their ability to siphon magic from his chosen victims, just by laying his hands on them. He thereby gained any ability *that* person possessed, for a short time that is. The effects unfortunately never lasted long."

Father pauses as a guard enters the room carrying the Wartal's tool bag. He sets it on the little side table, bows to my father, and quickly backs out of the room. Father begins unpacking it, laying out pinchers, clamps, spreaders, knives, scalpels, and tiny bottles of I don't even know what. He cheerfully glances back over his shoulder to wink at me before continuing, "But listen, and this is the most amazing part, Rommal ate so many Ribbitters, for so many years, that he began to take on more and more of their qualities. He started to secrete his *own* toxins from his skin, particularly from his palms. Not a poison, he'd explained, but more like sperm, or bellyworms even. Invasive little parasites. And suddenly he found that he was no longer forced to suck up as much magic as he could, in the few seconds of contact he had with his intended targets."

"Rommal theorized that his secretions were actually small bits of himself, tiny Rommal parasites that left him and entered into his victims." Father pauses momentarily to grin, "Rommalites, he'd called them. Once in place, the Rommalites went to lunch, slowly eating his victim's magic from the inside. And amazingly, all the magic that they consumed, somehow, miraculously went straight to Rommal himself, as if there was an invisible tube connecting him to his parasitic minions."

"Now, as you know, magic usually regenerates itself in time, so any lost magic eventually gets replaced. So theoretically, the Rommalites could eat forever and provide him with an endless supply of magic, at least until the host died. The parasites never grew, never took over the host, and they never died...so long as Rommal himself stayed in close proximity to his Rommalites. The instant that they strayed too far apart from one another, the Rommalites broke down, dissolved and eventually got discarded along with the rest of the host's waste!"

Father takes up a scalpel and makes his first cut across my lover's chest. Krispin doesn't even flinch, but I know that will soon change. He's tough, powerful and stubbornly strong, but he'll not be able to stand the upcoming pain. I don't think anyone could. Father is going to flay the skin right off of him, and he'll do so in small, excruciating strips by the looks of things, because once he has a six-inch rectangle sliced into Krispin's chest, he sets the scalpel aside and takes up a pair of pinchers. He clamps the pinchers down tight onto the edge of the little flap of skin and gives it a quick, sharp tug. It rips free with a loud, wet, tearing sound.

Krispin grits his teeth and grunts. Yeah, he felt *that*. Father glances back at me to calculate my reaction, and frowns when I calmly, sleepily meet his eyes. He orders the Hobglin to remove all but one of the Ribbitters and put them back into their cages. Apparently, he believes that it's their effects that have me feeling so unconcerned at the sight of my lover's pain. If he only knew how much I *adore* the sight of Krispin's blood, he may have thought up different torture methods. The thought of Father trying to manipulate me by bleeding Krispin makes me laugh out loud, and he frowns even harder at the sounds of my giggles. He turns and gets back to work unwrapping Krispin, bit by bit. He wants me to suffer, he wants me to hurt over what's being done to my mate, but that's not his only reason for doing it. He is also exacting his revenge on Krispin for daring to touch what he believes belongs to *him*.

The little man responsible for my capture now sits in a chair in the corner of the room, his eyes averted from the current events that he is largely responsible for. Apparently, all that power I'd felt before, that huge, angry energy, had been nothing more than my father's Night Shades possessing his body, and also, that incredible magic net of his. *That* thing has a power like I've never felt before. I (briefly) wonder how such a weak little man got his hands on something so incredibly magnificent.

Now that my father is no longer possessing him and his enchanted toy has been taken away, he is exactly what his appearance suggests. He's nothing but a weak, pathetic, and ordinary little man. He also has no stomach for torture, seeing as he has emptied his, loudly and violently, three times already. Watching my father flay the skin off Krispin, in small strips to make it all last longer, is apparently something he hadn't signed up for. But he really has no other choice than to sit through the torture session. Not if he wants his net back, that is.

The absurdity of that makes me snort out loud. Stupid little man. Does he *truly* believe that dear, old daddy will just let him go on his merry way and deprive himself of such a handy tool? That's hilarious. Father will take his spidder-web snare for himself, once he knows how to work it and/or how to replicate it. But if that proves impossible and can't be done, the little man will become his prisoner too, forever forced to use his net to service my father. He'll become just another tool, another weapon in my father's arsenal. Either way, he's about to lose something precious to him. His net, or his freedom, and quite possibly both. Stupid, stupid little man, I think to myself once more, as I close my tired eyes and drift away into the darkness.

I regain consciousness in stages, slowly coming back to awareness. I realize that I've been released from the magic net while I slept. Surprisingly, *humorously*, my hands and feet, bound with a simple rope, seem to be the only restraints placed upon me. Like those will *ever* hold me. But then it's not so amusing anymore when I glance down to see what the heavy weight in the center of my chest is. A huge, disgustingly fat Ribbitter has nestled itself down into my shirt, and every minute or so it lazily slips out its tongue to lick my skin. Each leeching swipe sucks out just enough power from my already weakened state to ensure that I remain docile and helpless.

I don't even have enough energy to raise my arms and knock the foul creature off of me. I guess this is my father's plan for the time being, leave the Ribbitters on me permanently to keep me enervated and powerless. But I really don't understand his reasoning. I mean, what good am I to him without my magic? I can't find his precious Ecko without it. Why even bother with me at this point? Unless it's just for good old-fashioned revenge and the need to feel like he's in control. Or possibly to gloat, as if he's won an epically glorious battle against me. I really don't know, but then again, I guess his reasons really don't even matter.

Krispin appears to be asleep, his weight held up mostly by his arms. His head is hanging down, his chin resting in a bloody, exposed patch on his chest. Father must have grown bored without me as a captive audience of one and decided to put the punishment on hold.

Krispin immediately feels my stare and lifts his head up to meet my eyes. He is so in tune with me, he sometimes knows what I am thinking, what I'm feeling before I know it myself. And he knows exactly what I'm feeling now. I…Am…Pissed. How dare he let this happen to me. I snort out a nasty little laugh. So much for his so-called love for me.

"Get me the hell out of here, Krispin," I grit out from between my tightly clenched teeth. He flinches and replies in a deep, wounded rumble, "I cannot. I have already tried extensively to free myself. Be patient, my love. I *will* get us out of here sooner or later."

Uuggh. Pathetic, useless waste of oxygen. Krispin looks away from my accusing eyes; he's ashamed that he can't save me. Well, shit on him. I don't need him to save me. I'm no damsel in distress, looking for her knight in shining armor. I *am* the knight in armor, but it's not shiny. It's tarnished and bloody and I wouldn't want it any other way. I'll free my own self. Just wait and see.

The geezers choose that moment to come into the room to carry out my father's orders. The stooped, old man stands in the doorway to watch over his wife while she spoons thin, disgusting gruel into my mouth. 'Yes, Father, mustn't let your enfeebled, captive daughter starve to death. Keep her alive, so you can punish her some more' I bitterly think to myself. I glare at the decrepit old woman and order her to remove the Ribbitter from my chest. Her face pales and her lip trembles but she says nothing, just keeps shoving spoonful after spoonful into my mouth as quickly as she can manage it.

She's in a huge hurry to be done with her chore, so she can retreat back to the imagined safety of her bedroom. I turn my attention back to the doorway and demand, "Well, old man. What about you? Are you going to help me, or don't you care that the girl you raised is being tortured and abused?"

He refuses to even acknowledge me, his eyes lighting on everything... *anything* but me. The bowl is finally empty, and the woman wipes the mess from my face, just as if I were a disgusting little baby. "You gonna change my nappy too, because I really have to piss. Or will I just be forced to lay in my own filth?" She silently stands up to go and her refusal to answer me fills me with a sudden intense anger. "Do NOT ignore me, old woman!" I scream.

Something nags at me, some errant thought, fluttering around in the back of my mind, but I'm too angry at the moment to sort it out. My eyes move from the woman to the man and then back again. "If you two dolts do not help me this very instant, I swear to you, right here and right now, that you will be very, *very* sorry. Do not walk out that door and leave me like this." They stop and look desperately at one another. They know very well that I mean exactly what I say. But they don't let me go. They believe my father's retribution will be worse than anything I could ever do to them. Oh, how very wrong they are. They'll regret their decision to abandon me in my time of need. I'll make sure of it.

"I'm sorry," the woman whispers, as they quickly close the door behind them. My blood absolutely *boils* inside me. It's all I can do to not scream out my rage. If I were rational, I'd say that I understand their decision to refuse me any help whatsoever. My father will make them regret every second they have left on this world if they go against him. But I am *not* rational. I'm infuriated and I imagine all the ways that *I* will make them regret living. Oh yes, they'd better shuffle their old bones as fast and far from me as they can if/when I get free. And then that tiny errant thought that had been lurking on the edges of my consciousness reveals itself. My anger is back! My beautiful, dark rage has been restored to its former glory. All those nasty little Rommalites must have finally died off. Now, if I could just get this loathsome creature to stop slurping up my power like a I'm some sort of magic appetizer long enough for me to put it to good use...

The hours pass slowly, with the previous events repeating themselves. Father/Wartal man comes in and takes the fattened Ribbitter from my chest and replaces it with a smaller, hungry one, so that *it* can constantly eat away at me and fatten itself up. Then he begins slicing away at Krispin again, watching me from the corner of his eyes all the while. He still expects me to get upset at his treatment of my lover. I can't help but laugh and his face flushes with anger.

"Don't you get it, old man? You keep waiting for me to cry over his spilt blood, but I honestly couldn't care less what you do to him. I don't care about *him*. He has never been anything but a plaything to me, a toy that brought me pleasure for a short time. Nothing more, nothing less. In fact, the only thing the sight of his pain does to me is turn me on. It *excites* me. You will *never* see me cry over him. I don't cry when my toys break. I just find better ones."

Krispin's head jerks up and he glares at me through the sweaty, messy locks of hair in his face. My father's face clouds with rage for a moment, but then he throws his head back and laughs uproariously. "Girl, you are too much like me. It's such a pity that you're not stronger. You are correct though. I *had* thought to kill two pixies with one stone, punish him for his crimes and punish you at the same time, by making you watch his suffering."

He turns back and yanks off another flap of Krispin's beautiful, blue skin and shrugs, "Oh well. I shall have to think on *your* punishment later. *This* one still has to bleed. Oh, and by the way. Thank you for your generous contributions." Father slices away, waiting for my response. I absolutely refuse to ask. I won't give him the satisfaction.

"No comment? No questions? Well, I'll tell you anyway, Daughter, just because I'm so very excited about my new project. The Ribbitters, the ones grown fat from your magic, well…they've been given to Vellina, a most loyal female subject. She's consuming them right now, as we speak, filling herself with *your* magic. You see, Rommal spent years eating Ribbitters, slowly gaining his abilities over time. Now that your little boy toy here has killed him," *Slice, slice, rip the skin from Krispin's chest,* "I have to start all over at the very beginning. You, my dear, will continue to provide the magic-stuffed Ribbitters and Vellina will continue to eat them, for years and years to come."

Krispin grunts as another strip of flesh is ripped off his body. Father takes the flap of skin and sticks it to Krispin's forehead. "Here, hold that for me, will ya?" He laughs uproariously for a moment and then continues, "As you are well aware, fully developed magic cannot be stolen from its rightful owner. Not even I can manage that. The only way to acquire an adult's magic is if they willingly give it up. Problem is, there's not too many people out there willing to lose their magic, and possibly their lives right along with it."

"But you *can* steal it from children. Children that are too dumb and too weak to hold onto what they have. That is why I choose the women that I mate with very carefully, to create infants that will inherit magics that will be beneficial to me. You would *think* I'd be able to take the infant's magic as soon as their bitches birthed them and then I'd be free to dispose of the useless little parasites right away. But no. When they are tiny, helpless babes, their magic is too wild, too unpredictable and dangerous to steal and absorb into myself. Terrible things can happen with wild magic. And so, I'm forced to wait until the magic settles down, when the child is just old enough to come into their full potential. And *that* is when I reach in and take what was rightfully mine all along."

"I mean, it was *I* that made that magic possible, brought it into being. Created it, if you will. Was I not? It was I who was strong enough to mate with their dangerous, deadly mothers in order to beget them in the first place. I, who allowed them to live past birth, *if* they'd proved to be worthy and promising, that is. I allowed them to live and to grow. So, did I not make the magic within them also? Was it not my right to take it back when I wanted it back? Of course, it was. If one is strong enough to do a thing, then they will always, always do the thing. Might equals Right."

I gag a bit when I hear him say that. I didn't know that those words were just one more thing that had come from him. I thought they were mine, *my* words and ideas. I wonder how many other things about me, my personal thoughts and expressions, are actually his and not mine at all. Who am I? Am I just an extension of *him*, nothing more than one of his Night Shades for him to use as he sees fit and then bring back and reabsorb into himself? My head spins and I can't think straight. I'm too tired and dizzy and confused.

Slice, slice, rip. The sounds distract me from my own thoughts, and I glance up at Krispin's face. He's hurting, *badly* but he still refuses to cry out. The sweat runs down his body in rivulets as it becomes harder and harder for him to hold his screams inside.

"And that's just what I'd planned to do to your sister," my father rambles on. "Your bitch of a mother ruined that for me, though. I wanted the magic that your sister would inherit in the worst way, needed it, in fact. That's the whole reason why she'd been bred, after all. A thousand years and I've never discovered the way out of this blasted EverRealm. I needed the magic that only a Mirror Walker could provide. A Wandelaar imprisoned me, and it'll take another Wandelaar to release me. I'll never be free of Sheol Castle without it."

Father selects one of the tiny bottles from the table, opens it and sprinkles the contents onto Krispin's newly exposed, skinless flesh. I hear sizzling and watch as tendrils of smoke rise up off of him. He groans loudly, but still, he refuses to scream. Blood trickles down his chin where he's bitten through his lip in order to suppress his cries.

All the while, Father watches me watching Krispin. "You really don't care what I do to him, do you?" he remarks in incredulity. At my disinterested shrug, he takes up his tools and continues the flaying. "Ah, well. Moving along then. Where were we? Oh yes. Can you just imagine if I had found Rommal years ago? Had I known about his Ribbitter- induced, magic stealing abilities back then, things would be so different now. For instance, had I known all of this years ago, *you* never would have been born. Oh, how pleasant life would have been! Had I known, I would have simply borrowed your mother's mirror magic when I'd had her here as a guest in my home. I only impregnated her because she refused to give up her magic. She *forced* me to breed with her. I'd needed her offspring to steal it from. Hell, the greedy slut didn't even have to *give* me her magic, not really. She could have just opened a mirror and let me go!"

"But she refused to do it, stubborn bitch that she was. No matter how much I tortured her, no matter how bad I hurt her, she never gave an inch. I'd almost admired her for that. For a while anyway, before her stubbornness just became tiresome." *Slice, slice, rip.* "Well, too late to worry about what might have been, although it seriously infuriates me to think of all the time I wasted trying to get your mother to cooperate, and then all the time it took to impregnate her. Irredarrians cannot get pregnant unless they choose to, did you know that?"

"Can you imagine how long it took to trick your mother into believing that I was her old lover, come to rescue her? *Years.* I spent years breaking her mind and then even *more* years filling it with thoughts and images of her chosen mate. But something unexpected happened when I'd finally managed to impregnate her. She somehow snapped herself out of her own insanity. I guess the thought of becoming a mother helped her. Her mind healed itself enough to know what was going on, to remember all I'd done to her. She realized that her lover had never come for her at all, that she was carrying *my* offspring inside her. She ran then and managed to escape from the most inescapable of all the seven EverRealms."

"Her sanity lasted long enough for her to whelp her brats and hide them away from me. And then her mind cracked again, really cracked. There was no coming back from where she went, after she lost her heiress. But I got her back in the end. And I made her so very, very sorry for what she'd done, for what she'd stolen from me. Those were *my* brats. They were *my* idea. *I* made them. She'd had no right!" *Stab, slice, stab, slice, riiippp.* Krispin grunts with every angry plunge of the knife and every swath of flesh that he loses.

Father sucks in a deep breath and visibly tries to calm himself. "All that is over and done with now. I've obviously moved on. I've had a thought, a gloriously brilliant epiphany and I want you to hear me out now. See if you can follow where I'm going with this. If this new method of magic thievery works like Rommal promised it would, there may yet be another way for me to escape this cursed place." *Slice, slice, rip.* "I, of course, have already started my Ribbitter diet and have tried out the effects on some of my lovely lady volunteers, here in my castle. It worked every single time, successfully allowing me to borrow magic from every woman that I've tried it on. None have been able to stop it from happening, although I thoroughly enjoyed all their efforts."

"Unfortunately, just as Rommal said, the effects never last long. But I'll keep working on it over here. I'll continue feeding the Ribbitters the magics that I desire the most and then I will gorge myself on them. Meanwhile, Vellina will do the same out there, with *your* Ribbitters. And when she finally gains the ability to produce her own toxins (and we are going to supply a full, steady diet for her, won't we?) I'll bring you both here, to Sheol Castle."

"You will take your place in the EverRealm with me, right where you should have been all along. I have high hopes that you will be of great use to me once I have you here. I can't help but wonder if, as Laelynn's daughter, you will be able to detect where the secret exit is located, just as your mother had. And if you cannot, or *will* not, well, I'm wondering just how much Irredarrian magic you carry inside you. Will it be worth leeching it from you with my own Ribbitter induced ability? Or, would you be able to pass it on to your own offspring? Could your child possibly inherit more Irredarrian magic than you yourself possess? What sort of child would we create together? Oh, the possibilities! Uugh, but then again, you *have* proven to be such a failure, I'm sure any child you spit out will be just as disappointingly pathetic. It's so tiresome having to constantly deal with subpar creatures such as yourself."

Father slams the pincher and its current flap of skin down onto the table in disgust. "*This* is becoming tiresome. I'm actually quite surprised. Your man is tougher than I imagined he'd be. Why are you not screaming yet, boy? Do you not feel pain?"

I start giggling then, I can't help it and Father turns his crusty, pustule- infested eyes to me. "I told you, Father, he likes it. I mean, he *really* likes it. I'm shocked that he hasn't gotten an erection a single time during all of your foreplay. I have *never* seen him go so long without one. You must not be any good at it!"

Father/Wartal's face is a terrible thing to behold, especially when it's angry, but for some reason the sight of it sets me off even more. I lay on my bed, bladder so full that it hurts, weak and pathetic as the day I was born, and I giggle. Hysterically, helplessly, endlessly.

Father finally storms out in disgust, probably so he wouldn't be tempted to try and shut me up, permanently. Although Krispin's head is lowered in exhaustion, I see his lips twitch slightly in response to my mirth, and also at my father's displeasure.

The old woman comes in then, carrying a pot in her hands. Three guards follow close behind her and they all crowd around. I am so weak that I can't even sit up on my own. They stand me up and yank down my pants, and the old lady positions the pot between my thighs. It's barely in place before I let loose. The relief is instant and immense, and I can't stop the soft sigh of bliss that escapes me.

I'm so relieved that I'm not going to be forced to piss on myself and then have to lay in it that I don't even care about the indignity of having to relieve myself in front of an audience. When I'm done, they right my clothing, toss me back to the bed, and place a new Ribbitter on my chest. Then they all leave, carrying the piss pot with them. They don't offer Krispin help in any way, shape, or form. But I guess when he can hold it no longer, he can just go where he stands. At least he won't have to lay in it.

Krispin and I are left alone for hours and hours and hours. The only interaction we have with anyone, other than each other, is when they come in to take the fattened Ribbitters away and replace them with hungry ones. I've had plenty of time to think things through and I have a plan, well, an argument actually, a plea offer, if you will. Because I can think of no worse fate than being tossed into the EverRealm, trapped for all time in Sheol Castle with my father.

I would rather have a Sluggeellian mate with me and impregnate me with its disgusting offspring. No one can survive *that*, and it is a most horrific way to die. But I would willingly, happily choose that fate over the one Father has in mind for me. I believe I can get myself out of this 'worse than death' fate though. All I have to do is get dear old Dad to go for it.

Father finally returns to take up where he'd left off, removing the skin from Krispin's belly, working his way lower and lower. (I can't wait to see if he's going to continue on down and peel the skin from Krispin's penis or if he'll skip over it altogether. The suspense has been driving me mad! Will his testicles look like peeled globberberries when he gets done with them?) My eyes never leave my father's hands. I want to see everything.

I clear my throat and nonchalantly say, "I've been thinking, Father." He snorts and interrupts my rehearsed speech.

"Such a dangerous pastime for you to engage in." he replies.

I ignore his sarcasm and determinedly continue. "I have a proposition for you. If you release me, if you remove the Ribbitters, and allow me to recover my magic, I'll find Ecko for you. And then

I will get her *here.* We know for sure that she has what you need and can do what you want. She's the one with our mother's Irredarrian abilities, after all. It's *her* magic that you need, not mine. But I will only do this if you agree to let me go afterwards. I want nothing more to do with you, or with her for that matter."

Father calmly sets the pinchers aside and turns to face me, but he isn't fooling me a bit. He's pissed and trying hard to contain it. "Do you take me for a fool, Daughter? You've spent years, YEARS trying to do just that. You have failed me time and time again. Why would I give you another chance? Besides, I *know* you. You'll run as soon as you're able to do so. No. I'm done with wasting time trying to get your sister here. I'll just have to make do with you."

He takes up the scalpel again and turns his back to me. I am not deterred. "There's something that you're forgetting, something you've not considered," I tell him. "Ecko has not yet come into her powers, as I have. Remember, my mother's binding spell had my magic suppressed. I wouldn't have gotten the full extent of my magic until I came of age on my next birthday, had I not removed her spell from my body."

Father turns and studies me very closely, intently, just like a slithery thing with beady eyes. "Surely," I continue, "Mother did the same for my twin, gave her the same protections and bindings. She would have wanted to protect her own heiress even more than she'd have wanted to protect yours. Oh yes, Mother spelled her, same as she did me. The only difference is, Ecko would have had no reason to remove her tattoo, so her magic is still suppressed. For the time being, that is."

"But as you know, our birthday is coming up fast. And I am willing to bet my life that the first time Ecko gets near a mirror after that spell vanishes and her magic hits, that mirror will open up for her. And if, IF I happen to be watching her from this side when it does, it will open to *this* world, to me. Chances are, she won't even know what's happening. It will all be so chaotic and overwhelming, completely out of her control and she won't even know what she's capable of. And *that's* when I'll make my move."

I fall silent and wait for him to process my suggestion, to think it all through. There's really nothing more I can say. I won't beg, I absolutely *refuse* to beg. Not that I think it'll come to that. I'm fairly certain that Father won't deny me this. He's greedy and so very desperate to escape his castle. No way will he be able to pass up the chance to finally get his hands on the prize that he has coveted for so long.

But there is so much indecision on his face right now, I'm beginning to worry that he really will refuse just for spite, just to do whatever will make me the most miserable. Father roars with angry frustration, spins around and slams his hand down, burying the scalpel deep in Krispin's chest. "I'll just wait right here for your answer," I call to his retreating back as he storms out of the room. The door slams with an angry, resounding crash. I guess he didn't find that as funny as I had. All that's left now is to wait for him to return with his answer. I'm tired anyway. I'll just take a nap while he makes up his mind.

"Wake up, Daughter." I open my sleep-crusted eyes to see Father (in his stolen Wartal meat suit) standing over me. He removes the Ribbitter from my chest and passes it to a waiting guard behind him. "I have some conditions of my own," he says. "First, you will have exactly one week after you and your sister's birthday to make good on your promise. No excuses, no exceptions. You will remain in this room at all times, and you will not try anything foolish. You will obey me, you will not try to escape, you will keep your magic to yourself and leave my men alone. You will watch your mirror like your eyes are glued to it. Or I will peel them from your head and glue them to it."

"This is it. You will never get another chance from me. If you disobey me in any way, if you fail to deliver what you have promised, I won't bother waiting even one more hour. I'll have you dumped into this EverRealm with me, and it will become my life's mission to make you miserable for the rest of your life. You think your life is terrible now? Think again. Any one of my lovely ladies would trade places with you. They would *kill* to trade the life they live for the one you've been privileged with."

I know he's speaking nothing but the absolute truth and I am so relieved that I can't even speak. I gratefully nod my head instead. "Say it, Daughter. Say that you understand. Tell me that we are perfectly clear on these terms."

I clear my throat and make my promises. "I understand, Father. And I agree. I won't fail you this time, you'll see. I won't let you down again."

He turns away and walks to the door but stops and looks back at me. "Oh yes, I almost forgot." He points to Krispin. "That one is mine. You will not release him. You will not help him. You will not interfere in any way. Are we clear?"

I turn my head and let my eyes slowly rove from the top of my lover's head, down his ravaged body to his feet and I feel the tiniest twinge of regret. It's positively disrespectful that even with all the blood and sweat and damage that he's taken, he's still the sexiest damn thing I've ever seen. I wrinkle my nose in disgust. "Can you at least take him away? He's really beginning to stink."

Father laughs uproariously while Krispin glares daggers at me. "He stays, smell and all. You leave him be," he orders over his shoulder as he leaves the room.

I stand up on weak, shaky legs and slowly make my way over to Krispin. I gently stroke his face while I breathe him in. I'd lied. He doesn't stink. He smells deliciously like strong, virile man, just as he always does. Mixed with the coppery smell of blood, of course. But I don't mind the blood. A little blood never hurt anything.

I run my hands over his body one last time and sigh with true regret when his body immediately responds to my touch. "Sorry, Lover. I wish it didn't have to end this way. But it's every Samara for herself. You've always known that I am the most important person in my life. Always have been, always will be. But we had fun while it lasted, didn't we?" I kiss his lips and, watching him all the while, I step back and sink back down onto my dirty mattress. I keep my face an emotionless, blank slate. I will never, ever admit it, but the single tear that runs down his cheek almost slays me.

Nearly a week later, Krispin, almost completely skinless and bloodless, closes his eyes and they do not reopen. The skin *had* been removed from his genitals, after all, and it had been the only screams Father had been able to get from him. I force myself to watch as the guards unchain him and let him drop to the floor.

They drag him out and toss him away like so much rubbish. They don't even give him a proper burial, they just dump him out into a filthy, deserted alley where he's left to rot away. I show no emotions outwardly, but inside they are churning like a bubbling stew of hatred boiling inside me. No matter what, Krispin deserved better and I vow that if I get the opportunity to avenge him, without risking myself, of course, I will take it. If the fates allow it, I will make them pay for what they've done. They broke my most favorite toy, and I hadn't been done playing with it yet.

Down the Rabbit Hole

Ecko steps out onto the cabin's porch and breathes in the crisp morning air. Leaning against the railing, she sips her coffee as she watches the sun rise up over the trees, again. She's done this every morning since her arrival, and it never loses its allure. It's a breathtaking sight, to be sure, but she longs to move on and experience the sunrise in at least a thousand other places.

Fifty...Eight...Days. She's been waiting for fifty-eight days. She's been waiting in the New Hampshire wilderness for so long that she has begun to question everything. Why exactly was she sitting out here waiting her life away for something that she wasn't even sure was going to happen? The forest around her is beautiful, just as beautiful as she remembered it. But she's beginning to feel like a prisoner, trapped here as she is. Waiting, waiting, forever waiting.

She's ready to *go*, to move on and do other things, exciting things. She feels as if she's traded one prison for another, although admittedly, this one is appealing and really can't be compared to the horror of Regal Falls. But a bird living in a gilded cage is still a prisoner in a cage, just in a pretty one.

Every day Ecko places her mother's ring back into its box so that she can reopen it and replay the message. She knows it word for word, has memorized every beautiful detail of her mother's face. She does not doubt that the magic is real, the rose pendant and the box containing the message prove that. But she's not so sure about the rest of it. She's going to receive some huge magical abilities, and that she's destined to save the world? Or more precisely, worlds. Plural. *That* she seriously doubts, but her mother had certainly believed it. Laelynn had also believed that the influx of such powerful magic could cause unpredictable side effects that could possibly be harmful to others around her. Hence, the reason for her self-imposed imprisonment that keeps going on and on, with no end in sight. So, the question of the day, was Laelynn delusional for her beliefs? Or is she, herself, the delusional one for following her mother's instructions?

She sighs heavily and steps back inside the cabin to get ready for the day. Every morning after she watches the sunrise, she hikes over to Charlie and Susan's cabin to check on them and to let them know that she's ok too. They all have their cell phones, but the signal is usually too weak and sketchy to make use of them.

The car that she had rented stays with Charlie, just in case they have an emergency. Once a week he and Susan drive the thirty-two miles to the closest town to restock their food and supplies. This morning she'll be going with them to buy all the supplies that she'll need for her upcoming hike.

She has walked all the short distance nature trails around her already and has decided that it's time to tackle a more serious trail. The one she's chosen is just over twenty-three miles long and ends at a large waterfall. It should only take a day for her to make it there and another day to get back, but she's giving herself four days total. She doesn't want to rush it. She wants to take her time, see all the sights, photograph everything.

Charlie, of course, could always be counted on to argue with any decision she makes that takes her out of his comfort zone. And argue he does. This is so far out of his comfort zone that he is downright miserable. "You've already taken thousands of photos of trees and mushrooms and squirrels," he grumps. "Why do you need to take more? How many can you possibly need?"

But deep down, Charlie understands. She's ready to do things on her own. He knows that he has to learn to let her go. Even if he clearly doesn't like it. And he doesn't, not one bit. He wears his sourpuss face all the way into town, but thankfully doesn't argue about it anymore. Ecko thanks God for small miracles as she steps out of the car, and they all go their separate ways.

She sets off to buy a tent, a sleeping bag, and enough supplies to last a week in the wilderness. When her oversized hiking backpack is stuffed as full as it can get, she walks down the tiny town's only street towards the diner. Charlie and Susan are supposed to meet her there for breakfast before she sets out on her hike. She pushes all her worries about birthdays, magical abilities, and a destiny that she'd never asked for, nor even wanted, into a new box in her mind. She labels it, 'Later' and slams the lid shut.

She smiles and focuses instead on her upcoming adventure. This feels good, feels right somehow. That terrible weight on her shoulders that's been dragging her down has shifted. It isn't gone, it's just become a lighter, easier burden to bear. Suddenly overcome with joy, she flings her arms open wide and spins in a circle, right there in the middle of the street. She throws her head back and laughs merrily up at the sky, before continuing on her way.

There's a happy little bounce to her steps as she passes by the few small shops and local businesses. She's eager to be out there on the trail, alone with her camera and surrounded by Mother Nature. And she just can't wait to see that waterfall! But Ecko never gets the chance to see it. In fact, she never gets to go on that hike at all.

Because at 9:53 a.m. on that 18th day of May, she came into her magic, right there in the middle of the street, in the middle of that small town. One minute she's skipping and spinning happily down the street and the next she's suspended forty feet in the air, held in place by the streams of electrical currents shooting out of the town's power lines and straight into her. Her gaze drops down and somehow lands on Charlie's horrified face staring back at her from a window in the diner.

Unbelievably, she feels no pain from the electricity flowing into her body. She feels amazing, wonderful, in fact. She giggles uncontrollably as people pour out of the shops to stare and point up at her. She's having the time of her life, floating in the air like a bobbing balloon, until it's not so fun anymore.

The electricity pouring into her has nowhere to go, no outlet, so it just continues to build up inside of her. Now it's becoming uncomfortable and frightening. She has a clear mental image of her body filling with electricity and swelling up, just like the balloon she had pretended to be only moments ago. She'll get bigger and rounder until she pops, her skin bursting open and spewing her insides to the outside.

She's suddenly terrified. Something strange is happening to her vision now, as well. The sunshine from moments ago seems to have fled, turning the morning to deep twilight. The people below her all appear to be glowing, shining with a strange silvery tint. They look as if they'd all been dunked into vats of silver, glow-in-the-dark paint. Other things are lit up as well, smaller things. Animals, she realizes, as she recognizes the shape of a cat lying in a nearby windowsill. She can even see the glow of a tiny mouse scurrying behind the dumpster next to the diner.

Sounds are suddenly, dramatically amplified and every little noise becomes excruciatingly loud in her ears. The terrified onlookers below her sound as if they're all yelling into megaphones. The honking of a car horn miles away becomes small sonic booms inside of her brain. Even the wind whispering through the leaves of nearby trees becomes screams in her ears.

It's all too much, the power is too big for her body. She begins to twitch and spasm violently, as she draws in more and more energy, and blood begins to trickle from her nose, mouth, and ears. Her mouth opens wide in a silent scream as her body arches back. She's bent backwards, almost in half, before the electrical currents finally let go of her and she crashes back down to the ground.

She's sprawled there in the street, writhing in agony as the people gather round to stare at her; she can do nothing else. She can't speak, or breathe, or even think. The overwhelming pain is felt in every single one of the billions and billions of atoms that make up her body, and it's excruciatingly, agonizingly decimating. The ordeal of, 'receiving her magic' becomes all too much for her fragile mind and body to endure. Mercifully, unconsciousness claims her and drags her down into the darkness where nothing hurts anymore.

Beep. Beep. Beep. Ecko wakes to the irritating sound of steady, chirping machinery. Hell. She has to be in Hell. There is no other explanation for the agony that she is currently experiencing. Her entire body is one giant bruise, inside and out, and her head is pounding ferociously. She feels as if there's a tiny man stomping around inside her head, turning her brain into sludge, like the old wine makers stomping grapes into wine.

She slowly, cautiously cracks her eyes open, but immediately slams them shut again at the brightness of the light. An involuntary whimper escapes her lips as the evil little man picks up the pace and does a frantic tap dance inside her skull.

"Susan, draw the shades. The light's hurting her. And get a nurse!" she hears, just before her hand is encased in a soft, old wrinkled one… Charlie. Relief surges through her and sudden tears leak from beneath her closed eyelids. She places her other hand on top of her head, as if holding onto it will somehow ease the pain. "I'm here, Sweetie. Just lie still. You're gonna be just fine."

Somehow, she swallows down the lump in her raw throat. "Hurts" she whispers, her voice hoarse and raspy. "Sshhh, baby girl. Just rest. The nurse will be here soon." Then there are sounds of people entering the room, but she dares not open her eyes again. The bed whirs softly as she's lifted into a sitting position.

She flinches as unfamiliar voices question her, and cold hands touch her without her permission. A high keening wail begins to build inside her mind...Is she back in Regal Falls? Oh God, she *can't* be back in the hospital! "Ecko, my name is Dr. White. You had an accident and were brought here to Memorial Medical Center. Can you hear me? Can you open your eyes for me?"

Not Regal Falls then, but still a hospital with doctors and needles and drugs. "Hurts," she repeats. It's the only thing she can say.

"Yes. I imagine you are in quite a bit of pain" the man replies. "I'm sorry for that. I'll give you something that'll help in just a few moments. But the medicine will make you sleepy again and I must speak with you before you go back to sleep. Who is your primary care physician? I'll need to get in contact with them and have them send me all your medical records, every detail they have. I need to go over everything they can provide, because honestly, I just don't know how to treat you. The results of your CT scans and your X-rays are astounding, unlike anything I've ever seen ..."

The pounding in Ecko's head gets harder and louder, momentarily drowning out the doctor's voice. "...heart is unusually large, and it beats faster than it should, almost double what a healthy adult heart rate should be. As for your brain, well, I just don't know. Every time we've tried to look at it, our machines somehow malfunctioned, on every *single* attempt. The malfunctions appear to be solely in connection to *you*, or more precisely, to *your* brain. They've worked properly on everyone else we've scanned before, *and* after our failed attempts with yours. I can assure you that our machinery is not faulty. Have you ever had any head scans, or any other scans actually, before now?"

The doctor pauses his seemingly endless spiel, waiting for her to answer. But her head hurts way too badly. She can't seem to form any kind of rational thought, much less speak them aloud. When she continues to lie there mutely, Dr. White pats her hand consolingly and continues. "That's ok. That's why I need to contact your primary care physician, so I can go over your previous records. Now moving along, the rest of your major organs, lungs, kidneys, liver, all appear to be normal and healthy. And your reproductive organs seem healthy, as well, but we've discovered that you have a congenital abnormality called uterus didelphys bicollis."

"Basically, all that means is that you have two uteruses instead of one. It is very rare, but it's not life threatening in the least. Most people don't even know…" Painful explosions going off inside her brain have her crying out for Charlie. He rushes back to her side and takes her hand in his. The doctor doesn't seem to notice, or care about her distress as he drones on. "And your lab results are just, well, *bizarre*. Your blood is not consistent with any blood type I have ever seen. It doesn't even appear to be human. It's close, but there are some major discrepancies. At first, I thought there was some sort of mistake. But we ran the tests six times, and they all came back inconclusive. I've never seen anything like it. I…"

But Ecko no longer hears the doctor's words. The screaming white noise inside her head has steadily gotten louder and louder until it's all she can hear, and the pain becomes too intense for her to handle. She grabs her head with both hands and shrieks at the top of her lungs. She's vaguely aware of Charlie yelling for the doctor to stop harassing her and to help her immediately. She hears metal clanging and plastic rustling and then there's a cold rush of fluid in her veins.

Her heart rate speeds up, causing the machines to beep out of control. The sounds are amplified, almost as if someone has plugged hearing aids into her ears and turned the volume all the way up to max. The beeping reverberates throughout her head, bouncing off each pressure point before slamming into the next.

Then all sound abruptly ceases as if she's been plunged back into the sensory deprivation void that she remembers from her first months at Regal Falls. It is not comforting. It is not a relief. The silence screams just as loudly as the machines had. The icy solution in her veins speed- travels to her heart, which then pumps it back out to all corners of her body.

Fire replaces the ice and then she's burning up, burning from the inside out. Flames lick along her skin, as a windless breeze whips her hair about her face. The pain is unimaginable, and she writhes in agony on the bed, trying to put out the fire. Steam begins to rise off her skin and her hair crackles and sizzles with static electricity. The pressure builds and the fire inside her rages out of control.

Something terrible is about to happen! Her eyes shoot open, finally, and she hears the nurses cry out in alarm. Her vision has that silvery infrared night-vision thing going on again and everyone that is crowded into her room is lit up with a silver luminescence. She ignores them all and focuses only on Charlie.

He's terrified, but not *of* her. He's scared *for* her and refuses to budge from her side. "Run Charlie! Get out of here. Something's happening and I can't stop it! You have to leave. Now! Get everyone out! Hurry!" But Charlie doesn't have to make *anyone* leave. They're already running out on their own.

She catches a glimpse of her reflection in Charlie's eyes and whimpers in fear. Her own eyes, usually a deep green flecked with tiny bits of silver, have gone completely silvery and shiny metallic. They look like pools of melted mirrors. As she watches, electric blue shooting stars begin to fall inside her mirror eyes. It would have been beautiful if it weren't so utterly terrifying. The stars fall faster and faster as the pressure inside her builds and the fire burns ever hotter. The lava flowing through her body, incinerating everything in its path is all-consuming.

"GO NOW!" she screams, and Susan drags Charlie from the room. Just as the door slams shut behind them, a massive wave of pure energy bursts out of her, causing the whole hospital to shake and rumble on its foundation. The lights flicker a few times, off and on, off and on, off again and then they stay off.

The sudden absence of light and the silence of the machines gone quiet around her is startling. She cries out and blindly reaches for help that just isn't there. And then she's falling, sinking back into that deep dark nothing. It really is nice here, she thinks as she begins to float away, alone in a sea of black. It's quiet…peaceful. Her mind is calm, her body no longer in agony. The little man in her head has finally ceased his relentless stomping. The pressure's gone and the flames have been snuffed out. Maybe she'll stay here. There's no pain, no fear or guilt or sadness. There's just...nothing. With a grateful sigh, Ecko closes her eyes, lets go of everything and gives in to the darkness beckoning her towards oblivion.

"Come on now, Sweetheart. Wake up. You gotta wake up. Open your eyes." Ecko awakens to Charlie's persistent voice and the soft pats to her cheeks. Her eyelids flutter and Charlie grunts in relief. "That's it, Ecko. Wake up. Open your eyes for me."

She smiles and stretches like a cat, reveling in how amazing she feels. "Five more minutes Charlie. Just five more minutes," she murmurs as she tries to roll over and go back to sleep.

But Charlie is determined and relentless. "Sorry, but we got problems, big problems. I don't know what to do. I NEED you to wake up. Now!"

Okay, that sounded serious. Her eyes snap open. "What is it? What's wrong?" She looks around at her unfamiliar surroundings. "Where are we…" she starts to ask, but stops with a sharp intake of breath, as the memories come flooding back into her mind. She suddenly remembers everything, how she received her magic, there in the middle of the street and the scene that she'd caused, waking up in the hospital and having that crazy reaction to the medication…all the pain.

Charlie sighs in relief. "Oh, thank God!" he rejoices. "You're awake and you're back to normal. Susan! She's ok!" he yells over his shoulder.

Then Susan is standing next to the bed too, smiling and looking relieved. She quietly asks, "How are you feeling? You gave us quite a scare!"

They're interrupted by a brief knock on the door, and a nurse walks in before Ecko has a chance to answer. "Oh! You're awake!" she blurts out and then smiles in an anxious, brittle sort of way. She's obviously nervous and she quickly shuffles backwards, right back out the door. "I'll just go let the doctor know…" Then she slams the door shut and is gone.

The three of them stare at one another in silence for a moment. "I have to get out of here, Charlie. I can't let them run any more tests on me. I can't let them give me any more of whatever it was that they put into my IV. I don't know why, but it did *not* mix well with whatever magic is inside me now. Maybe my body can't handle human medicines anymore. Or, at least not that one! That whole crazy thing earlier was my body rejecting those meds. The magic incinerated it, burned it right out of me. I was so scared. I really thought I was going to die." Ecko shudders in horror as she recalls how much pain she'd been in.

"I knew it!" Susan exclaims. "I told them that you were having some kind of reaction to the medicine. The very instant that doctor administered it, your heart rate shot up and all the machines started going nuts. And then...well, you know the rest of it. Thank God they listened and took me seriously when they put the IV back in. It got ripped out at some point."

Susan nods her head towards the IV tubes sticking out of Ecko's hand. "That's just a saline drip. I've been watching them like a hawk to make sure they don't slip anything else in there. But honey, that all happened yesterday. You've been unconscious for almost 24 hours!"

Charlie waves his hand in the air and grumbles. "No time for that now! We can discuss it later. That Dr. White is up to something and no good can come of it. He blames you for that earthquake yesterday. Seems it 'mysteriously' only hit this one building. No one else in town was affected by it at all. There was a lot of damage to the building and the power was knocked out. It took hours to get everything back up and running."

"Don't worry!" he rushes to assure her, as panic fills her eyes. He knows exactly what she's afraid of. "No one was hurt. Not even a single band-aid was called for. But the quake (and that whole incident right before the quake) combined with what was found in your test results and lab work has that doctor spooked. I heard him talking on the phone. He has the CDC and the FBI and God knows who else on the way here, right now! We have to hurry and get you out of here and as far away as possible. Now, I already have a plan. I'll go out first and bring the car around while Susan helps you get unhooked from those machines. I'm gonna pull the fire alarm on my way out, so you'll have to get dressed and into this wheelchair as fast as you possibly can. Susan will wheel you out to the elevators. They're not far."

She frowns and insists that she can walk out on her own, but the stubborn man is even more insistent. "No. You've been hurt and there's no way of knowing exactly how badly. What if you need to run but can't? What if you fall? The wheelchair's our safest and best bet."

Charlie takes off his ball cap and hands it to her. "Here, put this on and stuff your hair up under it. All those wild red curls of yours are like a beacon, drawing attention straight to you. Hopefully this helps and no one will recognize you. They probably won't even pay you much attention in all the confusion from the alarm going off. You'll be fine. We'll have you out of here in fifteen minutes, tops."

Ecko sits up and swings her legs off the bed and onto the floor. "We have to hurry! I can't let the government get their hands on me. They'll lock me up and turn me into a lab rat! I can't go back to that Charlie, I can't! I'd rather die!"

Charlie grabs her shoulders, looks right into her eyes and vows, "I won't let them have you. That's a promise. This *will* work! Now, are you two ready?" Ecko and Susan nod their heads and watch him with wide, terrified eyes. He pulls them both in for a group hug and tells them he loves them and assures them that everything will be fine.

Then he steps back and walks to the door. He reaches for the door handle, takes a deep breath, then turns back and smiles at them one last time. "See you soon, ladies!" And then he's gone.

As soon as the door shuts behind him, Ecko's up out of the bed, ripping off wires and tape. Susan quickly and efficiently removes the IV from her hand for her then helps her get her clothes on. They ball her hair up on top of her head and she slips Charlie's baseball cap over it. All that's left is to put on her shoes.

While she's tying the laces she asks, "Where's all my stuff? My mother's box and Sir Didymus is in my backpack. I'm not leaving them behind." Susan points to the little closet space and she rushes to retrieve it. Her tent, bed roll, and camera are all clipped to the backpack, everything still bundled together in preparation for her hiking trip.

"What's taking so long? Where is he?" Ecko worries aloud as she sits down in the wheelchair and settles the backpack onto her lap. "Shouldn't the alarm be going off by now?"

Susan cracks the door open and takes a peek down the hallway. "I don't know! I can't see anything beyond the clerks at the desk. I'm going to walk down there and ask them if you can have some water. That way I can see all the way to the elevators, see if Charlie's even made it off this floor. Hopefully someone just held him up, maybe with more paperwork or something like that. Don't worry, sweetie. I'll be right back" she says as she shuts the door behind her.

Ecko stands up and slips the backpack on, settling it comfortably in place. She wants her hands free in case she has to make a run for it. She was completely serious when she'd told Charlie that she'd rather die than go back to being locked up and strapped down. If she has to, she will run, and she *will* fight. They'll have to shoot her to stop her. She nervously peeks out the door like Susan had done just moments ago.

A nurse is coming down the hall, heading straight towards her. She smiles at Susan as they pass by one another. Susan worriedly glances back but continues on her way. It would look suspicious if she turned around now. Ecko slowly, quietly shuts the door. She turns back to look around the room, desperately searching for some sort of magical exit.

But of course, there's no other way out. There *is* a small restroom that she can hide in, though. Never taking her eyes off of her only escape route, she backs up until she's standing in the restroom's doorway. If all else fails, she'll lock herself inside. Maybe she can make the nurse believe that she's on the toilet and she'll leave, give her some privacy and come back later.

She holds her breath and watches the handle go down and the door to the hospital room begin to swing open. She backs the rest of the way into the bathroom and prepares to slam the door shut, but a horrible, dreadful feeling washes over her. Alarms start ringing in her head and all the tiny, fine hairs on her body stand straight up. Someone is in here with her. She can *feel* them, can almost hear them breathing.

She slowly turns her head to seek out the intruder, just as the nurse steps into the room. "What are you doing out of bed? Who unhooked…" But Ecko isn't listening. She no longer cares about one insignificant, human nurse. Her gaze is locked on the one person that she *should* have been worried about the most, the one person that she had completely forgotten about.

In her haste to escape the hospital, Ecko hadn't even once thought about avoiding mirrors. She was trying to hide in a bathroom, of all places, *and all bathrooms have mirrors!* Samara is here, now. She's finally found her again and things are different. They can both feel it. Samara smiles that terrible smile and hisses, "Got you! No more running, sweet sister. Now that you've finally gotten your own powers, *my* magic can sense it and I'll be able to track you. You will *never* be able to hide from me again."

She bounces up and down and claps her hands gleefully. "We are going to have so much fun, just like when we were kids! I can't wait to show you what I have planned for those two old geezers that you love so much!" Samara throws her head back and laughed like a madwoman as Ecko's face flushes with fury.

"No! I won't let you hurt them, *Sister*" she snarls back. The Rage that has been locked up inside her head for so long is suddenly very much awake and roaring to be released. She tries to calm herself. The last thing she wants is for that monster to be let out. She's always been terrified of what she will be capable of, if it ever broke free. And now that she has this unpredictable power that she knows nothing about, or how to control, well, nothing good could come of Rage taking control *and* having magic to back it up.

She has to get herself back under control this instant. She can feel the pressure rising inside her; she already recognizes that as a sign of the magic coming to life, but she is just so *very* angry. It wasn't enough for Samara to make her childhood a living nightmare. It wasn't enough that she had taken her family away from her and turned her whole world upside down and inside out. No, she had to have it all. Every scrap of love and joy and hope.

Samara wouldn't be satisfied until she manages to take away every single thing that Ecko loves, everything that brings her happiness. She wants Ecko to suffer, immensely and eternally. But ENOUGH! Ecko's had enough of this sister that hates her for no reason, has *always* hated her. Her hair begins to whip and snap about, and she can feel her eyes changing, filling with the magic.

The mirror in front of her begins to ripple as if its surface has turned to liquid, changing from a solid sheet of glass into a gently swirling silver pool. Samara's eyes open wide in wonder, and she reaches up to touch her side of the melted mirror. Her hands meet no resistance, and they pass right through, as if it were nothing more than an open window.

Ecko watches in horror as those two hands emerge, straight into her own world. Samara grins wickedly, triumphantly, as she steps forward, pushing her head and shoulders through also. Ecko slams her hands into Samara's shoulders and pushes her backwards with a strength born of desperation. She must stop this! She cannot let this evil be unleashed into this world.

But Samara shoves back, just as hard and just as determined. For the moment, they're at a standstill, locked together in an angry, hate-filled embrace. The sudden shout of "Oh, my God!" causes Ecko to jerk her head to the right. Susan's standing there in the restroom's doorway, staring in horror at the scene before her. The terrified nurse has plastered herself back against the far wall, her mouth and eyes opened wide with shock. The distraction allows Samara to gain an inch and Ecko pushes back desperately, harder than ever, determined to keep her loved ones safe.

"Run, Susan! Get Charlie as far from here as you can! MAKE him go! If I can't hold her back, she's coming straight for you two. Tell Charlie I love him and that I will find him when I can. Now, go! I don't know how much longer I can hold her!"

Samara laughs evilly and shoves her back another inch. Ecko struggles against her sister with all her might, but she knows that it's only a matter of time. It seems that the two of them are twins in physical strength, as well as in appearance. They're evenly matched in strength and determination, and the struggle continues on for ages, neither one of them able to overthrow the other. That is, until the ugliest pair of creatures Ecko had ever seen comes into view in the room behind Samara.

Her eyes widen at the appalling sight of the abominations and Samara uses the distraction to her advantage. She stops pushing on her sister's shoulders and wraps her hands around Ecko's forearms instead. Then she suddenly jerks her forward, towards the mirror, using her own momentum against her. Samara steps aside to make way as Ecko flies through and lands right on top of the disgusting creatures. The three of them go down in a pile of tangled limbs.

"Seize her immediately!" Samara orders. "She's the one your master has been seeking all these years. Get her safely to his castle and you will be rewarded beyond your wildest dreams for your loyalty." One of the repulsive brutes grunts and wraps its steel-strong hands around her in a bear hug, squeezing the breath from her lungs, while the other one deftly ties a rope around her hands and another around her neck like a leash.

"Better gag her as well, so she can't put a spell on you," Samara snaps. "If you let her get away, you'd better run as fast and as far as you can get. My father will punish you in ways you can't even imagine." One of them hastily stuffs a filthy rag into Ecko's mouth, causing her to gag uncontrollably. She can't breathe! Panicking, desperate for air, she begins to struggle and thrash about until the larger of the two creatures balls up his fist and strikes the side of her head.

While she does not lose consciousness, the blow is hard enough to addle her senses and forces her to momentarily stop fighting. She falls heavily to her knees. The only thing keeping her in an upright position is the rope around her neck, pulled taught in the goon's hands.

Samara realizes that Ecko's magic is retreating, and the mirror has begun to solidify again. She quickly steps through, out of her world and straight into Ecko's. She turns back and grins evilly. "Welcome to Hell, dear sister. Enjoy your vacation in my world; it'll be a permanent one. Good luck finding another mirror to escape through. Oh, I almost forgot! I left a little surprise for you in the master bedroom. Give my regards to those two old fools who raised me, and thanks for getting me here! I never could have done it without you. I just know I'm going to love this world! Bye, bye now, Sister! I hope you have a positively dreadful life."

Samara presses her hands to the surface of the mirror, just as it finishes closing. Her eyes go completely black and smoke flows from her hands and into the mirror. The glass swells and bulges as more and more smoke fills it, until it can hold no more. The mirrors in both worlds shatter explosively, sending shards of glass through the air. The twins have, for better and for worse, switched worlds and are now both very much trapped on them, respectively.

Samara is no Mirror Walker. She does not possess the ability to open up the way and travel through, so there's no going back for her, even if she wanted to. And there are no more mirrors in the world that Ecko's now trapped in. Mommy dearest had made sure of that years ago.

Samara throws her head back, screaming and howling with laughter. Doom on you Ecko, she thinks, and Doom on you too, Earthlings…All of you.

Epilogue: Samara

A Whole New World

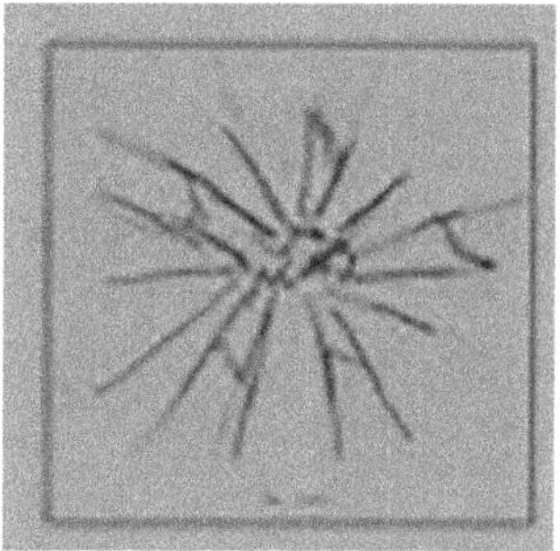

Samara throws her fists up into the air and screams triumphantly, reveling in the satisfaction of finally, *finally* escaping her father's clutches and the hellish world that her mother had abandoned her on. Now, to celebrate her victory, she's going to have some fun with Ecko's old geezers. But the old woman is no longer standing there in the doorway. She has wisely fled the scene, as Ecko had instructed her to.

Burning rage fills her at the missed opportunity, but she realizes that not all is lost. She grins with pure, unadulterated malice when she notices the petrified woman backed up against the wall, whimpering in terror. "Oh goody! Something for me to play with, after all," she crows as she stalks up to the nurse.

She leans in close, almost as if she plans to kiss the frightened woman. Then she gently blows out a thin stream of black fog from her lips, straight into the woman's open mouth. The woman chokes a bit and then her eyes go blank, staring out at nothing. "Kill yourself," Samara whispers into her ear.

She watches as the woman calmly turns and walks out the door, then down the hallway to the nurse's desk. "Stop me. Please stop me! Help meeee!" the nurse begs her coworkers, as she picks up a pair of scissors. Samara cannot suppress her delighted giggles as the nurse stabs herself in the throat... repeatedly, all the while begging for someone to stop her. But the other three nurses on duty are frozen in shock, staring in horror at the macabre scene unfolding before their very eyes.

A dinging noise signals the arrival of the elevator. The doors open, revealing a man in dark clothing and a ball cap with the word 'Security' embossed on them and another wearing a white coat. The nurse can no longer stand on her own. She drops to the floor, still steadily impaling herself with the scissors, over and over again.

"What's going on here?" the doctor shouts as he rushes over to the fallen nurse. He snatches the scissors out of her hands and tosses them away. Then he quickly presses his hands to her throat to stop the bleeding, but he's too late. Sheila McIntyre takes one last gurgling breath as the light fades from her eyes forever.

Dr. White stands back up, his eyes immediately landing on the girl standing off to the side, watching it all. Her shoulders are shaking with mirth, her hands thrown over her mouth to hold back her delighted laughter. "That's her!" he tells the security man. "She's the one responsible for all these recent disasters. Frank, you can't let her leave. We have to hold her until the FBI arrives."

The security guard draws his weapon and aims it at Samara. "Miss, I need you to put your hands up, nice and slow, where I can see them. Slowly, now. That's good." Samara raises her hands up, as if she has every intention of surrendering, but the mischievous look in her eyes and her giggles seriously unnerve him. Something is very, *very* wrong here, he thinks to himself, just as strange black tendrils of smoke pour out of the girl's hands.

The foul, inky black ropes wrap around him, then disappear up his nose and into his mouth. His body betrays him by locking down and freezing in place when all he wants to do is run the other way, just as the girl leans over and whispers into his ear. Frank has no choice but to change direction and turn the gun back on the doctor, Samara grinning maliciously over his left shoulder all the while.

His hands shake uncontrollably as he tries to fight the compulsion. "I'm sorry Dr. White! I can't stop myself! I have to do it!" Frank squeezes his eyes shut, turns his face away from the impending horror, and then pulls the trigger. Samara claps her hands and jumps up and down, laughing maniacally as the gun booms.

The bullet enters the doctor's right eye and splatters all those years of extensive schooling onto the wall behind him. The nurses at the desk scream and try to run. Samara sticks her pointer finger and thumb out in a facsimile of the guard's pistol and points it at the closest nurse. The guard unwillingly copies the movement, his gun swinging towards the terrified young man. Samara cocks her thumb back and yells, "Bang!"

Frank screams as the gun recoils in his hand and the nurse drops to the floor. "Bang! Bang!" she repeats, and the gun roars two more times, killing the last two nurses instantly. Frank drops to the floor, wailing, the tears pouring down his face. "What have I done? Oh, what have I *done*?" he cries aloud.

Samara kneels beside him and gently strokes his head. "Thank you for that. Don't be sad, now. You did what you had to do." She stands up and backs away. "Now, finish it," she commands, and he lifts the gun up into his mouth, firing it for the last time. Samara smiles and walks away, leaving poor Frank sitting there on the floor with his last thoughts behind him, dripping down the wall.

Samara waves cheerfully at the people that she passes on her way out the hospital doors. "Living in this world is going to be such fun!" she says to a slightly balding, middle-aged man as he's getting into his car. "Hey. You want to give me a ride? Yes. I thought you might. Let's go, let's go! I haven't got all Pale!"

He opens the door and helps her in, then goes around and lets himself into the driver's seat. As the man pulls out of the parking lot, Samara turns back and watches the hospital receding behind them. "I'm going to miss that place. I had so much fun there! Maybe I can go back some time for a longer visit!"

She turns back to the driver and smiles. "But first, you and I are going to go see what other mischief we can get ourselves into. Isn't that right, handsome?" The man nods and drives, mindlessly awaiting Samara's next order.

Epilogue: Ecko

We're not in Kansas anymore, Didymus

Ecko violently jerks awake with a scream tearing from her lips. She's lying on the cold, hard floor, her body sore and her head pounding. The blast from Samara's magic that obliterated the mirror had thrown her and her two would-be captors back against the wall and sent them all to la-la land. Her eyes snap open and focus on the nastiest little bug thing she has ever seen, twitching and skittering and gnashing its double sets of mandibles only inches from her face.

It looks like some sort of disgustingly mutated crossbreed of roach and beetle. Its hard-shelled body is covered in needle-sharp spines, and it has four large slimy eyeballs, which are staring straight at her. Suddenly, all four of those eyes pop out and rise up about an inch off of its head on thin antennae appendages, just like a snail. It blinks at her several times and then skitters off, disappearing into a crack in the floor.

Unbeknownst to her, the bug had just taken several still images of her with its camera lens-like eyes. The images are being sent back to its Collective to be processed. If the info proves to be of interest, it will then be passed on to the Lokskell. The bug titters gleefully from its hiding spot; it *knows* that this is definitely something HE will want to see. It extends its eyes out as far as it can, watching through the crack to see what this new female will do next.

She sits up and looks around her. Thankfully, the two hideous creatures are still unconscious. She realizes that she may have only minutes to make good her escape before they regain their senses.

She stands up on shaky legs and tiptoes from the room, quietly closing the door behind her as she goes. She knows that she must get as far from those two as she possibly can, but what sort of nasties await her outside? What she needs is a weapon. She has magic inside her, but until she has a chance to figure out what all she can do (and how to do it) she needs something a bit more tangible to wield.

There's a Swiss Army knife in her backpack, but what good will that do against an enemy? It certainly wouldn't do much good in a fight, but she wishes that she could reach it and dig it out of the backpack anyway. At least she would be able to cut the ropes off her hands and from around her neck. She quickly searches the tiny, rundown home for something, anything, that may serve to rid her of her bonds and to help her protect herself.

The small, dirty bathroom certainly has nothing she can use, not that she would be willing to touch anything that came out of there anyway. A quick search of the kitchen turns up a single dull butcher knife. Better than nothing, Ecko thinks as she picks it up and drops to the floor. She positions the knife handle between her sneakers, holding it steady as she saws through the ropes that bind her hands, just as fast as possible.

It seems to take forever to hack through it with the dull blade. Every second sees her more and more paranoid that her would-be kidnappers will wake and come after her again. She keeps her eyes fixed upon the bedroom door, determined to be alerted the very second that her situation changes.

Finally, after long torturous minutes of hacking at it, the rope falls to the floor, freeing her hands. She wastes no time in reaching up to untie the knots around her neck. She hurriedly searches the small living room and front closet but has no luck in finding a better weapon than the one she's already found. That leaves only one other room that she has yet to explore.

The door to that room is closed, but even so, she can smell the stink seeping out of it. Her mind screams at her to turn around, to just leave it, but her hands refuse to obey. They defiantly reach out, turn the knob, and push the door open.

The nauseating scent of death, decay, and feces blows right into her face, causing her to gag uncontrollably. But the sight, oh, the sight that greets her will forever be etched onto the back of her eyelids, a terrible picture saved and stored in her mind for later reexamination. Something that was once alive had exploded in there. Whatever it was… it's now splattered on every inch of the walls and ceiling, left there to rot.

"Yep." Ecko whispers to herself. "I've seen enough. Time to go." She opens the front door and cautiously steps out into the murky gray light. She looks left and then right, trying to decide where to go from here and what she's supposed to do now. An angry roar from inside the house quickly makes up her mind for her.

"Left it is!" she shouts as she turns and makes a run for it. She runs as fast as she can make her legs go, down the crumbled remains of the old cobblestone street, looking into the old, neglected buildings and shops as she passes by. The 'people' and creatures she sees inside them are truly the things of nightmares. As she flees for her life, she finds herself begging God over and over again to turn her into a bird so that she can fly far away, just like Jenny did in the movie Forrest Gump. But just as God did not turn young Jenny into a bird that day, neither did he turn Ecko into one.

Krispin

"Oh, I am *not* dead yet" he whispers to himself. They'd tortured him for weeks, beaten and then skinned him alive. His body had finally grown cold and stiff from the loss of so much blood, and his heart rate had slowed so drastically that it had been virtually undetectable. That's when they'd made their biggest mistake. They'd failed to *ensure* that he was truly dead, before they'd tossed him out to rot.

He'd been forced to lay there for hours, playing dead in the rubbish and the filth. But finally, the Pitch had arrived. His old friend Darkness had come out to play hide and seek with him, and he'd at last, been able to pick himself up and crawl away. But he hadn't gone far. He only went as far as he needed to go to steal food and drink to help replenish himself.

Then he'd hidden himself away and he waited, and he watched. All the while his body had healed until he was almost himself again and he vowed to himself that he would get her back. He would reclaim his lover no matter what it took. He would show her the error of her ways, teach her to love him as much as he loves her.

So, now he's lying upon a nearby rooftop, waiting for just the right time to move in when, unbelievably, his love, his Samara opens the door and cautiously steps out. She turns her beautiful head from side to side, as if searching for something. Then his little demon-love takes flight, running so fast she becomes a blur.

"That's my girl! You did it. You're free. You looking for me, Baby?" he whispers softly to himself. He crawls down the wall, lizard-like, digging his razor-sharp claws into the wood for leverage. He freezes in place, still carefully camouflaged, as the door opens again and the two ugly Hobglin guards rush out, tripping over one another in their haste to catch her before

She gets too far away. He doesn't waste time worrying about the guards. They won't recapture her. They won't even be able to get near her. His lover is fast, even faster than he is, and Hobglins are slow, with their short legs and hunched backs. He grins as he drops the rest of the way to the ground and turns to go the other direction. He knows exactly where his beautiful, filthy lover is heading…and he knows a shortcut.

Mirror's Ecko

Don't stare at the mirror too long. Don't look too closely at it. Don't go searching for buried secrets and hidden truths. You may not like the things that surface. And don't speak to it. Never speak to it.